The Favour

The Favour

Nicci French

W F HOWES LTD

This large print edition published in 2023 by
W F Howes Ltd
Unit 5, St George's House, Rearsby Business Park,
Gaddesby Lane, Rearsby, Leicester LE7 4YH

1 3 5 7 9 10 8 6 4 2

First published in Great Britain by
Simon & Schuster UK Ltd, 2023

ISBN 978 1 00410 687 5

Typeset by Palimpsest Book Production Limited,
Falkirk, Stirlingshire

Printed and bound by
T J Books in the UK

MIX
Paper from
responsible sources
FSC
www.fsc.org   FSC® C013056

To Kersti

PROLOGUE

A scream ripped through the air. She didn't know if it came from her, or from him as his hands flew up to cover his face, or from the car itself as it left the road with a screech of tyres on tarmac. Then silence, the tree filling the windscreen, its leaves black in the headlights. A crunch of metal and the lights went out. Her face rammed hard against something, pain flowered in bright colours inside her skull. She tilted her face and opened her eyes, seeing blues and reds and nasty purples. There was a silence in the car. Terror washed through her, and the terror was bigger than the pain.

'Please help me,' Jude said to no one at all.

They had been driving back from a party in Liam's rusty old Fiat, with one of its wing mirrors held in place by tape and an ominous rattle on steep hills. Jude and Liam were in the front, Yolanda and Benny in the back, though Benny was passed out, his head on Yolanda's shoulder and his mouth open, and Yolanda was also fast asleep. Jude looked at the clock on the dashboard: it was two in the morning, but still warm after a sweltering day. It felt like the sky might split open at any moment and a flood of rain would soak into the parched, cracked earth.

It had been a hot summer. Jude thought of sitting her A levels in May and June, the sun glaring through the large windows and her fingers slippery on the pen, beads of sweat on her forehead and damp patches under her arms. That seemed like another world away because since the middle of June she had been in love. Stupid and dizzy and glorious with love, in love as never before. Her body ached with it. She could feel where his fingers had touched her; her lips were sore. At the party he had taken her into the garden and kissed her until she would have lain down on the lawn in full sight, but he'd whispered, 'Later,' his breath hot in her ear. And now it was later: they would drop off Yolanda, haul Benny out of the car and onto his front steps, and drive into the woods. He had a blanket in the boot of his car. She didn't mind if it rained; she imagined their wet bodies pressed against each other and a shiver of anticipation rippled through her.

She looked over at him and he felt her looking and put his hand on her thigh, through the thin material of her dress. Liam Birch: not her type at all. Liam was not on track; Jude was. She had known she was going to be a doctor since she was at primary school and she had worked for years

2

to get there, never letting up. She had a place at medical school and as long as her results were all right, and she was sure they would be, in six weeks she would be heading to Bristol.

Liam didn't know what he was going to do next. He was good with his hands. He could fix almost anything and he could pick up a pencil and in a few strokes create something vivid, startling. Jude had said he should go to art school and he would shrug his shoulders and say he would see what happened – as if it wasn't really his decision to make, as if life just rolled him over and carried him along. Maybe he would go travelling, he said; get away from this medium-sized town in the middle of England where he had lived all his life with his parents and his little brother. She looked down at the hand that lay warm and heavy on her thigh. What would happen when she went to university? They hadn't talked about the future, just as they hadn't talked much about the past. She didn't know a great deal about Liam's family, his childhood, his previous relationships. What mattered was now, and here, and the lovely loosening of her body when he touched her, when she thought of him touching her, and the way he looked at her and said her name.

They hadn't been at the same school. Liam had gone to the large sixth-form college on the outskirts of the Shropshire town they both lived in, Jude to the comprehensive. But she had been aware of him, a tall lanky figure with dark hair that needed cutting and clothes that never looked new: ripped jeans, T-shirts with mysterious words on them, a weird green jacket that on someone else would have looked terrible but he carried it off. She had seen him over the past two years, walking along the streets in a group of other teenagers, smoking, swigging from cans, looking cool and impossibly worldly.

A few days after her last exam, a friend introduced her to him at a party. She waited for him to say, 'Hey, Jude,' and laugh at his own wit, but he didn't. She waited for him to turn away and go back to his gang, but he didn't do that either. He told her about a baby fox he had run over that day, how he'd thought at first it was a little child who'd run into the road. The fox was still alive and squealing piteously and passers-by had quickly gathered to watch. He'd had to kill it, he said, smashing a stone from the kerbside against its head, and then take the body and dump it in the woods. He had carried it for almost half an hour, hot and rank in his arms. He was a bit stoned. His pupils were large; his eyes dark, almost black, in the dim light. Jude was surprised by how friendly he seemed, and how young. Almost – well, almost *ordinary*. Just a handsome boy.

For the first few weeks, it had been a gorgeous secret that she hugged to herself. She didn't tell her friends, because she didn't want them rolling their eyes or saying anything that would make it seem unimportant or too important or too surprising. She didn't want to hear that one of them had been with him, or knew of someone who had, or had heard something about him, about his recklessness and his sudden inexplicable bursts of anger. She didn't want anyone to say: 'You need to watch out for that one.' Even now, she was reticent about telling people. Every so often they went to parties together, like tonight, and only yesterday they had spent the day by the river with a group of friends. She had talked about him to Rosie, lying in the long grass by the river and speaking to the blue sky. But she hadn't told her parents: she knew they would be alarmed by Liam, who smoked weed, took pills, sometimes looked a bit unwashed, and wouldn't be going to university. Maybe that was the attraction: he was someone her parents wouldn't approve of. In any case she was leaving for Bristol in September. He was her in-between time, her summer, her escape.

'I feel a bit sick,' said Yolanda, half-waking in the back of the car.

'Wind down the window,' Liam said.

'I might *be* sick.'

'Not in my car, you won't.'

'It won't be long till we're at your house,' said Jude. 'Tell us if we should pull over though.'

But Yolanda didn't answer because she had fallen back to sleep. A gurgling snore came from her, then a grunt.

Jude felt a bit tipsy herself. Liam had drunk a lot, too, and taken who knew what else? But it was only a short journey. A few large drops of rain landed on the windscreen. She put a hand up to touch his face and felt his lips smile.

Then: 'Fuck,' he said, or shouted.

Because there was a sharp bend in the road but the car sped onwards, off the road, towards the tree. Terrible slow motion. Terrible clarity of disaster, and a world that would never be the same again.

A scream ripped through the air.

Jude couldn't tell which way her body was facing. Her head rang with pain, one side, then the other. Yolanda was sobbing wildly in the back. Benny wasn't saying anything at all.

'Are you hurt?' said Liam urgently in the darkness.

'I can't see.' Jude put up a hand and found her face, which was warm and sticky. 'I'm bleeding,' she said.

'Can you get out of the car?' said Liam.

'I don't know. Yolanda? Benny? Are you okay? What's happened? What's going to happen?'

Liam climbed out, came round to her side, helped her out too. She couldn't stand, her legs were shaking too much, and he sat her on the grass bank. She could make out his pale face. He returned for Yolanda, who stumbled away from the car and was violently sick on the road. Jude heard the splatter of vomit.

It started to rain. She heard Liam talking to Benny.

'Is he breathing?'

'Yeah, he's breathing. He needs help, though. I'll make a call.'

'Do you have to?'

Liam squatted beside her and wiped the blood from her face with the hem of his T-shirt. He seemed remarkably calm, almost nonchalant. 'It'll be all right.'

Tears and rain were stinging her face. Her tongue was swollen in her mouth. 'This is a nightmare.'

Liam was talking into his phone. How could he be so calm? Jude leaned forward and cradled her face in her hands. She heard Yolanda sobbing and the wind blowing in the trees and somewhere an owl out there in the wet darkness.

Then from far off a siren.

The ambulance arrived first and, a few minutes later, a police car, then another, blue lights flashing on woods and on the car's bonnet buried in the tree, on the pale scared faces of its four passengers. The paramedics lifted Benny onto a stretcher and he opened his eyes at last.

'Get off, will you?' he said. 'What's going on?'

A woman bent over Jude speaking in a kind voice, but Jude couldn't make out the words. There was a roaring in her head. But she heard the words a police officer spoke to Liam, asking if it was his car.

He said it was. She lifted her head and he looked at her and smiled. As if it was a joke, thought

Jude. As if none of this really mattered: just one of those things.

He was asked if he had been driving, whether he had been drinking, whether they had all been wearing seatbelts. He was told that he was going to be tested.

She saw Liam shrug. The blue light flickered over his face. Everything became confused once more until she saw him being led towards the open door of one of the police cars. He looked round at her and lifted a hand in what looked like a gesture of farewell.

That was the end, really. The end of Liam and Jude and the glorious agony of first love, the end of her summer, the end of her childhood.

Jude stayed in hospital for two days. She had received a head injury and they wanted to keep her under observation. She had a broken nose that the young doctor assured her would mend and leave no scar. A gash in her forehead needed twelve stitches. The day after the accident, she didn't recognise herself in the mirror, her face swollen, her skin all purples and deep browns and murky greens.

'You could have been killed,' said her mother.

'What were you thinking, getting in a car with someone who was drunk?' said her father.

Her parents looked at each other and asked about Liam. Who was he? Why had she been in his car?

Jude winced. 'He's just a boy I know,' she said.

Just a boy. Her boy. She tried calling him and he didn't pick up. She sent a text, several texts, saying she urgently had to see him, and he wrote back saying things were a bit complicated, but not to worry about him. He was fine. He probably wouldn't be going to prison, just have to do a bit of community service. 'Travel plans on hold,' he wrote.

Prison. The word made her feel sick.

When Jude got out of hospital she went to his house. The door opened and she felt a sudden rush of panic and excitement at the sight of Liam but then saw it wasn't Liam. It was someone who looked like Liam but was younger, less formed, less assured. He said that he was Liam's brother, Dermot. He said that Liam wasn't there, that nobody was there. Apart from you, Jude said, and he blushed. She asked if Liam was all right and Dermot said he was all right, a bit shaken up.

She looked at this boy – what was he? Fifteen? Sixteen? – and asked him to tell his brother that she wanted to see him. No, she corrected herself: she *needed* to see him. She added with a shake in her voice that it mustn't be like this. Please, she said. Please. The words hung in the air between them. Liam's brother looked for a moment as if he wanted to say something, but instead he simply nodded and she turned and left.

For several days, she sat listlessly in the living room at home, a blanket over her in spite of the heat, her head throbbing and her face turning to mauve and yellow, and watched daytime TV. Friends came to see her, exclaiming over the exciting awfulness of what had happened. She tried to smile and tried to talk. They brought body lotion and brownies they'd baked. Rosie gave her a vast pot plant which she said Jude should take to university with her, but which died within a week.

The crash was like a garish nightmare, remembered in fragments. Liam was like a figure in a fading dream. Sometimes she woke in the early hours and found she was crying.

She collected her results, which were better than predicted. So she would go to Bristol and she would become a doctor. Her life was still on track.

Liam's life was still not on track. Benny told Jude that his results weren't great. 'He knew they wouldn't be,' he said, as if that was a comfort. 'He's not that bothered. You know what he's like.'

What was he like?

For weeks she thought about him all the time and then, bit by bit, it was easier not to think about him.

It had only been three months of her life: three intense, giddying months that had burned a hole in her life.

A few days before she was due to leave for Bristol, she saw him in the street with a girl. They were walking away from her, but she would have recognised him anywhere: the tall figure in tatty jeans; the slightly loping walk as if he couldn't be bothered to lift his feet; the dark, unruly hair. She started to cry, thick tears sliding down her cheeks that weren't bruised any more, into her mouth. But she didn't try to catch up with him; instead she turned away and walked in the other direction.

She thought that she would never see him again.

CHAPTER ONE

It had been a routine night shift. Jude had been called down multiple times to the casualty department. Three women in their eighties, one woman in her nineties. Three had fallen. One had been brought in unconscious. Two were severely confused. The wards had been quiet. Not literally quiet. A patient with dementia was calling for her mother over and over again. A male patient woke up repeatedly and shouted something unintelligible in a frenzied tone and went back to sleep and then woke up again and shouted the same fearful words. Jude had talked to the duty nurse about his medication but decided to leave it as it was.

Years before she'd had a placement in an A & E department at a hospital in south London. Friends of hers who had done that job said they enjoyed the adrenaline, the sense of not knowing what you would be doing in five minutes' time. Jude had never felt that. She didn't feel much adrenaline in treating the drunken fights, the drunken accidents, the drunken car crashes. You would fix them and send them away. Or you couldn't fix them and you would send them on to someone who could fix them. And sometimes, horribly, there were the mangled dead or the dying and she never got used to that.

When she chose geriatrics, her friends seemed surprised. Didn't she find it depressing? No, she didn't. She did the things other doctors did, making diagnoses, prescribing drugs, ordering tests. But she also felt like a doctor from an earlier age, when sometimes all one could do was to sit with a patient, hold their hand, talk to them, listen to them, attend. Behind everything, the mask of old age, they were as funny and complicated and fucked up as everyone else. Every time she was able to send a patient home, a little better than when they came in, without pain perhaps, able to walk unaided, it felt like a victory.

She looked at her phone. The 94-year-old woman should be having her X-ray. Jude made a mental note to check up on her before she left. Then she got cross with herself and made a real note. Mental notes were useless.

She looked at the board on the wall next to the nurses' station. Nothing she hadn't dealt with. She walked across to the nurse behind the desk and asked if anyone had called from A & E.

The nurse shook her head. 'They're terrible down there. They never get back to you. They never return calls.' She tapped her finger on the desk. 'But then as soon as *they* want something.'

'I know,' said Jude. 'Tell me about it.'

These shared complaints about the inefficiency and the arrogance of other departments – that was how they bonded.

'Someone called for you,' said the nurse.

'Did you take their number?'

'No, I mean called. Came here. Asked to see you.'

'Which department?'

'I don't think he's from the hospital. I said you were working. He said he'd wait downstairs.'

Jude was puzzled. Who would come to her work? In the middle of the night?

'That's weird. Was it something serious?'

The nurse shook her head.

'I don't think so. He just said he'd wait. It didn't seem so urgent. He's down at the main reception.'

Jude looked up at the clock. Six-thirty. Half an hour left, and this was often the busiest part of her shift. She had to carry out all her usual duties while preparing to hand over to the incoming registrar and then actually handing over. At times it felt that some vengeful God sent in a really tricky case just as she was preparing to leave. The unconscious woman was proving complicated. It was probably a stroke but the woman had a multitude of other conditions and after a confusing and inadequate conversation with the carer, an inconclusive examination and a series of phone calls, Jude looked up and saw it was twenty past seven.

She walked into the little office where she kept her coat and her bag and her keys and, as she always did, she took a moment, letting her thoughts settle. Was there anything she might have missed? She couldn't think of anything.

She got out her phone, looked at it and blinked. There was a faint aura around it as if it was glowing. Sometimes this was just tiredness but usually it wasn't. Usually it was the sign that a migraine was coming. It almost never happened during work. It was as if her brain was politely waiting until she did what she had to get done. It would give her enough time to get home and then the headache would start. Sometimes the medication would stop it, if she took it in time. She started to check her messages.

She and Nat had a wedding to prepare. Often she wished they could have simply gone to the register office the two of them, with a couple of friends for witnesses. But Nat had said that it was a great excuse for a party and his mother would never forgive him if her son didn't have a proper wedding and from there it had grown like a fungus. It had taken months to settle on the right venue and now that that was settled, there was the catering and the flowers and checking the numbers and there was her dress. The gathering migraine sent out a little flash of pain as Jude allowed herself to think about that. She didn't wear long dresses and shoes with heels; she wore men's suits from charity shops, jumpsuits, jeans, walking boots and sandals and pumps, anything that made her feel agile, ready for a quick getaway. But Nat wrinkled his nose when she said that and then laughed anxiously, trying to make it into a joke. He wanted her to be a bride; he was anticipating her in soft focus, wearing something pale and feminine as she looked at him with tenderness and said, 'I do'.

She felt guilty complaining, even to herself. Nat was doing the hard work. Every so often he would come to her with a choice. Would she like this or that? This food? That wine? This decoration?

Her phone rang and she knew who it was before she even looked. When she worked nights, it was as if she and Nat were in different time zones, even though they were living together. She would get home, exhausted, just as he was leaving for his office in Lambeth, where he worked as public health project officer. Sometimes she would miss him altogether.

'Good morning,' she said.

'Any dramas?'

'Just the usual.'

The events of the night were already fading, like when she woke after a deep sleep and could feel the memories of her dreams slipping away.

'Shall we meet for breakfast? I can set off in a few minutes.'

'Lovely. Usual place then.'

Normally she left the hospital by the side entrance, but when she reached the ground floor she turned and headed for the main entrance.

In the reception area, there were a number of

people around, sitting on benches, clustered in groups, talking, reading, waiting.

'You look different,' said a voice. 'But you also look exactly the same.'

Jude had forgotten that someone was waiting to see her.

She turned her head and there he was: he was tall, about her own age, dark tangled hair, bearded, eyes that were almost black. He was dressed in jeans and a battered grey jacket. He had a richly patterned cotton scarf knotted around his neck.

'You're hard to track down,' he said.

She didn't recognise him.

And then she recognised him.

'You're kidding,' she said, a smile forming.

It was Liam.

CHAPTER TWO

'You're a doctor.' And Liam smiled that soft slow smile that brought the past back so vividly that Jude felt it in her stomach.

She looked around, as if she needed to reassure herself that this was true, that she really was a doctor and this really was a hospital.

'Yes, yes, I am. Just about.'

'It was what you always wanted.'

It was impossible to exchange small talk with this ghost who had come out of her past.

'I never thought I'd see you again.'

'Yes, I know,' he said slowly. 'I mean, I don't exactly know. But it was complicated.'

She looked at him and couldn't look away. She didn't know what to say.

'Can we get a coffee?' he said. 'Unless you've got somewhere to go.'

'I'm on my way home. It's my bedtime.'

'Maybe decaffeinated coffee, then.'

She shook her head and smiled. 'Nothing keeps me awake after a night shift. I'd like to have coffee.'

They left the hospital and crossed Whitechapel Road and Jude led them up Brick Lane to a small café that had recently opened, all soft chairs and rough wooden tables. She suddenly remembered Nat, about to set off to the hospital to meet her – she hoped he hadn't left by now. She took out her phone and texted him: *Sorry! Emergency. Can't do breakfast. See you this evening. xxxx*

They faced each other across the table. Jude felt giddy with the strangeness of it.

'Do you want breakfast?' she asked. 'Eggs or something?'

He shook his head and ordered coffee for them both. Her hunger had vanished. As the young woman behind the counter prepared the drinks, Jude and Liam simply looked at each other without speaking. The silence didn't feel strange or embarrassing.

When the coffee arrived, Jude took a packet from her pocket, extracted two pink pills and swallowed them with a gulp of coffee. Liam looked quizzical.

'I've got a migraine coming on. This sometimes stops it.'

'You never used to get them, did you?'

'No. They began shortly after . . .' She stopped. After the crash; that was when they had begun. 'I get them a lot. Colours start looking strange and then I go to bed for a few hours.'

'Anyway, congratulations,' said Liam, holding up his coffee cup.

'What about?'

'About your upcoming marriage.'

'How do you know about that?'

'Someone told me. When I was tracking you down.'

Jude laughed. 'Tracking me down? What are you, a private detective?'

'Just an old friend.' He sipped his coffee. 'A doctor, like you always said you'd be. You did it.'

Jude's throat felt tight. She had thought she would never see Liam again, and yet over the years she had imagined meeting him: by chance, on a bus, on a street, in a crowd of people, walking in the Clee Hills by her parents' house in Shropshire. Because there were things that she needed to say, had needed to say for over a decade, although now the moment had actually come she didn't know how to start saying them.

'I should be the one tracking *you* down,' she said, haltingly. 'I know that you . . .' She stopped. 'I've never forgotten.'

He frowned, as if he was considering this. When he spoke, he didn't seem angry or even sad. Just reflective, as if he were talking about someone else.

'I made some choices,' he said. 'Not always good choices. You probably heard about how I messed up my exams, on top of everything else.'

'I'm sorry.'

'That's all right. It happens. And things are better now, on the whole. I've got some stuff to sort out but I'm fine.' He paused a beat and then smiled – not ironically or one of his knowing half-smiles, but a smile that transformed his face and made him look younger. 'I've got a little kid,' he said. 'Alfie. He's one now.'

21

Jude blinked. 'Wow. A son! Does he look like you?'

'People say so. Poor little guy.'

'That's so nice.' She wanted to cry but didn't know why. She smiled instead.

'Yeah, well.'

Jude took a deep breath. 'I need to say something.'

'All right.'

'First, before I say it. I'm with Nat and I'm lucky to have him and we're going to get married, well, you know that, and we're buying a place together.'

'Good.' His tone was dry.

She put out a hand and gripped his; it was dry and warm and his fingers curled around hers.

'No, listen, I'm being serious. I had to say that first, because I really want to say something else.' She took another breath. 'I loved you so much, Liam, back then. I was smitten. Blown away. You were all I could think about. And for ages after, I thought about you. For years, really.'

Jude almost gasped as she had said this. She had never said anything like this to him at the time. She had never said anything like this out loud. She thought of Nat and felt a stab of guilt.

Liam shook his head slowly. 'You turned my life upside down too, you know.'

'And then it got taken away. After the crash.' Now Jude spoke very carefully and slowly. 'When I look back on it, it's like a kind of fairy tale. This awful thing happened and at the end of it, I got everything I wanted and you lost most of what you wanted.' Jude looked at Liam but she couldn't see any response. She couldn't tell what he felt. 'Afterwards, you rejected me. You didn't want to see me. I felt you hated the sight of me because of what we had been through and then I went into a tunnel and tried to pretend none of it had ever happened. I'm ashamed of that.'

'It was ten years ago,' said Liam softly.

'Eleven,' said Jude. 'More than eleven.'

'We were just kids.'

'I know. And here we are, all grown up.'

She looked down at her coffee. She had barely even touched it. She took a sip. It was cold. Without asking her, Liam picked up the two coffee cups, took them over to the counter and came back with two fresh ones.

'Here,' he said. 'Drink it before it gets cold too.'

Jude sipped her coffee; her head buzzed mildly.

'You haven't asked me why I got back in touch with you.'

'It's a shock. I'm still processing it all. Okay, so why have you got back in touch with me?'

Liam grinned and suddenly he looked just like when he was a teenager, when she was in love with him, and she could feel it right in her chest.

'I want you to do me a favour,' he said. His eyes were black as sloes.

'A favour?'

'Yes.'

'What kind of favour?'

He took a piece of paper from his pocket and pushed it across the table. She took it. It was an address: Springs Cottage, with a postcode she didn't recognise, but clearly out of London.

'What's this?'

'I want you to go there on Saturday.'

Jude had thought he might want some money. Or help with getting a job. Something that would make them both awkward. But she couldn't make any sense of this.

'I don't understand. You want me to go to this cottage? Why? Where is it?'

'There's nothing complicated. I've booked it for the weekend. It's an Airbnb place. I'll meet you there on Saturday evening and tell you what the favour is. It's nothing big.'

'You mean go there and stay the night?'

'Yes.'

'Where is it?'

'Norfolk.'

Jude felt lopsided; the table seemed to tip away from her. She didn't know whether it was her oncoming migraine or her sense of utter confusion.

'I don't understand what you're asking.'

He smiled, but his eyes were watchful. 'It's very simple.'

'Why me?'

Liam hesitated before replying.

'I thought of you,' he said finally. 'It felt like you were the only person I could ask. I think we're important to each other. We always will be.' He leaned forward. 'But I want to be clear, Jude. I'm asking a favour and you can just say no and I won't be cross and I won't reproach you. I'll just finish my coffee and we'll say goodbye and you'll never see me again.'

Jude took a sip of her coffee.

'It's gone cold again.' She replaced it on the saucer. She gave a funny little laugh. 'I feel embarrassed even saying this but . . . you're not asking me to do something wrong, are you?'

He shook his head. 'I wouldn't ask you to do anything wrong. Though you mustn't tell anyone. Not even this Nat of yours. Nobody at all.'

She looked at him full in the face and felt a lurch of memory so intense that it almost made her swoon: she could feel the heat of that summer, the feel of him, his touch and then its end in that screaming smash of metal.

'You know I can't say no, don't you?'

'I don't know that at all.'

'I go to this place on Saturday and come back on Sunday?'

'Yes.'

'Norfolk?'

'Yes.'

'And that's all?'

'Yes.'

'All right.'

CHAPTER THREE

Jude held her migraine at bay all the way home, pushing her bike for the last mile as if a moment of clumsiness might tip the pain over her like scalding liquid. The morning was misty and windless, wet leaves underfoot in a slimy carpet. The pale sky throbbed and shimmered above the Olympic Park. People loomed towards her and then were gone again. She opened the door to their little flat, steered herself into the kitchen, took off her coat, poured herself a glass of water.

The coffee in the cafetière was still faintly warm. Nat had left fruit and yoghurt out for her – or maybe he hadn't put them away after his own breakfast. Either way, she couldn't eat anything just now, though her stomach felt hollow. She needed to lie down but it was hard to make the effort, so she rested her head on the table, feeling the cool wood against her cheeks. Through the window she saw that someone else's cat was in the yard, next to the barbecue with the broken leg. She and Nat had talked of getting a cat when they moved to the place they were in the process of buying, which would, fingers crossed, be before Christmas, before their wedding in January.

Jude thought of Liam, his dark eyes watching her, watching the woman she had become: a doctor, about to get married, about to own a property and maybe even a cat.

She was feeling sick with her migraine and with old memories, ones that she had pushed deep inside her for years.

Making her way into the bedroom like a blind person, she closed the curtains, took off her clothes and climbed into bed, where she lay curled up in the merciful darkness, waiting it out.

Nat called her a super-sleeper. After years of working different shifts, she could lie down anywhere, at any time, close her eyes and be asleep within seconds. But for a long time that morning she couldn't sleep. Her eyes pulsed and dark shapes moved through her head.

Liam Birch, with his dark eyes and his smile. She saw him at eighteen and as he was now. He looked older than thirty, as if life had duffed him up. One of his teeth was chipped. He had tiny wrinkles round his eyes. He had a beard and smoke-stained fingers. His jacket was old – but he had always worn old clothes, rummaging through second-hand shops for things that took his eye. He was still beautiful.

Now this. It felt almost comic, like a practical joke. Perhaps that's what it was. It felt like a child's game, with the instructions about where to meet

27

and the secrecy. Cross my heart and hope to die. She would collect his car, drive up alone and when Liam arrived he would tell her what it was all about and that would be the end of it.

And she had promised not to tell anyone.

Which meant not telling Nat.

Which meant she would have to tell a lie.

'What are our plans this weekend?' asked Nat. 'You're off, aren't you?'

They were eating spicy coconut dhal, which she often made after working nights. She felt ravenous after her migraine.

'Dee invited us to theirs on Saturday,' he said. 'Some kind of party, and then there are the fireworks in the park.'

Jude put her fork into the creamy mess on her plate and stared hard at it. This was the moment she had been dreading. She was tempted to tell him a partial version of the truth. A friend had asked her for a favour. It was nothing. But as she'd played the conversation over in her head, it kept coming out wrong. Nat would start asking questions. What if he objected? It was easier just to lie. It made it simpler.

'I'm sorry, I can't,' she said, and stepped across a line. 'I've just arranged to go to see my granny.' Jude's grandmother had been ill and she had been talking about going to see her. She lived in Gloucester. It was plausible enough and she knew that Nat wouldn't want to come with her.

'Would you like me to come with you?'

'No,' she said quickly. Almost too quickly. She saw the look of relief that he tried to hide. 'I mean, that's really nice of you, but it's just a short visit and it would eat up your weekend when you've been working so hard all week. We'll probably just be sharing memories.'

'If you're sure.'

'I'm sure.'

'I'll try and manage without you,' he said lightly.

She looked up to meet his gaze, took in his grey eyes, his smooth face, the dark blond hair cut neat and short, the linen shirt. He looked clean and cool and trustworthy. She knew that if she pressed her face into his neck, he would smell of sandalwood.

It was quite easy to lie after all.

CHAPTER FOUR

Jude stood outside Blackhorse Road station in the drizzling rain, sipping the coffee she had bought. People hurried by with their heads lowered. She had arrived with plenty of time to spare and now she kept glancing at the time on her phone. There was a cold wind blowing, and she wished she had packed warmer clothes.

It was typical of Liam, she thought: when she had known him, he had always arrived late, strolling along, never in a hurry, never apologetic, as if it couldn't be helped.

Perhaps he wouldn't come at all and then she could go home and pretend this had never happened. It would be a relief. Yet at the same time she felt a touch of disappointment or even regret.

A car horn sounded and she turned to see a blue car drawing up on the double-yellow lines. It was old, with a dent in the rear door, and it didn't look in much better condition than the car they'd been in that night eleven years earlier. Liam opened the door and climbed out, leaving the engine running.

Jude hurried across.

'Ready?'

'I guess so.'

'I wrote down the full address. It's on the bit of paper in the cup holder. This road leads you on to the North Circular, so you'll be on the A12 in no time, heading east. The key is hanging on a nail in the porch.' The drizzle was thickening into chilly rain. He handed her a thin wallet. 'It's almost out of petrol.'

'I can pay.'

His expression hardened.

'You're doing me a favour, I don't want your charity as well. Promise you'll use my card.'

Male pride, she thought, and felt a twinge of pity and irritation.

'Okay.'

'The pin is 6613. I've written it under the address.'

A car horn sounded from behind. Liam's car was blocking the way. A man leaned out of his car window and shouted angrily. Liam casually gave him the finger. The man started to say something more but then Liam looked round at him and he subsided.

'I've left a bag of my stuff in the boot. Put it in the bedroom when you get in, will you?' He saw her face and grinned. 'There are two bedrooms,' he said. 'You don't need to worry.'

She just wanted to be on her way. She got into the car, slung her backpack on the seat beside her and adjusted the seat and rear-view mirror. Liam held the door open.

'I'm going to get a train that arrives at Ixley at half past nine this evening. Can you pick me up? It's just a few miles from the house.'

'Ixley,' Jude repeated. 'Nine-thirty.'

'Maybe you can buy some food. With my card, mind. There's a little shop in the village. We can have a late meal.'

'I should go before one of these cars rams me.'

She stared up at him. Raindrops were glistening in his dark hair and she had the tingling feeling that if she pulled him towards her and kissed him, then time would fold back on itself and they would be eighteen again, and the future would be different this time round. She could do things better.

She shrank back in her seat and frowned at him. 'This really is all right, isn't it, Liam?'

He smiled cheerfully. 'Don't stress. I'll tell you everything later. If you're not comfortable, you can say no.'

He leaned forward and kissed her on the cheek. Smell of cigarettes, bristle of beard. A stranger.

'Thanks, Jude.'

'See you at half past nine this evening,' she said.

He shut the door at last, and in the rear-view mirror she saw him walking away.

CHAPTER FIVE

The ancient Honda rattled its way out of London. Jude's phone told her it should take two hours and fifty-five minutes, because the A12 was clogged with traffic, presumably still escaping London for the weekend. As the car moved at walking pace, she nervously looked at the petrol gauge hovering on empty. What if she ran out? She pulled off at the first service station she saw and dutifully used Liam's card. Before setting off again, she examined the inside of the car. There were a few empty cans on the floor by the passenger seat, an apple core and chewing gum in the door compartment, a ripped road atlas, a tangle of wires under the dashboard, half a bottle of water. In the back was a child seat, a single miniature red wellington boot and a half-eaten pack of Skittles. Alfie.

Jude wondered about Alfie's mother. Did Liam live with her? Was he married? Did he see his little son every day, tuck him up in bed at night? He had said nothing about that, nothing really about anything, although he knew about her partner, her job. He had told her that he had messed up his exams, which she knew and which was a long-ago setback, but that his life was good now. On the whole, he had added, with one or two things to sort out – was she helping him sort out one of those things?

It wasn't too late to turn around and for a moment she let herself imagine that: turning off at the next junction, driving home, hugging Nat, going for a run to shake off the strangeness of the day. It would fall from her like a dream. But she drove on, of course. Anyway, where would she leave Liam's car? Not only did she have no idea where he lived, she realised that she didn't even have a number for him, an email address, any means of contacting him.

What had she been thinking?

The car inched forward and the rain fell.

Gradually the road became clear. Ahead the landscape was widening out and the grey sky grew larger. Jude, wrestling with the gear stick of the cranky car, focused on practicalities, remembering her to-do list on her bedside table that she added to each day, putting a neat line through the tasks accomplished. Their wedding was in late January, which some of her friends thought an inhospitable month to get married in, but Jude and Nat liked the idea. Nat had found someone who arranged wedding parties in a restored barn down in Shropshire with a view over the Clee Hills, near her parents' house. It looked beautiful, ornate, complicated. So much to arrange. All the people. There would be presents and speeches. Jude still couldn't quite believe it was going to happen.

She couldn't imagine Liam sending out invitations and getting a formal suit made. Unless he made it himself or had it done by someone he'd met somewhere. He had let things happen to him and let them go. Let her go. Jude knew that she and Liam would never have lasted; she had always known it. They were too different and their lives on such opposite trajectories. The crash had just accelerated what was inevitable. But if the crash hadn't happened and if they had simply drifted apart, Liam would be a nice, bittersweet memory now – a youthful summer fling without this power to drag her back to her past and stir up old desires.

During her first years of university, Jude had had relationships: lovely, terrible, brief, occasional. It had always been clear that they weren't going to amount to anything. There had been a fallow patch when all she thought about was work. Then, three years ago, she had met Nat on a blind date and it was as if she'd been waiting for him: steady, trusting and trustworthy. More than that, he was funny and straightforwardly affectionate and he didn't irritate her, which lots of people did. He was always attentive. Even sitting in Liam's car, she could feel the way Nat would stroke her hair, run his hands under her shirt. She could picture a future with him.

She was driving along a small road now, through a beech wood where some trees stood bare of leaves and others shone orange and gold. Then out again into a bare landscape, huge sky and marshes. Her feeling of unreality grew.

She slowed, glancing frequently at the map on her phone which was taking her down an even smaller lane, muddy and potholed, past a field edged with muddy piles of sugar beet. In the distance a tractor like a toy was moving across the muddy earth. She drove through a little village of flinty houses with a post office, a pub and a tiny supermarket. It was twenty past two. A sign-post pointed straight on for Ixley, where she was to meet Liam that evening, but she turned left, up a hill; then left again down a short driveway.

Springs Cottage.

Jude switched off the ignition but didn't get out of the car straightaway. She rested her forehead against the side window and waited. The cottage was small, square, painted white, with a grey slate roof and a chimney that was missing a few bricks at its crown. A rose bush growing up the wall still had a few tenacious yellow flowers. There was an enormous chestnut tree at the side of the cottage, its branches heavy with a mess of twiggy nests. Jude saw the dark shapes of rooks and then heard their harsh calls.

She opened the door and cold air rushed at her. The wind was getting up, and leaves flurried along the ground at her feet.

36

She collected her backpack and Liam's wallet and went towards the cottage. Sure enough, there was a key hanging on a nail in the porch, out of sight behind a wooden beam. Stepping inside, she dropped her backpack in the little hall. It was cold and smelled musty and unused. Probably people came here in the summer when they could go for long walks, swim in the sea which must be just a mile or so away, not in early November when everything was rain and mud and harsh winds sweeping in from the east.

The kitchen was small, red tiles on the floor, and a wooden table with a cactus on it and a laminated booklet of instructions. Jude opened the cupboards: there was four of everything, dinner plates and side plates and bowls, glasses and tumblers. She opened the fridge and it was clean and empty.

The living room was also small, with a bulky grey sofa, an armchair, an open fireplace but no wood to put in it, and a large flat-screen TV. The window looked over marshes and tall spindly trees that swayed like dancers on the horizon. The sea must be out there, she thought, and glanced again at her phone to check the time. If she was quick, she could have a walk before it got dark.

There was a message from Nat: *How's it going?* She sent him a thumbs-up icon and a heart.

Up the narrow stairs, where there was a bathroom, a moderate-sized bedroom with a double bed, and a tiny bedroom with a single one where she laid her backpack, plugging her phone into the charger. It was colder up here. She wished she had packed a hot-water bottle.

She remembered Liam's bag and jogged back down the stairs and outside to retrieve the holdall from the boot of the car. She put it on the double bed.

She had just over six hours before Liam's train arrived. She couldn't remember when she had last had so much unplanned time.

She drove Liam's car further down the lane to the coast, and walked along the track with marshland on one side of her and mudflats and choppy grey sea to the other. Her feet sank into the claggy earth. Her trainers and the hem of her jeans were soaked and muddy. Wind coming off the sea pummelled at her, and the light was thickening. But she felt exhilarated. She took pleasure in the scouring wind on her face, the rumble of the waves. There was nobody around. Nobody apart from Liam knew where she was. By the time she got back to the car, it was hard to see where she was walking. She liked this darkness that she never experienced in her city life.

She stopped at the little shop on the way back. Liam had said to get in some food. What? She wandered the shelves, then bought some onions, mushrooms, garlic and rice. She would make a simple risotto. That meant buying oil. She added parmesan to the basket and a bottle of red wine and some crisps. She remembered salt and stock cubes at the last minute. The thought of sitting in the kitchen, eating a meal with Liam, was unnerving.

She texted Nat. *Missing you.*

At the checkout, the woman looked at her curiously.

'I'm staying at Springs Cottage,' Jude said brightly.

'It's been empty a while,' said the woman.

Jude tried to make the heating work but only one radiator got warm. She thought she might run a bath but the plug seemed to be missing.

Outside, it was completely dark. There wasn't even a moon. Water dripped from the gutters.

She'd brought a book with her but couldn't concentrate on it. She made the risotto. She flicked through TV channels, read the news on her phone. She wanted to open the wine but couldn't because she was going to be using the car.

At ten past nine, she left the house, locking the door and sliding the key into her coat. She drove to Ixley station, the headlights making a tunnel of light through an unfamiliar world of woods and fields and marshland. Little creatures spun across the road.

There was a bang, and in the distance she saw a spark arcing into the sky and then exploding into petals of light, then another. She was missing Bonfire Night. She imagined her friends gathered in the park, setting off rockets and drinking mulled wine, and here she was in a place she had never heard of, meeting a man she hadn't seen for eleven years.

The car park was empty. The little station was deserted. She sat on the bench, in the darkness and the cold, and waited. She tried not to think about what Liam was going to say to her, what this favour actually consisted of. She tried not to think about why he had specifically chosen her, rather than one of his friends. The more she tried not to think about these things, the more she thought about them. What was it that she could do that nobody else could?

She made herself a promise. When Liam arrived, she would make sure she was absolutely clear about what it was he wanted her to do and then, whatever the obligation she felt to this man she had once loved, if it was wrong, she wouldn't do it. It would be embarrassing, he would probably be angry with her, but there was a line she wouldn't cross.

Did he expect an emotional attachment? A sexual attachment? She had felt immediately relieved that there were two bedrooms in the house. She had made it clear that she was engaged, she was committed. Had she made it clear enough, though? She considered it from his point of view and then from her own. Liam had been her first, and she could still remember the shock of that intimacy. It had been terrifying as well as thrilling. She had

40

left herself so open, so exposed. She'd heard of people, she'd even known people, who had met up with old boyfriends from years before and rekindled something. Sometimes it had been disastrous and sometimes it hadn't. She pushed away the idea. That was then and this was now, and in the now she was happy and in love with the man she was going to marry.

Liam was a stranger to her. She would carry out this favour for him, without doing anything she didn't want to do, and then she would go back to her life.

She heard the tell-tale rattle of the rails. A train was coming. She looked at her phone: 9:24. Yes, this was the one. She stood up and took a step forward and looked in the direction of London. In the darkness she could see the glow of the approaching train, surprisingly distant. She felt nervous. She wondered if Liam was feeling nervous as well. Probably not. After all, he had planned this, and in the past he had never seemed to feel apprehension about anything at all.

The rattling of the rails increased and she heard the clacking sound of the train itself becoming louder and the lights on the front of the train becoming larger. As it approached, she could see the figure of the driver, silhouetted, and she reflexively stepped back from the edge of the platform.

It slowed with a screeching sound. As it drew to a halt she glimpsed the outlines of passengers in the lit windows. It stopped. No doors opened. No one got on and no one got off. And then, after a couple of minutes, it was gone and Jude watched the red lights in the back disappearing into the darkness.

CHAPTER SIX

Jude was so startled that for a few moments she had trouble thinking straight. She took out her phone and looked at the time. There was no doubt about it. The train had arrived on time but Liam had not got off. Was it the right train? Perhaps the real one was about to arrive.

She would give it ten minutes. Now she found it impossible to sit calmly on the bench. She walked up and down the platform. She constantly checked her phone. The passing of the minutes was agonisingly slow, but finally ten minutes had gone and there was no sign of another train.

Perhaps Liam had missed the train, in which case she might have to wait for the next one. Using the torch on her phone, she was able to find a timetable on the wall and quickly saw that there was no next one. And the previous one had been fifty minutes earlier. There was no doubt about it. That had been the train and Liam hadn't been on it and if he was going to arrive by train it wouldn't be until tomorrow.

Jude cursed herself and him for not having given her any means of contacting him. What was she supposed to do now? For a horrible moment she thought Liam might have been playing a weird practical joke on her. But this practical joke involved her taking his car and his credit card and buying petrol with it.

She shivered. She was getting cold. Once again, she was tempted just to give up and return to London. He hadn't turned up. What was she expected to do? As soon as she thought of this she started to see the complications. She would have to go back to the house anyway, to collect her stuff and the food and Liam's bag. What then? Meanwhile, if Liam had missed the train, he would probably arrange another means of getting to Ixley. He might have rented a car or got a lift from someone. He was probably already on his way.

So she drove back to Springs Cottage and when she let herself in it felt twice as strange and lonely as before. She opened the wine and poured herself a glass. She didn't feel hungry but she opened the packet of crisps and took a couple and chewed on them almost without thinking. She didn't know what to do. The idea of watching TV or listening to the radio or reading her book seemed completely out of the question. She just sat at the table and refilled her glass of wine and slowly finished the crisps.

Suddenly she heard a sound, very faint and, it seemed, very far away, so far away that she couldn't make it out except that it sounded musical, repetitive. She moved her head, trying to find out where it was coming from. It was inside the house, upstairs. What could it be? A clock radio that had suddenly come on? She padded upstairs, her heart beating fast so that she could feel it in her temples. It made her feel faint.

It was coming from the main bedroom. She entered and the sound was louder but still muffled. She realised it was from inside Liam's bag. She unzipped the bag, opened it and the sound became clearer, more insistent. She pushed her hand inside, through clothes, rummaging, and her hand closed around something. She pulled it out and saw she was clutching a ringing phone. She stared at it as if it was an alien object. The caller ID said 'Erika'. She clicked on it.

'Hello?' she said.

'What?' said a voice. 'Hello, Liam, is that you?'

Jude looked at the phone, horrified, frozen. She didn't know what to do. She switched it off and put it back in the bag and stared down at it. She felt utterly confused. Why had Liam packed his phone in his bag? Could he possibly have done so by mistake? If it was his phone, did that mean he had another with him? Or no phone at all? Or was it somebody else's? That made even less sense and the voice had asked for Liam.

Jude left the room and started to walk downstairs but then she stopped halfway, thinking furiously. She couldn't make sense of anything. Liam hadn't arrived on the train. Was that part of his plan? Liam's phone was in his bag. Was that part of his plan too?

She walked back upstairs, picked up the bag and put it on the bed. She didn't know if this was right or wrong but she had to do it. She started to unpack the contents onto the bed. She did it slowly and carefully so that she would be able to replace everything, leaving no sign.

It was just what you'd expect in the luggage of someone staying away from home for a day or two: a heavy-duty blue shirt, a zip-up sweater, underwear, socks, a pair of trainers, a pair of jeans, earphones. She unzipped a grey cloth spongebag and found a toothbrush, toothpaste, a miniature deodorant can, a bottle of scent, cotton wool, a plastic razor. It seemed as if Liam had packed in a hurry. Everything looked as if it had been tossed in, without being folded properly. She picked up a small, carved piece of wood attached to a leather thong. She held it in the palm of her hand for a moment. It was a tiny wishbone, beautifully cut and shaped, and it reminded her of the Liam she had known, always fixing something or making something. He would do it absent-mindedly, whittling at a piece of wood with a penknife.

She was aware that Liam could arrive at any moment and it wouldn't do to be caught rifling through his bag. So she carefully replaced everything, trying to do it in the right order and trying also not to do it *too* carefully. She had to pack the bag the way Liam had packed it, not the way she would have done it, which meant the clothes weren't neatly folded and arranged but crammed in anyhow.

She picked up his mobile. She thought for a moment of checking it, to look at recent calls, emails, but as soon as she tried, it asked for the passcode. It was probably just as well, she thought. She pushed it back into the bag, under a shirt, the way it had been. She zipped up the bag, put it on the floor, and went downstairs.

The risotto was ready on the stove. It just needed heating up. Jude didn't know what to do. She didn't want to eat. She felt like a drink but she had already had two glasses of wine, maybe a bit more than two, and she had never had much of a head for alcohol. She probably wasn't thinking clearly as it was. She had already rejected the idea of leaving as impossible. But what about staying? She had lied to her fiancé. Now Liam had failed to appear and his bag was upstairs with the phone.

She couldn't think of what to do, so she simply sat in the armchair and stared in front of her.

CHAPTER SEVEN

At midnight, Jude finally climbed into the narrow bed. She had dozed off downstairs, waking with a jerk, unable for a moment to remember where she was, and when she did remember, she was flooded with unease.

Liam obviously wasn't coming tonight. Tomorrow, then. The first train got in at 8:25. She would meet that, and if he wasn't on it . . . She rubbed her face. She had no idea what she would do if he wasn't on it. Drive back to London and leave the car somewhere, to be towed away?

She set her alarm for seven, saw a WhatsApp from Nat and sent him a string of hearts in reply, cleaned her teeth, pulled on pyjama trousers and an old T-shirt. The sheets were chilly and she curled herself up into a ball, pulling her knees to her chin, rubbing her cold feet. She imagined being with Nat in their double bed at home, snuggling up to the warmth of him.

She closed her eyes and heard the wind in the creaking branches, the rain falling steadily. If she let herself, she could panic, lying here in the unfamiliar darkness, surrounded by marshland and then the sea, sweeping in over mudflats. Something had gone wrong. Something was going wrong right now.

She wanted to sleep and wake up to morning. In the morning she could sort things, get a grip on this mess. But sleep eluded her and time became a sludge, barely moving; she was adrift in the small hours, when dread can clutch.

Perhaps she slept a bit, she didn't think so, but then she was fully alert, sitting up in bed and her eyes straining in the darkness. A sound. What was it? Yes, it was Liam's phone ringing again, ringing at one in the morning. Jude stumbled from the bed and into the other bedroom, turned on the light. In the sudden dazzle, she unzipped Liam's bag, pushing her hand deep to find the phone before it stopped ringing.

'Hello,' she said. 'Hello. Who is this? Who's there?'

'Hello,' said a woman's voice. 'Who am I speaking to?'

'What?'

'Who am I speaking to?'

Jude sat on the bed. Her heart was pounding unnaturally fast and hard. Should she answer this question? She couldn't think clearly enough to decide the right thing to do.

'Jude Winter,' she said, then, ridiculously, amended this. '*Dr* Jude Winter. Who are you?'

'I'm Inspector Leila Fox. I'm a police officer. Where are you?'

'What?'

'Can you tell me where you are?' repeated the voice patiently.

Jude gave the address.

'Stay there. Don't leave the property. Don't call anyone. Someone will be with you shortly.'

'Someone? What do you mean, someone?'

'A police officer.'

'I don't understand. There's been a mistake.'

'This is Liam Birch's phone?'

'Yes.'

'We'll see you soon.'

When the call was finished, Jude thought furiously. The police. What could it be? She wasn't sure whether the panic she was feeling was for Liam or for herself.

Upstairs, she contemplated once more the inside of Liam's bag. She rumpled the clothes a bit. She unzipped the sponge bag and took out the bottle of scent. She sprayed her wrist and sniffed jasmine and green tea. She liked it. She replaced the bottle. After she had closed the bag once more, she noticed that while she had been rearranging the clothes, the necklace with the little wooden wishbone had fallen on the floor. She picked it up and held it in the palm of her hand. It was so delicate it weighed almost nothing. Reflexively she put it round her neck. She would consider it as payment for a favour.

CHAPTER EIGHT

It was over half an hour before Jude saw head-lights approaching and a police car pulled up. She opened the door and stood watching as two officers, a man and a woman, got out and walked towards her. She stepped back into the house and the officers followed her. They stood in the front room looking around.

'What's this about?' asked Jude. 'What's happened?'

'We were just told to come here,' said the woman.

'What do you mean? You must know something.'

'Someone said something about a phone.'

'What do you mean, a phone?'

'A phone that belongs to someone.'

'I've got a phone that belongs to a friend of mine,' said Jude. 'It rang and I answered it.'

'Where is it?'

Jude pointed to the table.

'We'd better just leave it there,' said the officer.

'I wasn't thinking of doing anything with it.' The atmosphere was awkward, as if they were people who had been introduced at a party and

had swiftly run out of things to say to each other.
'So what do we do now?'

'We wait.'

'What for?'

'Someone's coming up from London.'

'That'll take ages.'

'So we'd better get comfortable.'

'Do you want tea or something?'

'We're all right.'

The thought of sitting with these two officers for however many hours it was going to be felt unbearable.

'Is it all right if I go and lie down?'

'That's fine,' said the female officer. 'I'll have to come with you.'

'What for?'

'We were told to keep an eye on you.'

So Jude and the female police officer went upstairs to her bedroom and Jude lay on the bed, on top of the duvet, and the officer sat in a chair in the corner. Jude closed her eyes, not because she thought there was any chance at all of going to sleep, but just so she wouldn't feel any need to talk. But she did go to sleep, because the next thing she knew, she was being shaken awake.

'They're here.'

For a moment, Jude didn't know where she was, who was talking to her, who it was who was here. Then she recognised the policewoman leaning over her. She got up from the bed and felt terrible. It would have been better not to have slept at all:

her head was thick and woozy. She had a sour taste in her mouth.

'What's the time?'

'Quarter past three.'

The two detectives were sitting in the living room when Jude was led in. She had been expecting men in sharp suits, but they looked more like two teachers on a field trip, a bit dishevelled. The woman was tall and strong-looking, broad-shouldered. She was wearing a mud-streaked jacket and her T-shirt was inside out. Her hair was a tangled mass of brown curls and she had clear grey eyes that were gazing at Jude in a way that made her feel she was being assessed. The man was younger and was wearing what looked like walking gear: a wind-cheater, jeans and hiking boots.

They introduced themselves as Detective Inspector Leila Fox and Sergeant Brendan Patterson. Jude sat in a chair facing them.

'Our colleagues are making you some tea,' said Leila Fox. 'I think you'll need some. I certainly do.'

Jude swallowed. What had happened? What was this about? She wanted to know but couldn't think what questions she should ask. She was aware of Fox looking at her with interest and curiosity.

'We're a bit puzzled by things,' she said. 'We were hoping you could help us out.'

Jude couldn't think of anything to say so Leila Fox continued.

'You're a friend of Liam Birch, is that right?'

'I knew him when we were younger. Years ago.'

'But you're friends?'

'We completely lost touch but we met up again a couple of days ago. Briefly.'

Leila Fox wrinkled her brow and turned to her colleague. He was sitting slightly to one side as if he were observing not only Jude but also the other detective. She looked back at Jude.

'I'm afraid I've got bad news for you,' she said. 'Liam Birch was found dead late last night.'

As soon as she had heard that detectives were driving up from London, Jude had known it would be something bad, but even so she felt as if she had just suffered a blow to the head. The room seemed to be moving around her. She couldn't speak. She heard a voice beside her. The uniformed officer, the woman, had put a mug of tea on the table in front of her and was urging her to drink it. She leaned forward and tried to pick the mug up, but her hand was shaking and some tea spilled so she put the mug back down. Liam was dead. He had come back into her life and now he was dead. Somewhere deep inside her a feeling dislodged itself. It felt physical, sharp and heavy. She knew it would work its way up through her. Later, she thought, not now.

'What happened?' she said at last, in a voice that sounded unfamiliar to her. 'Did he have an accident?'

'No.'

Everything seemed to be happening slowly and she couldn't think clearly. At the same time she was aware that she was being looked at, scrutinised. She could feel the detectives' eyes on her, studying her reaction.

'What do you mean?' she managed to say.

'He was found by the side of a path on Walthamstow Marshes,' said Leila Fox. 'You know that area?'

'No, I don't,' said Jude faintly.

'It looked like a mugging that had gone wrong. Wallet and phone missing, but there was a business card in his pocket. Then a strange thing happened. We rang the number, not expecting anything. But you answered. In a cottage in Norfolk.'

'I didn't know it was here. It was in his bag. I answered it earlier in the evening.'

'Did the caller identify themself?'

'The name came up on the screen. Erika.'

'What did this Erika want?'

'I don't know. I ended the call.'

The detective looked at her for several seconds. 'Is anyone else here?'

'No.'

'Has anyone else been here?'

'No.'

There was a pause.

'What are you doing here, in Norfolk, with Liam Birch's phone? And his luggage.'

'I was waiting for him. He was meant to arrive this evening. I mean, yesterday evening. I went to the station to collect him but he wasn't on the train.'

Leila Fox smiled sympathetically. 'You're going to have to say more than that.'

Jude thought about what she could say and decided she had no choice. So she told the whole story of Liam arriving at the hospital and their conversation in the café and what he had asked her to do and while she was talking she was listening to herself. She had thought and thought about this, but now that she was putting it into words and saying the words aloud, it felt even stranger. Absurd even. She could tell as she spoke that this wasn't what they had been expecting. When she was finished, the two detectives looked restless and dissatisfied.

'I have so many questions,' said Leila Fox after a pause during which they stared at her and she wanted to scream. 'I hardly know which one to ask first. For a start, I have to ask, were you in a relationship with Liam Birch?'

'No.' Jude didn't know if this was another lie. They had been in a relationship eleven years before, but that was different. 'I knew him when we were seventeen, eighteen. Friends, that's all.'

'I mean now.'

'Not at all. I'm getting married in a couple of months.'

'To someone else?'

'Of course to someone else.'

'This someone else: does he know you're here?'

Jude hesitated for a fraction too long. 'No, he doesn't.'

'Where does he think you are?'

'I'm sorry,' said Jude in a distressed tone, 'but what does it matter where my fiancé thinks I am?'

Leila leaned forward. 'Put yourself in our position, Jude. A man has been murdered and for some reason his phone is over a hundred miles away.'

'I have his wallet as well,' Jude blurted out.

'You have his wallet?'

'Yes.'

The woman raised her eyebrows. 'This is all very confusing. For example, you're saying that Liam Birch asked you for a favour but I'm not clear what the favour was.'

'I'm not clear either,' said Jude. 'He said he was going to tell me what it was when he got here.'

'Why you?' said the male detective. He had a sharp, metallic voice that Jude disliked. 'You said you haven't seen him for more than ten years. Why does he suddenly turn up and ask you for a favour?'

'I don't know. We were close once. But it was a long time ago.'

'I'm sorry,' said Leila. 'Forgive me if I'm being stupid, but can we look at it from the other point of view. I mean your point of view. This man from your past asks you to do him a favour and you say yes, even though you don't know what it is.'

'That's right.' Jude tilted her chin defiantly.

'Weren't you worried that it might be something illegal?'

'I asked him and he said that he wouldn't ask me to do anything that was wrong.'

'And you believed him?'

'Yes.'

'But you didn't tell your fiancé what you were doing. Why was that?'

'I thought it might seem strange to him.'

'Is he the jealous type?'

'I don't think so. Not particularly. It just seemed hard to explain.'

'It's definitely hard to explain,' said Leila with another slight smile, 'because I don't understand it at all. Someone you've completely lost touch with pops up and asks you to do a favour, even though he won't say what it is. Why would he do that?' She paused but Jude didn't say anything. 'I feel that most people would say no, sorry, that sounds worrying or too weird or whatever, but instead you not only say yes but you don't tell your fiancé about it. Why would you do such a big thing for someone you don't know any more?'

'It's hard to explain.'

'I know,' said Leila. 'But we're the police and you really do need to explain things like this. Even if it's hard.'

Jude took a deep breath.

'I knew Liam when we were both teenagers. He was nice. I liked him.' She paused and looked towards the window and the darkness beyond.

58

Nice. Liked. She saw Liam's beautiful face, his dark eyes. 'But he was a bit reckless, a bit, I don't know, adrift or something. When I went to university, it always felt like a fork in the road. We went in different directions. I did everything I always planned. I went to medical school and had a wonderful time. I became a doctor and got a great job. I had relationships. Now I've met Nat and we're going to get married and buy a place together.' Jude could feel tears running down her face. She took a tissue from her pocket and wiped them and blew her nose. 'During all that time, I never saw Liam, but he was somewhere in the back of my mind.'

'The love that got away?' said Leila Fox.

'No, I told you.' Jude stopped. 'I just had the feeling that everything had worked out for me and it hadn't worked out for him. I'd been lucky and he'd been unlucky and there's a kind of guilt attached to that. Being okay when all around you there are people who aren't. So when he came to me and asked for a favour, I just said yes. I felt I had to do it. And then this happened.' She looked at the two detectives. 'What do you think? Could it just be terrible, terrible bad luck?'

'What do *you* think?'

'I don't know. I don't have any other information apart from what I've told you. I don't know anything. As you said, I was a hundred miles away.'

Leila Fox's face looked more sombre. She thought for a moment then told Jude that they would be driving her back to London. One of the uniformed officers would accompany her as she got her things. They would take care of Liam's car.

CHAPTER NINE

Jude climbed into the rear of the car with her backpack, her head thick with exhaustion. The car set off, its headlights sweeping across the rough-surfaced lane, the trees and the marshes. She didn't want to think and she certainly didn't want to talk to the police or answer any more of their questions.

She closed her eyes and tried to breathe deeply and evenly, to concentrate only on her breathing: air going in, air going out. She heard the low rumble of conversation from the front of the car, the occasional swish of the windscreen wipers. Every so often lights coming from the other direction shone on her closed lids.

What did they think?

It wasn't hard to guess. They thought Liam had been her lover, because why else would she have done him this favour? She had seen their expressions when she talked about the guilt she felt at her luck. They didn't believe her. But what favour did Liam want? What did they think? What did Jude herself think?

Now they were driving her back to London, where Nat would be waiting.

She opened her eyes cautiously to look at the time illuminated on the dashboard. They had been driving for nearly an hour. It was just gone five o'clock; with no traffic they would probably be back in London by about six-thirty. What would she say to Nat when she stumbled in? She tried it out in her imagination: *I told a lie. I didn't go and visit my grandmother. I went to a cottage in Norfolk because someone I hadn't seen for over eleven years turned up and asked me to do him a favour.*

She had told Nat about other relationships, but she had never told him about Liam. She'd just said, shrugging it off casually, that she'd had a couple of flings before university. No names. Just the general act of growing up, discovering oneself, having fun.

Fun.

She remembered the agony of being head over heels with Liam. It hadn't been fun. It had been all-consuming and then it had ended. She had never talked about it to anyone, but buried it deep inside.

Now Liam was dead.

The car sped on.

Someone had killed him. He had a little boy called Alfie. He had a few things that needed sorting out.

Fields gave way to edgelands. There were more cars on the road now, heading into London. The clocks had gone back the week before and there was a faint smudged light on the horizon. The rain was starting to fall again; a new day was beginning.

What should she say to Nat?

'You can drop me here.'

'We're not there yet,' Leila Fox said. Jude saw her eyes in the rear-view mirror.

'Here's good.'

The car drew up and she opened the door.

'Obviously we'll need to see you again,' said the detective.

In the light, Jude saw how tired she looked, shadows under her grey eyes, and her hair a spectacular mess.

'I've told you everything,' said Jude.

Leila Fox gave her a faint smile, sympathetic or perhaps tolerantly amused.

'We'll be in touch.'

Jude climbed out of the car, hauling her backpack after her. The wet wind slapped at her. She watched as the car drew away.

CHAPTER TEN

It was one of November's grim, lowering mornings, not fully light, the sky dull grey, leaves flurrying and twitching like litter, vans sending up sprays of water from the puddles: an admin day, a baking-and-board-game day, a duvet-day in front of the TV.

Jude fished out her mobile. It was ten past seven. It was too early to go home. She wandered down a side street in search of a café but it was Sunday and most places weren't yet open. She was chilly and damp and tired, and behind that, like a heavy shadow, she was scared. She set off in the direction of the Olympic Park whose helter-skelter slide was a smudgy shape in the rain, but long before she reached it found a café that was open. There was no one else there, and she sat at a Formica-topped table with a cappuccino and sipped it, staring out at the rain, thinking, trying not to think, seeing Nat's face and seeing Liam's. They hadn't told her how he had been killed: was he shot or stabbed or punched or pushed? Had he suffered? And was he really dead? Had she really been crouched in a little cottage near the Norfolk coast last night waiting for him? Was this really happening to her?

She ordered another cappuccino but drank only half. As she got up to leave, she saw her reflection in the glass of the door, like a ghost. She noticed the carved wishbone on the little leather thong around her neck. She had completely forgotten about it. Would Nat ask about it? Normally he didn't notice things like that. But she didn't want to take it off. She felt, strangely, that it would be disloyal to Liam. She tucked it inside her shirt.

She walked through empty residential streets and reached her own door at half past nine, took a deep breath, stood up straighter, went inside.

Nat was on the phone as she came in, talking in a low, calming voice. When he saw her standing there so obviously tired and spent, his face went blank with surprise for a moment, but then he ended the call and took her in his arms as if she had been away for weeks. He smelled clean; his hair was still wet from the shower and he was freshly shaved. Jude sat at the kitchen table while Nat made tea for them both. He placed a mug in front of her then leaned down and kissed her on the top of her head. Then he sat opposite her with his own mug. Jude wondered: was there something about his expression? Did he suspect something?

'You're back sooner than I expected,' he said. 'I didn't know there were such early trains.' Panic flooded Jude; she couldn't bring herself to speak.

But Nat didn't expect an answer. 'Was she glad to see you?' he asked.

Now was the moment. Jude looked into his face, still a bit puffy from sleep. Now, she thought. Her imagination ran ahead of her, hearing the words she was going to say, seeing his confused face.

'Yes,' she said. 'It was the right thing to do.' As she spoke, she told herself that she would never lie to Nat again after this. Not ever. This was a one-off and it would be a lesson to her. 'She's so old now,' she said. 'I get a bit of a shock each time I see her.'

Nat took her hand, turning the engagement ring on her finger, nodding.

Jude shut her eyes because she couldn't bear to look into his believing face. There was no reason that he should ever have to find out about this wreckage of a weekend.

'What did you talk about?'

'Oh, you know, the past. Memories. That's where she lives now, in her memories. Then I cooked her a meal and she went to bed. I had trouble sleeping though,' she added, to account for her obvious weariness.

'That's not like you. Migraine?'

'Yes.'

Another lie. Little lie upon big lie.

'Everyone missed you at Dee's last night.'

'So you went?'

'Yeah. Shall I run you a bath?'

'That would be good.'

'Then brunch?'

'Great. Thanks. Did you have a good time?'

'It was fine. I missed you, though.'

Jude forced a smile.

'You're allowed to have a good time when I'm not there, you know.'

'All right. I had a reasonably good time.'

'Were there fireworks?'

'It rained. Nobody stayed long. I came home early.'

She got up and walked round the table and kissed him.

'I do love you,' she said.

'You'd better,' he said easily. 'What with the wedding and everything.'

Leila Fox rang her that afternoon. Jude snatched up her mobile and took it into the yard.

'Would tomorrow be convenient?'

'I'm working.'

'I was just being polite. We can come to you before you go to work or after you get back.'

Jude felt a rush of panic.

'I'll come to you.'

CHAPTER ELEVEN

When Jude woke the following morning her head felt clear. She would go to the police station, answer any remaining questions, and then it would be over. She would have learned a lesson. Nat was still asleep, bundled up in the duvet with his forearm over his eyes, small comforting snores coming from him every so often. She stood by the bed for a moment, looking at him. It would be okay.

She made herself a pot of tea, then boiled an egg, dipping toast into the yolk and eating slowly while she scrolled through messages on her phone: drinks after work, a movie tomorrow with a group of women friends, yoga class on Wednesday followed by a meal out and she was supposed to have booked the table for six and hadn't. Did she want to sign up for a half-marathon? No, she didn't, she could barely run six miles. Did she and Nat want to go to a gig at the weekend? Did she want to go halves on a friend's thirtieth birthday present? How about a pizza and board-game night sometime soon? She sent messages, washed up her breakfast things, hung her lanyard round her neck, feeling the little leather string of Liam's necklace like a guilty reminder, and left the flat.

Jude didn't think she had ever been into a police station before, and it felt unreal as she pushed open the door and stepped into the windowless reception area, as if she was in a play whose lines she hadn't learned. There were a few rows of plastic chairs and a large desk behind a Perspex screen. It felt rather like the waiting area in A & E, except that was always crammed and noisy. Here there was only one other person: a thin elderly woman in slippers, sitting very straight and holding a large bag on her lap with both hands.

There was no one at the desk so Jude rang the bell and waited. The woman gazed at her fixedly. A burly man appeared. Even though the room was chilly, he had beads of sweat on his forehead and damp patches under his armpits.

She told him she was expected and he found her name on the computer system and then pointed his thick finger at the chairs.

'Take a seat,' he said.

Jude didn't want to take a seat. She wandered across to the noticeboard but the only notice on it was one about where to park in the area.

She heard her name being called and turned round. Leila Fox was there. Even in a police station, she still didn't look much like a detective to Jude. She was wearing a green corduroy shirt and her unruly hair was held back by a colourful headband. She smelled musky, something with patchouli, thought Jude. Her handshake was vigorous.

Through the door at the back, down a corridor that could have been a hospital corridor, into a room with unpleasantly harsh lighting and chairs ranged round a rectangular table. There were filing cabinets under the window, and a picture of a vase of flowers on the wall. It was hanging askew and Jude automatically straightened it.

The young male detective, Brendan Patterson, entered the room, carrying three paper cups that he set on the table. He produced packs of sugar and milk from his jacket pocket, scattering them in front of her.

'I don't know how you like it.'

'This won't take long, will it?' asked Jude.

'We just want to clear up a few things,' said Leila.

It was more than a few things, and it was recorded on a large machine that looked as if it belonged to a previous age and made Jude jittery: her fumbled words were becoming evidence, stored.

Leila asked all the questions. Jude had to go through the whole story again, tripping over words, suddenly worrying that she was contradicting what she had said before.

'You really hadn't seen Liam Birch for eleven years?'

'No.'

'And you say there was no sexual involvement?'

'No. I mean, yes, I do say that there was no sexual involvement.'

'So you just did what he asked for old time's sake.'

'Yes.'

Every true thing she said sounded like a lie. Her voice was scratchy. She took a sip of the coffee. It tasted bitter.

'You do see the problem,' asked Leila Fox.

'No, I don't.'

The detective readjusted her headband, gathering up her unravelling hair.

'With your . . .' She paused, apparently searching for the right word.

'He's not my anything.'

'With him being murdered in London and you up in Norfolk with his wallet and his phone and his car.'

'I'm as baffled as you are.'

'You think?' Leila Fox's expression was bland. 'Jude, we know you're in an awkward position with your boyfriend – fiancé,' she corrected herself. 'We're not judging you. We don't care if you were having an affair with Liam.'

'I wasn't.'

'It's quite common, people reconnecting with old flames from their past. We get that. But if you're lying to us, you're wasting our time and energy and, even more seriously, you might be messing up our investigation, just to hide your embarrassment.'

'That's not right.'

Fox frowned. 'You're a doctor. You have to be clever to be a doctor, don't you? When Liam asked you to do this, what did you think it was about?'

'He said he was going to tell me when he arrived.'

'Did you think of any possible explanation that was harmless? That was legal?

'I didn't think. He told me it wasn't wrong and I believed him.'

'But you didn't tell your partner.'

'That was for a different reason.'

'On that subject, I recommend that you do tell him, because it looks like it's going to go public.'

Jude felt the breath going out of her. She tried to stay calm.

'What do you mean?'

'A journalist somehow got hold of the story,' said Leila. 'We don't yet know how.'

'About Liam?' Jude whispered.

'That was public already. I mean about your involvement.'

'But I wasn't involved. How did they find out?'

'I don't know.'

Jude thought for a moment. Desperately.

'Someone must have leaked it. I mean you must have. Someone in the police.'

'I don't accept that.'

'Who else knew?'

Neither of the detectives replied. Jude blinked several times. 'When will it appear?'

Leila Fox shrugged. 'I don't know. It could be anytime. Today, tomorrow, next week. The press might even decide not to run it.'

'I've got to go.' Jude lurched to her feet, putting a hand on the table to steady herself.

'Are you all right?'

She couldn't speak for a moment. Hot tears filled her eyes and her throat was thick.

'I think I've messed things up,' she said.

'Tell us what happened. What was Liam up to?'

'Stop,' said Jude. 'I don't know anything about Liam. But I've ruined things.' She looked at Leila. It was as if Patterson wasn't even in the room. 'What should I do?'

'Speak to him. Tell him the truth.'

CHAPTER TWELVE

Jude made it out of the station, into the cold wind. She took her phone from her pocket and called Nat. Her breath came in shallow gasps as she waited for him to pick up. It went to voicemail. She tried again. He'd be at work by now. He was probably in a meeting. She sent him a WhatsApp – *please call me asap*. She could see he wasn't online.

She stood for a moment, undecided what to do. Should she bike to his office? She would be horribly late for work but that didn't matter. Not today, not this once. She stared at the ticks beside the message but they didn't turn blue: he hadn't read it yet.

Perhaps the story wouldn't be published. Perhaps it would be published but he wouldn't see it. Perhaps it would be tomorrow, or next week.

She gnawed at her knuckles, trying to think what to do. What she really wanted to do was to go back in time and say no to Liam's request. It was stupid, but she kept replaying that short meeting between them. She had thought she had no choice. How could she have been so stupid? And how

74

could she have lied to Nat? That wasn't her. She didn't do things like that.

She looked at the phone again. He still hadn't seen the message. Perhaps she shouldn't have sent it. It might be better to risk it and wait until this evening when they were together and she could tell the story properly, face to face.

She hovered a finger over the delete icon, and as she did so, the arrows turned blue.

She waited for him to call, but he didn't. She hesitated, then called him and he didn't pick up.

She cycled to work along the main roads, late and weaving dangerously in and out of traffic; when she finally arrived at the hospital she called again, and again he didn't pick up.

She held her mobile away from her, as if it was a bomb that was about to go off. Nat was busy, that was all. He had said it was a day crammed with meetings.

When she arrived at the hospital, Jude put her phone in the locker. She was ferociously energetic and concentrated as she went from patient to patient. She didn't give herself time to think; she held the mess at bay.

During a break, she went to the locker and took out her phone. Still nothing from Nat, but there was a message from a friend called Carmen. *What the fuck, Jude?*

A jolt of panic went through her. She turned off her phone, went to the Ladies and sat on the toilet with her head in her hands, trying to breathe slowly and deeply.

What the fuck, Jude?

At the end of her shift, Jude collected her coat and bag and turned on her mobile. The screen filled up with missed phone calls and messages: ping, ping, ping, ping.

'You're popular!'

She turned to see her consultant and made a meaningless gesture; a weird sound came from her, halfway between a laugh and a yelp.

'Stuff,' she said. 'You know.'

She half-ran towards the exit, scrolling down the questions and exclamations until she got to Nat's name. *Tell me this isn't true.*

Meet me at home? she wrote and pressed send.

I'm already there.

On my way.

CHAPTER THIRTEEN

Nat was in the kitchen when she came in. He didn't smile and Jude didn't smile. Panic was like a bird in her chest.

'I've been trying to reach you all day,' she said.

He was wearing his glasses, which always made him look older and more serious. If she touched him now, he would be like wood.

'I want to explain,' she continued.

'Is it true then?' he asked. Then, as her mobile in her pocket gave a series of beeps, 'Turn off your bloody phone, for once in your life.'

He had never raised his voice to her before. He had never sworn at her. Jude fumbled with her mobile. Her hands were trembling and her fingers felt useless.

She didn't know what he knew or what he thought. In her blind fear, she hadn't even done a search for the article yet, as if she could hold the ghastly mess at bay by pretending it didn't exist.

'It's true I was in Norfolk,' she said, and watched the way his face tightened. 'I should have said. I've been such a fool.'

'A fool?' Nat gave a harsh laugh. 'Is that what

77

you call it? You tell me you're going to see your grandmother, you race off to some cottage in Norfolk to be with a man I've never heard of, you get embroiled in a murder investigation, and you still carry on lying. Fool? Is that the right word?'

'It's not what you think.'

'What do I think?'

'Probably that I was cheating on you. I get that.'

Nat stared at her. He took off his glasses and laid them on the table, then rubbed his eyes violently.

'What am I supposed to think? I thought we were happy.'

'We were – we *are*. I love you. I love you very much. I swear there was nothing going on.'

'You lied,' he said, laying it down flat like a trump card. 'Why would you lie like that?'

'Can I try and tell you?'

She told him the same story she had told the police, and he listened without interrupting her. And again, the words sounded flimsy and unreliable. She no longer felt that she was telling the truth.

'I felt guilty about him,' she said at the end, when Nat remained silent. 'About how his life had gone so wrong while mine had gone so right. He made me feel how unfair life is. I thought I had to agree. He made me promise not to say anything to anyone. Including you. He said he would tell me what he wanted when he got to the cottage, but then he got killed and everything blew up in my face. I can't believe now that I agreed to any

78

part of it. I hate that I lied to you. But I haven't been unfaithful. I never would. Nat? Tell me you believe me.'

'I don't know. Why should I?'

'I swear it's the truth.'

'This time, you mean?'

He stared at her and she flushed and looked away.

'Yes,' she said.

'I thought you trusted me,' he said eventually.

'I did! I do.'

'If you'd trusted me, and if this weird tale was actually true, then you would have told me what he had asked for as soon as it happened. We would have talked about it. I would have said it was a completely crazy thing to do; ridiculous and wrong and out of the question. We might have had a discussion or an argument. But you just made up a story. A convincing story, Jude, and what's more, one that made you seem kind and considerate, the lovely granddaughter. You did it so *well*.'

'I'm sorry,' said Jude. 'I'm really, really sorry.' Her voice wobbled and hot tears started rolling down her cheeks. 'I'd do anything not to have done it. I can't understand now why I did. But there was nothing between me and Liam. You have to believe me.' She leaned forward, her hands pressed together as if she was praying. 'I hadn't seen him for eleven years. I just – I just – I don't know. Honestly, Nat, I only want you. I will never do anything like this again. Tell me it's all right.'

'All right? Everyone will know. I look like a complete idiot.'

Was *that* what he cared about? Jude didn't reply.

'I can't think,' said Nat, standing up abruptly, screeching his chair along the tiles. 'I'm going for a walk, clear my head. We can talk about it tomorrow.'

He left the flat and Jude sat with her head resting in the crook of her arms, limp and wrung out.

She felt cold and tired and she was probably hungry, though it was hard to tell because she felt sick. Maybe a migraine was on its way.

She had told Nat there was nothing going on with Liam now. But telling him that she and Liam had been together all those years ago had been too complicated and messy, so she hadn't said anything about that at all.

CHAPTER FOURTEEN

It was easy enough for Jude to find the article: she just put Liam's name and her own into Google search and there it was on a news website she had never heard of called The Pulse. Jude read it rapidly, feeling sick. It was all there: Liam's murder, her mysterious involvement, the cottage in Norfolk, the clear implication of their secret affair. A photograph of Liam looking sleepy and amused sat alongside an old one of her, tired and unsmiling, in her hospital scrubs.

Nat didn't come back that night. Jude slept fitfully and each time she woke she put out a hand to feel for him. She called him and she sent him messages but there was no reply. She didn't know what else to do except wait, and she hated waiting.

At six, she got up and went for a short, damp run, came home and showered, dressed, then ate a poached egg on a crumpet for breakfast.

At work, she realised that as the day went on a few people were giving her sidelong looks. They must have read the story, she thought, and felt shivery with shame and a kind of itchy misery. But she knew that the way to deal with humiliation was to confront it and, at last, as her shift was ending, she made herself do exactly that, stopping a colleague outside the ward. He rubbed his face, smiled nervously.

'Just say it.'

Piers was a very thin, very pale young man and Jude watched as a flush spread up his neck and into his face.

'You've read the story about me. Say something!'

'I did,' he admitted, not looking at her. 'But only after someone sent me the picture of you.'

'Picture?'

'On Instagram.'

'Someone posted a photo?'

'It was from years ago,' said Piers.

She hurried to her locker, not meeting the eyes of anyone in case they too knew something about her that she didn't, trying to look as if nothing was wrong.

It was only when she was out of the hospital grounds, sheltering from the driving rain under a sycamore tree whose fallen leaves were spread in a circle around her, that she took out her phone.

The photograph had been posted by someone called Flo Duncker. Jude couldn't immediately place her, but then she remembered. Hair in a thick braid, played the saxophone, had glandular fever in her GCSE year. She'd been on the fringes of Jude's friendship group, but they hadn't kept in touch. And now Flo Duncker had posted a photograph of her. Jude's fingers were clumsy as she pulled up the image.

A slender girl in ragged denim shorts and a bikini top, her short black hair spiky and wet. Jude could see her ribs, the silver chain round her ankle. She had her arms round the neck of a bare-chested, barefooted youth in jeans, who held her round the waist, his hands on her bare skin, his head lowered towards her. Both of them half-smiling. They are about to kiss, or they have just separated from a kiss.

One afternoon of a long-ago summer. What the picture didn't show, but Jude knew was there, was the river behind her and Liam where the willows dipped their leaves and swans floated by in flotillas, raising their wings to threaten swimmers. She remembered that afternoon, remembered it as if it was not long gone. A group of them lying on the bank in the blazing heat, eating over-ripe cherries and spitting the pips, drinking warm white wine from the bottle, passing joints between them. Liam was there, and even when she closed her eyes she could feel him. Just a week or two before the crash.

If her colleague had seen it, someone who wasn't even a friend, who else had? She looked back down at her phone and her stomach turned: already there were 5,293 likes and 1,077 comments, and as she looked the numbers rose. She wanted to be sick.

Nat, she thought. There was no way he wouldn't see it.

She thought of the police officer, Leila Fox, with her grey eyes and horribly amiable smile, looking at this image, tapping her fingers on the table.

She didn't know what to do. She thought of calling Nat, but instead she called her friend, Dee.

'Are you at home?'

'On my way. I'll be there in ten minutes or so.'

'Can I come over?'

'Sure. I'll put the kettle on. Or maybe open the whisky?'

'You've seen it?'

'You look pretty good in it.'

Jude ended the call and made her way to her bike.

'Dr Winter? Excuse me. Dr Winter?'

Jude turned. A woman about her age was gesturing her. She had a friendly smile, but Jude didn't recognise her.

'Yes?'

'I was wondering if I could speak to you?'

'What?'

'About Liam Birch.'

'What do you mean? Who are you?'

'It would be great to have your side of the story as well.'

'Are you a journalist?'

'You might find it helps . . .'

Jude turned towards the woman. She looked like someone she could have been friends with. She forced herself to be polite.

'I'm sorry. I can't.'

'I thought you might want to tell your story.'

'I'm a private person. I can't do that.'

'I want to give you a chance to respond,' said the woman, putting her hand on Jude's arm. 'People are saying things about you.'

To Jude, it felt like a threat. Talk to me, or else. She pulled away from the woman's hand and shook her head.

'I'm sorry,' she said. 'Or rather, I'm not sorry at all. Go away. I've absolutely nothing to say to you.'

She walked away as quickly as she could.

It rained on the way and Jude arrived at her friend's flat cold and wet. She was glad Dee's flatmates were away for a few nights, at a wedding in Scotland. She couldn't bear the thought of being with people, being looked at, pitied, criticised, judged. Dee sat her on a sofa and brought her a thick cardigan, a pair of walking socks and a glass of whisky. Jude took a gulp and felt a warmth spreading in her chest.

Dee sat opposite Jude, waiting for her to speak. The wind was strengthening. Jude looked through the uncurtained window at the cranes on the horizon, with lights picking out the giant raised arms. She thought of her and Nat's flat, miles from here, which had felt like home but now seemed tiny and precarious.

'I'm in a bit of trouble.'

'Tell me.'

Jude told her everything from the dreamy teenage

passion that had ended in the crash, up to the police interview room. Dee just nodded and looked at her and, when Jude had finished, she didn't say anything.

'Well? Do you believe me?'

'Believe what?'

'That I wasn't involved with Liam. Not in the past. I mean now, sexually.'

Dee hesitated, narrowing her eyes.

'Would you have? If he'd come to the cottage as he'd planned.'

'No.'

Dee nodded slowly, considering. This was why Jude had turned to her. She was a friend but she was also sternly dispassionate, turning things over to see them from every angle, careful in her reactions. 'Does Nat believe you?'

'I don't know. Yesterday he was . . .' She considered this. 'He wasn't just angry. It was worse. He was *disappointed* in me, that was the worst thing. Then he went out last night and didn't come back, and that was before this photo started going viral. I haven't talked to him today.'

'Did he know about you and Liam, how you used to be together?'

'I know it sounds weird. It's complicated. Liam was complicated. My feelings for him. It ended strangely. It wasn't something I could talk about. I didn't have the words.'

'So the answer is no.'

Jude nodded slowly. 'I didn't tell him. Not even

now, when we talked about what I'd done, how I'd lied to him and everything.'

They sat in silence for a few moments. Dee held up the bottle and Jude nodded, so she poured her some more.

'What shall I do?'

'Talk to Nat. What else is there?'

'You're right. Of course Nat is angry with me. I've deceived him. Do you think he'll forgive me?'

'I don't know.'

'I keep thinking of him at the fireworks, while I was in that creepy cottage. Missing me, trusting me, before it all exploded. I wish I could turn back the clock.'

'If it makes you feel any better,' said Dee, 'you didn't miss much. It rained all evening. Most of us left the fireworks early.'

Jude stared into the empty tumbler.

'So he didn't even have a good time. I should go back and see him. Try and make things right.'

CHAPTER FIFTEEN

How long does it take for a life to unravel? Jude and Nat faced each other across the kitchen table. He looked tired – he had spent the previous night on a friend's sofa – and wore an expression of solemn distress as she told him how, in the ghastly tangle of lies and truths withheld, she had never been unfaithful to him.

'It's you I love. I've monumentally fucked up. Can you forgive me?' She reached a hand out, touched his briefly.

He stared at her for a long moment.

'I love you too,' he said. 'You know I do. But after this, can I trust you?'

Jude held his gaze. Unexpectedly, she felt the stirrings of anger. It was like a clean wind that blew through the murk of her thoughts and she suddenly felt clearer.

'I am saying that you can,' she said eventually. 'But if we're going to get through this, you're not to hold it over me – Jude the sinner, and Nat the saint who forgave her and took her back. I didn't sleep with Liam. I was never going to.'

He nodded slowly, not in agreement but as if considering her words.

'Nat, if you don't believe me about that, we're done.'

Nat turned away for a moment, so Jude couldn't see his expression. After a few seconds he looked back at her.

'You made up a story.' When he next spoke it was in an imitation of her tone that made her want to hit him. '"Oh, my poor grandmother, she's so ill, I've got to go and see her." You told me this sob story so you could go away for the weekend with an old boyfriend of yours. That's what this is about.'

'I've already told you the truth about that. I've said I'm sorry. I feel terrible about it but I've apologised. You need to decide if you can accept that and go forward, or if this is the end.'

'And you made an idiot of me.'

'Is *that* what you're thinking about?'

He shrugged. 'I need to think about everything,' he said. 'Before I decide if I can forgive you.'

'Can you hear yourself? Nat, this isn't us. We . . .'

But she stopped. The anger left her and she just felt a dull, flat dreariness. Nat's face was blank now, as if he had been wiped clean of all emotion. He was like a stranger, this man she had been two months away from marrying.

'It's over,' she said. 'We're over because – oh well, look at us, Nat.'

★   ★   ★

Jude slept on the sofa that night and the next morning she worked her way through her contacts searching for a spare room. She knew she could sleep on Dee's sofa, but Dee's flatmates would be back at the weekend, and Jude hated the thought of being surrounded by other people when she felt so raw and ashamed and all she wanted to do was hide away. After several calls, she was put in touch with Simon, a friend of a friend who was off to Berlin for a job. By the time she left for work, Jude had arranged to flat-sit for him, feed his cat, water his plants, send on important mail. She would move in the following day, which she had free before working nights.

There was no way back, she told herself, and to stop herself from having second thoughts, she sent messages to a few of her closest friends telling them that the wedding was off. She would tell her parents face to face, and they could tell her brother Michael.

She waited for the grief, but it didn't come. Instead, she felt a kind of weightlessness. She was alone; she had no home and she had no partner. As easily as stepping out of clothes, she had shed her imagined future. No wedding, no party, no honeymoon, no buying a flat, no children in the near future. All the plans, the arrangements, the plaiting together of two lives – gone, leaving this sense of emptiness.

The story wasn't going away; fuelled by the

photo on Instagram and the mystery around Jude's presence at the Norfolk cottage, it was gathering a horrible momentum. There were three journalists waiting for her today at the hospital entrance, and a man from the TV with a camera and mic that he thrust in her face.

She didn't hear all they asked, just a babble of questions and phrases: *What was the reason for your weekend jaunt? What did you do and why did you do it? Secret affair. Teenage obsession. Love nest.* Camera flashes in her eyes, a woman with a notebook, the man's mic pushing at her.

She wanted simply to tell them to leave her alone. She knew that she mustn't say anything but then, out of nowhere, she said it anyway.

'Liam Birch is dead,' she said. 'Someone killed him. I'll never be able to make it all right. Never.'

She was standing her ground, glaring at them and trying not to shout or cry or curl in a ball. Then she felt an arm go round her and she leaned into a bulky overcoat.

'Come on, Jude. This way.'

It was her consultant. He bought her a coffee and she told him, between hot and comforting gulps, that she was having a bit of a crisis, as he had probably gathered by now, but she was fine to work. It would help, in fact: the structure and purpose. Her hands trembled so much that she could barely steer her mug to her mouth. Hot liquid slopped onto the table.

'You're sure?' he asked doubtfully, looking at her

shaking hands, her tired face, her flannel shirt that she realised was wrongly buttoned up.

So it was that Jude was signed off work for two weeks. She returned to her empty flat, packed two bags of clothes, her laptop and chargers, and other basic things she thought she would need to tide her over the next few days. She stayed that night at Dee's. Jude didn't want to talk and Dee didn't press her. She was peaceable like that. They ate takeaway pizza and watched a film and then Jude slept on the fold-out sofa bed and looked through the uncurtained windows at tower blocks and cranes and the winking lights of planes, climbing higher, going somewhere far away.

She woke in the early hours, when the rain had stopped; there was a slice of moon in the window. She lay staring out at it, feeling the strangeness of her life now, so abruptly hollowed out.

The following morning she moved into Simon's flat. It was in Tottenham, in the basement of a narrow Victorian house wedged between two modern blocks of flats. The rooms were dark and Jude could smell the damp. There was nowhere to put her bike, so she leaned it against a counter in the kitchen area. The sofa was stained. The stove was small and rusty, and there was no electric kettle, just a stainless-steel one you had to put on the hob that took ages to boil. In the windowless bathroom, the shower dripped steadily. The plants that Simon wanted her to water were ferns and succulents, and the cat was a narrow, grizzled tabby with a torn ear and an unfriendly gaze.

She had a fortnight off – or rather, she realised as she unpacked her meagre belongings into the drawers that Simon had cleared for her – she had even more than that because of time owed after her night shifts. She and Nat had planned to go away somewhere for a long weekend.

She plugged her laptop into the socket by the small table in the kitchen, then opened up the mailbox. Emails started appearing from friends. There were dozens and most were about the same thing. She winced and connected to her work emails instead.

Her mobile rang. No caller ID. Jude hesitated, then answered.

'It's Leila Fox.'

'What do you want?'

'I want to speak to you.'

Jude didn't reply at once. An email had caught her eye. It was from someone called Danny. The subject was 'Liam' and she could see the first two lines: 'My name is Danny Kelner. I got your email from . . .'

She clicked on it. The cat bit her ankle and she swore.

'Jude?' Leila Fox was saying. 'Are you all right?'

'Yes.'

Jude looked at the email.

My name is Danny Kelner. I got your email from the hospital website. I was Liam's partner and I would like to meet you as soon as possible. Please get in touch.

There was a mobile number and under that a website.

'Can I come to see you at your flat?' Leila was saying.

'I've moved out.'

'Ah.' She didn't sound surprised. 'Where are you now?'

'I'm in a shithole with a cat that doesn't like me. And they've told me not to come into work. So I'm free to see you whenever you want!' Jude gave a cackle that sounded worrying even to her. 'I'll come to the station.'

CHAPTER SIXTEEN

Jude looked across the table at Leila Fox and Leila Fox looked back across at Jude. She waited a long time before saying anything and sat gazing at her with a friendly expression. Jude didn't trust it. She didn't feel like trusting anyone at the moment.

'Are you having a difficult time?' the detective said finally.

'Yes.'

'Do you want to enlarge on that?'

'I don't think you want to hear about my problems.'

'I want to hear about everything.' Leila Fox gestured around the interview room. 'This is all unofficial. Nothing's being recorded. It's just a chat.'

Jude gave a smile, although it felt like an effort.

'I've always thought of myself as someone who can control things. Ask me to take an exam and I'll pass it. I pay my bills on time. I remember birthdays.' She frowned. 'I don't know which order to say it all. I'm currently taking a break from work because I'm considered to be unsafe. I agree with them. I think I am unsafe at the moment.'

'It's probably good to take some time off.'

'And, as I said on the phone, it looks like the wedding's off.'

'So he didn't take it well?'

'I know I was wrong but he was so pompous, deciding whether he was willing to forgive me. I wanted to punch him.'

Leila Fox gave a faint smile. 'And are you coping with the publicity?'

'I feel like I've had my skin ripped off. I'm being stalked by journalists.'

'Wanting you to tell "your side of the story"?'

'I suppose you're going to tell me not to talk to the media.'

'If you've anything important to say, I'd rather you tell me first.'

'I don't have anything important to say. I wish I did.'

'Also, if you think telling your troubles will be therapeutic, tell them to a therapist not to a journalist. I can promise you, even if they print exactly what you say, once it's there in black and white it won't read the way you think.'

'I've told my troubles to you instead.'

'Any more of them?'

Jude felt a cold shiver running through her.

'You know, when you tell friends about some bad situation you're in, they normally comfort you by saying, at least nobody died.' Jude made a vague gesture with her hands. For the moment she didn't trust herself to speak. She thought she might start crying. She waited for Leila Fox to say something but she didn't. So Jude felt she had to add something. 'I'm sorry but I don't know what I'm doing here. I keep saying I don't know anything apart from what I've told you.'

'Which keeps turning out to be not quite true.'

'Okay. But now it is.'

There was a silence. Jude looked down at the floor but she could feel the detective's eyes on her. When Leila Fox finally spoke, it was as if she was thinking aloud.

'It's all about you,' she said slowly.

'Sorry, I don't know what that means.'

'It's a bit complicated. We're really talking about two crimes and you're involved with both of them. If it hadn't been for you, we'd have been investigating the killing of Liam Birch as a simple mugging gone wrong. That was our first impression, until we talked to you on the phone. If it wasn't for you, the press would be talking about it as another example of London's problem with knife crime. I think that's what the killer wanted us to think.'

'How did it happen?'

'I told you it was on Walthamstow Marshes, didn't I?'

'Yes.'

'He was stabbed.' She paused. 'Several times. The body was found in some bushes just north of an area that's used for horse riding. It had been dragged off the path and there'd been a half-hearted effort to hide it. But someone was out walking their dog and found it not long after it happened.'

'Why would he have gone there?'

'It's only a short walk from where he lived.'

'You said there were two crimes. What was the second?'

'The second one isn't exactly a crime. It's more like a might-have-been crime.'

'What's a might-have-been crime?'

'If someone gets an old friend to go out of town with their phone and their wallet and their credit card . . .' She paused and seemed to remember something. 'By the way, did you use his credit card?'

'His car was almost out of petrol. I used it on the drive up.'

'Why didn't you pay for it with your own card?'

Jude swallowed before she replied. It sounded different when she spoke the words aloud.

'He said to use his card because I was doing enough for him already. He insisted.'

Leila Fox shook her head slowly. 'I feel sorry for you, I really do. What you're going through. And I feel worried about you as well. But what were you thinking?'

'I didn't know, I wasn't sure. I asked him and he said he would tell me when he arrived.'

'But couldn't you see? Wasn't it obvious?'

'What?'

'By the time he arrived, you would already have done the favour.'

98

'Sorry?'

'Oh, stop it,' said the detective, looking irritated for the first time. 'If you're driving out of London with his phone, if you're using his credit card to pay for petrol, then you're giving him an alibi. An alibi for a crime. And if you're going to all that trouble, then it's not for something small.' Fox pushed her chair back as if to give herself more of a view of Jude. 'Don't you see how it looks, to an outsider?'

'What?'

'Your involvement. Strange. Suspicious. Criminal.'

There was a long silence while Jude thought of how to respond. Was this the moment she should refuse to answer any more questions? Or ask for a lawyer? On the other hand, she wasn't actually being accused of anything. Yet. And none of this was being recorded.

'Haven't you thought that Liam's plan might have been something harmless? That he was going to meet me at the station and tell me something that wasn't illegal at all?'

'Yes, I have thought about it. For about five seconds.'

'And is it possible that it was a simple mugging? He could have been held up and when he didn't have a wallet or a mobile phone, the mugger could have got angry and stabbed him.'

'Is that the theory you'd pursue if you were me? Look for some fifteen-year-old with a knife?

'I'm just saying that it's possible. There are different motives for killing someone.'

'Well, what *I'm* saying is that I don't think you quite realise the situation you're in.'

Jude almost laughed at that. 'I think I do.'

'No,' said Leila Fox, with a serious expression. 'I want to say a couple of things to you. The first is that if there's anything you're holding back, anything at all that might be relevant to this inquiry, you'd better tell me.'

The detective paused as if she was waiting for Jude to reveal something.

Jude stared back, feeling the first shimmering of a migraine preparing itself.

'And the other?'

Leila Fox shrugged, disappointed. 'All right,' she said. 'I told you that your involvement with all of this was a shock to us. In my opinion, we aren't the only people who were shocked when you popped up. I think someone wanted to make it look like a mugging, and they might have got away with it had it not been for you.'

Jude started to say something but Fox held up a hand to silence her.

'Bear with me. I imagine this person or persons being surprised after killing Birch when they search him and find he doesn't have a wallet or a phone on him. What's *that* about? And then they must have been even more surprised when they heard about you. They must be wondering what you were doing there. They must be wondering what you know.'

'I don't know anything.'

'That's what you say. They don't know that.'
'What are you saying?'
'I'm saying that it's very much in your interest that we find out who did this. In the meantime you should be careful.'

CHAPTER SEVENTEEN

J ude clicked on Danny Kelner's website.

'Wow,' she said aloud.

It seemed that Danny Kelner ran an outfit in Clapton called Lines on the Body. She was a tattooist and on the homepage there was a photograph of a woman with dark hair and dark eyes, three beautifully drawn tears on one cheek and delicate, barely visible ripples of water around her neck. She looked like a woman who could tell your fortune or cast a spell. Jude clicked through the samples of Danny Kelner's work, photographs of snakes winding around necks, insects on breasts and the backs of hands, cats stretching down backs, flowers and vines curled around legs and arms. There was exotic calligraphy, networks of tiles, dots and splotches and swirls. There were stars, planets and comets. A sumptuously evoked dragon was winding round the bald head of a man and across his face. Was that legal?

So this was who Liam had ended up with. Just the sight of her made Jude feel small and pale and drab. She also felt confused. What was the right thing to do? To reply or not to reply? She had already damaged herself. Surely the best thing was to do nothing.

But of course, she dialled the number. It was answered so quickly that she felt unprepared. In what sounded to her like a nervous gabble, she introduced herself.

'It's Jude Winter and I'm so sorry about your loss,' she said. 'I don't even know what words to use.'

'Thank you,' said Danny. Her voice was husky and low. 'It's good of you to call.'

There was a pause and suddenly Jude had a sense of horror. She knew what she needed to say, but it also felt wrong and she didn't know how to begin so she just spoke, as if she were leaping off into space.

'I understand how terrible this is for you. The whole thing. It's the most awful tragedy. But on top of it all, you must be wondering who the hell I am and what on earth I was doing. I want to tell you, right upfront, that I had no involvement with Liam.' She paused. Involvement. What a stupid word to choose. Of course she'd had a kind of involvement with Liam, even now in the present. She had agreed to do this favour for him. 'When I say involvement, I mean there was nothing . . .' She paused again. She was sounding insane. 'I know what you must be thinking. But we weren't having an affair.' She had said it. She had got the words out. 'I want to be clear about that. We had a coffee together. That was all.' Stop talking, she said to herself silently. Just stop.

'I know who you are,' said Danny. 'Liam talked about you. I mean about him knowing you when you were at school.'

'But I hadn't seen him since then,' said Jude. 'I want you to believe that. Or everything would be even more awful for you.'

'It's easy for you to say that. But the fact is, you were one of the last people to see Liam alive. And then that arrangement. In Norfolk.'

'If you wanted to talk to me because—'

But Danny cut in. 'I wanted to talk to you because the only thing worse than talking to you was not talking to you.'

'I get that,' said Jude. 'If there's anything I can do to help, I'd be happy to do it.' What should she say next? 'Would you like to meet?'

Jude made the offer impetuously and she regretted it as soon as the words were out of her mouth. But she was sure Danny wouldn't accept.

'Yes.' Danny spoke firmly. 'I certainly would like that.'

'Great,' said Jude faintly. 'Of course. Where? Shall we meet for coffee?'

'I'm having trouble getting out of the house at the moment. There's so much to organise. And I have Alfie. It's all a bit chaotic. Could you come to me? I know it's a lot to ask.'

'No, of course,' said Jude. 'I'd be happy to.'

It wasn't like she had anything else to do.

CHAPTER EIGHTEEN

It was a ten-minute walk to the bus stop, then twenty minutes on the 158 to Bromley Road, where Jude got off and bought a bunch of yellow and red chrysanthemums from a roadside stall. From there, it was another ten-minute walk. Jude constantly looked at her phone to check the directions; she wished she had biked, which would have been much quicker, but it was drizzling steadily and she didn't want to arrive cold and wet. Walking through the residential streets of Walthamstow, she was almost dazed. These rows of terraced houses were familiar and unfamiliar at the same time. Although this part of north-east London was completely new to her, the streets felt like she knew them. They could have been anywhere from Richmond to Romford.

But when she arrived at the address Danny had given her, it wasn't like everywhere else. In fact, it wasn't like *anywhere* else. The house stood at the end of a close, slightly askew. It had clearly been there before the rest of the houses were built and it didn't seem to quite fit. It was set apart from its neat neighbours, detached, double-fronted, three-storied. It was bigger and much more neglected. At first glance you might even think it was abandoned. A driveway led down one side of it, as in a builder's yard or an industrial workshop. The house itself looked as if it had once been converted into a commercial premises and then partially converted back. It was clearly still a work in progress.

She wouldn't have imagined Liam in the suburbs but this was more his style. He was never quite like other people.

She rang the bell. When the door opened, she was preparing herself to say something soothing and apologetic to Danny but it wasn't Danny. Instead she was facing a tall bulky man, with stubble on his chin that was almost a beard, and sweeping brown hair. He was dressed in heavy-duty canvas trousers and a blue checked shirt with the sleeves rolled up to the elbows. He was dusty and his clothes were dusty. Even his beard was dusty.

'Does Danny live here?' said Jude. 'I've come to see her.'

The man frowned. 'Who are you?'

Jude didn't quite know how much of an explanation she was expected to give, especially as she might have come to the wrong house. She just said her name. He gave a slow nod.

'Aha! Now I know who you are,' he said. 'We've been talking about you. The mystery woman.'

'There's not much of a mystery.'

He gave an odd smile. 'Come in,' he said, and gestured her inside.

She looked around. Ahead of her was a staircase and there were doors on either side of the hallway. On the left wall was a large canvas: an abstract painting, with fierce reds, blues, yellows – like a fire or a torrent or stormy clouds. On the right wall, a mural had been painted directly on to the plaster: five stick figures with heads like pumpkins, dancing in a circle.

'That was Liam,' said the man, pointing at the painting. He turned to the mural. 'And that's Danny. She's good.' He lifted up his left arm to reveal, on the underneath, running from the elbow to the wrist, a branch adorned with green leaves and blossom. 'That's Danny as well.'

'That's beautiful.' Jude looked at him inquiringly. 'I'm sorry. You seem to know me but I don't know you.'

'Of course you don't.'

There was a pause. The man just looked at her as if he was amused.

'Fine,' she said at last. 'I'm just here to see Danny.'

He laughed, a booming sound. 'I'm Vin.'

He held out his hand. Jude was holding the large bunch of flowers and she had to move it under her arm to take his hand. As she shook it, she felt like her hand had been entirely enfolded.

'Liam and I are old friends. We work together.' He caught himself. 'We *worked* together. It feels strange and wrong to talk about him in the past tense.'

'I'm sorry,' said Jude. 'This must be so terrible for you all.'

Vin nodded slowly. 'We're still processing it. It's a lot to get your head around. Liam was the linchpin, you know what I mean?'

'Yes.'

'You do? You know what a linchpin is?'

'I know it's something important. Something that holds things together.'

'Not just things,' said Vin, looking serious. 'You know when you put a wheel on an axle?'

Jude hoped she wasn't supposed to reply to that.

'The linchpin,' Vin continued, 'is what you put through the hole in the end of the axle to hold it in place. We were like spokes in the wheel and Liam was what held us together.'

Jude wasn't quite sure how to continue this conversation and then she heard her name being called out. She looked round and recognised Danny immediately.

Like in her photograph, Danny was strikingly dark and pale, but Jude recognised the look that shock gives. As a young doctor, she had seen it in people who had suffered heart attacks or a stroke. But you could also see it in those who had been told they had cancer. It was something in the eyes, a pallor in the skin, of someone whose whole world has changed. Danny had the face of a woman who had been crying and not sleeping. She was a beautiful mess, tall, strong, dishevelled, tragic, gorgeous. Her clothes were layers of dark-coloured fabric that could have been pulled on without thought or could have been carefully chosen.

'I wasn't sure if you'd actually come,' she said in a voice that seemed blurred round the edges. 'It's good of you. Not everyone would do that.'

Jude held out the flowers. 'They may be too bright,' she said. 'But I couldn't bear the idea of lilies.'

Danny took them and looked down at them indifferently. 'They're perfect.'

She hates them, thought Jude.

'I'll get you some tea, love,' said Vin. He looked at Jude. 'Is that all right?'

'Yes, just normal tea.'

'It's all herbal here,' said Vin.

'I'll have what Danny has.'

CHAPTER NINETEEN

Danny led Jude through a door beyond the paintings, into a room that was halfway between a conservatory and a garage. It was very cold, very light. The far end was all glass, but some of the panes were cracked and one was covered up by a billowing tarpaulin. The ceiling was a work in progress, some of it stripped back to its beams. There was a trestle table against one wall, heaped with paint trays and brushes, saws, an electric drill, sandpaper, bottles of white spirit. Jude wondered about a toddler let loose in this room full of sharp-edged tools and toxic liquids. In the centre of the room was an enormous wicker chair, round-backed and piled with bright cushions. Water dripped into a bucket near the door that led into the garden, which wasn't really a garden at all, but a large dumping ground of miscellaneous objects: she made out a rusting bike, an old-fashioned commode, towers of chipped terracotta pots, a bathtub with clawed feet, a stone gryphon, a hammock stand, a clothes wringer, a bird cage, several ladder-backed chairs, two large speakers covered in see-through plastic and, in the middle of all of this, a small patch of garden with some straggly winter plants in it.

'Most of that stuff belongs to Irina,' said Danny, laying the flowers on the table.

Jude had no idea who Irina was but before she could ask, a door at the other side of the room was pushed open and a miniature person staggered in. Momentum carried him a few rushing steps, legs bandy and arms outstretched, and then he toppled into a soft heap in front of Jude and Danny. He stared up at them, dark curls and dark eyes and a mouth that was deciding whether to open into a wail.

'Up you get,' said Danny matter-of-factly, and put her hands under his armpits, lifting him to his feet. She turned him so he faced Jude. 'This is Alfie,' she said.

Liam's son. Liam's almost-black eyes and his wide mouth. Jude bent slightly towards him, seeing his white teeth, his long lashes, his soft cheeks. He was wearing striped dungarees that had paint splatters on them, and a buttery-yellow T-shirt.

'Hello, Alfie,' she said, self-conscious and shy.

Few of her friends had children. She wasn't really sure what to say to a one-year-old, or what to do. She pointed to herself. 'I'm Jude.'

'Say hello to Jude,' said Danny, lowering her son to the floor where he sat splay-legged.

He just stared at her, unblinking. Then he put his hands, fingers outstretched, over his entire face. His eyes glinted through them.

'He's like his father, isn't he?'

'Yes,' said Jude. Everything felt unreal.

'Did you ever see pictures of Liam when he was Alfie's age?'

'No.'

Of course Jude hadn't. She'd only been inside Liam's house once and had never met his parents.

'Tea for two.' Vin came in carrying two large mugs and put them on the table. 'Fennel.'

'Thanks.' Danny barely glanced at him, but she let her hand trail down his arm. 'Can you take Alfie for a bit, while we have our talk.'

Our talk. That sounded ominous. Jude took a sip of her tea, which was surprisingly pleasant. She was very tired, she realised.

'Sure.' Vin bent down, hauled Alfie up and onto his shoulders. Alfie yelped and clutched his ears. 'Come on, mischief, you can help me.' Vin made the sound of a motor, an aeroplane maybe, as they passed through the door.

'He doesn't understand,' said Danny, looking after them, her face briefly softening.

'It must be very hard.'

'It is. Have a seat.'

Jude glanced around. There was the wicker contraption, several mismatched chairs pushed against the table, and a stained beanbag. She pulled out one of the chairs and sat. Danny took the wicker throne, sighing and settling back against the cushions, tucking her legs under her. She was wearing wooden bangles that knocked against each other as she lifted her mug to her mouth. Her fingers were heavy with rings. There was a silence.

'You're a tattooist,' said Jude.

Danny looked amused. 'And you're a doctor.'

'Yes.'

'One of the people in this house is called Doc, I don't know why, he's not anything like a doctor. I don't really know what he does with himself. Mostly he plays the guitar and has loud sex with Erika, and burns toast in the middle of the night.'

Erika, thought Jude. The woman who had called Liam's phone the night he had died.

'Reminds me of university,' she said. Danny didn't reply so she felt a need to explain. 'You know, sharing a house with lots of people.'

Danny leaned forward and put the mug down on the floor, then straightened up again. 'Tell me about you and Liam.'

Upstairs there was a violent hammering sound. Jude waited for it to subside.

'There wasn't any me and Liam. I hadn't seen him since I was eighteen. And then he came to the hospital a few days before he died.'

Danny smiled, except it wasn't really a smile at all, more like someone baring her teeth. Jude saw her hands grip the side of the chair, as if she was trying to keep control over herself.

'Try and see this from my point of view,' she said in her ragged voice. 'There's this girl Liam mentions over the years, usually when he's drunk and maudlin, someone he was in love with when he was just a kid. Sometimes I felt almost jealous of her.' That smile again. 'And then he gets fucking murdered out there in the mud and the cold and the rain, my beautiful man, my darling, and it turns out he had been planning to spend the weekend with this woman from his past. With you.'

'Spending the weekend,' said Jude. 'That sounds different from what it was. He tracked me down at work, out of the blue. It was after a night shift, we had coffee, he told me about Alfie, he said he had a favour to ask me and told me to go to this cottage and wait for him and he would explain. That's it. There's nothing more.'

'I like stories,' said Danny. 'When people come to me for a tattoo, I tell them that each image I puncture into their skin, it's got to tell a story. It can't just be a passing fancy. Look.' She drew up the loose sleeve of her shirt and held out her inner arm. Jude stood up and went over to her. There were a series of what looked at first like delicate ticks in the pale skin between elbow and wrist, but she saw they actually represented birds in flight, their wings at different angles. Danny clenched and unclenched her fist and the shapes moved.

'Each of these is one of my dead. This one is my gran, this my father. Here's my friend who killed herself.' She pressed her forefinger on a dark red shape. 'This is my dog. I'll do one for Liam soon. I need to understand what colour he is.'

She lifted her head. Tears glinted in her eyes.

'Tattoos should have a secret meaning for the person who bears them. People tell me their stories and then I help them find the picture. I'm asking myself which story I should believe now. Should I believe that Liam was unfaithful, or should I believe that he had some secret you were going to help him with, this favour? And why would you do that, anyway? Just because he stepped back into your life after all those years and asked you? I mean, he could be pretty persuasive, but it sounds a bit weird.'

'It's all I can tell you,' said Jude, retreating to her chair. 'I don't know anything else; I wish I did.'

She thought of what Leila Fox had said to her: she was to have been Liam's alibi, but alibi for what? What had Liam been about to do? Did this woman, with teardrops inked on her cheek, know anything about that?

'You swear,' said Danny. 'Swear on your life?'

It wasn't at all funny but Jude almost laughed, desperately. Swearing on your life was like being in the playground when she was ten years old.

'Yes. On my life.'

'You're not what I expected,' said Danny.

'What do you mean?'

'I don't hate you.'

Jude gave a surprised laugh. 'Thank you, I guess.'

'Did you love him?'

'You mean, when we were young? Yes. Or I was in love with him at least. When I look back, I think

I was scared by how hard I fell for him. It was like I didn't know who I . . .'

She stopped, appalled at herself. Leila Fox had warned her that if she wanted therapy, she should talk to a therapist not to journalists. She certainly shouldn't be saying previously unspoken things about her feelings for Liam to his bereaved partner.

'It was a long time ago,' she said, trying to distance herself from her words. 'I was eighteen. And I was a young eighteen.'

Danny was smiling at her now, a real smile this time, sympathetic.

'Liam was powerful,' she said. 'It took me a long time to learn that I had to keep hold of my own self, not just give myself up to him. Women are too ready to lose themselves.'

Jude couldn't imagine Danny losing herself to anyone: she would be on the other side of that equation. But she nodded.

'Then along came Alfie,' said Danny. 'Nothing like that feeling you have for a child.' She looked dreamy now, staring out at the junkyard. 'Mind, Liam was a very devoted father.'

'I'm so sorry,' Jude said again. It was her refrain. Sorry sorry sorry. So sorry for your loss.

'Poor little boy,' said Danny. 'He won't even remember his dad. He'll just be a name, a face in a photo. Me, though, I'll always remember. I'll never get over him.'

She stood up suddenly.

'I think I might believe you, weird as your little tale is.'

Jude decided not to be insulted by this. Her little tale *was* weird, after all.

'Thank you.'

'Or I might not.'

'Right.'

'I needed to see you, look at you.' She stared at Jude with an intensity that made her feel like wincing. 'And you're not actually particularly beautiful or captivating.'

'You don't really need to say all this out loud.'

'Nothing like the picture I had of you in my head all these years. The girl no one could measure up to. Liam was, though. Beautiful, that is. Captivating.'

'I think this is a conversation you should be having with someone else.'

'Yet for some reason he chose you.'

'I chose him too, you know.'

Danny took on a sarcastic expression. 'I mean, he chose you to turn to. For this favour.'

'I don't know why he did that. As I keep saying.'

'You do keep saying it, yes. But he was having an affair with someone, even if it wasn't you.'

'How do you know?'

'Something had changed. He was different with me.'

Jude wasn't sure how to respond to this woman who was treating her like an intimate friend and insulting her at the same time.

'It must be complicated for you,' she said lamely.

'I'm going to find out.' Danny picked up the flowers Jude had brought. 'It's part of the mourning process,' she said.

'Acceptance,' said Jude. 'Isn't that how the mourning process ends?'

Danny nodded slowly. 'Yes, but there's anger as well. Anger is necessary, I think.'

Jude wondered how much of the anger was directed at her but then they were both distracted by a bump-bump-bump on the stairs. Danny's face softened, looked less gaunt. 'Here comes Alfie, on his bottom.'

There was a final bump and silence. Together they went out into the hall, where Danny lifted the boy and he squirmed his pliant body into hers, grasped hold of a hank of her thick dark hair. The flowers she held rested on his crown of curls.

The front door swung open and a young man in running gear stepped inside. He had red hair, a red, perspiring face, slightly jug ears, eyes so blue they looked unnatural.

'Excuse me,' he said awkwardly. He had a faint accent, Dutch perhaps, thought Jude.

'Jan,' said Danny. 'Meet Jude.'

'Hi,' said Jude.

Jan put out a sweaty hand then withdrew it, wiped it on his shorts, and shuffled on the spot. 'Hello,' he said. 'Pleased to see you.'

'Jan only arrived in September,' said Danny. 'I think he's got more than he bargained for.'

Jan started walking sideways towards the stairs.

'Shower,' he said, standing on the first step.

'He's a mathematician,' said Danny, as if Jan was out of earshot.

She spoke as if Jan was a small boy playing some game. He flushed even redder; the tips of his ears glowed.

'That sounds good.'

As Jude spoke, she wondered why everything she said sounded foolish. But he smiled.

'Yes, thank you. It is good.'

Jude decided it was time to go. She held out a hand. Danny took it and didn't let it go.

'I could do a tattoo for you,' she said. 'It's a way of marking a moment.'

Jude was appalled by the idea.

'That's an interesting idea,' she said.

'You're a doctor. You can't be scared of needles. Something beautiful and delicate, with a secret meaning.'

'I'll think about it.'

'Do that. We'll meet soon.'

Jude was puzzled by that. Meet soon? What for?

CHAPTER TWENTY

'Do you always walk that fast?' said a voice behind her.

Jude turned to find Vin. He was wearing a battered leather jacket that creaked when he swung his arms. Drops of rain glittered in his hair and beard.

'I thought I'd accompany you to the bus stop.'

'There's no need.'

'That's all right. I wanted a word.'

'What about?'

'You know. The mystery.'

'There's no mystery.'

'Liam was up to something. And you were in on it.'

Jude stopped abruptly and turned to face Vin.

'You're all wrong,' she said. 'I've had this conversation with Danny. Just ask her.'

'Liam was my friend, Danny's partner, Alfie's father. We need to know what was going on in his life before he died. So what was?'

'I don't know.'

Vin just looked at her, hands in pockets. Jude continued.

'Look, I'm really sorry about everything. I'm sorry you've lost your friend, but I've got a few troubles of my own.'

'Do you want to get a drink?'

'No,' Jude said. It was four in the afternoon.

'Something to eat?'

'I've really got to go.'

'I missed lunch,' he said. 'You never can tell what time it is in that house.'

'How many of you are there?'

'Six now that Liam's gone.' He thought for a moment. 'Seven, if you count Alfie. There's Danny and me, obviously. Irina.'

'Who owns the junk in your yard.'

'That's her. She clears houses for a living, takes away all the stuff no one knows what to do with, and a lot of it ends back at ours. You should see her room. She's great, a bit wild; dances when she can't get to sleep, like a restless ghost; brings back strange bedfellows. Then there's Erika and Doc. They've got the attic room.' He smiled faintly. 'They're loud.'

'I heard. And there's Jan the mathematician.'

'You've been paying attention. Jan's not really part of the house. He's a temporary lodger. Liam needed the money. He keeps to himself. He runs and stays in his room and keeps his own food in a Tupperware.'

'But Liam owned the house?'

'That's right. Or he borrowed the money to buy it, if that's the same thing. So I guess we're all

121

lodgers really. It's never felt like that. We all pay different rents and help out with the renovation. Some more than others,' he added, and pointed at himself. 'Master builder. It was a wreck when Liam bought it; once water gets into a building, it goes pretty fast. Still is a wreck mostly, but it could be amazing. Or at least . . .' He grimaced. 'It could have been. I'll show you the rest of it next time you come.'

They'd reached the bus stop. Vin surprised her by laying a heavy hand on her shoulder and staring into her face, as if she was a puzzle he was going to solve.

'Cut us some slack,' he said. 'We're all in shock.'

Why are you telling me this? Jude thought. *I don't care.*

'Maybe you can help us,' he said.

'I can't.'

Vin dropped his hand and stepped back. 'We'll see.'

CHAPTER TWENTY-ONE

Jude made herself a curried parsnip soup and ate it listening to a podcast so that she wouldn't have to listen to her own thoughts. The Tottenham flat was cold, silent and smelled of damp. She wasn't used to being alone. She had never lived by herself: she had always shared with friends and in the last year it had been her and Nat. She rarely spent an evening alone, and when she did it was a kind of luxury. It didn't feel like that now.

A group of friends were meeting at a pub in Islington later. She thought about joining them, drowning her sorrows. But outside it was cold, dark, wet. She could hear rain dripping from the gutters. She shrank from being with people who were still in their old lives: working, dating, laughing, making plans. She didn't want their curiosity or their kindness.

She made up her mind and stood decisively. She had to do this at once: the longer she waited, the harder it would get.

She reached for her laptop, opened it and pulled up the wedding list. She stared at it. She couldn't just send a joint email to everyone, because then she would be telling Nat's relatives and friends as well as her own, so laboriously she entered the addresses of everyone who she thought closest to her. She grimaced at the division into 'his' and 'hers'. There were several people who belonged to them both, and these she added to her own list. She blind-copied Nat into the message, so that he would know who she had told.

Dear each and all. Some of you have probably already heard by now, but I'm afraid the wedding's off!

She chewed the side of the finger, then deleted the exclamation mark. It was too perky. Then she deleted the whole thing, and began again.

Dearest everyone. I'm so sorry to be doing this in a group email, but I wanted to tell you all at once, and I will contact you properly soon. Nat and I have broken up. I've moved out. Obviously this means there won't be a wedding. There won't be lots of things. So I'm partly writing to tell you the party's off, no dancing in the barn, and partly to say I love you all.

Would that do? Was it too emotional? Not solemn or formal enough? Her finger hovered over the delete cursor, but then she thought, sod it, and pressed 'send'. There was a whoosh and it was gone. Jude imagined her friends hearing a ping, taking out their phones, reading it, calling each other . . .

She had left her parents off the email though. She hadn't been in touch with them over the past terrible days because even the thought of trying to explain what had happened was unbearable. She needed to call them. She needed to call them right now before someone else did, because surely they would find out any moment. She was lucky they hadn't already. She needed to go and see them and tell them face to face. She had nowhere else to be, and the neighbour could feed Simon's cat. She picked up her mobile and as she did so, it rang, startling her. She looked it and was even more startled.

'Hi, Mum,' she said. 'I was literally picking up my phone to call you.'

As soon as her mother asked how she was, it took an effort to stop herself from crying.

'There's something I urgently need to talk to you about,' she said. 'I should have called before.'

'As it happens, Judith,' – her mother and father were the only people who ever called her Judith – 'I'm not just calling to chat myself.'

Jude felt a wave of apprehension. She already knows, she told herself. I left it too late.

'What is it?'

'We've had a slightly odd message. It's about you. For you, actually.'

CHAPTER TWENTY-TWO

The train ride to her childhood home in Marsham was complicated. She had to change at Birmingham New Street on to a smaller line and then change once more and even then it was a fifteen-minute taxi ride. All the way, her phone buzzed and jangled as if it had come alive. Messages were pouring in. Friends were calling her. She switched it to silent.

She knew it was going to be a difficult conversation. Her father worked for the council, in the planning department, and his hours were rigid, but her mother, who was a community health visitor, had Fridays off. That made it easier. She would find a way to tell her mother and then her mother would find a way to tell her father. But the conversation was delayed. Her mother made tea and they sat down at the kitchen table facing each other. People who knew them both told Jude that she looked like her mother. She was small and slight, with a tipped-up nose and dark, thick eyebrows. She wore her soft, greying hair cut short. Jude's father, on the other hand, was bulky and tall, with large hands and feet. He towered over his wife and daughter. Jude sometimes thought that was why he stooped: to be nearer their level.

Sitting there in the kitchen that reminded her of her childhood and her teenage years, Jude felt hesitant. She wanted to tell her mother everything, to be held and comforted, but she also wanted to protect her. She knew it was also protecting herself. Her parents had got to know Nat and they liked him. They would be baffled, anxious, upset, and probably embarrassed as well about what their friends would think. Jude knew that every day she kept the truth from them only made it worse.

She took a deep breath and steadied herself, but her mother got in first.

'When Tara Birch rang me yesterday, I didn't even know who she was.'

'There's no reason why you should.'

'It was terrible. She was crying. She told that me that Liam was the boy in the car in that accident you were in, the one who was driving, and then in the same breath she told me that he was dead, that he had been murdered.'

She had said all of this to Jude already on the phone, but she seemed to need to talk about it.

'I know. It's terrible.' Jude spoke mechanically.

'I didn't know what to say. It's difficult to react to something that's so awful when you don't know the people involved.'

'It must have been strange for you.'

What was really strange, thought Jude, was that

her parents still had no idea of the mess she had got herself into. In London it had felt like everyone knew, everyone had read the online story or the subsequent reports in newspapers, had seen the endlessly retweeted picture of her and Liam as teenagers, had discussed it, drawn conclusions, made judgements. And yet, here in their village in Shropshire and outside of that bubble, her parents seemed blissfully untouched by the whole thing.

'All the time she was talking to me,' continued her mother, 'I felt I wanted to ask, why are you ringing me? Why are you telling me this? Of course I couldn't. Suddenly she said she was calling because they wanted to contact *you*. I didn't know what to say. You hardly knew him, did you? I didn't even know you'd stayed in touch.'

'We hadn't,' said Jude. 'Not really.'

'She said that they – she and Liam's father – wanted to talk to you. I said I'd give them your number but they said if it was at all possible, they wanted to talk to you in person.' She waited for an answer that didn't come. 'Do you know what it could be about?'

Jude felt she did know what it could be about. The police would have told them how Liam had been in touch with her just before his death. They would know about the night she had spent in Norfolk with his car and his phone, and of course they would have read the stories and comments. They must be curious, or more than curious:

hungry for information and knowledge about their murdered son. It wasn't a conversation Jude wanted to have but she owed it to them. If they needed to see her in person, she owed that to them as well.

'I suppose they want to talk about Liam,' she said.

'Couldn't they do that over the phone? I mean, getting you to come up all the way from London to do it. It's very good of you, but still.'

'Could I borrow your car?' Jude said. 'If I can't, it's not a problem. I can get a taxi.'

'Don't be silly. Of course you can borrow it.'

'I won't be very long.'

'It doesn't matter. Take as long as you need. Are you staying the night?'

'If that's all right. Maybe a few nights?'

'Are you taking time off work?'

Jude took a deep breath. She couldn't put it off any more.

'There's something I haven't told you.'

It was a relief to get in the car and drive away and be alone for a time.

It had been very different from what she had anticipated. In a way, it had been worse. Her mother hadn't been cross. She hadn't acted disappointed. Her only emotion had been sadness for her daughter. Jude had been prepared for an argument or for having to justify herself but she had just met unqualified sympathy and concern. The kindness had almost undone her. She'd found it hard to hold herself together and not collapse into helpless sobbing. That might have been a relief, but she felt like she couldn't allow herself to do it. Not yet. She needed to hold herself together for what was coming.

All those years ago, she had never met Liam's parents, although she had, briefly, met his brother, Dermot. They still lived in Marsham, in the same house. Jude had been inside that house, just once. It was eleven years ago and she remembered every detail. It had been an evening on a weekend and Liam's parents had been away and Dermot had been away.

That had been the evening when they first slept together, the evening when she lost her virginity. She remembered his bedroom. Liam didn't have posters of pop stars, the way other teenagers did. He had prints of paintings, impressionists, pop art. But what she really remembered was the fumbling, the undressing, the condom, the embarrassment and the awkwardness and the unbearably exciting feeling that this was it, it really was it. And then, much later, Liam driving her home and her wondering whether her parents could see it in her eyes, how she was changed.

When Jude met Tara and Andy Birch, she felt that they seemed younger than her parents, almost a different generation. Tara opened the door of the little terraced house and for a moment stood framed there, unsmiling, looking out at Jude. She was lean and tall, dressed in corduroy trousers, tatty trainers and a stained yellow jumper, the sleeves pushed above the elbow so that Jude could see a small abstract tattoo on her forearm. Perhaps Danny had done that, she thought. Her rich brown hair was bundled messily into a knot at the back of her head. She had thick brows, dark eyes that were Liam's eyes, a full mouth slightly quirked by a scar, multiple piercings in her ears, lines radiating out from her eyes, a frowning groove in her forehead. She nodded Jude in without speaking, and then called Andy from his workshop in the backyard. He came in with a heavy tread, a solid man, muscle turning to bulk, with a shaved head and a close beard. He wore ancient jeans and a long-sleeved T-shirt in washed-out blue. He rinsed his hands in the sink before shaking hands with Jude, a wringing grasp that made her wince.

'I'm so sorry,' she said to them both. 'I don't know what to say.'

'There's nothing to say,' said Tara. 'Our son is dead.'

'I can't imagine what it must be like,' said Jude.

'Of course you can't,' said Tara, almost casually. She turned to her husband. 'Have you got it?'

'It's upstairs.'

He left the kitchen and Jude heard his steps on the stairs. She wondered what 'it' was. Tara didn't offer her tea or coffee, so Jude asked for a glass of water. Her mouth was dry.

Tara filled the glass, gave it to Jude and led her through to the living room. Even in her fog of apprehension, Jude was surprised. She didn't know exactly what she had expected but not this. Liam had been good at making things and fixing things. He had a feeling for painting and drawing, for colour. She could see where he got it from. Everything, the sofa, the chairs, the pictures on the wall, the clay ornaments on shelves, looked home-made or rescued. Some of it was pretty basic, like the wooden boxes hammered together to hold oversized books; other objects were more complicated. How had she not noticed this? Her mind had been on other things.

She sat on the sofa, took a gulp of water and put the glass on to a low table that looked as if it had been made from reclaimed floorboards, rough and scuffed and richly grained. Then she saw a large framed photo on the windowsill: Liam, staring out at the room with a tiny smile, almost too good-looking, almost naff. She looked away, found Tara staring at her, took another gulp of water just for something to do.

Andy came into the room. He was holding a buff-coloured A4 envelope. The two of them sat in armchairs on the other side of the table from Jude.

'So you grew up here?' Tara said. It didn't sound like a friendly question.

'Yes.'

'Did we meet you?' Andy asked. 'There were so

many of you in those days. In and out of the house. It was hard to keep track.'

Jude wasn't sure whether she was meant to feel this as a putdown and a humiliation. But she looked at their faces. They were both hollow-eyed with grief. They'd gone through what no parent should ever go through. Still, she felt a creeping anxiety: why had they gone to the trouble of finding her and contacting her? She didn't want to ask. They would tell her in their own time. She waited.

'You were friends,' said Tara.

Jude wasn't clear whether this was an assertion or a question. Tara made it sound like an accusation.

'For a time. It was in our last year at school. We spent some time together.'

'And then you both lived in London,' said Andy.

'We'd lost touch by that time. Almost completely.'

'*Almost* completely?' Andy glanced at Tara.

'Yes,' said Jude. She had decided that she would answer any specific question honestly. But she wasn't going to volunteer any information that she didn't have to. She didn't know what they wanted or what they knew.

Andy leaned forward and picked up the envelope, then seemed to think better of it and replaced it on the table.

'You were close friends,' he said. It wasn't a question.

Jude looked to one side, meeting the eyes of Liam in the photo, seeing that secret smile of his.

The years seemed to dissolve and she was eighteen again and giddily in love. For a moment, she couldn't look away. She felt hot tears well up and bit her lip fiercely: she mustn't cry in front of Liam's parents.

'We went out together,' she said. 'For a bit.'

The words sounded horrible and false as she spoke them.

'If you don't mind me saying so,' Andy said, 'Liam never once mentioned you in that way.'

'Teenagers have secrets,' she said. 'I never mentioned him to my parents either.'

'Liam had lots of girlfriends,' said Tara. Her voice was harsh. 'It was hard to tell them apart. Girls always loved him. He had to fight them off.'

'He didn't fight me off,' said Jude, and then was appalled at the words. 'I mean,' she added, 'it wasn't like that between us.'

'We obviously knew your name though,' said Andy.

'You were the girl in the car.' Tara stared at her like a judge waiting to pass sentence.

Jude nodded.

'And,' Tara continued, 'you were the woman in the cottage.'

Here it was: the reason they wanted to see her then. They knew who she was: the woman Liam had been having an affair with. That's what everyone thought.

Yes,' she said softly. 'I was.'

'You were there that first time everything went so

wrong for him,' said Tara. 'And you were there at his death.'

'Hardly at his death,' began Jude, then wiped a hand across her forehead. She felt cold and shivery. 'But that's not the point. You're right that Liam got back in touch just before he was killed. It must seem odd to you.'

'Odd? Odd? You think it seems *odd*?' Jude shrank back at the tone of savage sarcasm. 'It doesn't seem odd, it seems nasty and wrong. Like someone's telling lies. Lies about my son who can't speak up for himself.'

'Tara,' said Andy warningly.

'The police are making out he was planning something dodgy. With you.' Tara pointed a long finger at Jude. Her mouth was drawn back, her dark eyes were slightly protuberant, and there was a look of accusation in them.

'I know,' Jude said. 'All I can say is what I said to the police. I don't know anything. I don't know why he got in touch with me. I don't know what he was planning, or wasn't planning. I don't know why he died.'

'I'm his mother,' said Tara. 'I won't have him smeared like this. Not by the police, not by you, not by anyone.' She leaned forward, eyes glinting, face contorted, but speaking very clearly. 'It's not right. *I can't bear it.*'

The words rang out in the little room, and then there was a silence. Tara put her fist into her mouth, biting her knuckles. Andy reached a hand out towards her, changed his mind, put it back on his lap.

'I'm not smearing him,' said Jude. 'I wish I could help but I can't. I don't know what he was planning or why he died. He was lovely,' she added, hearing the words before she knew she was going to speak them and only then understanding they needed to be said. 'He was special. Everyone who knew him saw that.'

Tara took her fist from her mouth, uncurled it, trailed her fingers across her cheek.

'I'm so bloody tired,' she said. 'But I can't sleep. And time stands still. I don't know how to get through time. I keep thinking he'll come whistling through the door with his laundry or something. My handsome lad.'

Jude nodded but didn't speak.

'And I'm angry. I'm so angry.'

She leaned back in her chair and closed her eyes, her tight face going slack.

Andy shifted in his armchair and coughed, a signal he wanted to speak.

'We actually had a specific reason for wanting to see you,' he began. It sounded as if he was saying something he had prepared. 'Aside from what happened.'

Jude looked at him expectantly.

'Liam used to come and visit. Not that often but occasionally. The last time he came here was about four months ago.' He looked at his wife. 'Is that right?'

'More like three,' she said.

'Three or four months ago. He came with his little boy Alfie, who was a baby then. Not walking, though he pulled himself up on the furniture. Anyway, while Liam was here he did a big sort-out of his old room. It's funny the stuff he still had here all those years after he moved out. He threw things away and before he left, he said there was a drawer in his room for documents. I thought it was strange. Documents. Liam didn't seem like the sort of person who would have documents.'

'He had documents,' said Tara, opening her eyes and sitting up straighter. 'Like his National Insurance card and his exam certificates.'

'There weren't many of those,' said Andy. 'Unless they give out certificates for failing.'

'Don't you dare speak like that,' Tara said fiercely.

He held his hand up in apology.

'I was just saying that there weren't many documents. But when . . .' He paused. He was finding it hard to say the words. 'When all this happened, we remembered that drawer. We thought we ought to check, in case there was anything important. It turned out there was one thing that Liam hadn't told us: he'd made a will.'

The two of them looked at Jude as if they were waiting for a response. She didn't quite understand why.

'Is that so strange?' she asked.

Andy pulled a face. 'A bit strange, maybe. We didn't expect it. Have *you* made a will?'

Jude shook her head. 'I know I should but I haven't got around to it. I haven't got much stuff and I don't know who I'd leave it to.'

'What do you know about wills?' Andy asked.

Jude couldn't make sense of this. Why were they asking her all this?'

'Not much. It's something you do with a solicitor, isn't it?'

'You don't have to. Liam did his himself. Downloaded the form, filled it out. Do you know what else you need?'

Jude thought for a moment.

'Doesn't someone have to witness it?'

'Two people,' said Andy. 'I don't recognise the names but judging by the addresses they must be local. They're probably just people he met around, in the pub. Do you know what else you need apart from them?'

'No, I don't. Isn't that all?'

'You need an executor. That's the person who makes sure that it's all carried out properly.'

'All right,' said Jude. 'I probably did know that but I'd forgotten.'

Andy picked up the envelope, pushed back the flap and pulled some papers out. He laid one in front of Jude.

'He named you one of the executors.'

'What?'

'Look.'

Jude picked up the paper. There was her name: Judith Winter.

'Is that your address?' asked Andy.

'It says "care of" and then my parents' address. I suppose that counts.'

'We were surprised, of course. But we thought we ought to tell you.'

Jude was more than surprised; she was so stunned that she could barely speak.

'I didn't know anything about this. Aren't you meant to get the person's permission?'

'You'd think so,' said Andy.

'Anyway, I'm not a lawyer. I don't know anything about things like this.'

'We looked it up,' said Tara. 'You don't have to be a lawyer. You don't have to be anything in particular.'

'You said executors. Is there more than one?'

'There is,' said Andy. 'You're a doctor, aren't you? So you're probably good at things like this.'

'I don't know about that.'

'You'll need to be because the other executor is Dermot, his brother.'

'Do you know why he chose you?' said Tara.

'No!'

'It looks to me like a sign of trust.'

CHAPTER TWENTY-THREE

Jude didn't look at the documents again until she was safely in her mother's car. Then she pulled them out of the envelope and gazed down at the top sheet in a daze of bewilderment.

Why would Liam even make a will? The obvious answer was that he had become a father. Parents start thinking of the future in a way that people like her did not. What happens after their own life has ended takes on a new meaning.

But why would he name her – the girl he had been involved with one heady summer but then abandoned after the accident – as executor? It made absolutely no sense.

She chewed the edge of her finger. Three or four months ago, Liam had named her as executor to his will, then a few days ago he had dragged her into the final days of his life and left her tangled up in a murder inquiry.

Was it all some kind of mad joke, a piece of troublemaking mischief? She wouldn't put it past the Liam she had known as a teenager: capricious, anarchic, with his own dark sense of humour.

She could refuse, she supposed. In fact, the more

she thought about it, the more obvious it was that she should do just that. Yet her mind snagged on the fact that this was Liam's *will*, the last wishes of someone who had been important to her and who, for whatever bizarre reason, had chosen her for this task.

At first glance, the will looked straightforward enough. It was a format document, with answers typed into boxes: his full name (she had never known he was Liam Craig Birch), date of birth, address. She flicked through the remaining sheets and saw that the last several were handwritten, Liam's bold script, with its slashed letters and words running into each other, the same as it had been when she knew him.

She pushed the documents back into the envelope. She would look at them later, decide later. She drove back through the growing darkness. Lights were turned on in houses, squares of yellow in the gloom, a few plumes of smoke from chimneys, a small group jostling outside the pub she used to go to, a gaggle of girls with skimpy skirts and goose-pimply legs and brave bright laughs marching down the road arm in arm, the weekend beginning.

Her father was home. Jude knew at once that her mother had told him: he looked awkward, solemn, fond. He held out his arms and hugged her so hard she could feel her cheek creasing against his jacket. He told her that he would always be proud of her and she was his favourite daughter, which was an old joke because, of course, she was his only daughter. She felt her eyes sting.

Her bedroom had barely changed since she'd lived here: the same wallpaper that she'd chosen when she was fourteen, the same moulting rug by the bed, the same sage-green duvet, and lines of paperbacks along one wall. The table where she did her homework. A round, deep-framed mirror she had stood in front of to put on make-up or thread earrings into her lobes. There were curling, faded photos pinned to the corkboard – herself and friends sticking their tongues out at the camera, herself and her elder brother Michael sitting cross-legged outside a tent, and she remembered that holiday and how it had rained every day, herself at the school prom, wearing a long, frothy dress she had hired for the evening and felt ridiculous in and someone had tipped red wine all over.

Her mother had made vegetable lasagne, which was the family comfort food. It was creamy and rich and full of carbs. Everything was a code for something else. They had a bottle of Chianti, which made Jude's head swim. She was so tired, so mugged by all the events, the losses and surprises and body blows of grief. She didn't tell them about Liam's will, because she didn't yet know what she was going to do.

At half past nine she went upstairs with a cup of tea, cleaned her teeth, put on pyjamas and climbed into bed with a hot-water bottle. Her friends would be getting ready to go out, pulling on finery, calling each other to check details, but that seemed a distant world.

She turned her phone back on and almost wished she hadn't. She was going to have to reply to all the messages and the missed calls, go through the edited story over and over again. Not now though. She would sort out the mess of her life later.

Turning on the bedside lamp, she pulled the documents out of the envelope and skimmed through the first pages. *I, Liam, presently of . . . sound mind . . . revoke all prior wills and codicils . . .*

Danny's name and her relationship to him.

Alfie's name: Alfie Kelner Birch. Jude looked at his date of birth: he was a year and one month old.

Then came the bit about the executors. Jude read through twice what the powers of the executor were. There were an intimidating number of them: to pay Liam's legally enforceable debts out of the estate, and all expenses to do with the administration of his estate. To take all legal action to have probate of the will quickly and simply (she didn't even know what this meant). To maintain, exchange, continue, dissolve or sell any personal property. To purchase or liquidate investments, to open and close bank accounts, to exercise voting rights in connection with shareholding. To maintain, settle, abandon, make a claim against or otherwise deal with any actions . . .

Jude laid the piece of paper down and rubbed

her eyes. There was no way she could do this. She turned to the end of the document where the other executor was identified: Dermot Robert Birch. There was no phone number or email by his name, just an address. He lived about ten miles away from here, near Shrewsbury.

She took a sip of tepid tea and adjusted the pillows, then turned back to the sheaf of papers. Liam had left everything to Danny. If she should pre-decease him, it passed to Alfie. He had appointed his mother as Alfie's guardian if both he and Danny died. That was simple enough. Presumably, Liam didn't own much except the mortgaged house and Jude had no idea what that was worth nor what his other debts might be. She couldn't imagine him with a pension, investments, money put by for a rainy day.

The last sheets were the handwritten ones, a scrawled list of objects with a name put beside each one, running over three pages: Liam's bequests. His circular saw to Vin, his acoustic guitar to Irina, his bike to someone called Dessie O'Toole, his fishing rod to his father, his photos and a gold chain to his mother (how her heart would break, thought Jude), his leather jacket to Bjorn Jansson, his chessboard to Graham Matlock, his favourite hat to Bill Friend and his hand-operated coffee-grinder to Megan Friend with thanks for all the coffee she'd made him, his lucky deck of cards to Benny Slater, the small wooden table with steel legs to Peter Cosco . . . Jude's eye skimmed down the list then, with a small intake of breath, stopped. Between the three-legged stool for Rainer Monk and the two-man tent for Sandy Balkan was the bequest of the wooden bowl he had carved for Jude Winter.

Jude sat quite still, propped up against the pillows, looking down at the papers. Tears stood in her eyes. She felt tired, sad, confused and very alone.

She turned to the final handwritten page. There were a couple more bequests, and then Liam had written that he wanted a secular funeral where everyone should laugh and dance and get blind drunk. He wanted his old leather boots to go on top of his wicker coffin. He wanted to be buried in Walthamstow cemetery with a simple headstone.

Jude put the papers back in the envelope and the envelope on the floor beside the bed. She turned off the bedside lamp and slid down under the covers but as she lay there, she felt something hard against her skin. She pulled off Liam's carved wishbone on its thin leather thong and laid it on the bedside table beside her. It hadn't brought him much luck.

CHAPTER TWENTY-FOUR

Jude woke early. She could smell coffee and hear the clatter of dishes. She climbed out of bed, pulled on the old dressing gown that still hung on the door hook, and opened the curtains. The sky was pale grey, and in the distance the green hills of Shropshire folded away. From here, she could just make out the renovated barn on the slope above the town. That was where their wedding party had been planned to take place. Nat would need to cancel that; they probably wouldn't get the deposit back.

'I got some croissants out of the freezer,' said her mother as she came into the kitchen.

'Great.'

'And the weather's cleared. I thought we could go for a walk.'

'There's someone I've got to see first. Can I use the car again?'

Dermot Birch lived over a shop selling ceramic tiles. Jude looked up at his windows. All the curtains were closed. Perhaps he was still asleep. She pressed the doorbell anyway, stood back, waited, then rang again. Finally she heard footsteps coming swiftly and lightly down the stairs and the door swung open.

For a moment Jude couldn't speak. The man who stood in front of her, barefooted, in jeans and a white T-shirt, looked so like his brother it was a mockery: the same dark hair, the same nearly black eyes and high cheekbones. But he was slighter than Liam, his face was thinner and beardless, his skin smoother. He was like a watercolour version, and when he spoke his voice was several shades lighter, though rough with sleep.

'Sorry. Did I wake you?'

'No. I thought I might be seeing you.'

'You know who I am then?'

'Jude,' he said. 'Jude Winter.' He smiled then, a quick, wary tightening of his lips. 'You've heard about the will?'

He was still blocking the doorway and Jude felt awkward.

'I thought, since I was in the area . . .' She trailed off.

He nodded, as if coming to a decision. Jude followed him up the narrow stairs, through the door at the top and into a space that was kitchen and living room combined. It was tidy, bare and neutral, nothing like Liam's crazy house or his family home.

'I've not been here long,' Dermot said, seeing her looking around the room. 'I was living with my girlfriend in Shrewsbury until August. But it didn't work out.' He shrugged, picked up the kettle and took it to the sink. 'What can you do?'

Jude made a vague, sympathetic sound.

'We met once before actually,' she said. 'You probably don't remember.'

'I remember. And of course I know you were the girl in the car.'

His mother's phrase. Jude winced. 'Yes.'

'You came to the house once and gave me a message.'

'That's it.'

She had stood in the doorway and told Dermot that she wanted, no, *needed* to see his brother. That he mustn't end things. She felt agonised and humiliated all over again for her ardent, frightened eighteen-year-old self.

'He really liked you,' said Dermot.

'It was a long time ago. That's why all this . . .' She waved her hand in the air, assuming that Dermot knew about everything. How could he not? 'I don't know what to say about it.'

'He used to say how clever you were,' said Dermot, putting tea bags into two mugs. 'How you were going to be a doctor. Maybe that's why he wanted you to be his executor. Because you're clever.'

'I don't know anything about things like wills. Do you?'

'I'm an electrician. That's how much I know about wills.'

'Did he tell you what he was going to do?'

'Liam didn't generally tell me things like that.'

They stared at each other. It seemed almost comic to her but Dermot didn't seem to be finding it funny in any way.

'At least you're his brother. I'm one of his teenage girlfriends. Of which, I've heard, there were many.'

'You've been talking to Mum.'

'Yes.'

'She thought the sun shone out of his arse.'

Jude watched him as he poured the boiling water over the tea bags.

'That must have been hard for you, as his kid brother.'

Dermot shrugged. 'It was all right.'

'Were you two close?'

'Close?'

He looked away from her, out of the little window.

'If you don't want to talk about it . . .'

Dermot turned back to Jude. He seemed to be making his mind up about something.

'Well,' he said at last. 'He pushed me around a bit when I was little. I used to trail after him, I badly wanted to be in his gang, you know. He was pretty fucking cool. He would get me to do his dirty work, cover for him to Mum and Dad. But yeah, we were brothers. He was my only brother and now he's dead.' He stopped, chewed his lower lip. 'So it's just me. I'll always be in his shadow now.'

'I'm really sorry. So sorry, Dermot.' Those useless words, over and over and over again.

Dermot nodded, muttered something Jude couldn't catch. His mouth was pulled tight but it quivered, as if he was preventing himself from crying.

They sat at the kitchen table, by the window that looked out on to the street. Opposite was a small car park. Jude propped her chin on her hand.

'So I don't know anything about the law and nor do you.'

'Not a fucking thing.'

'Have you looked at it?'

'A bit. It all goes to Danny, and I guess even if he hadn't made a will that's what would have happened, since she's his long-term partner and the mother of Alfie. No surprises there.' He shrugged. 'Maybe there won't be much to do. Maybe Liam just had to put down a name or two because it's asked for on the form, and so he put down us, but it'll turn out to be easy.'

Jude thought of the powers given to executors, the stuff about assets and debts and things being maintained or sold or liquidated.

'Did he have much except the house?'

'I'd be surprised. This is Liam we're talking about – he always treated money as if it was something dirty. I was amazed he ever bought a property, and I bet there's a socking great loan to pay off.'

'Why did he?'

'He was always making sudden decisions, changing his plans in a split second. You never knew what was going to happen next. Have you seen the place?'

'I was there on Thursday.'

'Did you meet Danny?'

'She invited me.'

'Then you know it's not like any other house. It's a wreck for a start. Did you go upstairs?'

Jude shook her head.

'I wouldn't want to sleep in one of those rooms. Liam never minded things like that, but the others . . .'

'So: a house that's a wreck and no savings.'

'Not that I know of.'

'Debts?'

Dermot shrugged.

'Then there are the bequests,' continued Jude.

'Yeah. So many of them! Some of those things are pretty niche. Did you see he's given his harmonica to someone – harmonicas only cost a few quid to buy new. It's like he just wrote down all the objects he owned that he could think of.'

'Do you know many of the people he's named?'

'A few, not all. But presumably Danny can hand most of the things out, and Vin as well. I can make sure Al gets the weights and Benny gets the cards.'

'Is that the Benny he went to school with?'

And the Benny, she thought, who was in the back of the car when we crashed.

'That's the one. He still lives round here. I don't know how much he and Liam kept in touch. Did you know him?'

Jude thought of the boy passed out in the back of the crashed car that long-ago night.

'A little,' she said.

'God, what was Liam up to?'

'It shows he trusted you,' said Jude, as Tara had said to her the day before.

A grimace of distress tightened Dermot's face. 'I guess he did. But look, one thing's for sure – you shouldn't have to get involved in this. I'd already decided that.'

'What do you mean?'

'As you said, I'm his brother. Why don't you leave it to me? This shouldn't be your mess to sort out.'

'Really?'

'Really.'

'How will you set about it?'

Dermot shrugged. 'I guess I have to start with finding out the basic stuff, like what his debts were, what he was owed, if anything, what was in his bank, things like that.'

'That sounds like it would be difficult.'

'I can always ask someone,' Dermot said vaguely. 'There must be people who deal in things like this. Leave it in my incapable hands. I'll let you know how it goes.'

Jude thought for a moment. The idea of leaving all this behind her was so tempting but she looked at Dermot, the straggly hair, the dark rings under his eyes. She couldn't. Besides, she had an idea.

'My brother's an accountant. He can suggest something. Or someone.'

'I guess we can keep him in reserve.'

'No,' said Jude decisively. 'He'll do it.'

CHAPTER TWENTY-FIVE

At first, Jude didn't recognise Benny. She remembered him as small, wiry, sharp-featured, but the man who came to the door was quite chubby, with a stomach billowing over his trousers, jowly cheeks and thinning hair. He frowned and for a moment looked more like the Benny she had briefly known.

'Who are you?'

'Jude.'

'Jude? *Jude!* What the fuck? Jude Winter. Of course you are. You've hardly changed at all. What are you doing here?'

Jude saw his expression change, saw him slowly understand why she was there.

'I'm up for a few days, staying with my parents, and I just thought I could call round.'

She let the sentence trail away. A woman had appeared behind him, her bright blonde hair tied back in a tight bun. She was alarmingly pregnant, and one hand was laid protectively over the tight dome of her stomach.

'Yolanda?' said Jude. 'Is that you?'

'Jude,' said Yolanda. 'Long time, no see.'

Jude had met Benny a couple of times after the accident and her break-up with Liam, but the last time she had seen Yolanda was when she was vomiting on the road beside the mangled car.

'Wow,' she said. 'I had no idea. I mean, congratulations. When's it due?'

'Six days ago.'

They both looked at her, waiting for her to say why she had turned up on the doorstep after so many years. Jude barely knew herself.

'It's probably a bad time,' she said awkwardly.

'I've got a few minutes,' said Benny.

She sat on the small sofa and he took a chair. Preparations for the baby were everywhere – piles of miniature Baby-gros, packs of disposable nappies, a Moses basket still wrapped in its plastic, a soft crocheted blanket beside it.

'Exciting,' said Jude.

'Terrifying,' said Benny, but he was smiling.

'I don't really know why I'm here. I – well, you've probably read about everything.'

'You mean, with you and Liam. Yeah, I guess. I didn't know you and he were still an item.'

'We weren't an item.' Jude thought of explaining, once again, the real situation but she couldn't face it. It didn't matter. 'It's made me think about things.'

'About Liam.'

'Yes.'

'He was a strange guy, that's for sure. My mum

used to say he had the devil in him. She thought he was a bad influence.'

'Was he?'

Benny laughed. 'He was a bad influence on me, that's for sure.'

'In what way?' Jude asked.

Benny shook his head. 'It doesn't matter now. I'm here. Things are all right.'

'He made me the executor of his will.'

'What does that mean?'

'I have to make sure that it's carried out the way he wanted it.'

Benny smiled.

'The same old Jude,' he said. 'Still running around trying to please Liam, even when he's dead.'

Jude felt like she'd been punched. She suddenly felt the old agonies and humiliations of being a teenager. They were so vivid and pungent that she could almost smell them. She didn't protest though. She just wanted to do what she had to do and leave.

'He left you a deck of cards.'

Benny snorted in disbelief. 'That old thing. Why would he do that?'

'I'm just the messenger.'

Benny rubbed his cheek. 'That makes me feel bad.'

'Why bad?'

'I lost touch with him. He tried to stay friends, he'd call me whenever he was back in the area. And he was loyal. He'd do anything for a mate.'

'But you didn't want to see him?'

'No.'

'Why?'

'He could be scary. I can't explain it better than that. I felt he was dangerous to be around, like literally anything could happen. He had no brakes.'

Jude made a small sound, waited.

'You do stupid stuff when you're a kid and then you grow up and you want to put it behind you. But Liam wasn't like that. You kind of felt that he wanted things to get out of control, life to blow up in his face. I don't know. And then me and Yolanda got serious and I just thought, I've got to distance myself from all of that.'

'Did he mind?'

'I don't know. He left me his deck of cards, didn't he?'

'He did, yes.'

'That crash,' said Benny after a pause. 'We could have all died that night.'

'I know.'

'I only remember bits of it.'

'You were pretty out of it.'

'We all were. That was it for you two, wasn't it?'

'It would have ended anyway,' said Jude, and stood up. 'I was going to university. It was always just a summer thing.'

CHAPTER TWENTY-SIX

Jude's brother Michael was married with two children and lived just outside Guildford. They met every Christmas at their parents' house. Although Guildford was an easy train journey from London, Jude had only visited his house a handful of times, for christenings and a housewarming party. Sometimes when he was in London, he would get in touch and they would have lunch or a coffee. Even now he still felt like an older brother to her. She felt that he looked on her being a doctor as something slightly amusing, as if it was a hobby she had taken up, like watercolour painting or horse riding.

When she phoned him, the first part of the conversation was more sombre than usual. Michael hadn't known anything about Jude's relationship with Liam. He had been doing an internship at the time of the crash. But he had talked to their parents about recent events, and Jude was at least relieved that she didn't have to tell him the story. He said that he was sorry about Nat but that, to be honest, he had never thought that he was good enough for her. Michael had only met Nat a few times, and Jude had to stop herself replying angrily. After all, she was about to ask him for a favour.

When she told him about Liam's will and being made executor, Michael started laughing.

'It's not actually funny,' Jude said.

'It is actually quite funny. You? Executor of a will? What's that about?'

'I don't know.'

'I hope there's another executor,' he said. 'A real one.'

'The other one's his brother. And I think he knows even less than me, if that's possible, but he did say he would do most of the work. If you'd just set us on the right track.'

Michael responded with a snort.

'Most of it seems quite simple,' Jude said. 'Just odds and ends he wanted to leave to people. But apparently we're meant to check his finances. I wondered if you could take a look at it.'

'You couldn't afford me.'

'I'm sorry. It was wrong to ask.'

He laughed. 'I was only kidding. No problem. Just send me copies of anything you want me to look at.'

'That's really good of you.'

'You'd do the same for me.'

'I would. If I could.'

'In fact, I've got this pain in my back.'

'Where in your back?'

There was another laugh.

'I was only joking again,' he said jovially. 'But seriously. This executor thing. How did it come about?'

'I've no idea. His parents contacted me when they saw the will.'

'You mean he didn't even ask you?'

'No.'

There was a pause. When Michael spoke again, he sounded more serious, more professional.

'That's weird.'

'I know.'

'Jude, you should talk to a solicitor. You can get out of it if you want.'

When the call was over, she considered this. Did she want to get out of it?

CHAPTER TWENTY-SEVEN

Jude thought that Danny might swear and shout, that she might be angry or upset, but when she took out the will and unfolded it and put it on the table in front of her, Danny just stared at it. As if she were in a dream, she picked it up and read it, page by page. Then she put the will down and looked at Jude.

'Who *are* you?' she said. 'No. Really.'

'I don't know much about things like this but I think it's straightforward. He's left little things to friends. But basically it all goes to you and Alfie.'

'You didn't answer my question?'

'I didn't understand your question. You know who I am.'

Without a word, Danny got up and left the kitchen. Jude stared round the room. It was large, and some of the floor had been ripped up so that she could see the pipes, and under that, rubble. But the rest was covered in beautiful rust-coloured quarry tiles that gleamed in the autumn sun coming in through the windows. The fridge was tall and had a rusty door. The oven looked ancient and something was bubbling away in a pan on its hob. The lid juddered up and down and every so often liquid sloshed out. In a saucepan next to the hob sat two congealed fried eggs. A huge brown paper bag of bread flour on the surface had split and the flour had leaked copiously. Packets of rice and pasta sat everywhere and there was a small metal wheelbarrow by the back door filled with potatoes and parsnips and onions. The wooden table was covered in candles and night lights; wax of all colours had spread across the wood in a muddy river. But there were also pots of herbs on the windowsill, and dried flowers hanging from a ring of metal that was suspended from the ceiling. Jamjars full of flowers and pieces of greenery were dotted round the room, on a stool, on the table, on top of a lovely wooden dresser.

Jude heard the sounds of footsteps going up the stairs. She heard the creak of movement on the first floor, then a door slammed and the footsteps came back down the stairs. Danny came through the kitchen door. She was holding a large wooden bowl and she put it down on the table, almost dropping it, with a crash.

'Did you have your eye on it?' she said.

'What?'

'It's one of the things Liam did in his spare time. He'd carve things out of wood: spoons, little dishes and then some more special things like this. They're almost like sculptures. This is one of the really special pieces, it took him weeks and weeks, he lavished care on it and he left it to you. Did you pick it out yourself?'

'Why are you saying this?' Jude protested. 'Look at the date on this will. When he wrote it, I hadn't had any contact with Liam since we were at school. I don't know why he left me that bowl. If you want it, you can have it.'

'It's not about the bowl. Look at it from my point of view, Jude. My partner has been suddenly murdered and then I hear that on the day it happened, he was planning to meet you in a house outside London. You and I meet and you tell me it's all very strange and a complete mystery to you. You've only seen him once since school and you were doing him a favour. I don't understand, but when we talk, I think you're a good person and someone I can maybe trust. The next thing I hear, he's done a will which he didn't tell me about and you're suddenly in charge of it. And he left you his beautiful bowl, which was special to him.'

Jude looked at the bowl properly – it was large and quite shallow and the wood was honey-coloured, swirled with darker grains. There was a knot near its rim. It was polished so that it glowed as if it was somehow alive. She had never owned anything as beautiful.

'And special to me,' added Danny, and she reached out and traced the rim with her forefinger.

Jude, feeling the stirrings of anger, took a calming breath.

'I know that you're going through something that should never happen to anyone, but I didn't choose this. You've read through it. Where do I benefit apart from this bowl? All right, I agree, it's lovely, but you can keep it. I don't want it. You say it all took you by surprise. It took me by surprise as well. You're meant to get the consent of the executor before you write the will, not just spring it on them. Do you think I want this job? Because I don't. I'm only here because my brother is an accountant and if I get stuff together he can have a look at things, give a sense of the larger picture. Liam's brother isn't exactly keen on being the executor either.'

At the mention of Dermot, Danny gave a faint smile.

'I can imagine that. It's not his kind of thing.'

'It's not my kind of thing either.'

'So if you're not the sort of person who does things like this, why did he ask you?'

'I don't know. Maybe my name just popped into his head.'

'So what does it all mean?' Danny asked. 'Do you start going around the house opening drawers and going through cupboards? Poking around.'

'If you've a problem with me doing this, fine. Absolutely fine. I'll just say I wasn't asked and I don't want to do it.'

'Who will you say it to?'

Jude thought for a moment and then grinned wryly.

'I don't have a clue. I don't know anything about being an executor apart from what I learned from spending about ten minutes online. You just have to get the assets valued, make sure debts are paid off and do what Liam wanted, like making sure that his harmonica goes to the right person. It would probably be sensible to get a solicitor to do it. It'll cost money but it'll get done the right way. Or you can lean on Dermot. He said he'd do it. I'm not sure he's quite . . .'

'Stable,' said Danny.

'Capable of doing something like this.'

Danny leaned forward to look at the document. Her dark hair fell across her face and she gathered it up with one hand. Her expression was stern, a little sad.

'You know what gets me,' she said. 'I look at the date, what is it? Four months ago? And I imagine Liam suddenly having the idea of doing a will and thinking about it and probably making lists of all those stupid little things he's leaving to people and all the time keeping it a secret from me. And then, just to make sure it's a secret, he goes back to his parents and does it there and gets witnesses I don't know, and then to carry out the will he names an executor.'

'Two executors.'

'Dermot,' she said. 'Was he in on the secret?'

'He was as surprised as I was.'

'Why would Liam do all that without telling me? That's what gets me.'

'I'm guessing he did it because he had become a father and that made him feel he had to put things in order. Maybe he didn't tell you because

165

people find it difficult to talk about dying. I work in geriatrics, so I see people die all the time and a lot of my job is to make their dying as good as I can. But I haven't made a will myself because I'm young and I still want to hang on to my belief that I'm going to live for ever. I think becoming a parent makes you feel mortal and makes you think about life going on after you've left it. What would really have been terrible is if he'd secretly written a will leaving everything to someone else. But whoever the executor is or isn't, basically it's all going to you and Alfie.'

Danny got up and filled the kettle, put it on the hob and then sat down again.

'So you need to look at bank records and things like that?'

'I think so. He left everything to you and Alfie. But to do that you need to be clear about what that is. How much it's worth. My brother said he'd look over it.'

'I'll warn you,' said Danny. 'It'll be chaotic. Liam was wonderful with his hands. He could make anything. He could fix anything. He could fix things that weren't designed to be fixed. But he couldn't deal with money stuff. He paid bills when he remembered to or when someone reminded him. But he didn't exactly have a filing system.'

'It probably doesn't matter too much,' Jude said. 'It's all going to you.'

Danny stood up again.

'Camomile? Ginger? Mint? The mint is fresh from the garden.'

'Whatever's most relaxing.'

'Camomile's best. It might send you to sleep.'

She sat back down with two steaming mugs.

'So what do you want to do first? The bills and accounts and things are all over the place.'

The thought of it made Jude's head ache.

'I'm tempted to say that we should start with the easy bit,' she said. 'The things that Liam wanted to give to friends. From the look of it, he must have put a lot of thought into it. But maybe you could show me where the financial stuff is.'

Danny got up, opened a drawer and pulled out a bundle of rolled-up shopping bags. She handed them to Jude.

'You're not going to find files and ledger books and spreadsheets. It'll just be papers scattered around. You can put them in these.'

As they got up, they almost bumped into Vin, who was coming in. He smiled at Jude.

'Can't keep away, eh?'

'She's here on business,' Danny said. 'Liam made her executor of his will.'

'Not just me,' said Jude, feeling the need to share the blame. 'He made his brother executor as well.'

She was wearily expecting the questions she'd got from Liam's parents and from Danny but Vin looked too surprised even to speak.

'You?' he said finally.

'I didn't ask to do it.'

'It's quite a document,' said Danny. 'Lots of little bequests. He left you his circular saw.'

'Oh, he did, did he?'

'You don't sound very happy,' said Danny.

'Well, we could have a bit of a philosophical discussion about whether it was his to give.' He stopped himself. 'It was nice of him to think of me, I suppose. But I'd have to look up the details to see which of us actually paid for it.'

'Jude here is going to be going through it all,' said Danny.

Vin gave a grunt. 'Good luck with that.'

'I'm not; I'm just handing it over to my brother.'

Jude and Danny were about to move away when Vin spoke again.

'When did he do this will?'

'Four months ago,' said Jude.

'Four months ago. And he named you as an executor.'

Jude didn't feel like justifying herself all over again.

'Are there papers over at the place where you worked?'

'What kind of papers?'

'I need to have some idea of what he owes and what people owe him.'

Vin frowned. 'As I said, it'll be interesting.'

'But are there papers there?'

He shrugged. 'If you want papers, we've got papers. Lots of papers.'

'Is there some kind of company accountant I can talk to?'

'No.'

'You mean there isn't an accountant?'

'That's what I mean. But you can come over and take a look.' He glanced at Danny. 'Most of the rest of the stuff will be in the back room, won't it?'

'I was about to take her there.'

Vin shook his head. 'Whatever you're being paid,' he said. 'It's not enough.'

'I'm not being paid anything.'

Danny led Jude up the stairs to the large first floor.

'The police came and poked around a bit,' she said. 'I don't think they found anything much. They took his laptop away.'

They went along the corridor to the room at the back. Danny looked back over her shoulder.

'This room's got a nice view on to the marshes. It's where Liam spent a lot of time.'

Danny opened the door and stood by to let Jude past. Jude gasped. There was too much to take in all at once. It looked more like a junk room than an office. It was full of apparently random things: a bike leaning against the wall, cardboard boxes piled up, tools of all kinds, papers strewn everywhere. At the far wall, under a window, was a wooden desk. More papers bulged out of half-open drawers.

The sight of it made her feel almost nauseous. She looked around. The walls were almost calming, beautifully painted, a terracotta red, like in a

Roman villa. And there were pictures on the wall that were pleasing, of fruit, lemons, apples. The view out of the window was the junkyard, which seen from above was even more chaotic, yet beyond it Jude could see the marshes, a wash of late autumn colours and the glint of water. The room itself felt like drowning, or like the inside of a disordered mind.

She looked helplessly at the shopping bags she was holding.

'I'm not sure I can do this,' she said.

'I'm not sure anyone can do this,' said Danny. She gestured around her. 'This was Liam. You knew him. He was amazing. He wasn't like anyone else. But he was also this.'

CHAPTER TWENTY-EIGHT

Danny left, shutting the door hard behind her. A howl of rage was coming from somewhere inside the house. Dimly, Jude could also hear a guitar being strummed, the same chords over and over again.

It was hard not to feel defeated before she'd even started. She stared around her at the unimaginable chaos, then strode determinedly towards the drawers of the desk from which papers erupted and yanked the deepest one fully open. Plunging her hand into it, she lifted out a heap and placed it on the desk; she scooped out the rest, then plonked herself onto the swivel chair, which spun on its wheels and slid sideways.

'Jesus,' Jude said crossly, and scooted herself back to the desk.

On top of the pile of papers was a shopping list, not in Liam's handwriting: light bulbs, loo roll, toothpaste, bleach, mousetraps. Jude crumpled it into a ball and chucked it behind her.

Then a violent blue and yellow scribble in wax crayon: Alfie's art, presumably. She chucked that as well, then felt a bit guilty; after all, Liam had cared about it enough to keep it.

It was quickly clear that Liam had kept everything. Receipts for tools and for nappies; doodles; reminders about paying the gas bill, and then final reminders; a drawing someone had made of the front of the house; scores from some card game; a recipe for tamarind aubergine curry; his NHS card; plans for a kitchen installation; flyers for a concert of folk music; takeaway menus; brochures; deft pencil sketches of things Liam had seen from this desk – garden birds, Alfie sitting next to the bird cage, the tree whose roots were splitting the wall separating the yard from the road. There were Post-it notes, ancient postcards, blobs of Blu-tack, leaking biros, an expired passport that turned out, when she opened it, to belong to Danny.

Randomly shuffled among everything else were those papers that Jude thought might be relevant to her task. Bank statements (she looked at a couple and winced), numerous utility bills, invoices, tax demands. She put these to one side.

In the next, smaller drawer were a stack of unopened envelopes. Jude slid her finger under the flap of one and drew out a final demand for council tax. Another contained the bank's refusal of a further overdraft. She pushed it back inside the envelope and bundled everything that looked remotely financial into a plastic bag. Michael was going to get more than he had bargained for.

She hadn't even started on the mess of papers on the floor. She squatted down and picked up a brown A4 envelope. Inside were images from an ultrasound: presumably that grainy little tadpole was Alfie. Jude suddenly felt incredibly sad. She sat back on her heels, surrounded by the debris of a life. Under her left hand was a letter that began, 'Dear Mr Birch, it has come to our attention that you are in arrears . . .' She put it into the bag. She had the nasty stirrings of a headache.

'Hello!' A voice sang out from behind the closed door. The handle turned, and a very long and slender lower leg slid through, holding open the door. On the foot was a lime-green pump.

'Hi?' Jude waited.

A tall, sharp-edged drama of a woman came sideways into the room, holding two large mugs in one hand and in the other a plate. Her hair was dyed pale red with dreads plaited into it. Her face was dramatic, with a beaky nose and carved cheekbones; her large mottled-green eyes were thickly outlined, giving her a tragic air. She had narrow shoulders, a protuberant collar bone, and her body, encased in a saffron-yellow jumpsuit with rolled-up sleeves, ripped knees and dirty hems, looked flat as a board. Jude, still squatting on the floor and gazing up at her, couldn't decide if she looked grotesque or glorious.

'I'm Irina,' said the woman.

Jude stood up, the nasty, mild pain shifting inside her skull. She felt very small and ordinary in this house of tall, extraordinary people.

'Jude.'

Irina put the mugs on the desk and the plate on the chair. She held out a hand and took Jude's, shook it very firmly. The muscles in her bare forearm rippled. She might be thin, but she was strong.

'I know,' Irina said. 'At last.'

Jude was starting to tire of the way people were treating her as an object of curiosity.

'Liam's mystery,' Irina continued, then: 'Liam's final mystery.' Her eyes looked even bigger. She was about to cry.

'I'm so sorry,' said Jude, bringing out those ritual words again, because they were all she had. 'It's terrible to lose a friend.'

'And such a friend,' said Irina, arresting a sob, while her green eyes examined Jude. 'A beautiful soul. Ginger okay?'

'What?'

'Tea. I brought us spicy ginger tea and banana cake that I found in some tin or other. I don't know how long it's been there.'

Jude tried to remember what Vin had said about Irina. She cleared people's houses and brought home lots of junk; she was a bit wild; she danced when she couldn't sleep.

'Thank you,' she said. 'I guess Danny told you that Liam asked me to be his executor?'

'Mmm.' Irina pushed half a slice of banana bread into her mouth and sat on the swivel chair, the plate on her lap. She spun herself round once, then picked up her mug of ginger tea. Her long bony fingers were nicotine-stained. 'That's weird, isn't it?'

'Yeah.'

'So?'

'What?'

'You know.'

'No.'

'Did he leave everything to Danny?'

'Oh! I see.'

Jude felt uncomfortable. She didn't know if it was the executor's job to tell people the contents of a will; it was supposed to be lawyers who did that, solemnly, in the presence of the family, in an oak-panelled room, and everything wrapped around in antiquated words that protected people from the hurting truth. *This person is dead; this is who they loved the most.*

Irina was humming softly to herself.

'Why don't you ask Danny?' said Jude.

Irina spun herself in another circle, put out her foot to bring herself to a halt.

'That's not as easy as it sounds. Not easy at all. Can I have your slice of banana bread?'

'Of course.'

'Wheels within wheels,' said Irina.

Jude's head throbbed. She'd left her pills back at the flat. She heard a child's voice outside and saw Alfie in the yard. He tottered towards the small bed and then tripped and fell. Jude waited for an adult to appear and lift him to his feet, but no one came and after a while he pulled himself up again and stood swaying on his unsteady legs.

'So I'm supposed to be finding out about Liam's financial affairs,' she said. 'But it's not easy.' She gestured round the room.

'His *financial* affairs,' said Irina, exaggeratedly raising her thin brows. 'I can't help you with them.'

What had Danny said to her the first time they'd met? *He was having an affair with someone, even if it wasn't you.* Jude looked at Irina in her yellow jumpsuit, her long legs crossed at the ankle; she was like a gorgeous flamingo.

'I can tell you that he did make you a bequest though,' she said.

'A bequest?'

'It just means—'

'I know what a bequest means. I clear people's houses for a living, and most of them are dead people. Dead people with too much stuff that nobody wants. Except me, sometimes. I see beauty where other people see dross. So what is this bequest?'

'His guitar.'

Irina's face fell.

'Really? Why would I want a guitar? I don't play the guitar and I'm not particularly keen to learn.

He should have given that to Doc, except I bet he didn't give Doc and Erika a single thing.'

No, thought Jude. He didn't.

'I wish he'd left me something that had real emotional value,' said Irina. 'I thought he'd do that. Like the chain he often wore. I would never take it off. Next to my skin.' She touched the sharp bones of her clavicle with her long fingers.

'That's for his mother,' said Jude, acutely uncomfortable. She thought of the wishbone on its leather thong that she had taken from Liam's bag.

'Or the gorgeous wooden bowl he spent such a time carving.'

'I'm afraid that's going to someone else as well.'

'Oh, I don't fucking care.' Irina leaned back in the chair and put her hand over her eyes. 'Not about the chain, or the bowl, or anything else. I'm not being greedy. I just want to know I mattered.'

'Right,' said Jude. She understood that.

'Why did he give me his guitar then?'

'Maybe because it meant a lot to him?'

'Maybe you're right. I can't believe he's dead. That I'll never see him again. I walk into the house and I expect him to be there. It's lonely here without him, like a fire's gone out.'

Tears welled in her eyes, and Jude made a sympathetic sound. She found it impossible to tell if Irina was being sincere or performing a grief she didn't feel. Everything about her was exaggerated, like a Greek chorus. At the same

177

time, there was something unexpectedly childlike about her that was touching.

'He was so alive,' said Irina. 'Don't you think?'

'I don't know. We hadn't been in touch.'

Irina made a scoffing sound.

'What?'

'Do you think anyone in this house believes that?'

Danny was nowhere to be seen when Jude came downstairs, nor Vin. But a woman came out of the kitchen carrying Alfie on her hip with practised ease. She looked Dutch, strong-boned with dark blonde hair and smooth round cheeks, but when she spoke she had a Liverpool accent. She was wearing loose-fitting jeans, a soft rollback jumper and shabby slippers, and the ordinariness came as a relief to Jude.

'I'm Erika,' she said, holding out a hand that was broad and warm.

Jude felt a spike of recognition. Here was the woman who had called Liam's mobile on the night he had been murdered.

'Jude.'

Erika nodded. 'I know. You look younger than twenty-nine.'

'How do you know I'm twenty-nine?'

Erika laughed. 'I know a lot more than that. We all do.' She disentangled Alfie's finger from her hair. 'Your full name is Judith Abigail Winter. You're a care-of-the-elderly doctor. You studied at Bristol. You were engaged to Nathaniel Weller but aren't

178

any longer and we all know why that is.' Jude felt her jaw tense. 'You lived with him in a flat in Stratford, but don't any longer. You grew up in Shropshire, same as Liam. You have one brother. Your father works for the council. Your mother is a nurse. You were Liam's girlfriend when you were eighteen. People who knew you both at the time say it was a very unlikely match. Liam was going to join you in a cottage in Norfolk the day he was killed. You're his executor. In the last week or so you've been described as slight, pretty, elfin, strong, frail, distraught, defensive, defiant. Plus lots of other things I can't remember now.'

'You've done your homework.'

Erika shrugged. 'Five minutes online. We're all curious. You can't blame us.'

Jude felt that she could blame them but she didn't reply.

'So what did Liam say about me?' Erika asked.

'He didn't say anything.'

'Come on. I don't mind.'

Jude picked up the bowl.

'I didn't know anything about you, or anyone in this house. Or that this house even existed. We meant nothing to each other.'

She was almost panting with frustration, but Erika just nodded at the gorgeous wooden bowl that Jude was clutching to her chest like a shield, at the bag stuffed with his financial documents.

'Strange way of meaning nothing.'

179

CHAPTER TWENTY-NINE

It was a slow bike ride back to Tottenham. Jude had to hang the plastic bags containing the papers and the beautiful wooden bowl on her handlebars; the bags swung when she went round corners and caught in the spokes. The bowl kept banging against her shin as she pedalled.

She stopped at the post office round the corner from the flat and bought a packet of extra-large envelopes, then, standing at the counter, filled three of them with the documents. She paid for recorded, next-day delivery.

She didn't really want to go back to the damp, unwelcoming flat, so she sat in a café, taking her time over a cappuccino and a pastry. She eased the bowl out of the bag, feeling its satisfying heft, running her fingers over its cool silky surface, following its grain.

She bought a few supplies from the little supermarket. She needed to think about where she was going to live. She needed to think about a lot of things. Later, she told herself, conscious that getting embroiled with the mess of Liam's life might be a way of avoiding the mess of her own.

She let herself into the flat and had to make two trips down the stairs – first with the bags, then carrying her bike. The cat nipped at her ankles and she shook some dried food into its bowl. She hadn't finished unpacking when the doorbell rang. It was Leila Fox. Jude led her down into the dingy basement, where the detective looked around.

'You've come down in the world.'

'Yes,' said Jude. 'It's the sort of thing that happens when details of a police investigation get leaked.'

Jude expected anger or some kind of apology, but Leila Fox just looked at her with an unyielding expression.

'Has something happened?'

'Did you think I wouldn't find out?'

'What?'

'That Liam Birch made you the executor of his will.'

'I only found out myself a couple of days ago. It came as a surprise.'

'Is that it?'

'What else do you want me to say?'

'Help me out here. You were his teenage girl-friend. You were waiting for him the night he was killed.'

'I told you what happened. I can't say this all over again.'

'You say there was nothing between the two of you. But you break off your engagement and move out of your home. Now it turns out you're the executor of his will.'

'It's just the way you're framing it,' Jude said.

'Framing it? How would you frame it?'

'I broke up with Nat not because of Liam but because I lied.'

'About Liam.'

'About the arrangement.'

'And you still persist in saying there was nothing between you?'

'I've given up saying that,' said Jude, taking a seat and resting her aching head on one hand. 'Nobody believes me. I just know it's true and that's good enough for me.'

'Don't you realise the situation you're in? We're going to find out who killed Liam Birch and we're going to find out how you're involved in his death.'

Jude almost stamped her foot with frustration. 'Except I'm not.'

The detective looked at her steadily. 'I used to think I could tell when someone was lying to me and when someone was telling me the truth. I learned a long time ago that I couldn't, but I feel certain that there's something you aren't telling me.'

'I don't know how many times we can do this,' said Jude. 'You're investigating a murder. I was a hundred miles away when it happened. I know it's weird he asked me to do this for him. Maybe it was for an alibi. Maybe he was going to do something terrible. But I don't know how you think I can help you.'

Jude looked at Leila but she didn't reply, just

stared back with a kind of curiosity that sent a shiver down Jude's spine.

'I understand it's strange that I'm suddenly executor of the will. It's strange to me as well. But I don't benefit from it.' She gestured at the wooden bowl. 'Except for that. That's what he left me in his will. I know it's all bizarre and unsettling, but what are you accusing me of? What's your theory?'

'Who are you trying to convince with all of this?' said Leila. 'Me or yourself?'

'Just because things are odd,' said Jude, 'it doesn't mean that they're connected with Liam being murdered.'

Leila gazed at her. Jude tried to hold her gaze, but in the end she blinked several times and looked away. Her scalp tightened and her face felt rubbery. She couldn't be sure what her expression was. For a moment she felt dizzy, the world swimming around her, things dissolving. She felt that the detective could see into her, the secret part of her, see everything that was there, and she wanted to hide from her unblinking scrutiny.

'Up to now I've been on your side,' Leila said eventually. 'I didn't understand why you set out to do this favour for someone you say you hadn't seen for over a decade. I've made every effort to see it from your point of view and I haven't quite managed it. And now this. If you can't do better than that, we're going to make you the focus of this inquiry and you won't like that. You won't like that at all.'

Leila Fox's grey gaze was still on her. Jude's body felt flimsy in the chair, her head unbearably heavy.

'What do you want from me?' Jude said feebly.

'Tell me about it.'

'You mean the alibi, if that's what it was? I've told you so often.'

'No, not that. Tell me about you and Liam, eleven years ago.'

'Why? What's that got to do with anything?'

'Please,' said Leila, almost in a coaxing tone.

So Jude took a deep breath and, in as clinical a way as she could manage, talked about how she and Liam had got together, even though they had been so different, *because* they had been so different. The parties they had gone to. She said that they had slept together. She didn't describe it.

'Was he your first?'

Jude felt her face flushing.

'Yes. He was my first. Why does it matter? What has that got to do with anything?'

Then she said how intense it had been and then she described the night of the crash, Benny and Yolanda in the back, the suddenness of it, how she remembered in fragments, and at the end of it Liam being taken away. And after that, it had all been over, like a dream that had faded.

As she spoke, Jude was aware of Leila gazing at her, leaning forward, almost with a hungry expression. When she had finished speaking, the detective was silent for a long time and then a slow smile formed on her face.

184

'What?' said Jude uneasily.

'I should have known all along. When you talked about feeling guilty about Liam going one way and you another in your lives.'

'What do you mean?'

'It was you.'

'I don't know what you mean.' But Jude did know. She felt she was falling into a great abyss that had opened beneath her, down and down and no end to it.

'You were driving that night.'

It wasn't a question. Jude closed her eyes.

'When the police arrived, Liam took the blame for you. That's what happened.'

A small sound escaped from Jude, a kind of grunt as if someone had hit her in the stomach.

'Maybe at the time, you were confused, concussed even, and you didn't realise what was happening. But later, you would have known and you didn't come forward. You would have lost your place at medical school if you'd had a criminal record. You would have lost everything.'

She paused and looked at Jude's pale face closely once more.

'What did you think, Jude? That he was messing his life up anyway? Or did you just manage to avoid thinking about it?'

There was a long silence, and when Jude finally spoke, the words sounded strange. She'd never said them aloud before.

'I didn't manage to avoid thinking about it. I

thought about it every single day. I'd think about it at night, lying awake. Whatever else happened, when I was at university, when I was a doctor, when I was alone, when I was in bed with someone else, a bit of me knew that my whole life had been built on that one lie. His whole life as well. When Liam came to see me, to ask me to do him a favour, I knew I had to do it, whatever it was. He didn't tell me what it was. I asked him if it was something wrong and he said it wasn't. But maybe I would have done it anyway. I don't know. Maybe not. I don't know.'

'Did he say that when he asked you?'

'About the crash? He didn't need to. We both knew.'

'And why did he do it? Why did he cover for you?'

'I've thought about that, over and over. I think about it in the small hours. He never mentioned it. He never asked to be thanked. I think he was just like that. He was idealistic, he was impulsive, he was passionate. He was the kind of person who would do some big, crazy gesture . . .' Jude stopped herself. 'Gesture. That sounds like something shallow. It was bigger than that. He put himself in front of a bullet for me. A bullet that was my fault. But it killed the relationship.'

Leila made an impatient gesture.

'Why the hell didn't you tell me this earlier?'

'For the same reason I didn't tell anyone, ever. My parents. Nat. My closest friends. I was scared

186

and ashamed. I was so ashamed.' Jude realised that she was crying. She took a tissue from her pocket and blew her nose. 'So what happens now?'

'What do you mean?'

'I committed a crime. And I covered it up.'

Leila shook her head, but she wasn't smiling.

'I don't think the prosecutors would be especially interested about the way you behaved all those years ago. I'm not going to blame you. Although you did the wrong thing, so that's a bit of blame. But you're a bloody idiot. You made us think you were involved in whatever Liam was up to. And if you've made us believe it, you've made other people believe it as well.'

'Unless it was a simple mugging after all,' said Jude wearily. She suddenly wanted to lie down in a dark room and close her eyes and sleep.

'You know as well as I do that was no mugging . . . and just when you should be steering clear of all of this, you're executing his will.'

'It'll only be a few days.'

'Jude—'

'I owe Liam this much at least.'

CHAPTER THIRTY

After Leila left, Jude folded forward with a small gasp and laid her head on the wooden table, closing her eyes. She thought she would cry properly now, howl like an animal with shame and grief. Her stomach ached and her head hurt and there was a strange tingling in her fingers and toes. But she didn't cry, couldn't, and after a few minutes she sat up. She felt dazed and her hands were trembling and the world around her went in and out of focus.

Finally, after all these years, she had spoken the words aloud. She had thought that some great change would have come over her; she waited to feel pain, relief, fear, but she didn't really feel anything except hollow and unreal, like a puppet of herself.

She forced herself to breathe calmly; after a few minutes, she knew what she needed to do. This wasn't going to be much fun, but she had better get it over with. She picked up her phone.

When Nat opened the door, he didn't even say hello. He just walked back into the flat, leaving her to shut the door behind her and follow him. In the living room, he turned and faced her.

'I've been going through your things,' he said. 'I've put clothes into bin bags.'

'I can't take them right now. I came on my bike.'

'I made some coffee. Do you want some?'

Jude wasn't sure what to make of this. She felt like an animal that had been hit and now was being stroked.

'All right.'

Nat went to the kitchen and returned with two mugs. They sat down, across the room from each other. Jude couldn't get over the strangeness of it, sitting in the flat they had shared, holding a mug she had bought. He hadn't put milk in the coffee, although he knew she took milk. She didn't say anything about it.

'So what are you up to?' he asked.

'Nothing much. I'm just trying to sort myself out.'

'I gather you've taken a couple of weeks off work.'

'How do you even know that?'

'You weren't answering your phone, so I rang the hospital.'

'You can always send me a message.'

'I didn't want to send you a message. I wanted to talk to you.'

Jude didn't know how to answer this, so she just looked around the room.

'Yes,' said Nat. 'As you can see, there are a lot of your things. At some point we're going to have to sit down and decide who takes what. Obviously, we're sitting down at the moment, but we should do it formally. I want you to have what's yours.'

'I wasn't thinking that.'

'But it's true.'

'I know. But at the moment I don't have anywhere to put all these things. I'm having a complicated time. Can we wait a bit and then do it calmly?'

'Calmly?' said Nat, with an edge in his voice. 'And cleanly too, I suppose. Maybe I don't find it as easy as you do to separate two lives that have got so intermingled. Undoing the arrangements we spent so much time working on. For example, have you written to all the people you invited to the wedding, uninviting them?'

'Of course I have,' said Jude. 'I did it almost at once, you know that.' A shocking thought occurred to her. 'Do you mean you haven't told everybody?'

Now Nat looked evasive.

'I've told a few people. I haven't contacted everybody yet. You'd better show me your list so we don't email the same people twice.'

Jude didn't know how to interpret this. Had Nat not got around to letting people know the way he didn't quite get around to picking up his dirty clothes and putting them in the washing machine? Or did he have some strange idea that she would come crawling back to him and beg for forgiveness and the wedding would go ahead?

'But you already have the list. I blind-copied you into my email,' she said. 'And I sent a text telling you. You must have seen it.'

'Very efficient,' he said, in a tone that dismayed her.

'What did you expect me to do? Let the word get out? I wrote to my friends and told my family. You can write to your friends and your family.'

They had a brief squabble about the friends who might be counted as belonging to both of them. Jude said that he should just look at the list of everyone she had told.

'Shall I contact the venue?' said Nat.

'Haven't you done that yet?'

'Why would I ask you if I'd already done it? I'll see if I can get the deposit back but they'll probably insist on keeping it.'

Jude didn't reply.

'A bit of a waste of money,' said Nat.

Jude still didn't reply.

'What's happening with the murder investigation?'

'I don't know,' said Jude. 'I don't know anything about it. I suppose they're interviewing people.'

'Did they interview you?'

'Yes.'

'Why?'

'They're interviewing people who met Liam in the days before he died.'

'They must have been interested in your connection with him.'

'They asked about it.'

'Old boyfriend and girlfriend suddenly reuniting. Did they believe your story?'

'There's nothing to believe or not to believe. I'm not a suspect, Nat. I was out of London when it happened.'

Nat gave a laugh that Jude found gratingly unpleasant.

'I wasn't saying you were a suspect. That would be ridiculous. Why would you want to kill someone who you hadn't met for eleven years? Why would you do that? It would be like lying to the man you were going to marry and doing a really big favour for someone you hadn't seen for eleven years. Ridiculous.'

Again Jude didn't answer. She just looked at Nat, at the anger rippling through his face, ticking under his temple. She couldn't believe that this was the man she had been planning to spend the rest of her life with.

'Did they believe that? About not having seen him for eleven years? And then doing him this huge favour?'

Jude's phone rang. She took it out and looked. It was her brother.

'You can take it, if you like,' said Nat.

'I'll ring back.'

'You didn't answer my question.'

'Which question?'

'The police. Believing you.'

'They were puzzled by what Liam asked me to do, just as I was puzzled by it. But I think they believe what I told them.'

'Did you tell them about how you lied to me?'

'I can't remember exactly. They know that I've moved out.'

'I don't believe you, as it happens,' said Nat. 'If you're interested.'

'Believe what?'

'That you hadn't met Liam for eleven years.'

'No,' said Jude. 'I'm not interested. As it happens.'

Nat sat back. His face had gone red. He was breathing heavily.

'So?' he said. 'You said you wanted to see me. What was it about?'

Jude genuinely had to think for a moment to remember why it was she was here, why she had put herself through this. Yes, she was here to tell Nat about the crash, about how it was her who had been driving. She had believed she owed the truth to him. Now the very thought of sharing this intimate, painful story from her past with the red-faced, angry man facing her made her feel nauseous.

'It was nothing,' she said. 'I think we've talked about everything we need to talk about.'

When she got out into the street, Jude took a few deep breaths to steady herself. Then she remembered her missed call. She took out her phone and rang her brother.

'I'm coming to London tomorrow,' he said. 'Can we meet?'

'Why? Is everything all right?'

'It'll be easier to talk about in person.'

'Is it about the will?'

'Yes, I've had a quick look through the papers.'

'Can't you tell me something?'

'Don't do anything financial,' he said.

'What does that mean?'

'With Liam Birch's estate. Don't pay any money out of it.'

'Don't worry. I wasn't planning to.'

CHAPTER THIRTY-ONE

The next morning, shortly after ten, Michael Winter stepped into the flat and looked around, visibly unimpressed. He was dressed for business and made Jude feel instantly shabby and unprepared. It was as if they were teenagers again, with Michael as the disapproving older brother.

'I'm so sorry,' he said. 'I didn't know you were living like this.'

'It's only temporary,' Jude said. 'Once things are settled, I'll get somewhere proper.'

Michael raised his eyebrows. 'Yes, *things*,' he said, putting a heavy emphasis on the word. 'That's what we're going to talk about.' He looked around once more. 'Is there somewhere we can sit?'

He sounded doubtful about there being any such place. Jude steered him towards the one armchair. She pulled across a small wooden stool.

'Can I get you tea or something?'

He looked at his watch.

'I've got a meeting near Old Street in fifty minutes,' he said. 'We'd better get a move on.'

He was carrying a leather case. He opened it

and took out a blue cardboard folder. In it was a single sheet of paper with his tiny, neat handwriting on it. It reminded Jude of their schooldays. He picked up the piece of paper, sighed and put it back down.

'Before we talk about all this, I think there are questions I should ask you.'

'What sort of questions?'

'Like: are you all right? I'm not good at that sort of thing. But the murder and everything. It must be awful.'

'Yes. It has been awful. I wouldn't say I'm completely all right, but I'm getting through it.'

'I've never known anyone who was murdered before – not that I actually knew this man, of course.'

'Nor have I.'

'And they haven't caught them yet?'

'No.'

'I looked it up online. All these stabbings. London's a frightening place.'

'I think it's quite safe. On the whole.'

Michael picked up the piece of paper and assumed a professional expression.

'Did you look through the papers before you sent them to me?'

'Not really. It's all a bit technical.'

'In a way,' said Michael. 'But in a way it's also very simple.'

'What do you mean?'

'For a start, you can't do this. I'm not sure who

196

can – this isn't really my speciality – but it needs someone qualified.'

'I thought anyone could be an executor.'

'Not in this case.'

'Are you going to tell me why? You were saying it's very simple.'

Michael sat back in the chair, collecting his thoughts.

'Well,' he began, 'if you're in a house that's on fire, you don't have to be an expert in chemistry and physics. You just need to get out. And I think you need to get out.'

'What does that mean?'

'As far as I could see, flicking through the papers, there are two areas. The first is Liam's work, which seems to involve joinery and carpentry. Judging by what I've seen, that business is insolvent. The finances seem completely chaotic, though I've not seen most of the paperwork, and I'm sure he did work that was simple cash in hand and no questions asked. But looking at the bills that haven't been paid, I think this business may be trading illegally. He was working on a big job and it seems he had trouble getting paid, which might be the last straw for a business that's already struggling.'

'That sounds awful.'

'It must have been awful to live through. You met him before he died, didn't you?'

'Yes.'

'Did he seem stressed?'

'Not really.'

'It must be scary to know your business is failing, bit by bit. I've heard of people in that situation killing themselves. It felt like the only way out.'

'But he didn't kill himself. He got killed.'

'Right.'

'You said there were two areas.'

'Yes, the other area is his personal finances, which is basically the house.'

'That must be better.'

Michael thought for a moment.

'It's hard to compare one with the other, but I wouldn't say it was better. The house was in his name, but he had a big mortgage and from what I can see, he's missed several payments.'

'Sometimes people need to renegotiate their mortgages.'

'Sometimes. But you don't do that by just not paying it.'

Jude considered this. 'Was Liam bankrupt?'

'That's a technical term. You have to declare bankruptcy to be bankrupt. The non-technical term is that it's a complete mess. People live like that, just hoping for the best. I don't know how they can sleep at night. Someone – not you – needs to come in and sort it out. Liam was owed money. In particular, this work he did for a man called . . .' Michael picked up the paper and looked at his notes. 'Leary. Anthony Leary. There are invoices amounting to thousands of pounds which haven't been paid. There may have been some problem.'

198

'Do you think there was some kind of falling-out?' asked Jude.

'I don't know. I've just seen some of the invoices and I've seen Liam Birch's bank statements. Maybe Mr Leary was just a slow payer. Cash-flow problems like that can be enough to sink a tiny business like this one. And this one was already under water. It's the job of the executor to sort out matters like this and I don't see why you should do it.' He looked at her pointedly. 'Or why you'd *want* to do it.'

'Isn't it something you could help with?'

Michael shook his head. 'It was painful enough just looking at this horror show.'

'Would Liam have known it was this bad?'

'Oh yes. That pile of papers was full of reminders and threats. It must have been like being inside the burning building.'

'So what'll happen to the business and the house and everything?'

Michael shrugged. 'On the face of it, your old boyfriend had nothing. Less than nothing. Mortgage not paid, overdrawn at the bank, bills not paid, clients not paying him. Sometimes you can come to some kind of arrangement. But it takes professional help and it takes time.'

'What about life insurance?' asked Jude. 'You hear about people who're worth more dead than alive. Wouldn't there be enough to pay off the mortgage and pay his bills?'

'I forgot about that,' said Michael. 'When I said

there were two areas, I should have said there were three areas. There were two life insurance policies. The first was connected to the mortgage, the second was taken out ten months ago.'

'That would have been shortly after his son was born. So that must be a reasonable pay-out, mustn't it?'

'Both of them had lapsed. He had stopped making the payments. There were warning letters printed in red for both policies. I doubt either of them will pay out a penny.'

'Poor Liam.'

'Welcome to the private sector,' said Michael, sounding strangely cheerful. 'You've spent your career working for the NHS. Your generous salary and pension plan are paid for out of my taxes. But for the rest of us, out in the real world, if things go wrong, really wrong, then the safety net gets pulled away. Liam must have known he was heading for a reckoning, one way or another.'

Jude was irritated by Michael's tone, the patronising tone he had always had for her, ever since they were teenagers. But she was aware that he had done this work for her in his own time.

'So you think that this isn't something I can sort out on my own.'

'I'm quite sure it isn't.'

'I could go and see that man who owed Liam money. That would help, wouldn't it?'

'Don't even think of it!'

'Why?'

'You don't know anything about the man except that he failed to pay Liam. I mean, he could be violent.'

'But I'm the executor and it's my job to call in debts, isn't it?'

'No. I mean, yes, in theory. But not by turning up on his doorstep. You could write him a letter.'

Jude looked at Michael dubiously.

'Anyway,' he said. 'It wouldn't sort out the mess Liam had got himself into. It would help pay the bills, I suppose, and there might even be a bit left over. But it wouldn't be enough to pay the mortgage. It's too late for those life insurance policies.'

'Those policies,' said Jude, 'were they joint policies? I mean husband-and-wife policies, not that Liam and Danny were actually married. Or did he do them himself?'

'If you mean, were they in his name only, the answer is yes. The beneficiary of the second policy was the woman he lived with.'

'So Danny will be left with nothing?'

'Is that a woman you're talking about?'

'Yes. His partner; the mother of his child and the person he left everything to in his will.'

'She'll be left with nothing and a terrible mess to go with it.'

When he left, he kissed her on the cheek and patted her arm awkwardly.

'Seriously. don't go poking around too much, Jude. It sounds to me as if you're in over your head.'

'Don't worry.'
He looked at her suspiciously.
'Why do I not feel reassured?'

CHAPTER THIRTY-TWO

Jude had the address of Liam and Vin's work-place but even so she had trouble finding it. The map on her phone took her to the outskirts of Walthamstow, down a potholed road lined with houses, several of which had boarded-up windows, and into the Jubilee Industrial Estate.

She couldn't tell from the names on the signs what most of them were: alongside a micro-brewery, and a storage and distribution company, there were also names like MaleCo, Formix, Vista Ready. She walked around the muddy yard, blowing on her hands and trying to find a name, until at last she came across a small, simple wooden sign: Liam Birch: All Things Wood. The shutters were open. She pressed her face to the smeared window and couldn't see anything, but she could hear the burr of a chainsaw. She knocked at the door and then, after a minute of waiting while icy rain dribbled down her neck, pushed at it. It swung open, and Jude stepped inside.

The single room was light, large and almost as cold as outside. There was a sweet, resiny smell of wood, and the floor was soft with sawdust. Apart from a glassed-in cubicle to one side, with a metal table that was covered in a mess of papers, everything was about the wood. A long trestle table ran along the room, with all manner of tools spread out on it – small and large saws with vicious-looking teeth, hand planes, rasps, chisels, measuring tapes, hammers, dozens of screwdrivers, boxes of screws and nails and rolls of wire. There were rolls of paper with diagrams on them, and pots of paint and varnish.

Against the walls were pieces of furniture, most unfinished: a beautiful little milkmaid's stool, a large kitchen cabinet without its doors, a set of simple units lined up to be painted. And there were planks of wood, propped against the walls or lying on the floor, all different colours and grains.

At the end of the room, his back to her, a man in headphones and wearing an orange helmet with a visor was bent over a hefty section of tree trunk with a chainsaw. Bits of bark and flakes of wood sprayed around him as he worked. The teeth sank quickly through the timber, and he straightened up, the saw still humming in his large, gloved hand.

He couldn't have heard her, but he turned, then lifted the machine as if in greeting, and walked towards her. Only when he reached her did he switch the saw off, lift his helmet and headphones from his head, his dark hair falling forward, scattering splinters of wood. He was sweating in spite of the chill of the room.

'Hello, Vin.'

'Dr Winters,' he said, and grinned.

He had even white teeth and his chin was dark with stubble. Jude couldn't tell if he was being friendly or sarcastic.

'I hope you don't mind that I let myself in.'

'I'm honoured.'

Vin put down the saw and rubbed his back. He took a towel off a hook on the wall and wiped his face with it.

'It's beautiful,' said Jude, gesturing to the room. She meant it: the seasoning wood, the gleaming tools, the skeletons of furniture.

Vin glanced around, furrowing his thick brows.

'Let's have some coffee. I've a flask. It might be a bit tepid though.'

Jude followed him to the cubicle, his feet in their heavy boots ringing on the concrete floor. There was barely enough room for both of them, and she saw to her dismay that alongside the paper-strewn table was a grey metal filing cabinet whose open top drawer was stuffed with bits of paper that looked like invoices and bills. Was there no end to them?

There was an overhead electric heater, but Vin saw her hopeful glance and shook his head.

'Doesn't work,' he said cheerfully.

He pulled a chair from the wall and gestured, then took a flask from the canvas messenger bag slung over the back of the other chair and poured coffee into two mugs. He sat next to Jude, so close in the small space that she could feel the heat of him.

'No milk or sugar, I'm afraid. Or biscuits.'

'That's fine,' said Jude.

'You can share my lunch, if you want.'

It was only half past eleven, but he took a package wrapped in wax paper from his bag and carefully unwrapped it. It was the size of a paperback, and thick: two grainy pieces of bread from which layers of filling spilled out. Jude could identify beetroot, broccoli, orange wedges of cheese, and something that looked like mustard.

'Leftovers from our fridge,' said Vin, carefully lifting the sandwich in both hands and taking a vast bite out of it. 'Sure you don't want any?' he asked through a full mouthful. His jaws worked vigorously.

'Sure,' said Jude, though watching him sink his teeth into the bread she suddenly felt ravenous.

He was only wearing a T-shirt over his jeans. A tattoo rippled on his upper arm as he lifted his mug and took a huge swallow. She lifted her own mug, which had a reindeer on it and a chip at its rim. The coffee was just about warm, but good and strong.

'There's something I should tell you. I thought it would be better in person.'

'Tell me then.' He smiled and then pushed more of his sandwich into his smiling mouth.

'As you know, I'm—'

He interrupted her.

'Yeah, yeah, you're the executor. You shouldn't be too serious about it, Jude. Liam probably named you as a joke.'

'I know. There's a really large part of me that just wants to let it all alone.'

'But?'

'There's another, small part of me that feels it's become a kind of responsibility. Like I owe it to him.'

'All right,' said Vin. 'So what was it you needed to tell me in person?'

'I showed some of his financial papers, bills, to my brother. He's an accountant. He was . . .' She paused, trying to find a kind way of putting it. 'A bit taken aback. Your company. It's not looking good. To say the least.'

Vin held up his broad, calloused hand.

'I really do not need to know that.'

'I think you probably do need to know it. Apparently you're insolvent.'

He made a snorting sound in the back of his throat. Was he finding this funny?

'I mean it. I looked it up. You're trading illegally, and that means that you can't—'

'Stop.' Vin had taken another bite of his food and he needed to swallow it before he could continue. 'You're a doctor. You get a steady salary, money when you're ill, money when you're on holiday. You get a good pension. Everything's sorted out for you. Now us.' He gestured around him. 'We are a tiny company. Two of us, working with our hands, doing jobs for multiple people at the same time, juggling. We live day to day, right. Sometimes we earn a bit more than we spend, and sometimes we earn a bit less. Sometimes companies go under and leave us a bit high and dry and we have to find ways round that. Sometimes we don't get paid on time and have cash-flow problems, and that's a pain in the arse. Sometimes we don't get paid at all.'

'But Michael said—'

'If accountants went round inspecting all the books and closing down companies that weren't sticking to the rules, we'd almost all be gone. Me and Liam, we got by. Touch and go, but we got by. We're good at what we do. We make lovely things. We take pride in our work. Some people piss us off; we piss other people off. But here we still are.'

He stopped, looked down at the remaining crusts of his early lunch.

'Of course, it's not "we" any longer, is it? So I've no idea if I can keep going. This was Liam's business before I joined him, and I was only his unofficial partner. It'll be hard to start over.' He shook his head, his thick hair rippling around his face. 'Ah well, if I have to.'

Jude waited. She finished her coffee and put her hands in her pockets for warmth.

'Anthony Leary,' she said.

Vin's head snapped up.

'Fuckwit,' he said. Then: 'Not you. Him.'

'He's one of the ones who never paid?'

'People like him,' said Vin, 'because they have money, they think they're better than everyone

208

else.' He folded the wax paper and slid it back into the bag. 'So not only did he not pay us, he not-paid us with a kind of sanctimonious self-righteousness.'

'He sounds pretty odious,' said Jude.

'Oh, you'd probably like him.' Vin was suddenly cheerful again, the anger wiped from his face like a cloth sweeps away dust. 'You're a doctor, after all, not a carpenter. I guess that's where you're headed?'

'I thought I should.'

At the door he surprised her by taking her shoulders in his hands and bending down to kiss her, first on one cheek and then the other.

'You're a stubborn woman, aren't you?' he said.

'I'm just doing what I'm meant to be doing.'

Vin shook his head.

'What you're meant to be doing is going back and being a doctor again.'

CHAPTER THIRTY-THREE

Jude didn't go straight to Anthony Leary's, but stopped off at the little Italian restaurant she had seen on her way to Liam's workshop. She was so hungry she felt almost sick, and she realised she hadn't eaten a proper meal since coming back from her parents on Sunday, just randomly snacked on things like the marinated anchovies past their sell-by date that she'd found in Simon's fridge.

It was cosily warm in the restaurant, and full of pungent smells. Jude ordered a pizza with olives and capers. It was far too big for one person, bubbling with spicy tomato sauce and with blistering cheese that hung in sticky threads when she lifted a slice to her mouth. But she ate almost all of it, and drank several glasses of water, followed by a large mug of coffee. She felt so full she could barely move and suddenly so sleepy it was hard to keep her eyes open. She didn't want to be going back into the cold rain, or return to a basement flat that smelled of damp, where the fridge leaked and the cat kept up its ankle-biting vendetta.

Jude checked the map on her phone. Anthony Leary was just a couple of miles eastwards. If she was going to visit him, she needed to do it now while she still had some will left in her.

Twenty minutes later she was very cold and very wet. The route had taken her along busy roads and she was splattered with muddy water sprayed up by passing cars. On the ride, the houses had gradually become more prosperous, larger, better maintained, set back from the road, further apart. Did the disputed money really matter to someone who lived like this? For Liam and Vin it had been about survival. Probably Leary wouldn't even be at home on a Wednesday afternoon.

But he was. He opened the door, eyebrows raised suspiciously. Leary was a middle-aged man with weathered cheeks and a snub nose that seemed out of place with the rest of him; his greying hair rippled at a side parting. He was wearing a beautifully cut grey suit that was slightly too tight, like he was about to go to or had just come from a meeting. A small dog stood beside him, barking ferociously.

'Sorry to disturb you,' said Jude, wishing she wasn't so damp and muddy, her hair flattened by her bike helmet and her fingers throbbing. 'My name is Dr Judith Winters.'

She waited to see if he recognised the name but his expression didn't change.

'I've been appointed executor to Liam Birch's will,' she said, thinking that the 'appointed' made it sound more formal than it actually was.

Now Anthony Leary's expression did change. His face darkened and his eyebrows drew together so that his forehead was corrugated with lines.

'Did you know he had died?'

'The police have already been and talked to me.' He ran a finger round the inside of his collar. 'As a formality.'

'I was hoping to have a quick word as well.'

Jude took a hopeful step towards the front door. The dog barked louder, its compact body quivering.

He looked her up and down.

'My son will be home from school in half an hour.'

'I won't be that long.'

Stepping back, he beckoned her inside.

'Perhaps you can take off your shoes,' he said. 'The cleaner's just been.'

Jude hung her wet coat on a hook, took off her muddy boots.

'I don't know what you want from me,' he said. 'And I don't know what you've been told, but whatever it is, I've done nothing wrong.'

'I'm just doing my legal duty,' Jude said. 'As Mr Birch's executor, I need to recover debts owed to him before his estate can be settled.'

She didn't know if she was using the correct terms, so in a rush she made herself clear.

'Even though he's dead, you still have to pay what you owe.'

Anthony Leary folded his arms and looked at her. 'No way.'

'It's the law.'

'Come with me,' he said, and stalked down the hall, followed by Jude, sliding on the polished wood in her socks, the dog ominously at her heels.

He flung the door open into the kitchen and beckoned her in.

'This is what they did.'

Jude looked around the room at the wooden cabinets, the thick wooden shelves above them, the granite surfaces near the sink, the large window that looked out on to a neat bare garden and, beyond that, ploughed fields.

'It looks lovely.'

'It's not what we asked for. I can show you what we asked for. What we agreed. We asked for stainless steel and he gave us this.' He rapped on the granite surface. 'Which cost an arm and a leg. We wanted glass-fronted units and he just ignored us, so when we got back from holiday – which we'd taken in order to get away from the incessant banging – we found these.' He pointed with a long, accusing finger at the cabinets. 'We wanted a double-sink but he found us something in the salvage place down the road that he thought looked better.'

'It does look nice,' said Jude, glancing at the large porcelain sink.

Anthony Leary took a step towards her. He smelled strange; it reminded her of something and she couldn't think what.

'It was over-budget and over-schedule and it wasn't what we asked for.'

'I can see—'

But he was in full flow now.

'And they were a bloody pain to have around. Liam burned a cigarette mark into the table and when I complained, he said it was a horrible table anyway and it looked better with a few scars. Like it was a joke.'

'It sounds as if they really got under your skin.'

Leary looked at her with an aggrieved expression.

'They didn't get under my skin. They behaved badly and they behaved unprofessionally.'

'You still owed them money.'

'You,' he said. 'Did you say you're a doctor? A doctor of medicine?'

'That's right.'

'Well, I'm a businessman and I know about what you owe and when you owe it and when you don't owe it.'

Jude looked around. 'I don't know much about you, but I'm guessing this money was more important to them than it was to you.'

'You're right,' he said. 'You don't know much about me. I tried to be flexible with them. I said I'd pay them when they'd done the job they'd promised to do. Does that seem reasonable?'

'That's difficult for me to say.'

'And they left with the door to the garden off its hinges, the radiator and the dishwasher unplumbed, mud all over the carpet, cigarettes in saucers everywhere, and they never came back. But I did get their bill of course.'

'Which you didn't pay.'

'Of course I didn't pay.'

'I see that there was a breakdown in communication,' said Jude. 'But the fact remains that they spent many weeks in your house, spent a lot of money on materials—'

'That I didn't want.'

'You're saying you don't intend to pay anything?'

'That's right.'

'You know that his being dead doesn't change anything. You still may face legal action.'

She didn't know if any of this was true, but she wanted to see how he would react. There was a flicker of what might have been concern on his face, but he seemed unmoved.

'Bring it on,' he said.

'Can I ask something?'

'What?'

'I don't know your circumstances. Can you actually afford to pay what you owe? Or some of it?'

'What?' he said again, sounding more agitated.

'I have to ask. As an executor. You'll have to pay something.'

Jude felt strange as she heard herself saying these words, as if she were fighting on behalf of Liam.

'The fact that things are a bit bumpy in my sector is not the point,' he said at last. His face was rigid with stifled shame and anger.

'Did you argue with Liam?'

'I tried to remain courteous.'

'Was he angry?'

Jude could imagine it. There was an anger in Liam that she had glimpsed, all those years ago, and never forgotten. Sometimes it was just a look, if she had said the wrong thing, but it had been enough to frighten her.

'I wouldn't say he was merely angry. I would say he was abusive. In the end I wouldn't take his calls. I felt threatened by him. I even thought of calling the police.'

Jude looked at this man, who she strongly suspected had hired Liam and Vin without having the money to pay them. She tried to imagine how she would have reacted if she had been Liam. Angry. Abusive. That sounded about right.

CHAPTER THIRTY-FOUR

It was dark by the time Jude returned to the flat. The cat hissed and the fridge whined. She took off her muddy boots and put on the kettle. She checked her phone and saw the unopened texts, emails, missed calls and WhatsApp messages.

She clicked on the first text. It started with 'Darling, darling Jude.' She put her phone face down on the table. Her chest ached.

She ran a bath, hot and deep, and tipped in the last of Simon's muscle-relaxing bath foam. Bubbles came almost to the brim and she lowered herself in with a sigh and slid into the water.

She thought about Liam stubbing his cigarette butt out on a table he didn't like and laughing. Then she thought about him taking the blame for the crash without any sense of martyrdom or virtue. She thought about him as she had last seen him, smiling at her, unreadable. She thought about him dead: a body pushed out of sight under a bush on the marshes, in the rain and darkness.

She thought about how she had been unable to tell Nat what she had done when she was a teenager: she couldn't have given her secret to the hard-faced stranger she had met up with yesterday. She closed her eyes and sank beneath the water and then, with a splutter of blown-out breath, she surfaced again.

A thought had snagged her.

Wrapped in a towel, she sat on the bed with her mobile, found DI Fox's number and rang it.

'I thought I should keep you up to date.'

'Up to date with what?'

'For a start, Liam's financial affairs were in chaos.' Jude paused, remembering Leary telling her that the police had already talked to him. 'I suppose you already knew that.'

'I did.'

'I went to see someone who owed Liam all that money. A guy called Anthony Leary. He and Liam clearly had a massive falling-out.' Jude waited but Leila Fox didn't respond. 'I thought it might be worth looking into.'

'Did you?'

Jude waited but Leila didn't say anything else.

'The thing I really wanted to say was about Nat.' She coughed. 'My ex.'

'I know who Nat is.'

'You asked me about him before and I told you that he hadn't known anything about Liam. I just thought of something. The morning when everything started, when Liam met me at the hospital and asked me to do him a favour. When Liam turned up, I texted Nat to say not to come.'

Jude waited for a reply. Nothing.

'Are you still there?' she asked.

'Yes.'

'So I was thinking, what if my text arrived too late and Nat had already left to meet me? What if he'd seen me and Liam together? I'm just saying, maybe he did see us together. He might have got the wrong idea.'

The way in which her feelings had swung so violently from love and affection to hostility and suspicion made her feel queasy.

'Is that it?'

'Yes. What do you think?'

'We'll look into it.'

'It's probably nothing,' said Jude. 'I don't know anything any more. That thing we talked about the other day, about the accident, about how I was driving, I couldn't tell Nat. It was impossible. I went to see him and confess, and then he was so unpleasant and angry that I couldn't.'

'I get that,' said Leila in a gentler tone.

'Yes.'

'Now I need to go.'

'Of course.'

'One word of advice.'

'What?'

'This executor thing. Go easy with it. Try to sort out your own life, not his.'

CHAPTER THIRTY-FIVE

Jude woke in the night and couldn't get back to sleep. Her head was buzzing with all that she knew about Liam and his life. He had been absent for years and she had sometimes wondered what had become of him. But she had never googled him. She had never looked for him on Facebook or Instagram. It felt like forbidden knowledge.

Now that he was dead, she was learning everything: about his family, his house, his business. She knew more about his finances than she knew about her own. She knew more about his finances than *he* had known. She knew the places in his life, where he had grown up, where he had lived, where he had worked. But then, as she turned all this over and over in her mind, it occurred to her there was one place that she hadn't seen. She decided to go there and found the idea strangely soothing; she drifted off to sleep.

It wasn't until she was drinking her second cup of coffee the next morning that Jude remembered those thoughts from the middle of the night. Even in the grey light of morning, it still seemed a good idea. She had nothing else to do. Why not now?

What was it that Leila Fox had said to her? Walthamstow Marshes. She took out her phone and looked at the map. It was a big area, running for a mile or more along the west side of the River Lea up to the reservoirs. Would she be able to find the spot? Then she remembered something else that the detective had said. It was near a place where people rode horses. Near? Had that been her word? She couldn't remember. She looked at her map again and saw the Lee Valley Riding Centre. She could go there and see. At least she might get some sense of the place where Liam had died.

She looked out of the window. It was just after nine but it still didn't feel properly light. She put on a sweater and a jacket, a hat, gloves and a scarf, and got on her bike. She cycled down through Stamford Hill and Clapton and on to the Lea Bridge Road. She passed the ice rink and then locked her bike outside the riding centre. She walked along the path that led along the left side of the centre. It was called a park, but it quickly became more like scrubby heathland, an oasis wilderness surrounded by new residential tower blocks on the west side and an industrial estate to the east. There was the hum of traffic and, every few minutes, the rattle of a train. But even now, on a weekday morning, Jude could see that it was a place where a person could be killed without anyone noticing and a body could be stowed away out of sight.

As she moved further from the road and the landscape became wilder, with unkempt bushes along the right side of the path, Jude could also see why the body was found so quickly. There were the usual runners but mainly across the heathland. To her left, she saw people with dogs, dogs off the lead, sniffing, curious.

She was just deciding that this was enough when she noticed it. Ahead, just off the path, there was a little assembly of colour. As she got closer, she could see that it was an arrangement of bunches of flowers and messages and photographs. It was an impromptu shrine to Liam.

She stood quite still, feeling the wind cold on her face and a hint of rain to come. Her chest felt tight and her throat raw with the tears she hadn't shed. This was the last sight that Liam had seen. Those brambles were where his body had been dragged and partially concealed. Here, where she was standing, must have been the actual spot where he drew his final breath. Had he known he was bleeding out? Had he been scared to die? She had never seen him scared. Even that night of the crash, he had only seemed ruefully amused, as if he was shrugging his shoulders at the vagaries of life.

It was the perfect place for a murder. Closer to the road, there were lights, there were more people around. But right here, there was a pretty good chance that nobody would notice.

She stared back in the direction she'd come from.

Yes. If you stood where she was standing now, you could have seen Liam coming but you would be in the dark, hidden.

Jude looked down at the sad little collection. At the centre of it was a piece of laminated card with a photograph of Liam. It was a slightly blurred snapshot but she could see why it had been chosen. He was turning towards the photographer and smiling in surprise. She wondered who had been taking the picture.

'What are you doing here?'

A man was standing next to her. He was tall, bulky and concealed by the hood of his jacket and the large woollen scarf wrapped round his neck. Jude was suddenly aware of how isolated she was. People were in the park but nobody was near.

'I knew this man,' she said.

The man pulled his hood back from his head. He had curly hair and a light beard.

'Where from?' he said.

Jude wasn't quite sure what to say. Did she really need to justify herself to this stranger?

'I knew him at school.'

The man broke into a smile. 'I know who you are. You're the one . . .' He stopped. 'You've been to the house.'

'Yes.'

He held up his hand. He was holding a single flower.

'I come most days,' he said. He knelt down and placed it on the ground. 'I'll do it until the funeral.'

He stood up again and looked at Jude with interest.

'How did *you* know Liam?' she asked.

'I lived with him.'

Jude thought for a moment. 'You're Doc, is that right?'

'You've been paying attention.'

'I've heard about you.'

'Really?' he said. 'What have you heard?'

She realised with a feeling of embarrassment that the one thing she remembered hearing about him was the loud sex in the house. That and burnt toast.

'Just your name. That you live in the house. With Erika.'

'You're doing the will,' he said.

'It's complicated,' she said vaguely.

The two of them stood together and looked at the shrine.

'You see them around, don't you?' he said. 'On railings by the side of the road where a bike has been hit by a lorry. Or you see a photo of some teenager who's been stabbed. I've always thought they were a bit too much. I thought they were like a performance of being upset. But not now. We're all in shock. When I was at primary school, a girl in the next class got hit by a car and died. But apart from that, I don't know anyone of my age who's died.'

Jude looked round at Doc, at his solemn expression, his almost theatrical posture of grief.

224

'He didn't just die,' she said. 'Someone killed him.'

'We've been talking about you,' he said. 'Nobody had met you. Nobody had even heard of you except Danny, and suddenly you're the one he turns to, right before he dies. Then it turns out that he's done a will and you're in charge of it.'

'Not just me,' said Jude. 'His brother as well.'

'That's weird as well.'

'Why?'

'I guess I didn't know Liam that well. It's none of my business who he chooses to do his will.' He smiled. 'I don't suppose he left everything to me.'

'Sadly not,' Jude said.

Doc started to turn away, then paused.

'Walk with me to the house?' he said.

Jude pointed in the other direction. 'I left my bike there.'

He held out his hand. She took it and he held it slightly too long, as if he was weighing it.

'We'll see you again at the house.'

'I'm probably getting in the way.'

He didn't say she wasn't. He just shrugged and walked down the path towards home.

CHAPTER THIRTY-SIX

That evening, Jude went out with a group of friends. It was the first time since her life had unravelled so publicly, the first time since she had separated from Nat, and she felt horribly anxious and vulnerable. But she knew that the longer she waited, the harder it would be, and so she showered and washed her hair, put on nice clothes, sprayed perfume and held her head high when she walked smiling into the crowded pub.

They welcomed her in; of course they did. They were her friends, her familiars, the people who she knew best in the world and who would always be on her side whatever she did, however badly she behaved. Everyone hugged her, kissed her, put hands on her arm as they spoke. They bought her drinks, then more drinks, and soon her thoughts blurred and the tight knot of shame and fear loosened. She talked – about Nat, about Liam's death and being made an executor, about the grim flat and the unfriendly cat, about endings and shame and loneliness. She made it into a joke – a joke against herself. She waved her arms in the air and told them she loved them all. She laughed and, in the middle of

226

laughing, cried. A bit drunk and emotional, she felt she could say anything, anything at all – and yet she didn't tell them about the crash when she was eighteen. She still had a cordon thrown around that. Only Leila Fox knew.

The following day passed in a blur. She was hungover, dry-mouthed and wrung out and couldn't bring herself to do anything. She mooched around the flat, drank lots of water, ate a bowl of pasta for supper and went to bed early.

When she woke on Saturday, she was aware of two things: the first was the cat was loudly coughing up a fur ball by the side of her bed. The second was that her mobile was ringing.

She reached out a hand and found it, seeing as she did so that it was nearly ten o'clock.

'Yes?'

She felt as if someone had hit her over the head with a brick. She needed several mugs of tea.

'Jude, it's Danny.'

'Hello.'

Jude struggled to a sitting position. The cat retched air violently. Maybe it was ill; maybe it was dying, like the plants seemed to be.

'I'd like you to come round.'

'Round to yours?'

'How about midday?'

'I can't do that,' said Jude.

She could, but Danny's peremptory tone grated on her.

'What about later?'

'I can probably get to you about three-thirty or four,' said Jude. 'If it's important.'

'That's great.'

Danny finished the call without saying goodbye or thanking her.

Jude made herself a pot of tea, and then, when she had finished it, a pot of coffee along with two pieces of toast and honey. She fed the cat and tried to stroke it, and she watered the drooping plants; maybe she was over-watering them. She cleaned the kitchen, vacuumed, and then lay in a bath, half-listening to a podcast.

Leila Fox had told her to sort out her own life, not the mess that Liam had left behind, and she was right. Liam was dead and beyond rescue.

She thought of the muddy ground where his body had lain, the shrivelled bunches of flowers and messages. Liam had been so gorgeously, menacingly alive and now he was in a morgue somewhere. Jude had seen many dead bodies. Her work was among people at the end of their lives and much of what she did was to help them have a good passing. But she had never seen the dead body of someone she had loved and had held in her arms.

The rain of the past days had stopped and the skies had cleared to a milky blue. Jude walked briskly all the way to Walthamstow, stopping only to buy a little paper cone of roast chestnuts, and arrived shortly before four, blown clean by the east wind.

She rapped on the door and it opened almost at once. Danny stood in front of her. She was wearing leggings and an orange zip-through jacket, tight and high-necked. Her feet were bare. Jude saw a geometric tattoo on her shapely ankle. She had piled her hair on top of her head, which made her look even taller than she was.

'We've just finished doing a work-out,' she said. 'Haven't we, Alfie?'

Jude realised that the toddler was standing half-hidden behind his mother, his arms wrapped around her long legs. Jude smiled down at him and he poked his head out and suddenly his whole face lit up in a grin. She was absurdly pleased.

'Hello, Alfie.'

Danny scooped him up and stalked into the messy kitchen. Jude hung up her jacket and followed. Even Danny's back looked tense.

'Is everything okay?' she asked, taking a seat. There were several burnt-out tealights and a bowl brimming with tangerines on the table in front of her.

'How can everything be okay?'

'I mean,' said Jude, 'what's up?'

Danny lowered Alfie to the floor and handed him a wooden spoon, which he at once started banging vigorously against the table leg.

'What's up?' She gave a crackling laugh.

'You asked me to come.'

Jude flinched as Alfie whacked her leg.

'I want to ask you something,' said Danny.

You could have asked me over the phone, Jude wanted to say, but didn't. She just nodded slowly, inviting Danny's question.

'I mean, really ask you something. Between you and me.'

'Go on,' said Jude.

'What do you want?'

It sounded more like an accusation than a question. Jude held Danny's gaze for several long seconds. Alfie dropped the wooden spoon and started crawling purposefully across the room.

'I don't want anything.'

'Jude,' said Danny softly. 'I know that can't be true.'

Jude gave a shrug. 'Then I don't know what to tell you.'

'You're poking around in our lives. You even tracked Doc down.'

'What are you talking about? I just bumped into him in the marshes.'

'You mean the spot where Liam died.'

'Which is on the marshes.'

'Oh, please.'

'And I'm not poking around. I'm Liam's executor.'

'Which gives you the perfect excuse to pry.'

'Is this why you asked me here? To insult me?'

'I asked you so that you could tell me the truth.

230

It won't go any further. But I need the truth. I'm sure you can understand that. The truth can set me free.'

Was that a quotation?

'I can't set you free,' she said softly. 'You're looking in the wrong place. There's nothing more I can tell you.'

Danny gazed at her, her eyes glittering. Then, as if a switch had been thrown, she softened. Her shoulders relaxed and her face lost its tight hostility.

'Sorry,' she said. 'I didn't mean to be rude to you. I can be a bitch sometimes. Hang on there, Alfie.'

He had reached the door. Danny stood and picked him up, bringing him back to the table, where he reached out and swiped several of the tangerines out of the bowl, setting them rolling across the wooden surface.

'Everything's such a mess,' said Danny. 'His finances were a complete fuck-up, right?'

'It looks like it. It must be a shock to you.'

Danny picked up a tangerine and very deliberately began to peel one, her fingers long and thin and covered in rings. Only when she had completed her task did she speak.

'I tried to talk to him about it. I found bills he hadn't even opened. He didn't pay the mortgage. He took out insurance policies and stopped paying for them. What can you do?' She gave a harsh laugh. 'You know when they say someone was worth more dead than alive? That wasn't true of poor old Liam.'

She ripped a sheet off a kitchen roll on the table and blew her nose, then rested her chin on Alfie's soft curls.

'His funeral's on Tuesday afternoon.'

'I didn't know.' Jude thought of his instructions. She hesitated, then spoke.

'I'm sure you're already aware of this, but he said that he wanted a wicker coffin—'

'Yeah, yeah. And his old boots to go on top.'

'Yes.'

'What he really wanted was to be set alight in a boat and then pushed out to sea like a Viking, but it turns out that's quite hard to arrange. We're having a kind of thing, celebration of his life you could call it, near here. Then a wake back here and the day after he'll be buried in Walthamstow cemetery.'

'I'm sure it will be beautiful.'

'I don't know about that. We're all arranging it together, and I'm sure you'll have realised that this house isn't exactly the most organised. Lots of unrehearsed live music and people getting up to say things they haven't prepared.'

'Liam would have liked that.'

'Will you make some food for the wake?'

'Me?'

'Yeah. It'll be here.'

'I didn't even know if you'd want me at the funeral.'

Danny snorted, but it wasn't unfriendly.

'Seriously, I don't need to come if you'd prefer me not to.'

'You're joking, right? The woman he was going to meet on the day he died. The woman he named as his executor. The woman he left his beloved wooden bowl to . . . Anyway, if you could cook stuff for the wake.'

'What kind of things?' Jude asked warily.

'You decide. Not cucumber sandwiches or anything like that. And it's not just you. I'm asking everyone I can think of to bring something. As long as I don't have to do anything.'

'How many are you expecting?'

'No idea. Whoever decides to turn up. Liam knew loads of people; he drew them in somehow. Moths to a flame. People met him once and wanted to be his friend.'

Jude nodded. She watched Alfie reach up and dig his fingers into the soft mass of Danny's hair.

'So I'll bring lots of food that isn't sandwiches on Tuesday,' she said.

'And don't wear black.'

Tears glittered on Danny's lashes.

Jude stood up. 'I should go.'

'What's the time?'

Jude checked her phone. 'Twenty to five.'

'Fuck. Irina and Vin said they'd be back by now to look after Alfie. They promised.'

'Are you supposed to be somewhere?'

'I was going skating. It's my thing. I go every Saturday afternoon with my sister, come rain or shine. We've done it for years. Everyone was telling me how important it was I went today: a tiny piece of something normal in all this awfulness. And then they don't even bother to turn up. What am I supposed to do?' As she said this, her eyes slid to Jude. 'I don't suppose?' she said. 'Just until they arrive?'

How could Danny think of leaving her son with her?

'Are you serious?'

'It'll be fine. Read to him. Play hide-and-seek. Vin or Irina will be here any minute. I just need to grab my stuff and run, or I'll miss my slot.'

She didn't wait for Jude to agree, but stood and deposited Alfie on Jude's lap. He was warm and squashy and his hair tickled her nose. He twisted his head and stared into her eyes. His eyes were squinched and his bottom lip stuck out. He was deciding whether to cry.

Jude picked up a tangerine.

'Let's share this,' she said brightly, and started to peel it.

Danny left the room with a farewell salute, then ran back in to snatch up a torch.

'It's dark out on the marshes,' she said as she left the room again.

A couple of minutes later, Jude heard the front door click shut.

A friend of Jude's had recently acquired a manic puppy. She had said that you had to engage with them at their level, not tower over them. Jude thought it might be the same for small children, so she lifted Alfie from the chair and hunkered down beside him.

'What shall we play?' she asked hopefully.

Alfie put out his dimpled hand and pushed experimentally at her chest. Jude let herself topple over so she was lying on the tiles. Which, she discovered, were grimy and greasy.

Alfie howled with laughter.

Encouraged, Jude levered herself back up to a squatting position, was pushed, fell down again, received the same cheerful response.

She repeated the manoeuvre several more times. It seemed he would never tire of it.

'Blimey,' said a voice.

She struggled to a sitting position, trying to pull her jumper down over her naked tummy.

Vin and Irina were in the room, gazing down at her, and standing in the doorway was the student Jan, looking pained.

'Why, Dr Winter,' said Vin, smiling broadly.

'You look hot,' said Irina. She wasn't smiling.

'You're late,' said Jude. 'Danny had to go to her skating.'

'We were picking up drinks for the wake.'

'You're still late.'

She stood up. Everyone in this house was too tall: beside them, she felt puny and unimpressive.

'I'll be going then.'

'No worries.' The smile still hadn't left Vin's face. 'You turn up everywhere. In the house, in the workshop, at the spot where Liam was killed, in his will.'

Jan was still standing in the doorway. Alfie was pulling at Jude and making a grizzling sound, like a motor that had been left idling.

'I'm only here because you weren't,' said Jude crossly.

'Come on, little fellow.'

Vin lifted Alfie high in the air and settled him on his shoulders. Alfie grabbed him by his hair and chortled.

'Bye then,' said Jude.

'See you on Tuesday, at the funeral,' said Irina.

'Oh, and Jude,' said Vin as she passed him, and she turned.

'Yes?'

'You've got a smudge on your cheek. Here.' He touched his own cheek to demonstrate.

Jude rubbed furiously at her face.

'Better?'

'Yeah. See you.'

Jan followed her to the front door and stood beside her as she put on her jacket. He shifted from foot to foot and cleared his throat awkwardly several times. Jude thought he was about to say something, but then Vin called from the depths of the house and the moment passed.

CHAPTER THIRTY-SEVEN

'What kind of things do people eat at wakes?' Jude asked her mother on the phone that evening.

'Crisps,' she said firmly. 'Crisps and sandwiches and things like sausage rolls.'

It sounded more like a children's birthday party than a wake to Jude.

'It's got to be vegetarian,' she said. 'And no sandwiches.'

'Smoked salmon and cream cheese bagels.'

'Smoked salmon isn't vegetarian.'

'How about lots of pitta bread and dips. Hummus, guacamole, things like that.'

'Maybe.'

'I do a really nice one with peas and coconut.' Dee was becoming enthusiastic. 'And one with beetroot and horseradish. Though beetroot stains. And you can bake some wheels of camembert.'

'You should be doing this, not me.'

'I can come and help you. It'd be fun, like the old days when we lived together. I'm pretty free tomorrow. How about I come in the afternoon?

We could even make some chocolate fridge cake – people love that. Half past two?'

'Dee,' said Jude. 'That would be really, really lovely.'

Jude boiled chickpeas, peeled garlic and squeezed lemons. Dee vigorously smashed up digestive biscuits and melted dark chocolate. The kitchen, that Jude had thought of as grim, filled with warmth and good smells.

'I've missed this,' she said.

'Me too. So: tell me about this Liam Birch who's turned your life upside down.' There was chocolate round Dee's mouth.

'Tell you what? You know what happened.'

Dee shrugged. 'Describe him. What was he like when you were a teenager?'

'Impulsive,' said Jude. 'Charismatic, I guess. Angry. Reckless. Good at making things. Artistic, in a way. Kind of fatalistic, though.' She stared off into the distance, trying to separate the Liam she had known all those years ago from the one she had learned about in the last few days. 'I suppose he was kind of a leader of the pack, if that makes sense. He was powerful.'

'He sounds a bit of an alpha male.' Dee swept the crushed biscuits into a bowl.

'Perhaps.'

'Don't you find that a bit odd?'

'Odd in what way?'

'He doesn't sound like your kind of person at all.'

238

'You're right.' Jude laughed. 'He isn't. Wasn't.'

'But you've got a look on your face when you talk about him.'

'I was only eighteen.'

'It's like you never got over him.'

'That's crap. I was in love with Nat. I never thought about Liam. Or hardly ever.'

'When he turned up, it triggered something in you and then he died. So you never had time to see he was just another man who was used to getting his own way with women.'

'He didn't have his own way with me,' said Jude. 'Nothing happened and nothing was going to happen, and I didn't feel anything for him, except curiosity and gratitude.'

Dee cocked an eyebrow at her. 'Gratitude?'

Jude started to explain and then stopped. She couldn't, not just now, not just yet.

'Because he was important to me once.'

Dee poured the melted chocolate over the biscuits and dried fruit. 'Now you're getting all involved with his partner and his friends. That's a bit weird, isn't it?'

Jude considered this.

'It's probably easier than sorting out my own life,' she said at last.

Dee nodded and Jude looked down at the hummus she was making, but she could still feel her friend's eyes on her, scrutinising, waiting.

'It's a really strange household,' she said. 'I mean, everyone in it is strange.'

'In what way?'

'It's hard to describe. When I'm there, everything feels a bit glamorous and a bit menacing, and I never know if someone's telling the truth or just, well, kind of acting things out, as if everything's some kind of game. It doesn't feel like there are proper . . .' She searched for the word. 'Rules. Boundaries.'

'It sounds awful.'

'Everyone's watching everyone else. Including me.'

'You mean they're watching you or you're watching them?'

'I don't know. Both, maybe.'

'I don't understand why you go back. They sound creepy.'

'They're kind of amazing as well.'

Dee looked serious. 'I don't think you should go there any more, Jude. I don't think it's healthy.'

Jude gave a laugh. 'I'm going to go to the funeral at least. We've cooked all this food!'

'No, you need to stop all of this. You need to get out of this place and be normal.'

'I'll think about it. I promise. Let me get through the funeral first.'

240

CHAPTER THIRTY-EIGHT

Jude had been to seven funerals in her life before. Two of them had been in churches, four in crematoriums and one of them, for an uncle she had barely known, had been in a kind of conference centre just outside Birmingham. The venue for Liam's funeral was his workshop. When Jude first heard this, she thought it was a strange idea, almost blasphemous, and then immediately she changed her mind. It seemed like the right idea. Liam didn't do what other people did, even when he was dead.

When she got out of the Uber at the entrance to the industrial estate, she saw people arriving, an improbable splash of colour moving between the drab, dilapidated units. She felt oddly self-conscious as the only person who was dressed more for a traditional funeral. The instruction had been to dress colourfully but that morning, preparing herself, she had lost her nerve. She had colourful clothes. She had an orange jumpsuit. She had a skirt that was all fraying strips of silk in yellow and blue and red. She had a feather boa from some fancy-dress party long ago. She had a choice of bright and patterned tops. But most of them were still in her old flat, which was Nat's home now and not hers, and the ones she had brought with her she didn't even try on. She was an ex-girlfriend of Liam's. She was involved in his death. She was responsible for the administration of the will. This wasn't a time for her to draw attention to herself. She decided to wear one of her androgynous suits, grey, with a white silk shirt. When she had bought the suit, she had hoped that, in the right light, it might make her look like Marlene Dietrich, but now she just hoped it would help her to pass unobserved among all the carnivalesque costumes.

She didn't recognise anyone until she saw Leila Fox, standing just outside the entrance to the workshop. She walked across to her, feeling as always slightly uneasy. When the detective saw her, she gave a smile.

'Well, *we'd* better not go in together.'

'What do you mean?'

Leila gestured at what Jude was wearing and then at herself. Jude couldn't stop herself from smiling. They were dressed almost identically.

'People will think we planned it.'

'You probably think it's strange, my being here,' said Jude.

'I don't think it's strange at all. You're the ex-girlfriend. You're an executor. And now you're apparently a friend of the widow.' The way Leila said it, it felt more like an accusation than a description. 'Anyway,' she continued, 'I was hoping you'd be here.'

'Why?'

'You talked to me about your fiancé. Your ex-fiancé. Nat Weller. I just wanted to tell you that he's no longer a focus of our inquiry.'

'A focus of your inquiry. What does that mean?'

'You thought he might have known about you and Liam, that he might have resented your connection.'

'I thought it was possible,' said Jude warily. 'Though of course I never believed that he, you know . . .'

'Killed Liam.'

'Yes.'

'We've accounted for his whereabouts on the evening of the murder.'

'So he was at the party?'

An unexpected expression crossed the detective's face, something wary, almost furtive, but it was gone almost as soon as Jude noticed it.

'For a bit,' Leila Fox said.

'What do you mean, for a bit?'

'The party ended early. It was raining.'

'So where was he?'

'That's not the point. I just thought you should know that Nat is under no suspicion.'

'Okay, but why can't you say?'

'I just can't share details of the inquiry. It's as simple as that.'

Jude nodded. 'So Nat didn't kill Liam, which I knew anyway. But thanks for letting me know.'

'We should go in.'

Jude looked at the detective's face, which was amiably inscrutable. She remembered the expression she had seen chase across it a few moments earlier.

'What aren't you telling me?'

'There are many things I'm not telling you, Jude, because this is a murder investigation and you are not a detective but a witness.'

'Something about that night,' said Jude.

As clearly as if she was watching it on a film, she saw Nat when she had returned to their flat after her disastrous trip to the cottage in Norfolk. She had come back much earlier than expected and he had been on the phone, talking to someone in a voice that was both placating and faintly angry. What had he been saying? She strained to remember, but perhaps she had never known. She tried to bring to mind his expression when he'd first seen her there. Had there been something, a moment of panic, before he came towards her to take her in his arms? Or was she making that up?

'Was Nat with someone that night?' she asked in a small voice. 'Is that what you're not telling me?'

'I've said all I'm going to say and what I've said is not implying anything. If you've got any questions, you must put them to him directly.'

Jude put a hand to her head, feeling the familiar buzz of approaching pain.

244

'Maybe all the time he was being strange about me, he was the one who was actually being unfaithful.'

'I absolutely didn't say that. I didn't say anything like that. Do not jump to conclusions here, Jude. I am simply telling you that he is not under any kind of suspicion.'

'All right, then,' said Jude. She felt frail and unanchored. Her vision was blurry with it. 'If it's not true, you can say that. You can tell me that Nat wasn't being unfaithful.'

'I can only say what I've said. You must take it up with him.'

CHAPTER THIRTY-NINE

There was none of the paraphernalia of a traditional funeral. There were no ushers directing people. There were no orders of service. The doors of the workshop had simply been wedged wide open. Jude joined the people making their way in and when she stepped inside, she actually gasped. The floor had been cleared of tools and there were now lines of planks on trestles, forming rough benches. The walls were lined with roughly sketched paintings on vast sheets of paper that had been tacked up on all four walls. The effect was dazzling, a riot of brightly coloured rhapsodic human figures, dancing, swirling, swimming, mingling. The figures were surrounded by water and sky and sun and stars. Everything was in primary colours, blues, reds, yellows. It was almost like stained glass and the colours were so strong and bright it felt as if the sun was shining through them.

There were bare branches of trees hung with lights, and sprays of greenery dotted around the room. At the front was a slightly raised dais. On a workbench in the centre was the wicker coffin but it was scarcely visible for the flowers and leaves that had been woven into it. Liam's boots were on top, toes pointing towards the gathering. Surrounding the coffin were chairs and a host of musical instruments, guitars, a double bass, an electric keyboard, and other instruments that Jude didn't even recognise. She looked around and saw Vin and Danny at the front, deep in conversation. Every so often Danny would recognise someone and mouth a greeting. Doc was on the other side of the platform, adjusting a loudspeaker and occasionally gesturing at someone at the back of the hall. Every so often, he picked up his guitar and strummed it softly, picking out melodies and then letting them go. He looked ill.

Jude found a place at the end of a bench right at the back. She took out her phone and stared at it as if she were dealing with something important. Really it was just to stop herself from catching the eye of anyone she knew. If she saw someone familiar, they might come and sit down next to her and she didn't want to have to perform her response in some way. She just wanted to be alone with her thoughts.

There was a hum of chatter and the creaking of footsteps on the wooden floor. Gradually the noise subsided, the doors were closed, and there was a sense of expectancy that you could almost feel, like at a music event. Jude heard the sound of hands clapping. She looked up from her phone and saw that it was Vin, who had stepped up on

247

to the platform. He was dressed in amber crushed-velvet trousers and a black and white jacket. He looked like the master of ceremonies at a medieval banquet.

At moments like this, when someone was about to speak in public, Jude had often felt a sense of vicarious anxiety, of nervousness on the speaker's behalf. She didn't feel that now. Vin was so obviously at ease among friends.

'We're here to . . .' and he stopped and smiled. 'I was going to say that we're here to say goodbye to Liam, but that's not right. We're not going to say goodbye to him because he's always going to be with us. And we're not here to mourn him. We're here to celebrate him.' He took a few steps to the side of the coffin and tapped it softly. 'It's a party for you, mate. And I hope you'll enjoy it.' He turned back to the crowd. 'Some of us are going to play some music. A couple of things Liam liked. A couple of things that Liam may not have liked but that we like to play.' There was a tiny murmur of laughter. 'Then we'll have a few words. Then back to ours for anyone who wants to come.' He looked around. 'All right, guys?'

Two women and three men stepped up on to the platform and nodded at the crowd. One of the women turned out to be Irina, though her hair was dyed a darker red and rippled across her shoulders like live snakes. She was wearing a green cape. The group were a motley mixture of different fashions: grunge, hip-hop, jazz, hippy. They picked up their various instruments – one of the men took a violin from a case – and after some tuning and muttering among themselves started to play. The music they played was as varied as their different styles. Nobody said what they were about to play before they played it or what they had played after they finished. It just looked like a group of friends having fun. There was a folky reel, something Dylanesque, something Cohenesque, a solo violin piece that might have been Bach. Someone else came from the audience carrying a trumpet and they played a piece that sounded to Jude like Miles Davis or John Coltrane.

As they played, Jude looked at all these people she didn't know. Mostly she just saw their backs, but it was clear that almost everyone was strangely and beautifully dressed. She made out Liam's parents at the front: they too had followed the instructions to wear bright clothes. Alfie was next to Tara, his mop of soft curls just showing. It was like looking at a meadow of wildflowers. She and Leila in their grey suits were the sober bookends.

There, perched on the edge, at the back, she was taken back to when she had first known Liam. She had felt exactly the same then with his exotic group of friends: like an onlooker, gazing at these other people who had some kind of secret knowledge that she was excluded from. How did they know what to do, what to wear, where to get hold of the strange garments they wore, the frightening potions they drank or smoked or snorted?

Liam had been her one brief link to that existence that she was both drawn to and distrustful
of. For those months, he seemed to have seen in
her what nobody else had, something that she
herself had never seen in herself, only in others.
And now she was here again, seeing it in these
vivid, gorgeous people and not in herself. Jude
looked at the way they dressed: so much cleverness
and wit and panache. She looked down at what
she herself was wearing. It was meant to prevent
her from standing out but it probably did the
opposite. She and Leila seemed to be the only
people present who were playing it safe. Leila had
the excuse that she was dressed for work, so really
it was just her.

A lovely, cheering reel came to an end and the
musicians put their instruments down. There was
applause and they stood up and walked to the
front and stood in a line. Irina held up her hands
to silence the applause. When there was quiet, she
waited a few seconds then looked at her compan-
ions on her right and her left, gave a slight nod
and they began singing. The music sounded
ancient – the words Jude could make out were in
Latin – and suddenly it felt like the wooden walls
and ceiling and floor were resonating with the
sound. She felt it as a passionate expression of
fellowship, something she wished she were a part
of and knew that she could never be, and it broke
her heart. She thought of her and Nat, their messy,
compromised, dishonest relationship. That was

what she had had – and Liam had had this, and he had lost it.

When the song finished, quite suddenly, the singers turned to the coffin, gave a slight inclination of their heads and stepped off the platform in silence. Someone was sobbing hoarsely at the front, probably Tara, whose head was bent forward. Jude found her eyes full of tears so that she couldn't see. She took a tissue from her pocket and wiped her eyes and blew her nose, and then realised that Vin was on the stage, looking around at the building.

'It felt right to do this here,' he said. 'Liam was the luck I had.' He turned round to the coffin. '*You* were the luck I had. But I'm going to tell the others about you.' He turned back to the crowd. 'He was the brother I never had. He was the best friend I never had till I met him. I lived with him and I worked with him. We joined up because we both had a dream. I never thought we could really do it but Liam did and this is where we did it. This is where we dreamed dreams and made things and fixed things and we created a company and there were ups and downs, like there always are, but we made it work.' He gestured around. 'We said we'd do it and we bloody did it.'

There was a murmur of applause. Jude's eyes had been full of unshed tears as Vin began speaking but now she felt like she was sobering up slightly. This was the part of a funeral that made her uneasy, whether it was in a church or a beautifully decorated industrial space. Saying things that weren't true, or were only one comforting version of the messy truth, because that's what you say about the recently dead. You didn't make it work, she said to herself, and you know you didn't.

'But it was never just work,' Vin continued. 'With Liam it was always about family. It was about Danny. It was about little Alfie here.' There was a crack in his voice and he stopped, just nodding slowly. It was like he couldn't trust himself to speak. He took two deep breaths and laid his hand on the coffin. 'I just want to say to you, mate, that we're all going to look after this place' – he gestured once more about the building – 'and we're going to look after your family for you. We'll try and be worthy of you.' He gave another little nod. 'Now, we all said to Danny that she didn't have to do anything and she didn't have to say anything. But Danny is someone who won't be told. So this very special lady is going to say a few words. Come on up.'

He reached out a hand and helped Danny up to the stage. She turned to face the crowd. She was wearing black trousers with a satin strip down the leg and a scarlet tux and scarlet lipstick that stood out from the deathly pallor of her face. Jude thought she looked straight-backed and fierce and almost magnificent in her grief. As she spoke, her voice sounded firm, and so calm that Jude wondered if she was on medication.

'When Liam and me met, we were both a bit . . .'
Danny paused. 'All over the place. But I'd never
met anyone like him. He was handsome, he had
the kindest eyes I'd ever seen, he was the most
creative person I'd ever met, he was funny, he was
strange, he was unexpected.' She stopped again.
She was clearly thinking of what to say as she went
along. 'We never got married. But we did make a
sort of vow together. It was none of that love,
honour and obey stuff. We promised to look after
each other. And to trust each other.' She seemed
to have lost her thread for a moment. 'There were
other things as well. Love. We did keep that bit
from the marriage vow. We promised to love each
other. And we said we were going to grow old
together. We didn't get to do that.' She sniffed and
put the back of her right hand up to her nose.
'I'm sorry about that, Liam. I'm sorry we didn't
get to do that.' Now there was a long pause, so
long that there was a feeling of awkwardness in
the crowd, a restiveness. Danny seemed to have
forgotten where she was. She looked round at the
coffin. 'Bye, Liam,' she said.

There was a murmuring from the crowd. She
acknowledged it with a regal nod of her head.

'Thank you, all. Now his brother, Dermot, is
going to say something.'

Everyone looked expectantly at Dermot, but he
didn't move. After a few moments of awkward
waiting, Danny stepped off the dais and walked
to where he sat. She bent down and whispered in

his ear, then straightened up and held out her hand. Dermot took it and stood up. Danny led him to the little stage and waited while he climbed onto it. She gave him a nod, part encouragement and part command.

Jude hadn't seen Dermot before now. When he stood facing the audience, awkwardly, self-consciously, she felt that he was like her. He wasn't one of this group. He didn't belong. It was like he hadn't quite got the memo about dressing colourfully. Like her, he had dressed for a more traditional funeral. He was wearing a dark suit that was slightly too large. His extravagantly patterned tie was his concession to brightness, but its bulky knot looked as if it was pushing into his neck and up into his chin.

Dermot took a piece of paper from his pocket and unfolded it. As he held it up, it shook. He started to read from it inaudibly and someone shouted from the back for him to speak up. He was visibly disconcerted by this. He started from the beginning, slightly more loudly, but even so Jude wasn't able to follow everything he was saying. It was more like the spectacle of someone being nervous and grief-stricken at the same time. The result wasn't an outpouring of emotion but the opposite. It was a dutiful school essay about when his brother had been born and where he had gone to school and what jobs he had done. As a doctor, Jude recognised a person who was still experiencing the shock of loss and was stuck in it. There was nothing about what Liam had been like, nothing about what Dermot was feeling, nothing that acknowledged the shock of what had happened. In a way, it was more moving than the easy, theatrical sincerity of Vin or Danny because Dermot was standing in front of them and they were watching him suffer. His face, so like Liam's face, wore expressions that didn't quite fit – as if he wasn't in control of it.

Dermot's talk didn't come to a conclusion. There was no summing-up, no final expression of emotion. It just ended and when it ended Dermot looked at the people and then looked back at his piece of paper as if it was something he was seeing for the first time.

'That's it,' he said, his voice quavering. 'That's all.' He looked around.

Jude felt a sudden anxiety. She was reminded of being in a play and seeing an actor forgetting his lines. But now there was nobody to give him a prompt and he didn't seem to know what to do, how to get offstage.

'I don't know,' he said. 'I don't know what more to say. He was my older brother. I always thought he'd be there to look after me or something.' He wiped his eyes with his sleeve and started to say something else, but then Danny stepped up on the stage and she hugged him and whispered something reassuring and he allowed himself to be led down. There was a murmur of sympathy from the audience.

The musicians returned to the stage and then Irina announced that they were going to play one of Liam's favourite bits of music, an old Irish jig, while the coffin was carried out. A jostle of figures came on to the dais: Vin again; Erika; a man with a long grey beard and an embroidered kimono; a stringy youth dressed in vertical stripes like a convict; two other tall young men wearing almost identical paisley-pattered shirts. They positioned themselves around the coffin and grasped it. Vin nodded and up it went, tilting this way and that, the boots on its lid sliding. Jude imagined Liam inside, his body shifting in the cramped space. One of the men almost lost his grip and Vin said something fierce in a carrying whisper. But finally it was on their shoulders and they very slowly manoeuvred their way down the steps and off the dais, followed by the sweet swirling notes of the jig.

Danny stood up, then Tara and Andy, Alfie between them. Danny put out her hand and grasped the hand of her little son. He was wearing a knitted waistcoat, blue with flowers stitched into it, and he looked bemused as he staggered on his bandy legs behind the coffin. When they reached the door, Danny scooped him up.

Gradually the room emptied. Jude remained where she was as people passed her on the way out. She listened to the music and could picture Liam dancing to it; he was a good dancer, loose-limbed, in his own world. She thought of the strangeness of his loss and the strangeness that nobody had said that he had been murdered.

She saw Dermot, his tie pulled off and glassy-eyed, heading for the exit and she intercepted him, stood in front of him. He saw her and there was a slow arrival of recognition; she stepped forward and looked him full in the face.

'You're in shock,' she said. 'I know what it's like. But you'll start to feel it before long, and then you'll get through it.'

'Yeah,' he said dully.

'And it was good of you to come and do this. Liam would have appreciated it.'

He looked more intently at her, as if he were noticing her properly for the first time.

'Would he?'

Jude thought to herself that the Liam she had known probably wouldn't have appreciated it all that much.

'Of course he would,' she said.

CHAPTER FORTY

Jude stepped outside. The light was fading and there was already a moon. At the far side of the lot, the pallbearers had stopped by a hearse and were attempting to insert the coffin into its open back. It was shedding flowers. Two men in formal black suits, one very small and the other very large, stood by watching with obvious disapproval. The sound of the Irish jig could still be heard, and the mourners stood in huddles in the cold wind, waiting.

'Are you going to the wake?' asked Leila, pulling on a thick coat as she came towards Jude.

'Me? No.'

'Me neither.' Leila hesitated, then nodded. 'Bye then.'

'Goodbye.'

'And Jude.'

'Yes?'

'I don't know. Take care, I guess.'

Jude watched the detective leave. She replayed what Leila Fox had said about Nat and what she hadn't said. Nat had an alibi for the night of the murder and it wasn't only that he had been at the

Bonfire Night gathering with their friends. He had left early and gone somewhere else. If it was something innocent, why hadn't he told her that? Why had he let her think that he had been with Dee and their group of friends and then come home?

She tried to remember exactly what he'd said about the evening. He'd said that he had – what? A reasonably good time, yes. She was almost sure that was the phrase; the memory was clear because everything that had happened at the cottage and then the subsequent day was cruelly etched into her mind. And then he had told her that it had rained, so nobody stayed long. He came home early. Jude was certain about that, which meant he had been lying to her at the same time as she had been lying to him.

Her throat tightened when she thought of it: of Nat deciding whether to forgive her, that expression of hurt and solemn self-righteousness, when perhaps all the time it had been him, not her. Him with someone else, but looking at her as if she was the traitor.

'Shit, shit, shit,' she said under her breath.

'I'm sorry?' She looked round, startled, and saw Jan, the mathematician housemate. He was wearing an unequivocally yellow sweatshirt and his face above it looked uneasy and pink with cold.

'Something is wrong.'

'It's nothing.'

'Something wrong,' he repeated, and she realised it wasn't a question.

'What do you mean?'

'Jude. Thank goodness,' said a voice behind her. It was Erika, though she could hardly be made out behind a great armful of greenery.

'Hi. That was a nice service.'

'That was just the beginning. Can you take these?'

She held out the branches that had been in the workshop, birch branches with a few yellow leaves still attached, eucalyptus, holly, and twigs covered with clusters of orange berries.

'Sorry. I'm not coming to the wake.'

'Really? Well, it's only a few minutes from here and then you can go home.'

'Can't Jan—?'

But Jan had drifted away. Jude could see his yellow top being swallowed up in the shadows. She took the greenery and its sharp fresh smell filled her nostrils.

Jude walked to the house following the small, colourful crowd of mourners. Ahead, she made out Alfie, riding on someone's shoulders, sagging a bit, like a sack of flour. As she approached the house, she saw that there were lights in the trees outside.

The door was open and the hallway full. Jude pushed through the press of people, clutching her branches.

'Where shall I put these?' she asked Doc.

'Who knows?' he said, holding up his palms

and raising his eyebrows. 'Ask Erika. She's in charge of flowers.'

'Where's Erika?'

'Who knows?' He made the same gesture of exaggerated helplessness.

Jude made her way into the kitchen, almost beaten back by the heat and steam and the smell of something burning. A woman in a kaftan was standing by the hob, stirring a pot.

'Would you like some punch?' she asked, holding out a ladle.

'I'm fine,' said Jude. 'I'm just dropping these off.'

'I think they're for the conservatory.'

Jude manoeuvred her way into the conservatory clutching her armful of greenery. The room was crowded and full of the babble of voices. The trestle table was covered with plates and dishes of food, including the dips she had dropped off that morning, and a motley collection of glasses, tumblers and mugs. At the far end, she saw Vin opening bottles and heard his booming laugh. The doors to the garden were open and groups of people stood amid the clutter, smoking or vaping.

Danny passed by, a few feet away, but she didn't seem to notice Jude, or anyone. People reached out to touch her, say a few words, but her face barely changed expression. Her carmine lips were a gash in her chalky face and she had a glassy stare. She was just stumbling through the motions. Jude thought she probably just wanted to lie in a dark room and wait for the day to end.

261

She propped the branches against a wall and straightened up, brushing off the leaves and twigs from her suit. She took a canapé heaped with sour cream and some kind of herby mixture and pushed the whole thing into her mouth, licked her fingers, turned to go, and found herself face to face with Tara and Andy.

'Hello,' she said thickly, still chewing. 'How are you both?'

'How do you think?' said Tara, at the same time as Andy said, 'As well as can be expected.'

'It was a lovely celebration.'

'Do you think so?' Tara raised her eyebrows. She was wearing a long skirt and a jacket that was cinched at the waist, like a character out of a Victorian costume drama, and her brown hair was piled on the top of her head. Her eyes were red-rimmed and her face was angry.

'I think,' said Jude carefully, 'that it felt appropriate for Liam. The music, the place it was in, the words.'

'Andy wanted to read a poem,' said Tara.

'Not really,' said Andy, shifting from one foot to the other. 'I didn't really.'

'But Danny said it wasn't that kind of service.'

'At least Dermot spoke,' said Jude.

'He was very nervous,' said Andy. 'I'm not sure it went down very well.'

'It was good,' said Jude awkwardly.

'It's Alfie you should feel for.' Tara took a step forward. Her mascara was smudged. Jude could smell her perfume and see a tiny pulse in her jaw. 'My little grandson.'

'Of course,' said Jude. She badly wanted to leave.

'Liam adored his little boy.'

'I'm sure.'

'Alfie won't remember him, though. He won't remember how his father loved him and looked after him and was proud of him. It's terrible.'

'It is terrible. But at least he's surrounded by people who love him.'

'Tara and I want to see him regularly,' said Andy. 'That's the thing.'

'Of course.'

'So no matter what Danny says, you'll make sure of it?' Tara put a hand on Jude's arm, gripping it hard.

'Me?'

'You're the executor.'

'That's just the will,' said Jude, horrified. 'It's about possessions. I have nothing to do with anything else.'

'In the will, Liam said if they both died, I would take care of Alfie,' said Tara. 'I'm his granny. So I have the right to spend time with him. The legal right.'

'I can't do anything about this,' said Jude. 'It's nothing to do with me. But surely you will be able to see Alfie as much as you want, for your sake and for his.'

'You're a little fool.' Tara took her hand away; her lip curled.

'Tara,' said Andy warningly.

'You don't know anything at all.' Tara was speaking in a hiss; her eyes glittered. 'Little goodie-goodie doctor.'

Jude stepped back from her.

'I'm really sorry about everything,' she said. 'Talk to Danny, sort things out. Now I've got to go.'

She pushed her way through the press of people. In the hall she met Jan. He had taken off his yellow sweatshirt and was wearing a thick grey jumper instead. He looked thoroughly miserable.

'Hi,' she said. 'I'm just leaving.'

'I too want to leave.'

'It'll soon be over.'

'Why are you here?'

'I was just dropping off some branches.'

'No.' He frowned at her. 'Why do you come?'

'To the house, you mean?'

He nodded.

'Because, well, everything that happened and then the will.' Jude made a vague, expansive gesture.

'If you like it so much here—'

'I don't. It's not that at all.'

'If you like it so much here,' he repeated stolidly, 'then you can have my room.'

'I'm sorry?'

'If you like it so much here, you can have my room.'

'I don't want your room! I have my own place.' Though of course this wasn't strictly true.

'My room is at the top of the house and quite big. With a leaking radiator and dampness and much noise. Sex noise and quarrel noise and baby noise and drilling and hammering noise.'

'That doesn't sound fun.'

'It is not fun. It is bad for the mental health.'

'I can see that.'

'Also.' He folded his arms solemnly. 'Everyone is mad.'

'Do you mean angry?'

'Mad. Yesterday Irina hit me with a mop.'

'Oh!' A tiny burst of laughter escaped her and Jan gazed at her, disappointed. 'So you want to leave?' she said.

'I must leave. Without ado.'

'Okay, I understand that, but I definitely don't want your room.'

'You too should leave,' Jan declared. 'You do not belong.'

'I told you. I am leaving. Right now.'

'Good.'

He nodded at her and made his way upstairs.

CHAPTER FORTY-ONE

Jude buttoned up her coat and went to the door. Something bumped against her leg and she looked down to see Alfie waver and fall on his bottom. He was holding on to a soft, shabby elephant and gazing up at her with those dark eyes. His mouth became square and a sob escaped him.

Jude squatted beside him.

'Hello, Alfie,' she said. 'Where's Mummy?'

'Mummy,' he repeated. 'Mummy.'

Jude squinted back down the hall but could only see strangers. She stood and held out her hand.

'Let's find Mummy,' she said firmly.

Alfie put his trusting hand into hers and she pulled him to his feet. They went back into the party.

'Glögg?' The woman in the kaftan held out an enamel mug.

'Not for me, thank you,' said Jude.

'It's nice and warming,' said the woman encouragingly.

'Just a sip then,' said Jude, and took the mug.

It was warming and tasted of brandy and wine and nutmeg and cloves. It reminded Jude of the Christmas market in Ghent she and Nat had been to nearly a year ago. The thought of Nat sent a spasm of rage and distress through her, and she took another sip, steam rising into her face.

She thought she saw Danny's red jacket shimmering in the garden and crossed the room with Alfie towards the double doors.

'Jude,' said a voice, and Vin dropped a kiss on the top of her head and laughed at her expression. He ruffled Alfie's head and then turned back to the woman he was talking to.

In the light-festooned garden, Doc and Irina and a man with orange hair and a lovely Irish accent were smoking weed and building a small bonfire. It was rather close to the house. Danny was standing by a stone urn at the far end of the yard, with a woman who could only be her sister, though not as dramatically beautiful.

'There's Mummy,' Jude said to Alfie.

'Never mind, I'll take him,' said Irina, spinning round, her green cape skimming the flame Doc had just lit.

'Thanks,' said Jude.

Irina bent down and lifted Alfie to her flat chest and let her rippling hair spread over him. He nestled into her. His eyelids were heavy; even his hair looked tired.

'Danny can't even be a good mother on the day of his daddy's funeral,' said Irina bitterly.

Alfie butted his head under her chin.

'Daddy?' he said.

Irina's eyes filled with tears.

'My poor little Alfie,' she murmured into the crown of his head. 'We both loved him, didn't we?'

'What do you mean?' asked Jude. 'About Danny, I mean.'

'Look at her. She doesn't know where he is. He could be anywhere, with anyone.'

'But you all look after him, right? It seems a great way to be with a kid, getting him used to lots of different people.'

'Like a house pet?'

'Of course not like a house pet.'

'What would you know?' said Irina. 'You just look after old people and have affairs with other people's partners.'

'That's a lie, and it's also mean and cruel!'

'Oh!' Irina's eyebrows shot up and she smiled. 'You're angry.'

'Of course I'm angry. You're upset, but you don't have to be insulting and unpleasant – and a liar.'

'Quite right.' Irina nodded several times. 'That's the spirit.'

'I'm going now. I should never have come in the first place.'

'You shouldn't leave yet; there's going to be a toast and more music.'

'I think a spark just caught on the hem of your cape.'

'I don't care.' Irina gave an exultant laugh. 'Let it burn.'

'Maybe you should stamp on it.'

Irina sighed and put Alfie into Jude's arms where he lay like a warm sack of flour, untied her cape and let it drop to the ground, and then jumped on it several times.

'There,' she said finally.

Tiredness burned behind Jude's eyes and she felt the nauseating tickle of a migraine lying in wait. Her anger left her.

'What about Liam?' she asked. 'Was he a good father?'

'Liam,' said Irina emphatically, 'was completely amazing.'

'Really?'

'He did almost everything for Alfie.'

'But it's good that fathers do that, right?'

'Huh – I don't think she has any maternal instincts,' said Irina.

'Not all women have so-called maternal instincts, but that doesn't mean they're bad mothers. It just means—'

'Yeah, right,' said Irina sarcastically, and, stooping to pick up her cloak, she stalked back into the house, leaving Jude still holding Alfie.

'Toke?' asked Doc, holding out a joint across the little fire.

'It's okay,' said Jude. 'I'm about to go.'

CHAPTER FORTY-TWO

Danny and her sister were deep in conversation so Jude hefted Alfie, fast asleep, back inside.

'Can you take him?' she asked Tara. 'I really need to go.'

'Of course.'

Tara held out her arms and Jude carefully transferred the sleeping boy. Tara held him closely against her chest and murmured softly; the expression on her face was so avidly tender that Jude had to turn away.

Once again, she made her way into the hall. Dermot was sitting on the stairs by himself, a beer bottle held loosely in one hand and his head against the wall.

'Bye,' said Jude. 'Good luck with everything.'

He gazed at her, a stupid smile on his face.

'My fellow executor,' he said.

'I'm going home.'

'Going home,' he repeated, as if it was a foreign word, one he didn't understand.

'Yeah. Take care, Dermot.'

Dermot sat up straighter and screwed a fist against his eyes.

'Did you love him?' he asked.

'Love Liam, you mean?'

'Yeah. Everyone else did. Did you?'

Jude was thoroughly sick of people asking her about her relationship to Liam and then disregarding her answer.

'I was eighteen,' she replied shortly. 'I was in love in that moment. That was eleven years ago. Since that long-ago time, I did not see him and I did not love him.'

'The one that got away,' said Dermot, and gave a violent hiccup.

'Did you?'

'Love my brother? Yeah, Jude, I loved my brother. I used to trail after him like a little puppy. Sometimes he'd shoo me away but other times he'd let me hang out with him and his mates, do stuff.' He rubbed his eyes again. 'He was so cool.'

'Did you stay close?'

Dermot took a swig of beer.

'He always meant more to me than I did to him, and he always meant more to Mum than I meant to her, and sometimes that made me feel like shit, but he was my brother. My only brother. What can I say? He's dead. He'll always be dead now. For the rest of my life I'll have a dead brother.' Another swig of beer. 'A murdered brother.'

'Not everyone loved him, though.'

271

'What?'

She sat on the stairs beside him, suddenly realising how tired she was. 'You said everyone loved him. Not everyone. Someone hated him enough to kill him.'

Music started up behind them, a bass note pulsing through the house.

'Isn't love a bit like hate?' asked Dermot. 'That's what people say.'

Jude gave a small shiver. She needed to get away from this house.

A voice, Vin's voice, boomed out from the conservatory. 'Fill up your glasses, everyone; time for a toast.'

'We should go and drink to him,' said Dermot, standing up, his suit rumpled, swaying slightly on his feet. 'Come on.'

And Jude followed him.

CHAPTER FORTY-THREE

Jude found herself in a crowd just outside the conservatory. She could hear Vin but she couldn't see him.

'Has everyone got a drink?' he said. There was a murmured response. 'Can you all hear me?'

'That's a stupid question,' said a man beside Jude. 'If you can't hear him, you can't hear the question.'

'I'm not going to make a speech,' Vin continued. 'We've had the sad bit. We've mourned him. We've all shed tears. But that's not what Liam would have wanted. He would have wanted us to have a bloody good party. To drink a bit, or whatever, and then have a good dance and remember the good times we shared. So here's to Liam and the good times.'

There was another murmur and a clinking of glasses.

It was an opportunity to leave. Jude pushed through people she didn't recognise on her way to the door. Just before she reached it, she heard her name being called and looked around. It was Vin. She mumbled something about needing to get away.

'I understand that,' he said. 'But could we talk before you go?' He watched her, saw her hesitating, and gave a slight smile. 'It'll only take a minute. Come on, I'll show you something. I'm going to bring up some more wine.'

He took her by the arm and led her along the hall. With his other hand, he grabbed two clean wine glasses from a table. He pushed open a small wooden door under the stairs, flicked on a light switch and gestured to Jude to walk through. Inside the door were wooden steps leading down. There was a bare brick wall and she immediately noticed a musty, damp smell. He followed her, pushing the door shut behind him. The roar of the party became a murmur.

At the bottom of the steps, Jude looked around. The light was dim and patchy; the corners lay in pools of shadow. They were in a cellar that ran under the front half of the house. The floor was brick. She looked up and saw beams and planks. She could hear the creak of people moving above.

The room was piled with junk: fold-up chairs, a rusty barbecue, an unconnected washing machine, packing cases, tools and other objects that Jude couldn't even identify. Vin was pulling open the top of a cardboard box. He extracted a bottle of red wine.

'I need to bring some more up to the party,' he said. 'I thought we could try some first.' He unscrewed the top and poured red wine into both glasses. He handed one to Jude. He clinked his glass against hers and took a sip.

'A hundred years ago this space would have been full of coal. It would have been delivered by horse and cart and tipped through a hole at the end of the front path.' He looked around. 'Liam and I talked about making something of it. Liam thought it could be some kind of studio space. Now it'll be a project for the new owners, whoever they are.' He looked at Jude. 'You're not contradicting me. You're not saying, oh, but surely Danny will be able to keep the house.'

'It's not up to me. There's probably some way of keeping the house, if she really wants to.' Vin looked at her with a fixed expression that made her feel self-conscious. 'What?' she said.

He smiled.

'You're a woman of mystery,' he said. 'You're an object of fascination.'

Jude took a gulp of wine and it made her cough.

'I'm really, really not.'

'People keep saying to me: who is that woman? What does she want? And I don't know what to say to them.'

'You sound like the detective.'

Now he looked puzzled.

'Why? Why do I sound like the detective?'

'Because she asks me questions like that, why I'm involved in all of this.'

'And what do you say?'

'I say that I'm not involved.'

Vin laughed but not unkindly. 'For someone who's not involved, you certainly are here a lot.'

'I didn't even mean to be here for this. Erika asked me to help bring the flowers back from the funeral and then I keep being about to leave when . . .' Jude made a vague gesture with her free hand.

'People do things like luring you down to the cellar.'

'Yes, things like that.'

'You don't have to apologise for being here. I suppose I'm just curious what you make of us all.'

'That's a big question.'

'It's the day of our friend's funeral,' said Vin. 'It's a day for big questions.'

'Is that why you've brought me down here?'

'It's better to be in semi-darkness for conversations like this.'

Jude hesitated. She thought about saying something bland and meaningless, and then going back upstairs, into the light and music and away, but a feeling of impromptu recklessness rose up in her. So she answered him sincerely.

'When I came to the house for the first time, it felt like something I'd never really experienced. All of you living together, being so creative. I've lived with groups of people but it's never been quite like this. The way you make things and do paintings and stuff together. It felt – well, it felt marvellous. Or like a marvel.'

Vin smiled again. He had white, even teeth. 'You

said, when you came "for the first time". Is that what you still think?'

Jude took a sip of her wine and thought as she did so that she had better eat something before she left. Her head swam.

'Things obviously get much more complicated when you get to know people.'

'How do you mean? When you get to know them? Do you know us?'

'Not really. But I know there are tensions and conflicts in this house.'

'Like what?'

Jude drank some more red wine.

'It's just what happens with any group, and you lot turn out not to be so marvellous after all,' she said, only half-registering that she was being rude. 'For instance, Jan told me he was moving out.'

He frowned. 'I didn't know that. Why? What did he say?'

'I think he just needs somewhere more peaceful. But you should talk to him about it.'

'He should have talked to us,' said Vin. 'We could have sorted it out.'

'I don't think so.' She heard herself give a laugh. 'He believes you're all mad.'

'Oh, does he now?'

She told herself to stop talking.

'And that something is wrong with this house,' she said.

'Do you think that as well?'

But Jude didn't want to continue with this.

'Do you want me to take a couple of those bottles?' she said.

'To be continued,' said Vin.

'What do you mean?'

He took two bottles from the box and handed them to her. She clutched them awkwardly.

'This conversation.'

Jude wasn't at all sure that she wanted this conversation to be continued. She was glad to take the bottles and go back up the stairs.

CHAPTER FORTY-FOUR

When Jude got back to the ground floor, she put the bottles down on a shelf in the hallway. She would eat something to counteract the alcohol she had never intended to drink and then she would leave. She should have left at once. She should never have come in the first place.

She pushed her way through to the kitchen. Plates and bowls of food were laid out on every surface. Jude took a paper plate and heaped it with hummus and aubergine and rice and various salads and slices of bread. That would soak up the wine. She took it out into the garden, carefully avoiding looking to the right or to the left. As a result she bumped into someone, started to apologise and move on, and then noticed it was Erika.

She said sorry and hello and started to walk past her when she looked up at her face.

'Are you all right?'

Erika just shook her head. Jude saw that her eyes were brimming with tears and she clearly didn't trust herself to speak. She sniffed and took several deep breaths.

'Wait,' Erika said finally. 'Don't go away.'

Jude stood awkwardly as Erika ran back into the house. She re-emerged a minute later, clutching a bottle of wine and a glass.

'Come over here,' she said, and she led Jude to the side where there was a low garden wall. Jude put her plate of food down on the top of the wall with some regret. She was ravenous.

'I thought you might have gone.'

'I got myself something to eat first,' Jude said, pointing at her plate. 'Then I'm going. I'm not really sure why I'm still here. It's like the place won't let me out.'

'I'm glad you're still here. I've been wanting to talk to you,' said Erika. 'I don't think we've ever had a proper conversation.'

Jude mumbled something about how it was an emotional day for everyone.

'You've known Liam longer than any of us,' said Erika. 'You knew him as a teenager.'

'We lost touch, of course.'

'But you were boyfriend and girlfriend.'

Jude groaned.

'Was he your first?'

Jude was utterly taken aback by the starkness of the question. There didn't seem to be any room for ambiguity.

'It's not something I want to talk about with you,' she said.

It sounded curt, but Erika didn't seem to mind. She filled her glass with wine and took a gulp.

'I remember the intensity of those teenage relationships,' she said. 'I sometimes wonder if you ever feel anything as strongly as you do when you're sixteen, seventeen.'

'It was quite brief.'

'That doesn't mean anything. After all these years, you're the one he thinks of. You're the one he turns to.'

'I don't quite know why he did that.'

Erika looked round. 'God, I could do with a cigarette. I gave up a few years ago but at times like this I really miss it. Shall I go in and cadge a couple for us?'

'I don't smoke.'

Erika smiled knowingly. 'That's right, you're a doctor.'

'Actually, quite a lot of my doctor friends smoke,' said Jude. 'And my nurse friends.'

'But not you. You're sensible.'

Jude wasn't sure she liked being described as sensible. Erika took another gulp of her wine. She seemed well on the way to being drunk, and the party had only just begun.

'Anyway, I'm so glad you're here,' Erika said fervently, to Jude's confusion. 'I'm so glad you've become part of the household. It's such a strange, difficult time. I feel like you're someone I can talk to. You're a doctor. You must be used to people feeling they can tell you things that they can't tell other people.'

Jude was certainly used to strangers finding out

that she was a doctor and suddenly asking for an instant diagnosis about a pain in their back or a lump on their neck. She waited wearily to hear about Erika's intimate symptoms.

'We've got something in common,' Erika said in a low voice, looking around, as if to see if they were being overheard.

'Have we?'

'Isn't it obvious?'

Jude frowned. Was this a quiz? Was she meant to start guessing?

'Liam,' Erika said.

'Ah.'

Jude found that her immediate reaction was surprise: she would have thought that if Liam had had an affair with someone in the house it would have been Irina, flamboyant and theatrical and full of a wayward energy. When they had met before, Erika had struck her as being the more practical, phlegmatic member of the household. But it had been Erika calling Liam that night, when Jude had been at the cottage in Norfolk with Liam's phone.

'That's right.' Erika took another gulp of wine, as if she needed to slake her thirst. 'I haven't been able to talk to anyone about it. Not ever.' She looked Jude full in the face and shook her head. 'And no,' she said, as if in answer to a question Jude had posed silently. 'I haven't told Doc.'

Jude couldn't think of how to respond.

'I know what you're thinking,' said Erika.

Unlikely, Jude thought.

'How could we keep it secret in a house where everyone knows everything about each other? Danny had a difficult birth. She stayed in hospital for over a week. There were a couple of days when Doc was away. I was on my own and Liam was vulnerable and hurting. It didn't feel wrong. It didn't feel like being unfaithful. It was just two people comforting each other.'

Jude almost snorted. She took a sip of her wine to conceal the sense of shock and revulsion.

'I know what you want to ask,' said Erika. 'If it didn't feel wrong, then why was it a big secret? Why not tell Doc? Why not tell Danny?'

'Didn't you think they'd understand? That you were just comforting each other?'

Erika appeared not to notice the angry sarcasm in Jude's voice.

'To be honest, it wasn't that simple. It started out that way but it became like a kind of addiction. When Danny and Alfie came back from the hospital, it stopped, of course, but there was still something between us. We both knew it. So sometimes, just by chance, there'd be the opportunity and we couldn't resist.'

She put down her glass on the wall and, before Jude had a chance to retreat, Erika stepped forward to hug her. She felt the woman's warm, winey breath on her cheek, the tickle of her coarse blonde hair. She stood stiffly in the circle of Erika's arms, stretching her hand out so she didn't spill her wine. She didn't want to hug her back. She thought

283

about Danny in hospital with her new baby. Hadn't Liam felt like a piece of shit? Hadn't Erika? Apparently not.

What a household, she thought. Everyone with their secrets and their betrayals.

CHAPTER FORTY-FIVE

Jude left Erika abruptly and strode towards the house. She felt grubby, and wanted to go back to the flat and take her clothes off and shower, and never, not ever, come here again. It was a bad place, a place where anything could happen. There were no rules and no boundaries. There was no kindness here, she thought. It was a savage place.

Music was throbbing in the building, a deep bass thrum. Lights had been dimmed and someone had lit candles and placed them on high shelves so they threw guttering shadows. A few people were dancing. Someone handed Jude a glass and she drank from it without thinking. All her bones felt soft. She shouldn't drink any more, she thought, and lifted the glass to her mouth again.

'You think you've won.'

A woman's voice, clear and loud, cut through the music and the chatter. People nearby fell silent.

'You think you can just take Alfie away from us and we won't fight you.'

It was Tara, and she was clutching the little boy to her and facing Danny. Her face was fierce and her eyes like dark stones.

'Come on, love,' said Andy, putting his large hand on her sinewy arm.

'Yes, time for you to go, I think,' said Danny, smiling gently at Liam's mother. 'You probably need to sleep it off.'

'You nasty, two-faced, scheming bitch.'

Alfie stirred, opened his eyes, gazed round him.

'Give me my son,' said Danny, holding out her arms, her voice a sinister coo. 'Come to Mummy, Alfie.'

'I was always said he was too good for you.'

'He used to laugh about how you could never let go.' Danny's voice remained pleasant. She didn't seem to mind that everyone was watching; perhaps she even liked it. 'Some mothers, hey? I won't be like that with you, I promise.' She laid her long-fingered hand, heavy with rings, on Alfie's soft curls and he gazed up at her.

'You're a bad woman,' said Tara, her voice shaking.

'Yes, well, that's as may be.'

Danny took hold of her son and lifted him out of Tara's arms, while Tara tried to hold on to him. Jude shut her eyes for a moment in wretchedness as Alfie began to cry.

'It's okay,' Danny crooned. 'It's okay. Here's Mummy.' Her eyes surveyed Tara over the crown of Alfie's head.

'He didn't love you,' said Tara. 'He only stayed because of Alfie.'

'That's my darling boy,' said Danny, apparently

unmoved, though her eyes glittered in her pale face.

'He hated you.'

'Please, Tara.' Andy tugged at her arm.

'Mum.' It was Dermot, dishevelled, a stain down his shirt. 'That's enough. Everyone's listening.'

Tara wheeled round on him.

'Am I embarrassing you? Am I? Liam wouldn't have been embarrassed. He would have cheered me on.'

'You wish I'd died, not him,' said Dermot bitterly.

'That's not true,' said Andy helplessly.

'Isn't it? Mum?'

Suddenly he sounded like a small boy asking to be loved.

'What?'

'Is it true?'

'This is Liam's funeral,' shouted Tara. 'Liam's. My boy. He's dead. He's murdered. And you're standing here snivelling like a child, asking for my pity.'

'It's true, then?'

'Go away. I can't stand you looking at me like that.'

'No. You go,' said Danny in her low voice. She laid a hand on Dermot's shoulder. 'You go, Tara. Take her home, Andy.'

Andy nodded dumbly and put his arm round his wife. For a moment she stood rigid, then she wavered and crumpled against him, her face folding into lines of grief. Andy led her away. Jude could hear her sobbing in the hall.

'There,' said Danny. 'That's better. Are you all right, Dermot?'

'I don't know?' Dermot looked dazed. 'Am I?'

Then Danny saw Jude and smiled, though her face remained austere. 'Sorry about that. But she was right, you know, Liam probably would have enjoyed that little scene. He loved public arguments. Here, can you take Alfie for a few minutes? There's someone I need to talk to.'

She didn't wait for Jude to answer but placed Alfie's warm body into Jude's arms and walked away, swallowed up in the throng of dancers.

CHAPTER FORTY-SIX

Jude wasn't sure what to do. Surely Alfie needed to be put in his bed. He was obviously exhausted. She looked around and saw Doc approaching. His face was grim.

'What did you say to Erika?' he asked in a voice that was slightly slurred.

'Me?'

'She's upset.'

'Well, it is a funeral.'

'What was she talking to you about?'

'Ask her that,' said Jude. 'I think someone should put Alfie to bed right now.'

'You're playing a dangerous game, you know.'

'I'm not playing any kind of game.'

'Really?'

Without warning, Doc reached out a hand and placed it flat on her breast.

Jude stepped back sharply and heard a glass fall to the floor behind her and smash.

'I'm warning you. Go away, Doc.'

'I live here, remember? You go away.'

'Don't worry, I will. I'll go and I'll never come back, but first someone needs to take Alfie.'

'Good luck with that,' he said, and turned and walked off towards the kitchen.

Alfie shifted in her arms, whimpering slightly.

'Shit,' said Jude.

People were dancing, bodies were swaying in the dim, queasy light. Outside, the bonfire was blazing merrily and Jude could see figures in the garden throwing objects onto it with a kind of drunken euphoria. She thought she could make out Irina and, sure enough, when she pushed open the door to the garden, Irina was there. She had discarded her scorched green cape and was in a silvery sheath that made her look like a mermaid. She was clutching a guitar by its neck and, as Jude watched, lifted it up in readiness.

'Stop!'

Irina turned. 'What?'

'Are you going to burn that?'

'What if I am?'

'Is it the one Liam left you?'

'What if it is?'

A man on the other side of the fire lobbed in a ladder-backed chair with wicker seating. The flames briefly flared and Jude saw faces gleaming in the firelight, eyes watching. There was one she thought she had seen before – male, middle-aged, snub nose, small eyes – but she couldn't place it.

'He never loved me,' said Irina.

'I'm sure that's not true.'

Jude felt very tired and her head swam. People

around her came in and out of focus and behind her the music got louder, more insistent.

'Never, never, never. My dark star.'

'Don't burn the guitar. You'll regret it in the morning.'

Irina gave a shrill laugh. 'I regret everything in the morning. But then night comes round again.'

A second chair winged its way through the air and landed on the fire, sending up sparks and a hiss as the wicker caught.

In the sudden brightness she saw the man's face again, heard him laugh. A jolt of recognition went through her.

'Isn't that—?'

'It should have been me.'

'You mean—'

'He and Danny – puh.' She made a gesture, a hand slicing across her throat. 'But he humiliated me.'

'I don't understand.'

'Nor do I,' Irina said. 'Nor do I.'

'Can you take Alfie to bed please? I need to go home.'

As she said the words, Jude felt a sob lodge in her throat. She had no home any more. No work, no love, no place to be safe in.

'Sure.'

Irina held her arms out, the guitar dangling from one. She was standing on the rim of the fire, sparks crackling behind her. She looked frantic.

Jude hesitated. She looked at the fire and the wild woman, then at the little boy in her arms.

'Don't worry,' she said. 'I'll take him.'

'We've met,' she said to the man with a pug nose and rippled grey hair. He was wearing a flowery shirt, and his face was red in the firelight.

He focused on her with difficulty.

'You're the executor.'

It took a moment to put a name to the face, especially as it didn't seem to belong to this place, this occasion. Then the name came to her. Anthony Leary.

'What are you doing here?'

'I'm here to pay tribute. Why shouldn't I be?'

'I thought you hated him. And he hated you.'

'I wouldn't put it like that.' He laughed uneasily. 'When Vin invited me, I thought, good, let's put it behind us. Clean sheet.'

'Vin invited you?'

'Yeah. Why not?'

'Because it's weird to come to the wake of a man you fell out with and refused to pay? Because you were Liam's enemy not his friend, so how can you set foot in this house of people who are grieving for him?'

Leary smiled at her. His eyes gleamed and his small mouth was wet.

'They look to me like they're having fun. You should try it.'

Jude started to say something angry, then put

her head into Alfie's soft curls to stop herself. She wasn't Liam's guardian. If Vin and Danny could bear to have this pug-faced creep in the house, then who was she to object?

She manoeuvred herself and Alfie back through the conservatory, where Vin was standing on the table with his shirt undone, conducting the dancers. In the hall, she saw that some people were leaving, but the room leading off it was still tight with bodies.

'Right,' she said, and headed for the stairs, stepping across puddles of beer and upended bottles. There were several people sitting on the steps, including one young woman who was fast asleep, her mouth wide open, and Jude had to squeeze her way past them, the boy a dead weight in her arms.

'Please to pass,' said a voice above her.

Looking up, she saw Jan at the top of the stairs, wedged by large cases. He appeared to have put as many of his clothes as possible on his own body, and was wearing a quilted jacket beneath a thick coat, a wool hat on his head. He had a big rucksack on his back and his pink face was sweaty with heat and effort. The two figures seated a few steps down stood and pressed themselves against the wall. Jan hauled his cases down the stairs, banging them against the skirting boards.

'You couldn't wait,' said Jude.

Jan arrived at the foot of the stairs with a thump

and let go of the cases, kneading his hands together. He looked around.

'Not another day,' he said.

'Right. Bye then,' said Jude. 'Good luck.'

'I do not believe in luck.'

And he was gone. Jude mounted the stairs again.

She didn't know where Alfie slept. Her arms ached from holding him. She pushed at the door at the top of the stairs and it opened on to a bathroom. The bath was full, and a man was leaning over the sink. Jude muttered an apology and retreated. The door next to that was a small room with a lavatory and basin in it.

She took the landing to the left of the stairs. The door stood open and the light had been left on and Jude peered inside. It had unplastered walls and some of the boards had been ripped up so she could see copper pipes running the length of the room. Instead of curtains, blankets shielded the windows. It definitely wasn't Alfie's room; it couldn't be Erika and Doc's because she knew that they were at the top of the house, along with Jan. She looked at the canvas jacket and battered jeans chucked over a chair, the tools and manuals on the shelves, an empty bottle of vodka lying on its side, the overflowing ashtray: Vin's.

She'd been to the study overlooking the garden when she was going through Liam's papers, so she retraced her footsteps and knocked then pushed at the door on the other side of the bathroom, waited, stepped inside to darkness, fumbled with her hand for a light switch and found herself in a scene of vivid confusion. There were silky drapes that couldn't quite cover the flowering damp spreading along the walls; someone had decorated the ceiling with purple and yellow blotches that from where she stood looked like violent bruises. Garments had been tossed every which way, in a riot of colours. The bed was heaped with them. A small piano near the window was covered in tubs and tubes of make-up. Jude spotted a green cape with a charred hem. Irina.

Danny and Liam had kept the largest room for themselves. It had two windows with old blue shutters in need of repair, and a vast mottled wardrobe with a smashed door. Wallpaper hung in strips from one of the walls. The large mirror had a spiderweb crack at its centre. But the floorboards were beautiful polished wood, and taking up half of one wall was a charcoal drawing of a forest in winter that made Jude sigh with pleasure. The long rough shelves were dotted with tealights; clothes spilled out of drawers and a long linen coat hung over a chair. Jude could imagine Liam wearing it, loping along with his characteristic gait.

There was a rolled-up futon in one corner, but no cot or bed for Alfie. Jude very carefully laid the sleeping boy down in the centre of Danny's large bed and pulled a cover over him. He lay as if he had fallen from a great height, arms and legs flung out, breath puffing at his lips. She worried that if he woke, he might roll over and fall off the bed, so she put a pillow on either side of him, then turned to go.

He started to whimper, and she stopped. His eyes had flicked open and he was staring at her.

'Go back to sleep,' she whispered, and continued to tiptoe towards the door.

The whimpering grew louder, turned into a hiccupy sob, then another. Jude murmured to him, but his face screwed up and he opened his mouth loud and gave a howl.

Jude went back and sat on the bed. The howls subsided. He stared at her, as if making up his mind about how to proceed. She stroked his hair and made what she hoped were comforting sounds.

His eyes started to close and his breathing deepened. She waited a couple of minutes and then very gradually she straightened up. His eyes opened and his face puckered. His mouth opened again and he took a shaky, preparatory breath. She lay down on the bed beside him and he curled his fingers into her hair. Gradually she could feel rather than see that he was falling back into sleep.

She turned her head away from Alfie slightly. There was a bedside table, clearly home-made, a few inches from her, on which there was a pouch of tobacco, a razor, a book about sea birds, an oversized watch, some scattered coins, a happy deck of cards, and a little wooden whistle, also rough and hand-carved. This must have been Liam's side of the bed, where he'd lain night after night with Danny beside him, where he'd read, made love, argued, slept, dreamed his dreams.

It was so very strange and wrong and horribly sad to be lying where he had lain, with patterned wallpaper dripping off the walls and a drawing of trees so real she felt she could walk into it.

Beneath her, the music thudded.

Jude woke with a lurch that brought her to a sitting position before her eyes were open, and for a few seconds she had no idea where she was. Alfie was still fast asleep so she eased herself off the bed, fumbling for her phone to find out the time. It was a few minutes before two. She'd been asleep for hours. There was still music playing, but she could no longer hear voices or the clatter of glasses. She crept along the corridor to the bathroom and washed her face in cold water. Her suit was crumpled, her hair stood up in tufts and her eyes were puffy.

A man with a grey ponytail was asleep on the landing, curled up on himself and snoring slightly. Jude went down the stairs as quietly as she could manage. There were voices coming from the conservatory. She was trying to think where she'd left her bag. It wasn't on the hooks in the hall where coats hung, which was where she thought she'd put it. She peered cautiously round the door of the front room, which was empty of people. There were glasses and bottles everywhere, and an upturned bowl of the hummus she had made. No bag.

She turned towards the conservatory; she didn't want to see anyone but she needed her bag to get home. It had her wallet in it and the key to the flat. Danny came out, floating like a ghost towards her, her face quite calm. She didn't seem surprised to see Jude.

'Alfie's asleep on your bed,' said Jude, and suddenly felt a satisfying spurt of anger that burned away her awkwardness. 'He was completely exhausted and I couldn't find anyone to take care of him.'

'Good,' said Danny.

'Maybe you should check on him.'

'Maybe.'

'Are you all right?'

'I don't know, Jude. I just don't know.'

'Well, I need to go home, but I'm looking for my bag.'

Danny headed up the stairs and Jude took a quick look in the kitchen before going into the conservatory, where people were still dancing in the half-darkness, surrounded by empty bottles, smashed glasses, an overturned plant. There were figures in the garden, standing around the remains of the bonfire.

Dermot lurched towards her from the corner of the room. He looked awful, his face chalky and his eyes red-rimmed. There was a smudged circle of red lipstick on his cheek.

'Are you all right?'

'All right?' he said.

He lifted his fist and punched the wall violently, then staggered back at the pain, moving like a string puppet, jerky and articulated, towards the table that was pushed back on the wall. He was very drunk.

'You should go home,' said Jude. 'Or lie down, sleep it off. You don't look well. Are you staying here? Or shall I call an Uber for you?'

'No. No, no, no.' He sounded like an animal in pain.

'Please, Dermot, stop.'

'I won't,' he said. There was spittle on his lips and his dark eyes shone. 'My brother. I will not stop. You little cunt.'

'That's enough.'

People had stopped dancing and were looking across at them.

For a moment, Dermot looked as if he might crumple. His face was like the face of a small, terrified boy. He put his hand on the end of a long trestle table and closed his eyes, taking ragged breaths.

Then, without warning, his eyes snapped open and he turned sharply, bent down to seize the table with both hands, and violently upended it. For a moment, it was like a slow-motion film: objects lifting off from the toppling table and flying through the air. Bottles, glasses, bowls of food, a board of cheese and crackers, saucers heaped with cigarette stubs, knives, lit candles, jamjars full of flowers. Someone screamed. There was an explosion of noises, of chairs toppling, glass breaking, china shattering, things spinning across the floor in a widening arc. The pounding music stopped and there was a sudden silence. A woman lying in a heap by the garden doors began to sob.

'There,' said Dermot, but half-heartedly.

'Someone turn on the lights,' said Jude. 'There's broken glass.'

The light came on. Jude almost laughed out loud at the spectacular mess. Splinters of glass and broken bottles, multiple cans dribbling beer from their opened tabs, cigarette butts in sticky puddles of hummus and guacamole and chocolate mousse, oozing slabs of cheese and, scattered over it like some insane art installation, sticks of carrots and peppers and a few bright flowers.

'Wow,' said Vin, suddenly beside her. He sounded almost admiring.

'Oh my God!' wailed Irina, arriving from the garden. She fluttered her pale hands above her and her mouth made a perfect 'o'.

'You should go home now, Dermot,' Jude said. 'Get some sleep.'

'I can help clear up,' he muttered.

'Just go, mate,' said Vin.

'No hard feelings?' said Dermot to the room at large.

Vin clapped a hand on his shoulder.

'You know you're an idiot, right?' said Vin. 'But you're part of this mad little family.'

'I guess I needed to vent. Hard day. Liam's funeral.'

No one spoke. Everyone watched as Dermot

lurched sadly from the room. Jude stooped and picked a little squashy toy from the floor.

'We need to clear up the glass,' she said. 'It's everywhere.'

'Including my feet now,' said a large bald man, wading through the mess with his surprisingly delicate pink feet.

'Then don't walk it in! Jesus, stop!'

The woman lying on the floor lifted her head and spoke loudly and tragically.

'My leg is broken,' she said. 'It's very broken. It's completely broken.'

She started to yell, high and clear, like a kind of ululation.

'Really?' said Jude doubtfully.

'I'll get a broom and bin bags,' said Vin. He spoke cheerily, as if this was just in the normal run of a party.

'What happened?' Danny was standing in the doorway in a belted towelling robe, her face scrubbed bare of make-up.

'It was Dermot,' announced Irina. 'He turned the table upside down. He was upset,' she added unnecessarily.

'And drunk,' said Jude.

'Poor Dermot,' said Danny. 'What a day.'

Vin arrived with brooms and bin bags.

'Either help or get out into the garden,' he ordered them all. 'But mind the glass.'

Erika was pushing a mop round the room and Doc was picking up chairs. Irina sat on the floor.

'Here,' said Vin, and put a glass of whisky into Jude's hand.

Jude took a sip and then another. Its heat ran through her as if a fuse had been lit. Someone turned the music back on and Irina stood up and began to dance, a slow and writhing movement that Jude found disquieting.

'He was very drunk,' said Danny in her soft voice.

'He was,' said Jude. 'And upset.'

'Poor thing. Poor Dermot.'

'Yes.'

'Liam cast a long shadow.'

'I can see that.'

CHAPTER FORTY-SEVEN

'You all right?'

Jude hadn't been asleep. She was sitting in an armchair in the living room, feeling the last of the party subside around her. She heard people outside in the hall saying their goodbyes. She had felt tired earlier but now she was beyond that. She was fiercely awake, her mind racing. Sleep was now impossible. She was thinking about Nat, going over her feelings of suspicion and betrayal. At the very least, he had lied to her while refusing to forgive her for lying to him.

In her hyper-alert state, memories from their shared life were coming to her like slides being slotted one by one into a projector. Over-complicated explanations for nights he had been away from home; phone calls ended abruptly; sudden gestures of tenderness that now looked to her like hidden apologies. But perhaps this was just paranoia, she told herself. It didn't feel like paranoia, but like a sudden turn of the dial so that fuzzy images became clear.

She might have married him. A man who was cheating on her – or who she now believed might have been cheating on her, she corrected herself –

at the same time as they were planning the wedding. Had her life been an illusion, a fake? And if it had, how could she not have seen it? What did it say about her? So it was a lucky escape, really. She should be feeling grateful: why wasn't she feeling grateful?

She looked up to see who had spoken. It was Vin. He had been there with her and then he had gone away and now he had come back.

'I think I should go,' she said.

'Can I show you something first?' he said.

'Another cellar?'

'No.'

'What then?'

'That would spoil the surprise.'

He gestured for Jude to follow him. She hesitated visibly but he looked back and smiled and she thought: *Why not?* They walked up three flights of stairs. On the top floor, Vin reached up and from the ceiling pulled down a foldable ladder that led up to an opening. He clambered up and Jude, with some trepidation, followed him into the darkness. Vin switched a light on and Jude looked around.

'All right,' she said. 'It's not a cellar this time, it's an attic.'

'We're not there yet,' said Vin.

At the far end, the roof sloped down to the floor. In it was a large dormer window. Vin unfastened a catch and pull one half inwards. He reached a hand back towards Jude.

'What?' she said.

'It's okay,' he said.

She took his hand and he led her out into the darkness and the fierce cold hit her so that it almost hurt her face. She could hardly see anything. She couldn't even make out what she was standing on.

'Is this a terrace?'

'It's not anything. It's just somewhere we come up at night, for the view. Look.'

She could see him faintly gesturing. She could see the lights of east London and beyond them, against the sky, the glow of the Shard and Canary Wharf. She could feel Vin standing beside her.

'In daylight you can see all the way to the Surrey Hills,' he said.

Jude saw the flash of flame from Vin's lighter and then the glow as he lit whatever it was he was lighting. She saw the glow of it and smelled the familiar smell. He handed it to her and she contemplated it and then took a drag and handed it back to him. She looked around. She felt dizzy and also nervous.

'Is there a railing?'

'There's nothing. We thought of turning this into somewhere we could come and drink on sunny days. But we didn't and we probably won't now. So be careful where you step. It's a long way down.'

She looked upwards. It was a cold clear night and she could see the stars. It was almost like not being in London at all.

'So what do you make of it all?'

'All? Life, the universe and everything?'

'All right,' he said. 'What did you make of this evening?'

Jude opened her mouth to speak and then stopped. There was too much to say – about Tara, about Erika, about Dermot, about Danny – but she wasn't sure this was the right time, standing on a roof with a man she wasn't sure she liked and had no reason to trust.

'It was an intense day,' she said. 'The funeral was intense in one way and the party was intense in another.'

Vin laughed.

'That's a diplomatic way of putting it. When you came here, you didn't know what you were letting yourself in for. This household is a bit complicated.'

She turned to Vin. She could only see his silhouette against the sky. His tone sounded more serious than she'd heard from him before, but it was still disconcerting talking to someone when you couldn't see their expression, and when a few steps away the roof ended.

'It's strange. I knew Liam, in a way and a long time ago, when we were barely more than children, though we thought we were so grown-up. And now I know all of you. In a very limited kind of way. But I never saw Liam with any of you. I never saw him with Danny or with Alfie or with the rest of you. I keep trying to picture it.' Jude paused. She wasn't sure of the right question to ask. 'What did you think of Liam and Danny? As a couple?'

'I don't know how to answer that. I don't think you can ever judge a relationship from the outside.'

'But you lived with them. You saw them every day. You saw them at the breakfast table.'

'You know Liam and you've met Danny. They're not like everyone else.'

He passed the joint back to her and she took another drag and passed it back to him.

'But I've noticed what you're not saying.'

'What am I not saying?'

'The sort of thing that people say about couples. That they were wonderful together. That they were fun. That they were meant for each other.'

'They could be fun. But they were like everyone else. They had their problems.' Jude felt Vin's hand on her back. 'What about you? How are you doing on this strange day in this strange house?'

'I don't really know how I'm doing,' said Jude slowly, dreamily. 'And I don't know what I'm doing. A few weeks ago I was thinking about my job and my wedding. Now I'm on leave from my job. The wedding is off. Earlier today I learned that my fiancé was being unfaithful. My old teenage boyfriend has been murdered. I'm in charge of his will. And it's the middle of the night and I'm half-drunk on the roof of a house in wherever I am.'

'In Walthamstow,' said Vin, and she could hear the laughter in his voice. 'And it's not such a bad place to be.'

'You must all be so sick of me. Liam's been

murdered and nobody knows who did it and suddenly I'm here interfering with everything. I'm sick of me.'

She looked around. She could see the lights, but she couldn't see where the roof ended. It would be so easy to miss a step and fall three storeys on to the concrete. She would be found with alcohol and illegal substances in her blood. A doctor who was on unofficial suspension because of erratic behaviour, who had recently broken up with her fiancé, who – a few hours earlier – had been told of his betrayal, who had just been at the funeral of her first love. She felt the soft touch of Vin's hand on her back. It would take the smallest nudge and nobody would bother to investigate.

'We're not sick of you,' Vin said.

'Don't you just want it to go back to normal?'

'I think it's a bit late for that.'

The large shape of Vin beside her moved closer, she felt his breath on her face then his hand touching her cheek and his lips on her lips. Her first reaction was surprise followed by a strange detachment. She pulled back slightly.

'Do you want me to stop?'

Did she want him to stop? She didn't know what she wanted. She didn't care. She wanted to stop thinking and to stop feeling and to stop remembering. She leaned back into him and kissed him and tasted the alcohol and the weed and smelled a scent she didn't recognise.

Neither of them spoke and she let him take him her by the hand and lead her back in through the window. They both clambered down the ladder and then he led her along the corridor and down the stairs to his room at the back of the house, the one she had glimpsed earlier when she was looking for a place to lie Alfie down. He kicked the door shut and they were in complete darkness except for the faint blur of the window in the far wall. He pushed her into the room until she felt the bed behind her and sat back and he was half on top of her and they were kissing and then fumbling with each other's clothes.

She wanted to lose herself and be reckless, but she couldn't stop herself thinking about it all as she was doing it. She was being kissed and caressed, but she also was unable to kick her shoes off and had to stop and bend over and unlace them. As Vin pulled at her trousers and she felt them slide over her thighs and knees, she couldn't stop herself from remembering that these were the clothes she had selected for the funeral. She knew that she was a bit drunk and a bit stoned and that very possibly she wasn't in her right mind. Would she be allowing this to be done to her if she were stone-cold sober?

Finally, she felt like a swimmer letting go and allowing herself to sink under the water. She gave herself up to the sensation and it wasn't clear what kind of sensation it was, whether it was pleasure or confusion or desperation or just a relief from the pain and anxiety. It was all strange and dark with no sense of time or space.

Afterwards it felt like coming round from an anaesthetic into a waking that was itself a kind of confusion. Where was she? What had she done? What should she do? She was aware of a slow breathing beside her. Vin was asleep. Then she was asleep too.

In her dreams, someone was calling out for Daddy. A childish, piping voice with a question in it.

'Daddy?'

Jude half-opened her eyes. A small figure stood at the side of the bed, staring at them both.

'Alfie?'

'Daddy?'

'Go back to bed, big man,' groaned Vin. 'Away with you now.'

And Alfie disappeared, as if he had been a dream, except Jude could hear him softly shuffle along the hall.

CHAPTER FORTY-EIGHT

Greyness.

Jude felt it before she saw it. Her eyelids felt stickily joined together and she had to rub her eyes to open them. She didn't know what time it was, but it was clearly day now, which meant what? Eight? Nine? The window was thick with condensation. The room was stiflingly hot with a damp, stale smell. Her skin was clammy. She tried to swallow but her mouth was dry.

Vin was turned away from her, breathing slowly and heavily. His back was like a mound of flesh, hairy and glistening with beads of sweat.

Jude was overwhelmed by wave after wave of repulsion. She held the back of her hand up to her mouth. She was on the verge of vomiting and had to make herself breathe and count the breaths slowly until the sensation receded. She was disgusted by everything but mostly she was disgusted by herself. She thought of Vin on top of her, inside her, and it made her gag. How could she have done this? How could she have let it be done to her? What was wrong with her?

She needed to get out and away as quickly as

possible without anyone seeing. She would get back to the flat, have the longest shower of her life, wash all the clothes she was wearing, or throw them all away, that would be better, and try to pretend that none of this had ever happened.

She slid out of the bed. First she needed to find her clothes, and then get dressed and away without disturbing Vin. She tiptoed across the room and looked around. She had to get on her hands and knees to retrieve the different items of clothing. Somehow a sock had got under the bed and she had to reach for it. When she stood up, Vin was sitting up in the bed, grinning at her.

'It's down the hall,' he said.

'What?'

'The bathroom.' He pointed at a chest of drawers next to the window. 'There's towels in the bottom drawer.'

Jude thought for a moment. She so hated the easy intimacy of Vin's tone that she couldn't think straight. She hated the idea of him seeing her, standing naked in the ghastly cloudy morning light of his bedroom. All right, she decided. She pulled out a towel from the drawer, wrapped it around herself and went outside and along the corridor. The door was locked.

'Just coming,' a voice said.

Before she could respond or do anything, the door opened and Erika emerged in a funk of steam, pink-faced in a dressing gown. She smiled know-ingly at Jude.

'Good party,' she said.

Jude just walked past her and closed the door. There was a rudimentary shower in the bath and the water wasn't much more than a trickle, but she washed herself as best she could. When she re-entered the bedroom, Vin was standing in the middle of the room in boxer shorts, buttoning a checked shirt. He looked at Jude appraisingly.

'We could go back to bed,' he said.

Jude felt she couldn't even look at him.

'I've got to go.'

He stepped forward and put his arms round her. He slipped one hand inside the towel and ran it down her damp back. The towel came unfastened and she shook herself free of him and stepped back, clutching the towel against her. He smiled at her and she felt it like it was scalding water being poured over her. He leaned close to her and she thought, almost with horror, that he was going to nuzzle her or kiss her. But what he did was even worse. He whispered into her ear.

'I know you fucked him,' he said.

'What?'

He leaned back and looked at her with a kind of ebullience.

'All that talk about just seeing him once and doing him a favour. Did you think anyone believed that?'

'What are you talking about?'

'Don't get me wrong,' he said. 'I don't blame

you. Or him. Not after last night. I mean, it was fun, wasn't it?' he said.

Jude stepped away from him. She bent down and picked up her knickers and pulled them on, trying to keep the towel wrapped around her.

'This was a mistake.'

'Don't say that. You're beautiful. A class act. You should loosen up a bit. Let yourself enjoy life.'

Jude found herself unable to reply to this. She felt that if there had been a heavy object to hand she would have hit him with it, yet he hadn't forced himself on her. She had done it. She had given in. Getting dressed in her crumpled and stained grey suit in front of his gaze felt so ghastly and took so long. She had to sit on the bed to fasten up her shoes. When she had finished, she stood up and made herself look at him.

'It was the wrong time,' she said.

Vin smiled again. 'It didn't feel wrong to me. I'll always remember the feel of you. The taste of you. You're part of the family now.'

She flinched in recoil and then looked at him properly, big and fleshy, standing over her. It was like he was an animal who had left his mark on her. She turned and opened the door and left. As she walked down the stairs she heard his bare feet padding behind her.

CHAPTER FORTY-NINE

'We need coffee,' said Vin as they reached the bottom of the stairs.

'No.' Jude spoke more sharply than she had intended. 'I need to get my bag and coat and then I'm going.'

'Suit yourself.'

He smiled at her, friendly and at ease, then ambled towards the kitchen.

Jude's coat was still on the hook in the hall but her bag wasn't in the living room and she had no idea where she had left it.

She went quietly into the conservatory, praying there would be no one in there. To her relief it was empty. Discarded items of clothing were strewn around; a silky pair of tights was draped over the edge of a framed print and a beautiful cashmere jacket lay coiled among a plate of chocolate profiteroles. The branches of greenery she'd carried in yesterday – was it only yesterday afternoon? – were already withering. Pools of wax from burnt-out candles congealed on the window-sills.

But she couldn't see her bag.

She pressed her face to the glass door. Outside, it was misty and drizzling; the bonfire was a nasty smouldering mess with half-burnt sheets of paper lying in curls at its edge. She could make out the remains of the chairs that had been hurled on there last night.

Her bag must be in the kitchen, which was where Vin was. Where she didn't want to be. She took a gulping breath, stood up straight and pushed open the door.

'Oh,' she said.

Vin was in there, standing near the hob carving doorstep slices from an oversized loaf of wholemeal bread, seemingly oblivious to the mess all around him.

But so was Danny, sitting at the table with Alfie on her lap and a mug of coffee cradled in both hands. Her hair was pulled back into an intricate coil, and she was wearing baggy pinstripe trousers and a sage-green cardigan, buttoned up to her neck.

'Good morning, Jude,' she said with a horrible composure. 'Would you like some breakfast?'

'No,' she said. 'Thank you.'

She was violently hot and felt that her face must be burning.

'Jude is keen to leave,' said Vin, inserting several slices of bread under the grill.

Alfie was banging his spoon on the table.

'I just need my bag, my keys. I think it must be in here somewhere.'

She gazed around the room despairingly, at the stacks of dirty plates and pans, the glasses, many of which were still half-full, at the bowls of leftover food – soggy cake and limp potato wedges, mashed avocado that had turned grey and watery.

The kitchen door opened behind her.

'Morning,' said Doc's voice. 'Hello, Jude. I didn't know we had a guest.'

Jude saw the look on his face as he glanced from her to Vin, a smile creeping over his face. She remembered the way he had laid his hand flat against her breast last night. Nausea rose in her and she swallowed it back. Her skin prickled.

'I'm just going,' she said.

'Surely you can have some breakfast,' said Doc. 'Mop up the alcohol. I need to, anyway.'

He sat at the table, ruffled Alfie's hair, then messily poured granola into a bowl, before adding several spoonfuls of yoghurt.

'No, thank you,' said Jude. She felt like she was trying to impersonate a normal human being and failing.

'Coffee?' asked Danny sympathetically. 'You probably didn't get much sleep.'

'I don't want coffee. Or anything.'

'Aren't you coming to the interment then?'

She'd forgotten about that.

'I can't.'

'Shame.'

'I just need my bag.'

She turned to go and almost bumped into Irina,

who floated into the kitchen in a long black dress and with bare feet, her red hair in a single muscular plait.

'Jude? Jude! Well, where did you sleep last night, I wonder?'

Jude mumbled something, but Irina put up her hand.

'Don't tell me. Let me guess. It's not very hard, though. Actually, I thought I heard noises. But I told myself someone was just being sick in the bathroom.'

Jude had to stop herself from putting her hands over her ears. Her face felt rubbery from the effort of trying to look coolly indifferent.

'I'm just going.'

Irina didn't budge from the doorway.

'Vin,' she said exuberantly, as the smell of burning toast filled the room. 'Oh, Vinny, my man!' Her tone was a mixture of gloating and belligerence.

'You're embarrassing Jude,' said Vin. 'She's not used to our ways.'

He took a huge mouthful of toast and marmalade and crunched it noisily. Jude couldn't bear it any longer. She didn't care about her bag, her wallet, her keys; she just needed to get out of here. She pushed past Irina and Erika.

'It's in my bedroom,' called Danny. 'Your bag.'

Jude ran up the stairs and into Danny's room. Sure enough, there was her bag on the bed. It was gaping open and the wallet was also unzipped. Danny hadn't bothered to hide that she'd been going through Jude's things.

Jude grabbed the bag, checked her keys were still in there and ran back down the stairs, almost tripping in her anxiety to be gone. She wrenched open the front door and found herself gazing into the face of Leila Fox.

The detective's expression was incredulous.

'Are you here for the interment?'

But as she spoke, she was taking in Jude's stained and wrinkled funeral suit, her unbrushed hair, her chalky, morning-after face.

Vin came down the hall. He was holding his toast and marmalade in one hand, but with the other he laid a hand on Jude's shoulder as if he owned her. She slapped it angrily away.

'I'm leaving,' she said.

Leila Fox inclined her head.

'I see,' she said.

'You don't,' said Jude.

'You probably do,' said Vin, and laughed.

'Hold on one moment,' the detective said to him. 'There is something I need to ask everyone in the house. I'll be back in a minute.'

She took Jude's elbow and steered her out of the house, on to the road.

'Are you completely insane?'

'I don't know what you mean.'

'Stop it! Right now!' Then the anger went out of her face and she gave a small sigh. 'Is this because of what I told you – though I didn't actually tell you – about your fiancé?'

Jude met the detective's grey eyes.

'Maybe,' she said in a small voice. 'A bit.'

'I shouldn't have said anything.'

'I'm glad you did,' said Jude. 'I needed to know. The worst thing is not knowing. As for the rest, for last night . . .' She tried to smile, but her face felt tight. 'Don't worry. It won't happen again. I'm never going back to that house. I know it's a bad, bad place.'

CHAPTER FIFTY

Jude ran, her shoes hurting her feet and her bag bumping against her hip and her breath coming in gasps. When she reached the end of the road, she stopped by a huge plane tree and leaned against its mottled trunk.

'Stupid,' she said. 'Stupid idiot.'

She needed to have a long hot shower. She needed to clean her teeth until her gums bled. She needed mug after mug of black coffee.

She thought of the grim basement flat and the hissing cat with its unfriendly green eyes.

'Shit,' she said.

Tears were seeping from her sore, tired eyes. She started to walk again, under the little bridge and out on to the marshes. It was raining steadily; the buildings behind her were blurred and indistinct, the grass was turning to churned mud, and the skies were low and dark. One of those days that will never get quite light, she thought, and then she tried to remember what day it actually was. Wednesday, she decided: the grimy centre of a wretched week.

She wandered slowly along a rough path, then

wound back on herself. Not really knowing where she was heading. Her eyes were stinging, her head aching. She felt unsteady on her feet. The rain fell harder. She stopped under a tree to protect herself; the rain hammered on its glossy evergreen leaves.

She was drenched. The events of the night were like the jumbled pieces of a dream, with their own internal logic. Episodes stood out with a lurid brightness in Jude's mind, like spot-lit vignettes in a murk. Tara and Danny snarling at each other, fighting over Alfie and over the love of a man who was dead. Erika's confession, if confession was the right word for something she obviously didn't regret. Doc's baleful stare and his hand on her breast. Dermot upending the laden table, a look of misery and triumph on his face. Irina wild and vengeful by the bonfire. Danny regally calm, stalking the party like a tragic ghost. Vin standing on the table conducting the dancers. Vin leading her to the roof. Vin leading her to his room. Vin saying she was part of the family now.

Jude pressed her hand over her eyes, wanting to stop the whirl of thoughts. When she at last opened them, she was met by a strange spectacle. Across the stretch of muddy grass, she could see Liam's mourners walking together towards the burial site. They were too far away to make out their expressions, but she could see that they were holding hands and were proceeding through the pouring rain in a linked chain, Irina's dress trailing through the churned mud. Vin was at the back,

Alfie in a carrier on his shoulders, and Danny at the front; both held an enormous umbrella. From where she stood, Jude could hear they were singing.

They fought each other, betrayed each other, slept with each other and abandoned each other; sometimes they hated each other and it was even possible that one of them was a murderer – and yet now they walked hand in hand to a burial, chanting mournfully together.

She watched until the line of figures disappeared over the brow of the hill. The rain was easing, and as she left her shelter, the grey sky broke open and a streak of pale turquoise appeared.

Soon the mortal remains of Liam Birch would be underground. Jude, who had thought she would go straight back to the flat to shower and sleep, found herself making a detour to the place where he had been killed. It was only a ten-minute walk, past the reservoirs and along the path towards the wilder area. There, just off the path, were the still-flattened brambles and the remnants of the shrine that Jude had seen when she had first come here. The flowers were all dead now, except for one bunch of orange dahlias that looked almost fresh. She wondered who had left them, and half-wished she had brought something herself.

For years, Liam Birch had been untarnished in her memory, an abstract version of a man, beautiful and wild, quixotic in his generosity to her. In the past few weeks, she had come to know another far less shiny version. He had been selfish, heedless and cruel. He had cheated on Danny while she lay in hospital with their newborn son. He had hurt people and hadn't cared. As she stood and looked at the patch of ground where he had died, Jude held both of these men in her mind, all the contradictions that had made him squalid, beguiling and dangerous.

She walked on and the riding centre came into view. Beyond it, the skating rink.

Skating. Jude stopped in her tracks and looked back at the way she had come – at the path that led from here to the murder site, and from there across the marshes to Liam's house.

She forced herself to concentrate, to remember. She heard Danny saying crossly that Vin and Irina had promised to look after Alfie but hadn't turned up.

I was going skating. It's my thing. I go every Saturday afternoon with my sister, come rain or shine. We've done it for years.

What time had that been? Jude screwed up her eyes in the effort of remembering. Danny had asked her the time; Jude had looked at her mobile. Twenty to five: that was it. Danny had said if she didn't hurry, she would miss her slot, had thrust Alfie into Jude's arms, seized a torch and raced from the room.

Twenty to five. Presumably her slot would be something like between five and six.

When had Liam been killed? She didn't know. She was sure that Leila Fox had never said. She knew that his body had been dragged off the path into the patch of brambles where it was found by a dog walker late on Saturday night.

Jude walked to the skating rink and stood at the entrance. She looked at the map on her phone, then pulled up walking directions to Liam's house. She followed the instructions back along the path she had come from, and soon she was standing once more beside the forlorn shrine. It was the only route for Danny to take, every Saturday, come rain or shine. Right past the place Liam had been stabbed to death.

Jude walked all the way to the flat. By the time she arrived she had large soft blisters on the soles of her feet. She eased off her shoes, fed the cat and watered the plants. Then, before she even took off her damp grubby clothes or filled the kettle, she called Leila Fox.

'What time was Liam killed?'

There was a sigh at the other end of the phone.

'What are you up to now, Jude?'

'Do you have a time?'

'Not in the way you mean. But we do have a window: it was after five in the afternoon and at least two hours before ten-thirty in the evening, when his body was found; in other words, eight-thirty.'

Jude was thinking frantically. After five meant

that it couldn't have been when Danny was expected to be on her way to her skating lesson. But it could have been after, when on other days she would be on her way home across the dark marshes.

'Are you going to tell me why you are asking?' said the detective.

'He was killed on the path leading from the skating rink towards the Walthamstow Marshes.'

'Yes? And?'

'On a Saturday evening. Which is when Danny always goes skating with her sister.' There was a silence. Jude pressed on. 'Danny would have been right there. Right on the very spot.'

There was another silence.

'Don't you see?'

'Jude,' said Leila Fox, sounding angry now. 'How stupid do you think we are?'

'What?'

'Do you think that you, Jude Winter, are coming up with things we haven't considered. Seriously? Do you think we haven't investigated the movements of Danny Kelner on the day of Liam Birch's murder, and the rest of the household for that matter?'

'So where was she?'

'She wasn't anywhere near the place.'

'But she goes skating every Saturday.'

'Not that day.'

'Why? Where was she?'

'Take my word for it, Jude. She didn't murder

Liam Birch. Or actually, don't take my word for it. Look it up on YouTube.'

'YouTube?'

'I need to get back to work.'

CHAPTER FIFTY-ONE

A search for Danny Kelner first produced a short film about tattooing. Danny was talking while drawing a swan on the back of a young blonde woman. It wasn't what she was looking for, but Jude couldn't stop herself watching a few minutes of it. She had always felt that she didn't really have any creative skills. She couldn't draw, she couldn't play the piano. Danny was creating art, but this was art on human skin and there was no room for error. She couldn't rub a line out and do it again. And all the time she was talking to the woman, explaining what she was doing, and also talking to someone behind the camera. She explained the significance of swans as an image of purity and she talked about her use of colour.

She was good at this, Jude thought. Also, she was so striking, so charismatic. No wonder she and Liam had been drawn to each other.

Jude looked down at the clothes she was wearing. She raised her arm and sniffed her sleeve. It reeked of smoke and alcohol and whatever the smell is that comes from clothes that had been worn at a party, that had been taken off in the middle of the night and then put back on again in the morning.

She felt horribly contaminated. She couldn't bear it for another moment. She pulled her suit off and crammed it into the bin, then took off the rest of her clothes and pushed them into the washing machine. She stood under the shower and washed her hair and her body, scrubbing at it until she felt sore. She only stopped when the water turned cold. She rubbed herself down with the towel and dressed quickly in baggy jeans and a sweater.

She picked up her phone again and scrolled down. There: that was it. It was labelled Firework Night and had been put up by someone called Nico. It was almost unwatchable. People were dancing and it felt like the person filming them was also dancing. The image was juddering and shifting. It was night-time and the dancers were either illuminated by the rippling light of the fire or turned into silhouettes. But Jude clearly recognised the faces of Danny and Vin and, she thought, briefly, Irina. Sometimes Danny seemed lost in the moment, her arms held above her head, moving to the rhythm. She was a beautiful, sinuous dancer. Another thing she's good at, Jude thought to herself.

At one point, Danny noticed she was being filmed and gave a broad smile and said something inaudible. The little film lasted just under fifteen minutes, but there were repeated cuts and the music changed. Danny was seen over and over again.

When it was done, Jude thought for a moment. She rang Leila Fox.

'I watched the film,' she said.

'Good. You didn't really need to ring and tell me that.'

'There are gaps,' Jude said. 'Cuts.'

'What do you mean?'

'There are gaps in the film. She could have been filmed and then left the party and then come back and been filmed dancing again.'

'Please,' said the detective.

'Isn't that true?'

She heard a deep breath being drawn.

'I don't need to justify myself to you, Jude. But just this once: the party in question was in Brixton, which is a long way from the marshes and would have taken Danny a good hour to get to. Multiple witnesses attest to her arriving shortly after five forty-five, which was when the fireworks started. A colleague watched the full version, which is time-coded and extends over a period of more than two and a half hours, between six p.m. and eight-thirty p.m. Danny Kelner is repeatedly visible.'

So Danny's alibi covered almost exactly the stretch of times during which the pathologist had said Liam had died.

'It's possible she could have left and returned,' Jude said lamely.

'It's not possible.'

'Don't you think it's a bit convenient?'

'What?'

'I guess that one of the main things you do when you do murder investigations is that you ask the suspects where they were and normally it'll be something like, I was watching TV or I was going for a walk or I was having a drink with so-and-so. But this time you've got someone actually being filmed at the same time as the murder.' When Jude finished, there was silence. 'Sorry, are you still there?'

'I'm still here.'

'What do you think about that? Don't you think that Danny's alibi is *too* good?'

'You were just saying that it wasn't good enough. Now it's *too* good. What does that even mean?'

'How many people have photographic evidence proving they couldn't have done it?'

There was a silence.

'Well?' Jude asked.

'I'm just hearing the bit where you say, "proving they couldn't have done it".'

'You don't see my point?'

'Before I answer that, do you mind if I ask *you* a question?'

'No. I mean, no, I don't mind.'

'What were you doing last night?'

Now it was Jude's turn to pause.

'It was complicated. Things got confused. I'm not proud of it.'

'I don't need to justify myself to you and you don't need to justify yourself to me. But if I were a friend of yours, I would probably be trying to help you at a time like this. Do you have friends?'

'Yes.'

She thought of her friends, of the life she had been living just a few weeks ago. Happiness and sociability and a thick crowd of hopes and plans. She thought of how quickly things could fall away and be lost, and the ache in her chest almost made her gasp.

'I think you should talk to them. But those people in Liam's house. They're not your friends.'

Jude started to speak in reply, then she realised the line was dead. Leila had hung up.

CHAPTER FIFTY-TWO

Jude walked very slowly into the bedroom, which was dark and cold and smelled of damp. The rest of the day stretched ahead of her. And then the next day, and the next.

She looked at her phone, all the missed calls and the unanswered messages. She would look at them all later. She lay down on the bed and closed her eyes. She felt tiredness chewing away at her thoughts. She wanted to sleep and not wake until – until what? Until this was all just a terrible dream and she would wake up and be back in her old life: before Liam came and found her, before Nat had fucked another woman, before she had entered the house in Walthamstow.

Her phone was ringing. She opened one eye and saw it was Dee. She didn't move and the phone rang out. After a few seconds, it rang once again. Dee wasn't giving up. Jude stretched out a hand and turned her mobile off.

She curled herself up and closed her eyes again. Perhaps she slept. The sky outside looked darker. Then she heard a sound. The doorbell was ringing. On and on. She didn't open her eyes. She was too tired and too defeated and she didn't want to get up, or put one foot in front of the other, or speak words. She couldn't face the detective with her shrewd eyes, nor could she face her friends and pretend she was all right. Her mouth was dry but it felt too much effort to get up and find a glass and fill it with water.

The doorbell sounded again. Jude curled into herself more tightly and pulled a pillow across her face. Eventually it stopped.

She lay in the silence. Outside was the ceaseless rumble of traffic. Sometimes she heard footsteps from the flat above. The cat miaowed outside the door. She heard the cat flap rattle.

When she woke it was dark. There was the sound of rain falling. Had it ever rained as much? She was cold and parched and needed to pee.

She made her way into the bathroom without turning on any lights, sat on the lavatory and put her face in her hands. She didn't know what to do. She didn't know the way out of this place she had come to.

She sat like that for a long time, breathing through the cup of her hands, but eventually she stumbled back to the bed again, took off her jeans and sweater and climbed under the covers.

She lay awake in the dark and then she slept again, and when she opened her eyes it was light outside. She ought to close the curtains but she couldn't make the effort to climb out of bed again so she simply huddled further into the cave of the duvet.

Things stirred in her mind like the vague, fragile shapes of a dream. People melted into each other: Liam when he was still a boy, when he was a man, when he was dead and the shrine of dead flowers marked the spot where somebody had sunk a knife into him. She imagined his astonishment; he must have thought he was immortal. Danny, with her tattoo of tears on her calm face. Vin. She didn't want to think about Vin. Or she didn't want to think about herself, drunk and stoned and self-hating, letting him claim her. Doc's hand on her breast. Dermot gazing at the havoc he had caused, with a hangdog look on his face. Irina dancing by the bonfire.

Nat who she had loved and Nat who she didn't love any more, didn't even know any more. He had dissolved and in his place was a stranger with a self-righteous face and a sneering voice.

Her life had been a bubble and she had burst it.

She wondered what day it was. Yesterday had been Wednesday, when Liam had been buried in his wicker basket with his boots on top. She pictured the household walking across the marshes hand in hand and chanting.

Was it Thursday then? Or maybe it was Friday. But it didn't really matter what day, or whether it was morning or afternoon or night, because time was no longer a river carrying her forward but a thick sludge. She heard the cat outside, miaowing. It needed feeding. The plants needed watering.

She slept again, or at least she drifted in that murky world between sleeping and waking. Faces and figures and a thudding heart; the sound of rain.

Someone was ringing the doorbell again. On and on. Like a drill.

It stopped.

Silence again, and then something was making a noise at the window. Tap tap tap. She turned towards it and opened her eyes a crack.

Through the smear of her stupefied sleep-soaked exhaustion, she saw a face.

Her mother's face pressed against the window, mouth open and hair drenched. She looked terrified, but when she saw Jude looking at her, her expression changed. She put both palms against the glass, then banged them. She was calling something.

Jude groaned. She sat up and went to the window, heaved it open.

'Oh, Judith, my darling!'

'Mum? What are you doing in the garden?'

'Your neighbour let me climb over his fence. Let me in, for God's sake.'

Jude nodded. She felt dazed and unreal. She turned to leave the room but her mother called her back.

'Put something on first!'

Jude looked down at her naked body. She was

wearing only knickers. She pulled on her jeans and sweater and went to the garden door, unbolted it and yanked it open to a rush of cold, wet air. Her mother stepped over the threshold and banged the door shut behind her.

'Mum,' she said again. She felt excruciatingly ashamed and wanted to hide somewhere.

'Oh, sweetie,' said her mother, with a catch in her voice.

She was wet through, her hair sticking to her skull, her coat dark with rain.

'What's going on? Has something happened? Is Dad all right?'

'He's fine. I was worried sick. I've been calling and calling and you never picked up, and then your friend Dee called. She said she couldn't get hold of you and nor could anyone else. She was about to dial 999.'

'That's crazy.'

'It's not crazy. It's what friends do. So here I am,' said her mother with a stuttery laugh. 'In case you need rescuing.'

'I don't,' said Jude.

But she did. And she saw in her mother's face as she looked at her that she did. She wanted to hide herself, not have to see such tender concern. She turned away.

'What day is it?' she asked.

'It's Friday.'

No wonder she felt hollowed out. When had she last eaten?

'The car's parked outside,' said her mother. 'Illegally. Let's go before I get a ticket.'

'Go?'

'You're coming home for a few days.'

Jude didn't know how to process this.

'What about the cat?'

'Can't you get your neighbour to feed it?'

'I don't know the neighbour.'

'Grab what you need and I'll go and ask him.'

'Thank you,' said Jude meekly.

'It's going to be fine.'

'Really?'

'Yes. Really.'

'I've made such a mess of everything. Every single thing.'

CHAPTER FIFTY-THREE

For the first two days Jude was like someone recovering from a long illness: no longer sick, but weak and easily exhausted. She slept a lot, or sat downstairs with a book in her hand that she didn't read. She looked out at the garden in its winter bareness. She went for short walks with her father, who was awkward and solicitous. She didn't cry, but sometimes she found hot tears seeping from her eyes. She didn't think about what had happened to her, what she had done, but often thoughts found her out, especially in the small hours. She had dreams that she couldn't remember when she woke, but they left her feeling shaky and scared.

On the morning of the third day, her mother came into her bedroom with a mug of coffee and an almond croissant warm from the oven, put them on her bedside table and, instead of leaving the room, took a seat in the chair by the window.

'So,' she said and gave a preliminary cough.

'I know,' said Jude, sitting back against the pillow and taking a sip of coffee.

'What do you know?'

'I know I've got to pull myself together.'

She thought about that phrase. It made sense, for she did feel that she had unravelled and come apart, ripping at the seams of her old identity. But the idea of fixing herself made her feel wretchedly tired. She didn't know where to begin.

'I was thinking you should talk to someone.'

'You mean a therapist?'

'Yes.'

'I think that's a good idea,' said Jude. Her mother's face brightened. 'When I'm in London again, I'll do it.'

'You can stay here as long as you like, you know that.'

'I have to go back. For a start, I have a job.' She gave a miserable laugh. 'I hope.'

'What's happening with work?'

'They've been trying to contact me.' She thought of the dismaying pile-up of emails and voicemails and texts. 'I'll sort it out today.'

'Good.'

Her mother nodded at her vigorously, as if her encouragement could carry Jude over all the hurdles in her mind. Jude took a bite of the damp, buttery pastry and felt it comfort her. There were flowers on the little table and the room was clean and bright. She saw the wishbone necklace coiled up where it had lain since last time she had been here and had discovered that she was Liam's executor. She picked it up, holding its weightlessness in her palm.

'Also,' her mother continued. 'I mean, I know it's just temporary, but I don't think the flat you're borrowing is very good for your spirits.'

'You can say that again.'

'So what about finding somewhere else to live?'

'Yes.'

'With friends?'

'Maybe.'

'It might be nice for you not to be alone. After everything you've been through.'

'You're probably right.'

Jude put the wishbone round her neck, took another bite of croissant, another mouthful of coffee. She looked at her mother sitting across from her and smiled.

'Thank you,' she said. 'And you're right: I need to sort my life out. I'll call work first.' She dreaded that. 'And then get in touch with the gang, think about where to live. One thing at a time.'

Later that day, Jude went for a walk by herself, through the little wood, her feet rustling among the fallen leaves, up the hill, round past the barn where she and Nat were to have had their wedding party, back along the high street. She stopped at the bakery to buy a loaf of bread and when she came out found herself face to face with Tara Birch, although at first she didn't recognise her, because she was wearing a long black coat with a hood pulled over her head.

Both of them looked shocked. Tara didn't smile.

'I wasn't expecting to bump into you. I was visiting a friend nearby and then thought I'd look in on . . .'

She trailed off and they stared at each other.

'Are you all right?' asked Jude.

'Not really. Are you?'

'I've been better.'

'Do you want a coffee or something?'

Jude didn't, but couldn't find a way to say no. They walked in silence up the road till they came to a small café that wasn't warm enough. Tara ordered them both coffees and sat at a little table opposite Jude. With her hood pulled back, Jude saw how terrible she looked. Her face seemed to have shrunk so that all her features appeared over-sized; her skin had a chalky pallor, apart from a rash on one cheek.

'That night at the party,' Tara said. 'I'm not usually like that.'

'It was your son's funeral,' said Jude softly. 'You don't need to apologise for anything.'

'Yelling at Danny, yelling at Dermot. That's not me. Or maybe it is. I've a temper on me; ask Andy.'

Jude just shook her head.

'It was awful,' Tara continued. 'I felt like I was going mad. Maybe I am going mad. I wake up in the morning and I remember. Every single morning I have to remember all over again. Andy made me go to the doctor's and he prescribed me some antidepressants.'

'Are they helping?'

'I haven't taken them. It sounds crazy, but I don't really want to feel better. My son has been killed. Why should I get over that?'

'I don't think it's about getting over it,' said Jude. 'It's more about finding a way of living with it.'

'I don't want to find a way to live with it. Because it's unbearable. It should be unbearable. He's dead. I'm a mother of a dead son. A murdered son.'

Jude watched as a tear made its way down Tara's ravaged face, then another. She put a hand on the other woman's arm.

'I've lost my son and I've lost my grandson.'

'You still have Dermot,' Jude said uselessly.

'Poor Dermot.' Tara lifted her head and looked drearily at Jude. 'I know he's suffering. But what's his suffering compared to mine? I can't help him. I can't help anyone.'

'Do you think that perhaps he feels—?'

'What's that you're wearing?'

'Sorry?'

'Round your neck?'

'Oh.' Jude looked down. The wooden wishbone necklace on its leather thong was just visible in the V of her shirt. She pulled it out.

'It was Liam's,' she said.

'I know that. Did he give it to you?'

'No.' Jude felt herself flushing. It doesn't really belong to me. I – well, I took it. It fell out of his bag at the cottage, the weekend he was killed. I just put it on. I'm not sure why.' She remembered spraying herself with his perfume as well. 'I shouldn't have it,' she said.

'It doesn't matter,' said Tara lifelessly. 'Maybe you're the person who should have it, when all's said and done. The girl he was soft on when he was a boy. Better than Danny taking it anyway. I couldn't bear that. When Andy and I had been married twenty-five years, Liam made one for the four of us. To bring the family luck, he said. Luck. And now look at us.'

When they parted, Tara took Jude's hand in her own fierce grip.

'Come and see me before you leave,' she said. 'Please.'

CHAPTER FIFTY-FOUR

When Jude woke the next morning, she saw there had been a frost overnight. It was sunny, the sky was a steely bright blue and the air was clear. Everything looked clean. Jude felt it was an omen. It was time to go home. It felt strange to be saying this in the place that for many years really had been her home. It felt stranger still, because she didn't have a home to go to in London. But it was time to find one. Or to make one.

Her mother face crumpled when Jude told her. 'Today?' she said.

'Yes. I've got to bite the bullet.'

'But where will you stay?'

'I'm going to make sure the flat's ship-shape and then probably move in with Dee while I find somewhere. If she'll have me. But there are other friends I can stay with while I look for a place. It'll be all right.'

Jude took hold of her mother's hand and held it against her own cheek. Both of them were close to tears. 'You've been amazing,' she said. 'But I need to sort out my life and the longer I wait, the harder it will be.'

Then there was the problem of Tara. She didn't really want to go and see her again. This was a woman she barely knew. Hadn't they said everything they had to say to each other? Jude toyed with the idea of just slipping away and sending her an apologetic text once she was back in London. But then she thought of Tara's face. At least she should have the courage to phone her and apologise and explain that she was leaving today.

It didn't work.

'You're going today?' said Tara. 'That's perfect.'

'What do you mean?'

'Dermot's here,' she said. 'He's driving down to London later and he can give you a lift.'

There were so many ways in which this wasn't a good idea. After everything that had happened, she felt she'd seen quite enough of Dermot. More than that, she had been looking forward to a few hours on the train without having to make conversation.

'I really don't want to be any trouble.'

'It won't be any trouble at all,' said Tara in an assertive tone, and then shifted into a strange kind of stage whisper so that Jude could barely make out what she was saying. 'He needs to get hold of himself. It will do him good, having someone to talk to.'

That was exactly why Jude didn't want to spend three hours in a car with Dermot Birch but she couldn't think of any excuse that wouldn't sound intolerably rude. So she said that it would be lovely.

Her mother drove her to the Birches' house and when they arrived she pulled in and surprised Jude by switching the car engine off. She sat for a moment staring straight in front of her. Jude suddenly felt like she was a teenager again. She sensed that a lecture of some kind was coming. Finally her mother turned and looked at her with a serious expression.

'I think this visit has been good for you.'

'I hope I said how grateful I was.'

'You've been through so much.' She gestured towards the house. 'I know you're a doctor, but you can't cure everyone.'

'What do you mean?'

'They're dealing with something nobody should have to deal with. But you can't do their suffering for them. They just have to get to the other end.'

Jude smiled. 'I'm only getting a lift down to London.'

Her mother shook her head.

'They see you as a connection to their son, or to their brother. That's too much for you to take on.'

Jude leaned across and kissed her mother goodbye.

'It's just a lift.'

CHAPTER FIFTY-FIVE

Tara was looking slightly better than when Jude had last seen her, but Andy was sombre, with dark shadows around his eyes. 'Good of you to come,' he said gruffly.

'I know it's a very painful time,' Jude said.

'You don't have to keep repeating that,' said Tara. 'That's the problem with being bereaved. People feel they have to keep expressing their sympathy to you and then you have to do a performance of being in mourning.'

'Tara,' said Andy. 'She was just being kind.'

'I wasn't talking about *her*,' she said, and then corrected herself, turning to Jude. 'I wasn't talking about *you*. You knew Liam. I mean people we hardly know. It's as if they want to muscle in. All those people who talk about Liam as if they knew him.'

Jude thought to herself that she also was definitely one of those people who didn't know Liam.

'I think people sometimes struggle to think of the right thing to say,' she said.

'They don't know what it's like,' said Andy. 'They can't know.'

348

Jude felt even more self-conscious about anything she might say so she didn't say anything.

'Dermot isn't here yet,' Tara said. 'He said he would be here by now. Would you like tea or coffee? I bought some biscuits.'

There was a brief standoff when Jude said she would have what they were having and Tara said it was entirely up to her and Andy interrupted and said he would make both. Jude felt that, after all, she had managed to say the wrong thing. Andy went to the kitchen and, as Tara was starting to explain how Andy felt it difficult to express his grief, there was the sound of the front door opening and being slammed shut.

Jude heard Dermot's voice. She calculated that a cup of tea and maybe a biscuit would be enough and then she could start talking about how she really needed to get back to London.

Dermot walked quickly into the room and hugged his mother. Then he saw Jude and was visibly startled.

'Didn't you know I was going to be here?'

'What?'

'Tara didn't say?'

Tara and Dermot started to speak at the same time and neither would give way.

'I can just catch the train,' Jude said over the top of them, loudly enough to make them fall quiet.

'No, no. We can leave whenever you like.'

Jude looked at Dermot with dismay. His hair was

unkempt. He was wearing a tracksuit top streaked with dirt. She wasn't sure if she should point out that the laces of one of his shoes was untied. He was speaking slightly too quickly with a wide-eyed look that Jude associated with small children who were both overtired but couldn't sleep. She felt an intense sympathy but also an intense worry that this was the man who would shortly be driving her along the motorway. He came forward and gave her a brief hug and she smelled alcohol and sweat. He was a man in clear need of help and a shower and a proper night's sleep.

'Are you okay?' she said.

He ran his fingers through his hair.

'You're a doctor. My brother's been murdered. How should I be? What would be a healthy way to deal with that?'

'She was just asking,' said Tara. 'There's no need to bite her head off.'

Dermot started to reply, but then Andy came into the room with a pot of tea and a cafetière on a tray. Dermot moved towards him to help him and somehow they collided and Andy lost control of the tray. The teapot smashed and the cafetière didn't, but the coffee still poured out of it and the mess was startling. There were splashes of brown liquid on a woven rug and on a large sofa. They looked like the sort of stains that would never come out, whatever you did to them.

'I was just trying to help,' said Dermot in a sullen voice.

Neither Andy nor Tara said anything at all in response. They didn't seem cross or dismayed. They didn't say it didn't matter. They didn't say anything at all. It was as if Andy had collided with an inanimate object. He bent down and picked up the cafetière and the larger fragments of the tea pot. Tara fetched a bucket and a mop. Dermot said he would do it but she ignored him.

'I want to do something,' said Dermot.

'Just sit down,' said Tara. 'It doesn't matter.'

To Jude those few words, which could have been maternal and consoling, seemed the most devastating of all. It really didn't matter because nothing mattered.

A few minutes later Andy came back into the room with another teapot, strangely shaped and decorated with flowers. He looked at it as if he was noticing it for the first time and gave a twisted smile.

'It was a present. Not my taste. It's the first time we've ever used it.'

When everyone had their drinks, there was a moment of awkwardness.

'How's the will business going?' Andy asked.

Jude didn't reply. She couldn't face talking about all of that here, in this setting.

'Jude says it's a mess,' said Dermot. 'If someone killed Liam for the money, then they're going to be sorely disappointed.'

'Dermot, please,' said Andy, in a reproving tone.

'It's not a criticism,' said Dermot. 'It's just the truth.'

Tara looked at Jude. 'Is that true?'

'I don't know,' said Jude. 'There were clearly financial problems. Maybe something can be sorted out.'

'Who's going to sort it out?'

'If Danny wants to keep the house, she might be able to arrange something.'

Andy snorted and Tara glared at him. Jude glanced at Dermot.

'Maybe we should be . . .' she said meaningfully.

'I heard you were talking to the detective,' Andy said.

Jude didn't know how to answer this question. She was tempted to reply with another question: How do you know? Why are you asking? What business is it of yours?

'I've been interviewed,' said Jude. 'Like everyone else.'

'She was at the funeral.'

'Yes.'

'Did she say how the investigation is going?'

'No.' Jude tried to catch Dermot's eye, to signal her desire to leave, but he was staring at his shoes.

'Do they have a suspect?'

Tara interrupted sharply. 'Andy, why would the police tell Jude about things like that?'

'I've got a bad feeling. I've heard that if they don't catch someone in the first couple of days, they probably won't catch anyone at all.'

'That's ridiculous,' Tara said.

Jude didn't think it was so ridiculous. She had

no sense that the police had done anything except eliminate suspects.

'It's about closure,' said Andy. 'I don't think we'll achieve closure until someone is caught and pays the penalty.'

'Closure,' said Dermot bitterly. 'What does that even mean? If you found out that he was killed by a random mugger, would that make you feel better? Or what if he was killed by . . . ?'

He stopped.

'Killed by who?' said Tara softly. She leaned towards her son. 'What were you going to say?'

'I don't know what I was going to say. If he was killed by someone he knew. Would that make you feel better?'

'It's not a question of feeling better,' said Andy. 'It's just that we would know. We could draw a line under it.'

'Which would be better?' Dermot asked wildly. 'Would it be better if it were random? Or would you like to discover that there was someone who hated your son enough to murder him?'

There was a pause.

'It doesn't have to be one of the two.' Andy spoke slowly. 'It could have been a misunderstanding.'

'We'd just like to know, that's all. It's a torment, not knowing.' Tara looked at Jude and spoke more loudly, almost shouted. 'Can't you see that?'

'I can see that.'

'Stop shouting,' Andy said to Tara, in a voice at least as loud as hers had been. 'You sound insane.'

'Maybe I want to be insane. Maybe one day I'll go insane enough to believe he's still alive. I'm not sure I care much about whether they catch the person or not. When you lose your son, it's hard to really care about anything.'

'You've still got one, you know,' said Dermot.

'What?' said Andy.

'You've still got a son.' Dermot's face was blotchy. 'The way Mum was talking it sounded like she'd lost her only child. I was just registering the fact of my existence. Here I am. Here!'

He banged himself hard on his chest.

'That's right,' said Tara. 'Here we go again. Let's make this about you.'

'It's not making it about me, fuck it. I'm just reminding you that I still exist. Your son. Dermot.'

He was about to cry.

'As if that were ever in doubt.' Tara's voice was acid with contempt. 'Ever since he died, you've been going around feeling sorry for yourself. Poor little Dermot.'

A silence suddenly fell on the room; it felt electric with nastiness. Jude stared down at the floor. Dermot stood up and looked at her.

'We should go.'

Jude stood. She had an impulse simply to flee but she had to say something.

'Maybe you need to talk. I can wait outside.'

'I don't think we need to talk,' said Dermot.

'I think you need to apologise to your mother,' said Andy.

'Apologise to my *mother*? What the fuck is this?'

Andy slammed his mug down on the table and stood up. His face was flushed. Jude thought for a moment that he was going to punch his son. Tara must have been thinking the same thing. She shouted her husband's name and then started sobbing. The two men looked at her, both breathing heavily. Jude went across and sat by her on the sofa.

'It's horrible,' she said. 'Horrible for everyone.' She looked up. 'I can get a taxi to the station. I really think you all need to talk and support each other.'

'I think you should go,' Andy said. But he wasn't talking to her. He was talking to Dermot.

CHAPTER FIFTY-SIX

Outside in the car, Dermot and Jude sat for several minutes. Dermot seemed out of breath. Jude wasn't sure he was safe to drive. She herself felt she was in shock. She had mumbled a few words of thanks and regret but she wasn't sure that Tara had heard them. Andy had taken her by the elbow and led her to the front door.

'I hope you'll keep in touch,' he said.

'Yes, of course,' said Jude, earnestly hoping that after today she would never have any contact with any member of the Birch family ever again.

'You've been a comfort to Tara. A reminder of the old days.'

She had nodded dumbly. Dermot had walked past them without a word and Jude had nodded at Andy and followed him to the car.

'You shouldn't have had to see that,' Dermot said finally, looking at Jude. His eyes were damp as if he had been crying.

'That's all right.'

'You've seen the bit we normally keep hidden,' he said.

'When dreadful things happen, people go a bit crazy.'

'Or show who they really are.'

'I don't think that's true.'

Dermot looked at her more closely and then he rubbed his face with both hands, as if he was washing it.

'Are you okay?' asked Jude.

He lifted his head.

'Snap,' he said.

'What?'

He reached into the collar of his shirt and pulled out the same little wooden wishbone that she was wearing.

'So he made one for you?'

'No, this is his one.'

He looked puzzled. 'But when did he give it to you?'

Jude inwardly groaned. Everything she did seemed to be designed to make people think that she and Liam had been having an affair.

'Sorry, it was wrong of me. When I was in Norfolk waiting for him I saw it in his luggage. And borrowed it. Or stole it, if you want to be precise.' As she spoke the words, they sounded worse and worse. 'Tara said I should keep it, though.'

There was a long pause that took Jude by surprise. She could understand Dermot being irritated by what she'd done. It might feel like a violation.

'Anything to get at Danny,' he said. He switched on the car engine. 'Let's be on our way.'

'Are you sure you're safe to drive?'

'Are you thinking of the teapot? I'm fine.'

CHAPTER FIFTY-SEVEN

Dermot wasn't fine, though.

'I think the speed limit's thirty,' said Jude, instinctively throwing an arm up as the car whisked round a bend and then swerved to avoid a cyclist.

'What's that?'

Dermot twisted his head to look at her, taking his eyes off the road for longer than Jude was comfortable with.

'The speed limit's thirty. You're doing fifty.'

He braked sharply, making her head jerk.

'I'm a safe driver. You don't need to worry.'

'Perhaps this isn't the right time to be driving though,' said Jude. 'After everything you've been through.'

They were now going at twenty. The car behind them tooted its horn and Dermot gave an evil grin and slowed even more.

'Arsehole,' he said.

'Perhaps you could just drop me at the station,' said Jude. 'Please.'

'No. A long drive will be therapeutic. And we can chat: fellow executors.'

Jude tried to unclench herself. Her fists were tightly curled and her jaw ached. The low sun glittered on the smeary windshield and she wondered nervously about visibility. Dermot accelerated again as they left the town and began their journey south.

'What are you going to be doing there?' she asked as the car screeched round a corner.

He shrugged. 'Business,' he said. 'Nothing interesting. I hate London.'

After that, they didn't talk. Jude looked out of the window at fields, hills and trees in the gathering dusk. There was a small river winding through the valley beneath them. Two horses grazing placidly in a meadow. A man standing beside his neat bonfire. A kestrel hovering. Ordinary life, she thought, as they shot past, the needle on the speed dial rising ominously.

She glanced across at Dermot. He was gripping the steering wheel fiercely; his face was pinched and his hair wild; he smelled unwashed. He looked disordered and wretched and her heart went out to him.

'Maybe,' she said, 'you should think of talking to someone about all you've been through.'

Which of course was what her mother had advised her.

'You've no idea what I'm feeling,' Dermot replied, once more twisting his head to look at her while the car jolted over a pothole. He'd bitten his lip and there was blood at the corner of his mouth.

She started to reply but he interrupted her.

'Liam would have told me to just get on with things. Square up.'

'Like you're in a battle?'

'Exactly. He said you had to fight for yourself like a soldier fights. Or a warrior.' His whole face puckered as if it was a matter of painful importance to remember the exact phrase. 'Maybe he said warrior. That sounds more like Liam. You know – daggers and fists, not guns and tanks.'

'Who are you fighting?'

Dermot shrugged. He had taken off the tracksuit jacket and Jude saw there were damp rings under his armpits and little beads of perspiration on his forehead. 'Whoever's against you or gets in your way. It's them or you.'

'It sounds like a grim way of being alive,' she said.

'Maybe.'

He rubbed at his eyes with a knuckled fist. Her eyes felt sore as well, gritty with tiredness.

'I know he was your older brother and that you're mourning him,' she said. 'But that doesn't mean he was right.'

'He always did win, though. Whatever he wanted, he got.' Dermot slid his gaze across to her and the car drifted towards the verge. 'Like you, back in the day. He got you, didn't he?'

'He didn't *get* me.'

'And he got Danny. She was with this other bloke and Liam just decided he was going to have her and nothing was going to stop him.'

Jude closed her eyes. She didn't want to look at him, or hear him. She didn't want to be in this overheated car that smelled of cigarettes and sweat and misery, hurtling its way towards London.

'You can be a loser or a winner,' Dermot was saying in a voice that dragged at her. 'He was a winner.'

Jude's eyes snapped open.

'He was killed, for God's sake,' she said. 'That doesn't sound much like winning anything.'

They reached a roundabout and took the exit on to the motorway. Dermot swung out in front of a giant yellow lorry and didn't seem to notice the blaring horn. He was saying something about Tara. The lorry overtook them and Jude could see the furious red face of the driver shouting soundlessly out of the window and giving them the finger.

It was nearly dark. She closed her eyes again. Perhaps she fitfully dozed and the clamour of the motorway mixed with the clamour of her dreams. She lurched fully awake as the car juddered over the studs on the road's edge and she saw the flash of the metal barrier.

She yelled out and Dermot wrenched the steering wheel back.

'Sorry,' he said, stretching his mouth into a smile. 'My bad.'

'Your bad? You fucking fell asleep. You almost killed us.'

'It's all okay now.'

'We need to stop for a bit.'

'I'm all right. Maybe there's some chewing gum in the glove compartment.'

'You're not safe to drive.'

'I'm fine.'

'You are not fine at all.'

After a few minutes, Jude saw a sign for petrol and services and Dermot turned off the road.

She got him a large coffee and also a plate of egg and chips, which he covered with dollops of tomato ketchup.

'Sorry,' he said, sinking the point of his knife into the egg and watching the yolk seep out. 'I don't know what's come over me.'

He put a yolky chip into his mouth.

'You and your parents – you should talk to them properly.'

'It's too late for that.'

'That's not true,' Jude said feebly.

'He charmed everyone. Even after his death, it's like he's in charge. Pulling the strings.'

'What do you mean?'

'Well, look at you.'

'Me?'

'You say *I've* gone a bit mad. What about you?'

Jude stared at him, but she was no longer hearing what he was saying. She saw his tear-stained face, his reddened eyes, his unbrushed hair, his trembling fingers as he pushed chip after chip into his mouth until his cheeks bulged.

Was this what she was like? Was she looking at a version of herself?

Long ago, Liam had charmed her, won her over, left her with his reckless gesture of self-sacrifice, and then, years later, he had suddenly reappeared. With a single gesture, a tug on the thread, he had pulled her back into his life. She had blown up her own existence. In its place she had taken on the role of Liam's executor, his son's baby-sitter, an inappropriate friend to his parents, involved herself in a murder investigation, and finally, for a night she wished she could forget, she had found herself in the bed of his best friend.

She didn't even have grief as an excuse. An excruciating shame burned through her.

Dermot dropped her off at Hanger Lane underground station. As she unbuckled her safety belt, he said in a blurt, 'I hope you won't be offended, but I really think you should give Danny that necklace.'

Jude looked down at the delicate wooden wishbone.

'It just feels odd,' continued Dermot. His face was blotchy with awkwardness. 'If us three Birches have one and the fourth, Liam's, goes to his teenage sweetheart rather than his partner.'

'You're right.'

'It's not as if he gave it to you.'

'I've already agreed with you, Dermot.'

'Good. Shall I give it to her when I see her?'

She looked at Dermot and suddenly felt resistant.

'I think maybe I should hand it over in person, or send it with a letter,' said Jude. 'My last goodbye.'

CHAPTER FIFTY-EIGHT

Jude's mobile rang as she walked towards the flat. Her brother.

'Hello, Jude,' he said, rather formally. 'Where are you?'

'In Tottenham. About two minutes from the flat. I've been with Mum and Dad.'

'I know. I was hoping I could see you.'

'Now?'

'Tomorrow morning. I'm in London for a meeting at ten, so I could be at yours for half past eight.'

'Is anything wrong?'

'There's just something I need to talk to you about. Best in person.'

Jude signed inwardly. Couldn't it just be done over the phone? It was all too tiring.

'It'll be good to see you.'

Michael was fifteen minutes early. Jude was still in a tatty bathrobe when he arrived, and he was in a suit and a tie, with polished shoes. You can always judge a man by his shoes, someone had once told her.

'I've just made coffee,' she said as she led him into the flat.

'Lovely.'

'Have you had breakfast?'

'I'll only be a minute.'

He took a chair and leaned down to stroke the cat; it arched its back till its spine bristled, then spat at him. 'Nice companion you have here.'

'I know. I'm finding somewhere else to live.'

He looked around. 'That sounds like a good idea.'

'And I'm going back to work on Monday.'

'Good,' he said heartily. 'That's excellent news, Jude.'

She put a mug of coffee in front of him and sat opposite with her own mug. Michael sat up straight and fidgeted with the knot of his tie.

'I have been thinking,' he continued. 'And I've been talking to Mum and Dad.'

'About me?'

'They're worrying. Don't take this wrongly, Jude, but you've been behaving in a bit of a bizarre way.'

Jude pulled her robe tighter round her.

'That's in the past,' she managed to say.

'I'm glad to hear it. But added to that, and related to that . . .' He gestured vaguely. 'We think that you should give up this ridiculous notion of being Liam Birch's executor.'

'You've decided, have you?'

'Let's face it, you can't do it properly anyway, and it's all been too much. On top of everything else.'

367

'Is that what you came to say?'

'I'm going to take it over. At once. Everything. Leave it with me.'

'You?'

'Well, probably mostly my trainee actually, but essentially, yes.'

Jude's first impulse was to stand up and shout at Michael, to be furious with him for getting involved in her life and talking about her behind her back. But then she had a second impulse, which cancelled out the first.

'That's very generous of you, Michael.'

He held up his hand. 'Is there a but coming?'

'There's no but.'

'You mean you're okay with this?'

'Of course. More than okay. It's a massive relief. You're right that I can't do it. I don't know how to thank you.'

Michael's face broke into a smile. 'I thought you'd kick up a fuss.'

'No. I want to put all of this behind me now. Start putting my life back together. You can ring Mum and Dad and tell them to stop worrying.'

CHAPTER FIFTY-NINE

Jude walked to Walthamstow, even though the sky was a bruised purple and every so often there was a dull rumble of thunder from far off. When she got to the front door of the house, she took off the necklace and pushed it into her pocket. She would tell Danny that Michael was taking on the role of executor, free of charge, she would hand over Liam's wishbone, and she would walk out of the house and never return. Over the weekend she would set about finding a place to live, and in the meantime she would move in with Dee and her housemates. On Monday she would return to work.

Doc opened the door. He didn't seem surprised to see her.

'Is Danny in? She knows I'm coming.'

'In the kitchen.'

Jude found her sitting at the table with her laptop open in front of her.

'Thanks for making the time.'

Danny raised her eyebrows. 'Making the time? Jude, Jude, you're always welcome here. You know that. You're one of us.'

Jude wanted to shout out that, no, she wasn't one of them, but instead she forced a smile. She had just started to speak when the door opened behind her and she turned to see Vin. The blood rushed to her face, and she saw him notice her confusion. He smiled at her and then he kissed her on the cheek.

'Jude was just saying that she had come to tell me something,' said Danny.

'Is it a girls' thing or can I stay?'

'It doesn't matter.'

'Do you want tea?' Vin asked.

'Mint,' said Danny.

'Want some, Jude?' said Vin. 'It's fresh from the garden.'

'I'm fine,' said Jude.

Vin filled the kettle and Jude took a seat opposite Danny, who closed her laptop and gazed at her without blinking.

'I'm going back to work on Monday,' Jude said.

'Me too,' said Danny.

'I thought I should come and tell you that I can't be Liam's executor. I never should have said yes in the first place.'

'And yet you did.'

'It was a mistake.'

'Have you told Dermot that?'

'Poor sod,' said Vin, pouring water over the sprigs of mint in two mugs. He opened the fridge and took out a plate covered in foil. 'Last night's pizza,' he said. 'Want some?'

Jude ignored him.

'Don't worry about Dermot. My brother's an accountant. He said he'll take it on. Free of charge.'

'Why should he do that for us?' asked Danny.

'He's doing it for me.'

Vin took the seat beside Danny and lifted the foil off the pizza. He took an enormous mouthful and started to chew. They were both watching her.

'I came to tell you that,' said Jude. 'And, I guess, to say goodbye.'

She stood up, but then remembered the necklace.

'There's something else,' she began, sliding her hand into the pocket of her jeans to withdraw it.

The door swung open and Jude turned away from them to see Alfie totter in.

She turned back.

Danny very delicately, almost out of sight, was stroking the small of Vin's back. They both still had their eyes on her.

'Something?' prompted Vin.

'It doesn't matter,' said Jude.

She suddenly felt she had to get out of there. She left the kitchen and in the hall passed Irina, just in from the cold and wearing pink rubber boots and a shiny yellow bucket hat.

'Jude,' she said.

Jude walked past her.

A deft act of intimacy that had been hidden from her when she'd been sitting down. A hand dipping down the lower back into the cleft. A lover's knowledgeable hand.

Danny and Vin. Vin and Danny.

Jude's brain hissed; thoughts tumbled round in it. She thought of Alfie standing by Vin's bed in the early hours, calling him 'Daddy'.

The two of them had alibis. Cast-iron alibis. As Leila Fox had reminded her, stupidly perfect alibis are still alibis.

But still, Danny and Vin, sitting together at the table and looking serenely across at her while Danny stroked her lover's back.

It wasn't her problem, she told herself. That messy and ugly chapter of her life was over.

She looked back at the house and she thought she saw a face at one of the windows. Someone watching her.

She pulled out her mobile and found the number.

'Leila?' she said. 'It's Jude. Can I come and see you?'

CHAPTER SIXTY

Leila Fox hadn't shared Jude's sense of urgency. She had suggested that Jude could come and see her in the next day or two. It took some persuasion for her to agree to meet later in the day. Leila named a coffee shop in Holborn at five, after she had finished her shift. Jude arrived at quarter to five and she was halfway through her second cup when Leila arrived, looking weary and distracted.

'Can I get you one?' Jude asked.

Leila said that she could get her own. She went across to the counter and came back with a drink that smelled of sweet spices.

'Hard day?' said Jude.

'Not especially.'

Jude had the dismal sense that Leila was tired of her or, more likely, that she had better things to do in her free time.

'I'm sorry to bother you,' she said.

'I haven't got long.'

'I'll just say my say. All right?'

The detective gave the lightest of nods, so Jude continued. She described what she had seen when she had visited the Walthamstow house. When she got to the end, it felt anticlimactic.

'I thought I should tell you.'

'Why?'

Jude felt taken aback. She wasn't sure what she had expected but it was more than that.

'Did you know that they were a couple?'

'No, I didn't.'

'Doesn't it seem significant? That they're together but they've kept it secret.'

'I don't really know where to begin with this. I'm not sure it's significant. And I don't even think you've established that they really are a couple.'

'They're definitely a couple. You know those intimate things that people do when they're in a relationship. Touching each other. Exchanging looks. It's unmistakable.'

'I suspect that everyone in that house is involved with everyone else, one way or another.'

'That's the whole point. You're right. People have been involved with each other in different ways. So why would they keep it so secret? Did Danny tell you about it when you interviewed her?'

'Look, Jude, can I just say that you still haven't established that there is a relationship between them. And even if you did establish it, I don't think it would matter.'

'But why would they go to the trouble of concealing it? What's the motive of that?'

'Motive? What are you talking about? People have strange reasons for doing things. Or they do things for no reason at all. Or for reasons they can't explain.'

Jude didn't know how to reply. She picked up her coffee but when she took a sip it had gone cold and horrible, or maybe that was just the way she was feeling.

'So how's the inquiry going?' she asked finally.

'I can't comment on that.' Leila spoke in a brisk tone.

'I wasn't asking for a comment like at a press conference. I just wanted to know how it was progressing.'

Leila started to say something and then thought better of it, and when she spoke her tone softened.

'When we have anything to announce, we'll announce it.'

'So it's not progressing.'

Jude saw a flash of anger in Leila's grey eyes. The detective shifted in her chair as if preparing to get up and leave. She picked up her phone, which was lying next to her glass of tea.

'I think I'd better . . .'

She stopped suddenly and Jude saw a new interest in the detective's expression. She put her phone back on the table and leaned across, reaching towards Jude's face. Jude flinched slightly. She thought the detective was going to touch her face but instead she touched the little wooden ornament on her neck.

'Where did you get this?' she said.

'I saw it when I was going through Liam's bag

in the house in Norfolk. It fell on the floor and I took it. As a kind of souvenir.'

'You mean, you stole it?'

'No, no, I just took it. I wasn't thinking about it like that.'

Leila frowned. 'Are you telling me the truth? You found it? Liam didn't give it to you?'

Jude was confused. What did it matter?

'Why would I be lying? My version makes me sound worse.'

When Leila spoke it was like she was talking to herself. 'I've seen this before.'

'Where?'

'Never mind.'

'Liam made it. He made one for himself and for his family. For Dermot and for his mum and dad.'

The detective seemed lost in thought once more.

'So,' she began, speaking slowly, 'if you hadn't taken it, we would have found it in his things.'

'Yes, I'm sorry. I know I shouldn't have. I just thought it was a funny little thing that he'd made. It was on the spur of the moment. But does it really matter?'

'There's something I need to check out,' Leila said. She stood up. 'I'll get back to you.'

CHAPTER SIXTY-ONE

Back at the flat, Jude couldn't settle to anything. She felt restless, her mind whirring uselessly, until it eventually latched on to an idea.

She changed into shorts and a T-shirt and set off into the darkness. It was seven o'clock and very cold. She ran at full tilt all the way to her old flat in Stratford where, still gasping from the effort, she rang the bell and then hammered on the door. She was just pressing the bell for a second time when the door swung open and Nat stood in front of her, a polite smile dying on his lips.

'Jude? What's up? You must be freezing.'

Jude was hot to the roots of her hair.

'*You* cheated on *me*.'

'What?'

'That's all I want to say. I don't want to hear you deny it, I don't want you to tell me who it was, I don't want to hear your excuses. I simply needed to say that I know. I know who you are and, boy, did I have a lucky escape.'

Nat stared at her. She could see his Adam's apple bob as he swallowed and the muscles in his face working.

'Is that it?' he asked eventually.

'That's it. The end.'

She turned back the way she had come, trying to run off some of the rage she could feel bubbling through her veins. As she reached the end of the street where her flat was, she tripped on an uneven paving stone and fell heavily, full length under the yellow glow of the streetlamp. She lay there for a moment, feeling in pain and at the same time embarrassed.

'Are you all right?' a voice asked.

Jude pulled herself into a sitting position. A black puppy was sniffing at her interestedly. At the other end of the lead was a middle-aged woman looking down at her.

'I'm fine, thank you,' Jude said, and she pulled herself to her feet and realised she wasn't exactly fine. She had scraped the side of her right leg from the calf up to the thigh, and it was raw with spots of blood. As she put her weight on her right foot, a wave of pain rippled through her so that she almost cried out.

The woman was telling her that she should get her cuts properly cleaned and that there was a danger of tetanus. Jude wanted to say that this wasn't correct, but she was overwhelmed with pain. She knew it would recede. She mumbled something incoherent to the woman and headed for home. With almost every step she had to support herself by clutching a railing or leaning against a tree.

Back in the flat, she ran a bath and pulled her clothes off. She saw that her right ankle was already starting to swell up. She had to untie the laces of the shoe and then gently loosen them so that she could ease the shoe off, and even then she couldn't suppress a whimper of distress.

She eased herself into the bath. The sensation of the hot water on her scraped skin actually made her sob and she gave way to it, crying and crying, so that her face was wet with tears and sweat and snot. It felt like even her own body had turned against her.

As she got out of the bath, she placed her right foot gingerly on the floor. It was painful but it didn't feel as if anything was torn or broken. It would be better tomorrow or the day after.

She pulled on a pair of tracksuit bottoms and a shirt. She didn't know what to do. She knew she should eat something. She thought of ordering a takeaway but the idea of anything like pizza or sushi or curry turned her stomach. She looked in the cupboard and found some rice. She cooked it, and then grated cheese over it. She didn't watch TV or look online. She just sat at the table and ate half of the rice and drank water. When she was finished, she looked at the washing up that had accumulated, but couldn't face it. It could wait till the following day. Then she went to bed. She couldn't think of what else to do.

Tomorrow was going to be different, she told herself.

CHAPTER SIXTY-TWO

When she woke the next morning it was after eight. It took her a few moments to realise where she was and what day it was. She was brought to herself by the twinge of discomfort as she flexed her right foot. She eased herself into a sitting position on the edge of the bed and touched the ground with her toe. Not too bad. It felt sore but it was getting better. She stood up. Yes, she could do it.

She looked around. The flat looked awful. Dirty, disordered. She made a decision. She was going to put the flat into some kind of order before she left it. It would be like drawing a line under her previous life and starting again. She pulled on ancient jeans that were beginning to come apart at the seams, an oversized T-shirt she usually wore in bed and her scuffed sheepskin slippers that wouldn't hurt her foot. She gathered up all the rest of her clothes that were scattered on the floor and on the chair and crammed them into the washing machine.

Where to start with the horror of the flat? Jude decided that the kitchen was probably the worst.

She filled the sink with all the dirty glasses and dishes and knives and forks and four brightly coloured little carving knives. She washed them up and dried them. She put the glasses and dishes into a cupboard. She not only put the cutlery in the drawer but arranged them neatly by type. She was left with four coloured knives, arranged on the worktop: bright red, yellow, blue and green. It reminded her of a children's drawing of the rainbow. What were the colours of the rainbow? On the wall next to the toaster was a magnetic strip. She put the red knife on the left followed by the yellow, the blue and the green.

She vacuumed the kitchen, the living room, the bedroom and the bathroom. She found a bucket under the sink, filled it with hot water and mopped the kitchen and bathroom floors. Her slippers were soggy and her foot was throbbing. Normally she would have had the radio on or been listening to something on her headphones. Just now it felt good to have no distraction and no thoughts either. She was losing herself in the effort and the smell of disinfectant. Everything was being scoured. She caught sight of herself in the bathroom mirror: her hair stood up in peaks and she'd splashed dishwater all over herself. There was a smear of dirt across her left cheek. But she was beginning to feel better.

Back in the bedroom, she packed all the clothes she had brought with her into a couple of bags, except for a few things she decided to throw away and the clothes she would put on after she'd had a shower and washed her hair. She stowed the luggage under the stairs. Then she went around the flat, picking things off surfaces and either putting them away or into a bin bag. Just when she was looking around in search of more things to arrange or throw away, the doorbell rang.

She opened the door. It was Dermot. He looked even worse than when she had last seen him. Her first impulse was to ask why he was here but then, when she saw his pale, sallow skin, his bloodshot eyes, she felt a pang of sympathy. Was it possible that she was the only person he could turn to?

'Are you okay?' she said.

'Can I come in?' He spoke in not much more than a whisper.

She would really like to have said no, he couldn't, but it didn't seem possible and so she stood aside to let him enter. Once inside, he took his jacket off and laid it on a chair by the wall. He was wearing a red T-shirt decorated with the logo of a vintage motorbike. Twisty blue veins stood out on his thin, strong arms. Jude waited for him to speak but he was just looking around the flat as if he had no idea where he was or how he had got there.

'What have you been up to?' she asked.

He looked at her as if he was surprised to be spoken to.

'Just seeing people.' He rubbed one cheek violently. 'You know.'

'Were you up at the house?'

'What do you mean?'

'You know. Danny. Vin. That lot.'

His eyes widened slightly and he took a couple of spasmodic steps towards her. 'How do you know?'

'I don't know. I thought you said you were going. I was just asking.' She looked at him more closely. 'Dermot, are you all right?'

'I'm all right. Dealing with things. Things that need to be dealt with. I'm tired, that's all. I'm very tired.'

He looked twitchy, nervous, as if he hadn't slept at all. Jude wondered if he was on something.

'Do you want some tea? Coffee?'

'I don't know,' he said. 'I don't know what I want.'

'I'll put the kettle on.'

He followed her into the kitchen and she took the kettle from the stove, filled it with water, put it back and turned the gas on. She was aware of him behind her, bustling around. It was as if he couldn't keep still. She regretted having offered him tea. She should have said she was on her way out.

'So how's Danny doing?' Jude asked, trying to talk in a bright tone.

'Danny?'

'Yes.'

'Why?'

'I don't know. You said you'd just been there and it's an obvious question to ask.'

384

'Right. Right. Danny is Danny. A bit stressed maybe.' He rubbed his cheek violently again. 'She said you were there.'

'Yeah. I went to tell her that my brother is going to take over the stuff with the will. Sorry, I guess I should have told you as well. He's an accountant. He knows how to deal with things like this. So that's one thing less for you to worry about.'

'What?'

'I said . . . ' Jude looked at him. 'You don't look well.'

'Maybe I'm not. She said you told her you weren't coming back.'

'That's right. I won't be bothering her any more.' Jude took two tea bags from a jar and put them into the teapot, then turned round and said on an impulse, 'To be honest, Dermot, I was suspicious of Danny for a while.'

'What do you mean, suspicious? You mean—?'

'Yeah. Sorry. She's your sister-in-law and all of that. But anyway, it turns out that she and Vin are the only two people who couldn't have killed Liam.'

'What do you mean?'

'There's a film of the two of them on YouTube, dancing at a party. They were far away in Brixton all through the time when Liam could have been killed.' Jude smiled. 'I told the detective that I thought their alibi was too perfect but it turns out that isn't a thing.'

'What do you mean, it isn't a thing?'

'Apparently an alibi can't be *too* perfect. The more perfect the better.'

Dermot looked dazed. 'I don't understand. Anyway, why would you suspect them?'

'Various reasons. But it doesn't matter.'

'No, why? Tell me why.'

'For a start, it's often the partner, isn't it? And I know Danny and Liam had been having a rough time.'

Dermot nodded. He was rubbing his finger round and round a knot in the wood of the table.

'And then, that house – well.' Jude spoke in a sudden rush. 'There's something really wrong about it. All the boundaries have gone. I'm sure you know – everyone having affairs with everyone else. Your brother was no angel, Dermot.'

'He wasn't,' said Dermot in a voice that had dropped to a hoarse whisper. 'He was a bad man, who did bad things. Maybe he deserved to die.'

'Don't say that.' Jude looked at Dermot with concern. 'I don't think you should go to the house for a while. You need time to heal. Stay away. It does something to people who go there.' Jude stopped. She was hot and her head felt heavy, as if something was pressing down on the top of her skull, but she felt she had to speak.

'I had a thing with Vin,' she said. Her voice croaked. 'After the funeral. I mean, so what, right, it's not a crime, but it felt horrible after. Like I'd been toyed with somehow.'

'You and Vin?'

Dermot was still rubbing his finger round and round the whorl of wood. His eyes were shadowed.

'Yes.'

'Wow,' he said.

'Yeah, and then I discovered he's with Danny too.'

'With Danny?'

'Yeah. Musical chairs,' said Jude with a forced laugh.

'I don't understand.'

'He's having a thing with Danny. Though the morning after the funeral, she didn't seem to mind at all when she saw that Vin and I . . .' She stopped. Her head was throbbing violently.

'What do you mean, he's with Danny? What are you saying?'

'I'm saying that Vin and Danny are involved. Maybe they have been all long. Maybe Liam knew and didn't mind, just as Danny didn't mind about me and Vin. I think she found it funny.'

'That's a fucking lie. A fucking, fucking lie.'

Dermot was about to say something else when Jude heard a rattling sound from the end of the room. It was her phone, vibrating on the table. She hobbled across and picked it up and looked at it. Leila Fox.

'Sorry,' she said. 'I need to take this.'

She moved away slightly and turned her back on him.

'I've been trying to call you,' said the detective.

'It was on silent.'

'It doesn't matter. I just wanted to tell you that we've had a breakthrough. Things are moving very quickly now.'

'What do you mean?'

'You'll hear later. I just want to tell you something. It's . . . by the way, where are you?'

'In the flat.'

'Good. I thought I should give you a quick warning. It's probably not necessary.'

'What about?'

'I just wanted to warn you that you shouldn't get in touch with Dermot Birch. Or take a call from him. Have you got that?'

Jude froze. She could feel Dermot behind her. She shut her eyes for a moment and it was like being drunk. The ground tipped beneath her.

She didn't know how loud her phone was. Was Leila's voice audible? She made herself turn towards Dermot, who was staring down at the floor. He looked up, as if he could feel her gaze on him. She forced a smile that wouldn't stay in place, then held up a finger, signalling – she hoped – that this was all very unimportant and casual and would only take a moment.

'That may be a problem,' she said.

'What?'

Behind her, Jude heard a raspy high-pitched sound. She felt she ought to know it but she couldn't make it out.

'The kettle,' said Dermot. 'I'll get it.'

He stood up and went into the kitchen area.

388

Jude was suddenly nauseous. She couldn't concentrate. She could feel her hand trembling and she gripped her right wrist with her left hand to hold it steady and close to her ear.

'I think it might be a bit late for that,' she said into the phone, her voice too high.

'What do you mean? What are you talking about?'

Dermot returned to his chair. He was looking at her with a fixed, glassy stare.

'I think it's a bit hard to put into words. Just now. Over the phone.'

There was a pause.

'Is he there, Jude?'

'Yes, I think that's right,' said Jude, trying to talk as if she were reacting casually to something unimportant. But she could feel her voice trembling. It must be so obvious.

'Has he said anything?'

'No, no. It's all fine,' said Jude breezily. 'So is that all?'

Another pause. Jude didn't know how long she could keep this going.

'Right,' said Leila. 'If he's got a weapon, just . . . er . . . say, "I think so".'

'I don't think so. I don't know.'

'I'm ordering a car. It'll be there in five minutes. Just be calm. Keep talking, it'll be fine. We should probably stop the call but when you say goodbye, don't ring off.'

'Okay,' said Jude. 'That's fine. See you, then.'

She put the phone down on a shelf.

She turned towards Dermot. It was him. It was him all along. Why? How? But none of that mattered. It felt like they were underwater or in one of those dreams where everything happens very very slowly, great spaces opening up between the seconds.

'Everything all right?'

'Fine,' she said.

Five minutes, Leila had said. That was a short time, wasn't it? Almost nothing. But it might be longer. They might get stuck in traffic. And five minutes was actually quite a long time. Jude did the maths. Sixty times five. Three hundred seconds. One, two, three, four. It was a long time. She looked at Dermot looking at her. Be calm, Leila had said. She needed just to be calm. She needed to continue the way they had been talking before the phone had rung. Just normal conversation until the police arrived. But suddenly she couldn't think of anything to say. Not a word. Her mouth felt dry. She pictured herself running for the door but he was closer than she was and she had her bad ankle and was in slippers. She didn't know how quickly she could move.

What about pretending she needed to fetch something from outside? Like milk. But that sounded mad and meanwhile they weren't speaking.

She remembered the kettle whistling. A hot drink. That could use up some seconds.

'What did you want, coffee or tea?' she asked.

'I'm all right,' he said.

His voice was dry as straw. He licked his lips, then stared at her. They were both terrified, realised Jude. Anything could happen. The air felt electric, like when a storm is due.

'I'll make some tea for myself,' she said.

She turned and limped into the kitchen and again she was conscious of him behind her. She moved the kettle back on to the stove and the hideous whistling started again.

As she went to take it off the gas, she looked to one side of the stove, where the toaster stood, and saw something that didn't look quite right. What was it? Her mind was working so slowly. Then she saw: she was looking at the rack of knives on the magnetic strip. The colours of the rainbow.

She looked at the knives. Red. Yellow. Green.

There was a gap. One of them was missing. Blue.

Suddenly her mind worked quickly and with great clarity. Had he come knowing what he was going to do but not how? Now he had the knife, that he must have taken while she was talking to Leila Fox. The blue knife. He would probably like to do it while her back was turned, so he wouldn't have to see her. It was a matter of seconds. Should she just let it happen? It would almost be easier.

Or she could take a knife as well.

She looked at the knives. Jude's hands twitched in readiness but it was hopeless. She couldn't get into a knife fight.

The kettle. There was no time to think. She eased the lid off, the steam burning her wrist. She had to be quick. She would have to take it in her hands. Just a moment of pain. Three, two, one.

With a spasmodic intake of breath, she seized the handle in her right hand and the spout in her left and, howling with the agony, she turned and hurled it at his face. It felt like an explosion, everything became blurred, but then there was a scream. She saw a gap and she ran through the kitchen, pulling the door shut behind her – she didn't even look for any way of locking it or blocking it – and made for the stairs. She pulled the bike from against the wall and threw it behind her. She thought she heard footfalls but now she was at the front door. As she fumbled for the catch, she expected a hand on her, but she pulled it open and ran to the pavement.

Every movement sent a jolt through her ankle and leg and her left hand was raw and throbbing with the burn from the kettle. She turned left. Her slippers slipped on her feet, making it hard to run. Why was the road so empty? Should she bang on a door? No. She would only have one chance and what if they didn't answer in time?

She didn't dare look back. Maybe he was at her heels; maybe he was nearly on her and if she turned he would be on her.

She went into an alleyway between two houses that issued into a small council estate. She hobbled through a small corridor between two buildings and vaulted over a metal fence. She landed on her bad foot and she actually saw the pain as well as felt it, like a firework going off, all golden sparks. One of her slippers came off. She felt tiny stones and sharp objects jab at the sole of her good foot. But she was able to keep going, through the other side, where she knew there was a shopping street, and once she was out there, with people pushing buggies and old people walking slowly and a bus pulling up, she at last looked round and he wasn't there and she stopped with a moan and vomited on the pavement.

CHAPTER SIXTY-THREE

'That's disgusting,' said a voice.

A tiny old woman was staring at her, her lips pursed.

'I just . . .' said Jude, straightening up. Her eyes were watering, her foot was throbbing hideously. The palm of her left hand had a pulsing pain of its own. She could feel it up to the elbow.

'Someone's got to clear that up, that's what you people don't realise.'

She walked off and Jude stared after her. *You people?* She tried to think what to do. She had to call Leila, but she had no phone, no money. She wasn't even sure where she'd ended up in her frantic flight. She would have to ask for help, but who from?

Making up her mind, she limped into a newsagent on the corner, whimpering with pain.

'Excuse me,' she said to the man at the counter.

He looked at her and his expression changed from bland politeness to one of distaste.

'Please,' she said. She wanted to smile at him, but instead she gave a kind of snort. Her face felt snotty, and she wiped her forearm across her face. She reeked of sweat and vomit.

'Yes?' He wouldn't meet her gaze.

'Please,' she said again. 'Can you help me. I need to call someone urgently. Can I use your phone?'

'Sorry.' He turned away. 'You need to leave.'

'What?'

'I can't help.'

'Just a minute.'

'Please leave,' he said, stony-faced, not meeting her eyes.

Bewildered, Jude limped and shuffled to the door. She looked down at herself. Her swollen ankle looked enormous. One foot was bare and covered in blood. Her T-shirt was splattered with vomit.

She stood on the pavement and people moved to avoid her, even to avoid looking at her.

'Please,' she said to a trim middle-aged man in a suit. He had a pleasant face. 'Please can I borrow your phone?'

He didn't answer but looked away as if he hadn't heard.

'I need help,' said Jude to nobody.

'Here you go.' A rake-thin teenager with cavernous eyes was holding out his mobile.

'What?'

'You said you wanted to make a call.'

Jude blinked away her abrupt tears. 'Thank you. Really. Thank you.'

He jerked his shoulders, embarrassed. 'S'all right.'

She took the mobile and then she didn't know what to do. She didn't have Leila's number in her head, or barely any number except her parents, and they were three hours away from here. And Nat's: even more hopeless. Maybe she should call emergency services.

Then she had a thought: she knew her own number.

As she keyed it in, it occurred to her that she hadn't ended her call with Leila, so maybe it wouldn't ring. But it rang. And someone picked it up. A male voice, calm and inquiring, with an Essex accent. Not Dermot.

'I'm Jude,' she said with a sob. 'This is me.'

'Jude?'

'Yes. Who are you?'

'Hold on one moment.'

There was a slight pause, and another voice came on.

'Jude?'

'Leila? Is that you?'

'Yes. Are you all right? Where are you?'

'I don't know.'

'Look around you,' said Leila patiently. 'Tell me the street.'

'Um. Southwick Road where it joins with Talbot Street.'

'Wait there.'

Jude handed the mobile back to the boy.

'That was really nice of you.'

'Nothing.' He slid the phone into his pocket.

'You've no idea,' she said, and watched as he shuffled off.

She propped herself against a lamppost. Her body was a blizzard of strange sensations: pain and fear and confusion. What had just happened? Had Dermot come to murder her and had she thrown a kettle of boiling water over him and had she escaped? Was he badly hurt? Was she safe?

She suddenly realised how cold it was, how cold she was, in the winter chill. Everyone was in thick coats, gloves, hats, scarves wrapped round their necks and heads lowered against the hard wind. She was in a T-shirt, thin jeans and a single slipper. The knowledge made her start to shiver violently. She wrapped her goose-pimply arms against herself.

Dermot, she thought. It was Dermot all along. Liam had been killed by his younger brother. But why? And why had he targeted her? She was turning it over and over in her mind when a car drew up beside her and she jerked back, half-expecting to see Dermot's face at the window. There were two people in the front: a young man driving and, beside him, Leila Fox.

Jude let out the breath she hadn't realised she was holding.

Leila got out and looked at her in dismay.

'Are you okay?'

'Yes.'

'You must be freezing.'

'Yes.'

'Come on.'

Leila led her to the car and helped her into the back seat, leaning over her to buckle the safety belt as if she was a small child. She got in beside her. But they didn't drive very far, just a few hundred metres along the road and up a small side street where they came to a halt.

Leila undid her seat belt and turned to Jude.

'We'll get you looked at soon and cleaned up. But I need to ask you a few questions. First of all, your injuries. What happened to your foot?'

Jude looked down at her foot, almost as if it belonged to someone else.

'That was from yesterday. I went for a run and fell over. It was stupid, really.'

'And your hand?'

Jude lifted her throbbing left hand and looked at the inflamed palm, now starting to break out in large puffy blisters. 'It was the kettle. I threw the kettle of boiling water at him. I think some of it hit him because he screamed, but I don't know how badly he was hurt. Bacitracin.'

'What?'

'That's what I need to put on my hand. It hurts quite a lot at the moment.'

'Did he attack you?'

'I saw there was a knife missing. A knife with a blue handle. I knew I had to act quickly. Before he used it.'

'You think Dermot took it?'

'I know he did. I'd been cleaning. There were four different-coloured knives on the wall, and then he came and there were three. The blue one was missing.'

Leila Fox nodded slowly.

'Has he admitted it?' Jude asked.

'He was gone. We have a witness who saw him running down the road, shouting and holding a hand over his face.'

'So he can't have been that badly burned.'

'We'll get him soon.'

Jude shivered violently. 'Why me? I didn't know anything.'

'It wasn't what you knew.'

'What do you mean?'

In answer, the detective tapped the young man at the wheel and said, 'Pass me those photos, please.'

He took a folder from the pocket on his door and handed it back. Leila slid out a sheaf of glossy photos and shuffled through them.

'Here,' she said. 'This is a photo from the scene of the crime. Don't worry,' she added hastily. 'Not of Liam's body. Just things that were there.'

Jude peered at it.

A churn of mud and brambles and trampled grass; an old tin can and an empty crisp packet, a rusting bicycle bell, a couple of cigarette butts, a shredded plastic bag, a few scatterings of twigs, the grisly remains of a dead bird.

'I don't get it,' she said. 'Except it's a horrible place to die.'

'Look.' Leila tapped something small on the edge of the photos. 'Do you see what that is?'

'What?'

Leila selected another photo and put it on Jude's lap.

'This.'

It was laid out on a shiny blank surface, lit from above, and taken from close up.

'Oh,' said Jude.

A small, delicate wooden wishbone, minus its string.

She was bewildered, looking helplessly from the laboratory photo to the scene of the crime.

'I still don't understand.'

'When Liam died, one of the things we found by his body was this little wishbone. We showed all the objects to Danny Kelner, and she identified this object as belonging to Liam. He had made it and she told us that he wore it on a leather thong. We assumed it had come off during the struggle.'

'But—' began Jude.

'Exactly. When I saw you yesterday you were wearing the same wishbone round your neck and you said you'd taken it from Liam's luggage when you were staying in the cottage in Norfolk.'

'He made four of them,' Jude said slowly. She still didn't quite understand. 'For his family. Each of them has one.'

'I know that now. Now. So the question was, if it didn't belong to Liam, who did it belong to?'

Jude thought for a moment. Everything seemed so hard. Then she remembered. *Snap*, he had said, and shown it to her.

'Dermot was wearing his. I saw it.'

'He was wearing Tara's. I called Tara and Andy Birch and they confirmed that Liam had made one for each of them, but Tara said she had lost hers a week or so ago. She had looked for it everywhere. We believe Dermot took it. He must have realised he'd left his at the crime scene.'

'Poor Tara,' said Jude, running her hand through her sweaty hair. 'How will she bear it?' She felt a sudden shock of awareness. 'But why are you just sitting here? You need to find him.'

'Do you have any idea where he might go?'

'How would I know? He looked desperate, out of control. Home to his parents?'

'We've already sent officers there, although it seems unlikely he would go to the first place we would look.'

Jude thought about where someone would run if they wanted to escape being caught. She imagined forests, seas, dark alleyways, cartoonish disguises, as if Dermot was in an old-fashioned movie about a life unravelling. Where would she go, if it was her? She pictured him blundering around with his scalded face, terrified and nowhere to hide.

'I barely know him,' she said helplessly. 'I know nothing about his life.'

'All right,' said Leila. 'Now, you should go and get sorted. Go back to your flat and collect a few of your things. You're not staying there.'

'Because he might come back?'

'That's right, though it's highly unlikely. Do you have anywhere you can go?'

'I was about to move out to a friend's anyway.'

'Call them. Tell them you'll be there shortly.'

'I don't have my phone.'

'I do.'

Leila dipped her hand into her coat pocket and drew out Jude's mobile. Jude scrolled down to Dee's number.

'It's me,' she said when Dee answered. 'Can I come round now?'

As she spoke, a sob lodged in her throat.

'Of course! The sooner the better. I've invited a few of the gang for supper, is that okay?'

'Great,' said Jude wanly.

'I thought I could make a giant pie. And we could make some kind of lethal cocktail. We can play board games and get drunk. I'm in the shops now, but I'll be back at mine in less than half an hour.'

'Thank you, Dee. I should warn you, though . . .'

But Dee had gone.

CHAPTER SIXTY-FOUR

There were two police cars parked outside the flat. Inside, everything was clean and tidy after her clear-up, except for water all over the floor, several smashed cups, and an upturned chair. Her bike had been leaned back against the wall and Jude saw that its front wheel was buckled.

Leila went back to the station, while the young officer accompanied Jude inside and waited in the kitchen while she hastily showered and pulled on her warmest clothes.

She fed the cat for the last time and tried to scratch it under the chin, but it stared at her in outrage. Then the officer picked up her bags and they left.

In the car to Dee's flat, Jude sat back in her seat and half-closed her eyes. She was on her way back to her old life, but she was suddenly and over-whelmingly exhausted. Everything that had happened felt distant and unreal. Images spooled through her mind; faces and scenes that became tangled, the Liam Birch she knew at eighteen sliding into the man who had stood in the hospital foyer that day, waiting to turn her life upside down, his face morphing into the face of his younger brother, his killer.

It was like peering into a sunless rock pool – drifting fronds, things that crawled and jelly-like creatures with mouths that opened and closed; all in constant motion but going nowhere. The cottage in the wilds of Norfolk where the sea rolled across mud and shingle, the muddy site where Liam's body had been found, the line of figures walking across the marshes on their way to his interment, hand in hand. The baroque house where Danny sat on the wicker chair as if she was some ancient queen, the tattooed tears on her pale cheek. The funeral. The wake. People drinking, dancing, laughing. Jude remembered Dermot standing by the toppled table, mess everywhere and a look of strange triumph on his face.

Something snagged. A fleeting memory tugged. What?

Floating towards her out of the murk came a memory: Jude had gone downstairs from putting Alfie to bed and was heading for the conservatory in search of her bag. Danny had come out of the conservatory and they had briefly talked. Then Jude had met Dermot, moving jerkily. She could see his face now, ghastly pale with spittle on his lips and his dark eyes glittering. He had a red oval of lipstick on his cheek. He had smashed his fist against the wall and said, 'I will not stop. You little cunt,' or words like that, a howl of injury and rage.

Then he had tipped the table, and as he stood beside the havoc, he had said, 'There!'

Who was he saying that to?

Danny.

Danny who had just left the room. Danny with the red lipstick. Danny who was the partner of his brother.

And now Jude remembered how Dermot had reacted that morning, when she'd told him that Danny and Vin were lovers, and perhaps always had been. He'd told her it wasn't true, she was lying.

Suddenly, horribly, the confusion cleared and everything became sharply clear. Things slid into place, like a collection of blades, chains, cogs. Click click click, all the nasty parts locking together.

The car turned left down the road where Dee lived.

Danny and Dermot, Jude thought. Of course.

The car stopped and the officer got out and held her door open for her. Jude struggled out and he pulled her bags after her and carried them to the entrance. The lights were on: Dee would be making her pie in the small, messy kitchen, her hands floury. Later, they would eat and drink and play board games. Her old, merry world continuing and Jude was about to be pulled back into it, as if nothing much had happened: merely a glitch.

She stood at the door but she didn't press the bell. Her mind was racing now, trying to keep ahead of the thoughts streaming into this new structure. She felt on fire with fury and shame. She didn't ring the bell, just pushed the bags out of sight and limped back on to the road.

CHAPTER SIXTY-FIVE

She started to walk. If she'd been able to she would have run. She knew her foot was hurting and her hand throbbed, but she couldn't feel it. Later.

Soon she was on the marshes, past the filter beds and along the river. There were little patches of frost in the shade which crunched underfoot, and tiny films of ice on puddles. It was very cold, but Jude didn't feel cold.

Dermot had been having an affair with his brother's partner. He had killed Liam, while Danny had given herself a perfect alibi. All this on the evening when Liam had his own sinister plan and arranged his own perfect alibi: his teenage sweetheart, her, the unwitting spanner in the works.

Two crimes. Two mirror images.

Liam had been killed at the exact spot where Danny always passed, every Saturday except for that Saturday. He was waiting for her there, but he had met Dermot instead, Dermot with a knife in his hand.

Dermot had done it for Danny.

Or no: he had done it at Danny's bidding. And

then Danny had told him it was over between them, on the night of Liam's funeral. He was a murderer and he was also a poor, stupid, self-pitying sap.

Danny had planned it but Dermot had executed it, and now he was going to be punished while she would smile serenely and go free.

Then Jude thought: Vin. Of course.

Danny and Vin had planned it together.

Vin and Danny. Vin with his booming laugh and his hairy hands, his gargantuan appetites.

There were herons on the marshes. One of them stood a few yards from her, so still at first she thought it was made of stone. Only its eye moved.

There was the riding school, the skating rink. Jude lurched on, jolts of pain spiking through her and her hand throbbing so hard it made her feel sick – but it didn't matter. She needed to stand in front of Danny and say, *I know what you did. I know what you are.*

She briefly considered calling Leila to tell her what she had, in a flash, understood. But Leila was busy finding Dermot, and Dermot would surely confess everything: how he'd been played by his brother's lover to kill his brother. How he'd been in love with a woman who'd used him as deftly as a carpenter uses a saw.

Jude didn't want to think about Vin, but he crowded his way into her mind, broad-shouldered, white-teethed, fleshy, grinning Vin. She realised – or at least her squirming, horrified body realised – that he must have taken her to bed as a kind of gratifying strategy. He'd thought to make sure she really had nothing against them, or maybe he'd believed that sex with him would wipe away any suspicions and make her docile and compliant, part of the family.

A violent shudder ran through the length of her.

Was that their plan? Danny would have sex with Dermot, while Vin would have sex with Jude.

She came to the end of the marshes and stepped on to tarmac. Her foot would barely hold her weight now. She hobbled along the road, turned into the street she had thought never to walk down again, stopped in her tracks.

CHAPTER SIXTY-SIX

The sight was so unexpected that it took Jude a moment to make sense of it. The road was full, a riot of orange and white and flashing lights. She made out two ambulances and at least three police cars. They were parked at angles in the middle of the road as if they had been abandoned in a hurry. As she got closer, she saw that the whole road had been closed off with a 'no entry' sign. Two police officers in yellow high-visibility jackets were standing by the sign.

'Can I get through?' Jude asked.

A female officer shook her head. 'The road's closed off.'

'What's happened?'

'There's been an incident.'

'What kind of incident? Is it in number three? Has anyone been hurt?'

The officer shrugged. 'We can't talk about that.'

'Is it number three? If it is, I know the people who live there. I need to know what happened.'

'You'll just have to wait.'

Jude edged along the plastic barrier that had been set up, so that she could get a better view. Yes, it was definitely the house. She could see that the front door was open and there were uniformed officers clustered in groups. It looked like the aftermath of something. She became aware of the other officer standing in front of her.

But then she noticed something. Or rather, the absence of something. There were no paramedics. There were groups of police talking but no sign of anyone in green overalls, nobody sitting in the ambulance. That was a sign that something serious was going on, something that needed everyone inside.

'This isn't a show,' the officer said.

'I'm allowed to stand here.'

Both of them had to stand to one side as a police van drove up. The two officers moved the barrier to allow the van to pass. Then they quickly pulled it back into place. The male officer looked at Jude and shook his head.

'Nobody's going in,' he said.

'I know those people,' she said desperately. 'I need to find out what's going on.'

'You'll hear when everyone else hears.'

Jude thought she would explode with frustration. She didn't know what to do. She took out her phone and called Leila Fox.

'I'm at the house,' she said.

'What house?'

'Danny's. Vin's.'

'I told you not to do anything—'

'Something's happened,' Jude interrupted.

411

'There's ambulances and police in the road. They won't let me anywhere near. Have you heard anything?'

There was a pause.

'I'll be right over.'

As Jude was putting her phone back in her pocket, she saw someone emerge from the house and start walking along the street towards her. It was Erika, but she looked different. She was moving slowly and staring in front of her like someone who was sleepwalking. She stepped off the pavement without noticing and staggered slightly but she didn't stop or look concerned. She just kept walking.

As she approached the barrier, the female officer intercepted her and said something that Jude couldn't hear. It wasn't clear whether she was trying to stop her or offering help but after a moment she stepped back and Erika walked past her and edged round the barrier. She noticed Jude without any apparent surprise.

'They said I should get some air,' she said in a deliberate, detached tone.

'What's happening?'

Jude had the uncomfortable sensation that Erika was looking at her but not seeing her. Her eyes seemed focused on something far behind Jude's head.

'They're all working on her,' she said dreamily.

'What? Who?'

'I wasn't meant to see. The kitchen door was

open. They're surrounding her on the floor. I could see the blood.'

'Who's on the floor?'

Erika looked puzzled. Jude wasn't clear if Erika was even hearing what she was saying.

'He was shouting and shouting and smashing things. Picking things up and throwing them at the wall. He had a knife.'

'Was it Dermot?'

Erika seemed surprised by the question, as if her chain of thought had been interrupted.

'Yes, Dermot. He was shouting that she had used him and that she had destroyed him. He was just shouting and shouting and waving this knife. I couldn't believe it was really happening. It was more like some kind of a dream. You don't expect anything like that in real life.'

'What did he do?'

Erika looked at Jude blankly.

'Alfie was there. I picked him up and ran upstairs, up to my bedroom. I shut the door and pushed things against it so that it wouldn't open. I left her to it. Do you hear that? I thought I was saving Alfie but I left Danny to it. I was trying to keep Alfie calm and sing songs to him. All the time I could hear the smashing sounds downstairs. I was hoping that someone would do something, go and help. Nobody did. Irina stayed where she was, and Doc and Vin weren't there. Nobody could help. And then the smashing stopped and the screaming started.' She looked more directly at Jude. Her eyes were staring, bloodshot.

'You should be saying this to the police, not to me,' said Jude, who wasn't sure if she could bear to hear any more. 'You're a witness; they must be wondering where you've got to.'

'Have you heard an animal scream?' said Erika, as if Jude hadn't spoken. 'It was like that. It didn't sound like her. It didn't sound human. And it seemed to go on and on. I know I should have left Alfie there and gone down to help. I didn't. I was frozen. I felt like a child pulling the covers over their head because they're frightened of the dark. I dialled 999 but then I didn't do anything else. I sat there with Alfie and I tried to sing to him and stop him hearing what was happening downstairs.'

'There was nothing you could do. You saved Alfie. You looked after him. That's all you could have done.'

'I let him into the house. Me. There was this loud knocking at the door, banging, like someone was trying to break it down. I didn't think properly. We should have gone and hidden somewhere, locked ourselves in. But I went to the door and opened it. Dermot was on the doorstep. He was shouting: "Where is she? Where is she?" If Vin had been there, he'd have been able to stop him.'

'I don't think that's true.'

Once again, Erika continued as if Jude wasn't there. It was like she was talking to herself.

'He always looked up to Vin. He was like a puppy. He'd do anything for Vin and for Liam. I could have said that Danny wasn't there or that she was upstairs but I just froze. I couldn't think of anything to say and he burst past me. It was like he was going to explode. He was punching the wall as he walked along. I followed him and I saw the knife and I picked up Alfie and I ran. I left her. I left her to it. To him. You always wonder what you'll do in an emergency. Now I know. That's what I did.'

She started to shiver violently. Her teeth were chattering.

'We need to get you warm,' said Jude. She touched Erika's forehead. It felt clammy. She took her by the arm and led her towards the barrier. She explained that she was a doctor and that Erika needed to be warmed up and given some fluids. They looked dubious but Jude persisted. They told her not to go near the house but they let the two of them through.

When they arrived at the nearest ambulance, all doors left open, they met a paramedic. She was a young woman, red-headed, freckled, sitting in the rear entrance of the ambulance. She brought Erika a blanket and a bottle of water. As she handed them across, Jude looked at her. She looked exhausted. And she looked very young. She made Jude feel almost middle-aged.

'How's it going?' Jude asked.

'They're still in there. I'm just taking a moment.'

'Grim, is it?'

The woman pulled a face.

'He had a few minutes, just him and her. It was . . .'

She stopped herself.

'It's all right,' said Jude. 'I'm a doctor. I've seen this sort of thing.'

'No, you haven't.'

There was a silence. The woman clearly wasn't going to elaborate on what she'd seen.

'I thought they'd send a helicopter,' said Jude. 'It could land on the marshes.'

The woman seemed about to say something but then she just looked at Erika and then at Jude. Jude recognised the expression and what the woman wasn't saying. There was no need for a helicopter. There was no point in rushing Danny to hospital. Jude knew those times from when she had worked in casualty as a junior doctor. You work on a case of cardiac arrest for ten minutes, then twenty, then forty, beyond a moment when there's any real hope of recovery. She may not have seen what the paramedic had seen but she'd attended a scene where the patient was losing blood faster than it could be transfused. At the end, when it was finally called, everyone around the table looked like they'd been bathing in blood.

'Have they arrested him?' Jude asked.

The woman looked puzzled, as if she didn't know there was someone who needed to be arrested, or had forgotten it.

'I don't know,' she said. 'You get a kind of tunnel vision. But there were a load of police here when I arrived. They seemed to be with someone in a room off to the side. It was all a bit chaotic.' She looked back at Erika, who was staring in front of her, her lips pale and her face chalky. 'Are you all right? Are you feeling dizzy?'

Erika shook her head slowly. The paramedic stood up. She looked at Jude.

'You might want to keep an eye on her for a few minutes. I'd better be getting back inside.'

But before she could even move, a cluster of green-clad figures started to emerge from the house. As they got closer, Jude saw the dark-brown splashes on their uniforms. Brown, Jude thought to herself, not red. It didn't look the way you expected. There was no sense of urgency about them, just exhaustion. They weren't speaking and they weren't even looking at each other. One of them, a tall, strongly built man, shook his head slowly.

CHAPTER SIXTY-SEVEN

On the Monday, Jude went back to work. Her foot, still swollen up to twice its normal size and a virulent purple-blue, was strapped; her left hand was wrapped in a bandage and sending out pulses of pain. She wore clothes borrowed from her new housemates since most of hers were still at Nat's.

It had only been a few weeks, but her absence seemed like months to her, or a whole lifetime, her other life a kind of dream. On that first morning, she was horribly anxious that she would no longer remember how to be a doctor, that her colleagues would watch her and whisper behind her back, or that she would suddenly start crying. She felt obscurely disgraced and also shockingly vulnerable. As she limped through the revolving doors and into the foyer, she tried to appear professional and confident. Dr Jude Winter, reporting for business.

Within minutes, she was back in the thick flow of hospital life, marked by the bleep of the pager, the ward round, the hurried consultations. She had forgotten how comforting the sense of purpose was, every moment measured out, the minute hand on the large clocks in the dementia wards sweeping round.

By Wednesday, it was the violent hiatus of her time away that seemed unreal, a hallucination. Jude knew that tomorrow afternoon, when she had a day off before a string of nights, she had to go to the police station and give her full statement to Leila Fox – but that was just a bureaucratic necessity. The sense of dread was ebbing away. Mostly she was exhausted, and it was the kind of exhaustion best cured by daily routine.

So when she left the hospital in the early evening, stepping out into the biting cold, and looked at the messages on her mobile, she was startled to see she had three missed calls from Tara Birch, as well as a text, saying: *Call me!*

She didn't want to call Tara. She didn't want to think about her – a mother of two sons, one of whom had killed the other. How would you endure such anguish?

The answer, it turned out, was Alfie.

'He's with us,' said Tara, throaty and thick-voiced as though she had a bad cold. 'We're his family now.'

'I'm glad,' said Jude. 'I hope that's some kind of solace.'

Anything she might say seemed paltry and tasteless.

'I wouldn't go that far,' said Tara. 'But me and

419

Andy, we're going to do everything in our power to give him a proper childhood.'

'That's good,' said Jude. 'I'm sure you will.'

She put her mobile under her chin and pulled on her mittens, taking care not to scrape her injured hand. Her breath was smoking.

'Danny's mother died several years ago and her father's got a history of violence, so it was always going to be us.'

Jude tried to suppress the memory that flashed into her mind, of Danny and Tara pulling at Alfie like an awful tug of war.

'Right,' she said.

She put on her helmet. She'd borrowed a friend's bike while hers was being fixed.

'You know what happened?' asked Tara.

'Yes.'

'Of course you do. The whole world knows.'

'They'll forget again.'

'They're lucky.'

There was a silence.

'What did we do wrong?'

Jude groped for words but she didn't find them. She made a sound instead.

'I have a favour to ask you,' said Tara.

'Oh?'

Jude wanted to hurl her mobile into the road and watch the cars crush it. No more favours, ever again.

'It's not much. I just want you to go to the house.'

'I can't do that.'

'Please, Jude. I can't do it. I'm hundreds of miles away, with Alfie. And there are things that he wants. When he gets upset, which he does a lot, he asks for them.'

'Can't you get someone to post them?'

'Please.'

'There must be somebody else . . .'

So it was that the following morning, Jude returned once more to the house.

There were still crime-scene tapes up, and she could see that one of the windows at the front was broken. All the curtains were closed and she couldn't see any lights on. Perhaps no one was there – because how could you stay on in a house where a few days ago a woman, a housemate and friend, had been slaughtered?

But even as she was thinking this, a curtain on the first floor was pulled open and a face looked out. Irina, gazing down at the street, her face like a tragic mask with a gash of red lipstick across the mouth.

Then a voice came from behind her.

'Jude.'

She turned to see Doc.

'Hello.' She hadn't prepared herself properly.

'Have you come to help us?'

'What?'

'Come on in, then.'

The house wasn't empty but full and in a state of dynamic disarray: people were going up and down the stairs with boxes, coming down the hall carrying pieces of furniture. Someone staggered out of the conservatory with a stone statue in his arms.

Jude stepped into the hall. She heard the sound of banging from upstairs and someone shout something unintelligible. Then a clattering and a giant wicker laundry basket came tumbling down the steps.

She ducked into the front room to avoid a collision. A man was up a ladder, chipping away at the large plaster rose in the centre of the ceiling.

'Hi,' he said, looking down at her. 'Pass me that screwdriver can you?'

'I don't think you're allowed to take things like that,' said Jude, passing the screwdriver. 'It's part of the house.'

'Are you a lawyer or something?'

'No.'

'Vin told me to.'

Jude felt her stomach lurch. 'Is he here?'

'Vin? Nah. He's taken a load of stuff to the dump, but he'll be back in half an hour or an hour if you want to see him.'

'I don't.'

'Jude!'

Irina was in the doorway, her arms full of curtains.

'Hello.'

'You came in our hour of need.'

'I just came to collect—'

'None of us can speak,' said Irina. 'None of us have the words. We are in a state of shock. Of trauma. What can you say about a woman who lived life to the full, who made other people suffer but who suffered herself, whose partner was killed and who was butchered in her own house? What can you say? Nothing.'

The curtains dropped to the floor.

'Hammer,' said the man above them, reaching down his arm.

Flakes of plaster fell to the floor. Jude watched as a crack appeared in the ceiling and began to crawl towards the wall.

'I have a piano,' said Irina. 'What will I do with the piano?'

'Are you all moving out?' asked Jude.

'I think Liam and Danny had lots of debts,' said Irina vaguely. 'So it turns out that this house officially belongs to someone else now.'

'Who?'

'Exactly,' said Irina darkly. 'And anyway, who wants to live with Danny's ghost?'

Jude left the room and went upstairs. She had a list of the things Tara wanted for Alfie: a soft elephant that his grandparents had given him at birth, a xylophone, a favourite picture book, a particular plastic bowl, pyjamas with flamingos on them, a colourful quilt, a potty in the shape of a hippo.

It felt wrong to be here, tiptoeing into rooms, pulling open cupboards and drawers. She dreaded

Vin returning. She found the quilt in Danny's room, which looked uncannily the same as when Jude had fallen asleep on her bed with Alfie beside her. She remembered his flop of gleaming curls and the warmth of his breath on her cheek, while downstairs the horrible party continued. His pyjamas were rolled up in the corner, and when Jude picked them up they smelled faintly of urine. The xylophone was under the bed, with one of its metal slats missing. The potty was in the first-floor bathroom.

Jude hesitated, then went downstairs in search of the other things.

Erika was in the conservatory, sitting on the floor with her knees drawn up and surrounded by the chaos of half-packed boxes. She glanced up as Jude entered.

'I'm just having a rest,' she said.

'Of course. I'm looking for a couple of things for Alfie. I'll only be here a minute. I don't mean to get in anyone's way.'

'I don't want any of this stuff anyway. I don't know why we don't just set fire to it and have done. It's all horrible. Who wants a dead plant or a cracked picture or a porcelain bathtub or velvet curtains full of moths or rugs that are falling to pieces?'

Jude saw the picture book and bent to pick it up. She looked out into the garden; two men were emptying a brazier, and as she watched they lifted it up and carried it towards the conservatory. It was obviously heavy, so she opened the door for them.

'Thank you,' said the taller man. 'It weighs a ton and I've already dropped it on Nico's foot.'

Nico. Something stirred in Jude's mind.

'Are you Nico?' she asked the shorter man, who had blond hair in a top-knot and was wearing drawstring cotton trousers and a singlet, as if it was August not December.

'I am.'

'The Nico who filmed Danny dancing that night – the night Liam died?'

He gave a small, curious bow.

'The same,' he said.

'Out of curiosity,' she said, 'what did you think when she told you to film her at that party?'

'Danny? She didn't tell me to film her.'

'No?'

'That was Vin. Vin arranged it. And when he gave the word, he and Danny danced: it was like a show they were putting on. He was very insistent that I put it up on YouTube.' He gave a small smile. 'She was a great dancer, Danny, I'll say that for her.'

'Right,' said Jude. 'Right.'

Liam was dead, Danny was dead, Dermot was in a cell somewhere, and Vin was overseeing the packing up of the house, taking what he wanted, moving on.

Jude found the shabby soft elephant stuffed down

the back of a sofa, found the plastic bowl, left the house without saying goodbye to anyone.

As she limped down the road with her bag of Alfie's things, a large van drove past her, music coming from its open window. She caught a glimpse of the man at the wheel: Vin looked like he was singing.

CHAPTER SIXTY-EIGHT

By the time Jude had finished giving her statement to the police, it was dark outside. Soon, she thought, it would be the shortest day of the year. Then it would be Christmas and she hadn't even thought about that. Then the new year and the day of her cancelled wedding. She had barely thought about Nat recently either: did that mean she had never properly loved him, or was it just that time and the flood of events washed everything away in the end?

'Are we done?' she asked Leila Fox.

'Yes. All done.'

'So we won't be seeing each other again? I won't be a witness at the trial.'

'Dermot's pleading guilty. There'll be psychiatric reports but not much else.'

Jude felt a moment of alarm.

'Do you think he'll be found insane?'

'No. He won't. Anyway, whatever happens, this bit of your life is over, Jude.'

'Yes.'

'How are you?'

It felt a bit late, here at their last meeting, but Leila was talking to her like a friend.

'I won't be going on runs for a while, and my hand's a bit sore.'

'I meant, how are *you*?'

'I'm okay. I'm back at work and that's good. The media attention is dying down at last. I'm living with friends. You know, people ask me about what happened and I say that I got caught up in something. That's not right, though. I chose to do Liam a favour. I chose to get involved with that household. Don't tell me it wasn't stupid.'

'I'm not going to.'

'And when I was eighteen, I let Liam derail his own life in order to protect mine. Now he's dead and I'm a doctor.'

'He made a choice.'

'I made a choice as well.' Jude hesitated. She had one last question. She was almost scared to ask it. 'Can I confess it? Give myself up?'

Leila looked at her for a few seconds, her head slightly to one side, her clear grey eyes quite sympathetic.

'It's too late for that,' she said finally. 'I'm afraid you'll have to find some other way to atone.'

'How did Dermot know?'

Leila smiled.

'I thought you'd already asked your last question?'

'Just one more. How did he know?'

'How did he know what?'

428

'Liam knew, or thought he knew, that Danny would be there on the marshes at that time. But how did Dermot know that Liam would be there?'

'That's simple. Liam told him.'

'Why?'

'He thought Dermot was on his side. He had no idea that Dermot loved Danny more than he loved him. A lot more.'

'It seems so – well, so *wild* to kill someone just because they're going to leave them.'

Leila shook her head. 'All I can say is that we live in different worlds, Jude. If you saw what I see week after week, you wouldn't feel that. Men kill their wives because they say they feel nagged. There are several cases every year when men facing bankruptcy kill their entire family and then themselves, as if their partner and children are just an extension of themselves. I think that the Liam Birch who came to see you and ask you for a favour was a man at the end of his rope. He told Dermot that Danny was planning to leave him and take Alfie. What's more, she was apparently going to fight for sole custody.'

'God, she must have hated him by the end. Surely that wouldn't have happened.'

Leila shrugged. 'Maybe not, but she cited his drinking, his bouts of anger and violence, his various affairs.'

'What a mess.'

'Liam's business was going under, so he was looking at losing his house, which he had put his heart into, as well as his son who he adored. A man like that who feels that he has nothing left to lose can be very dangerous.'

Jude was silent for a few moments, thinking of the two brothers.

'So Dermot killed Liam in the very spot that Liam was planning to kill Danny.'

'Yes.'

'Liam's dead. Danny's dead. Dermot's going to prison for ever. What about Vin?'

'What about him?'

'He was involved. He must have been.'

'You have proof of that?'

'It's obvious. He set up the alibi. I met the man who filmed them. Nico someone-or-other. You should talk to him. He'll tell you.'

'Thank you for your suggestion, Jude,' said Leila drily. 'We have talked to him. We have also interviewed Vin. He was here for several hours, with his lawyer.' She held up a hand to stop Jude from speaking. 'We have also been through his laptop and phone.'

'And?'

'And nothing. You have to let it go.' She stood up. 'And this is where we say goodbye.'

She held out her broad, warm hand and Jude grasped it.

'Don't take this the wrong way, Jude, but I don't want to hear from you again.'

430

CHAPTER SIXTY-NINE

It was an early September day but it still felt like summer. Jude stepped out from the hospital into the bustle of Whitechapel. She'd been waiting for this all day. She had no plans, nobody to meet and she would make the most of this beautiful day on her own. She would go for a walk, maybe down by the river, clear her head.

Then she saw him.

It felt like she was in one of the nightmares she sometimes had, where the same event happened over and over again and she couldn't get away from it. She remembered that feeling of seeing Liam at the end of her shift. It was more than a memory. It was as if it was happening again. She felt it like a punch in the stomach.

He was standing by the kerb, a large man casually dressed in jeans and a blue T-shirt and a grey tracksuit top, bearded and his hair still long. He had his back to the traffic and had clearly been waiting for her.

Vin gave his broad smile.

'What are you doing here?' she asked, as calmly as she could manage.

'I wanted to see you.' He was still smiling. 'I'm glad I did. You look well. A bit tired, maybe.'

'I've just finished a shift.'

'What people like you do is amazing. Caring for old people. You're the real heroes.'

'Stop that. Why are you here?'

He look amused rather than dismayed by Jude's unfriendliness.

'Do I need a reason?'

'Yes.'

He seemed to think for a moment, frowning slightly, his head slightly to one side.

'Something has been nagging at me,' he said. 'I felt there was just one loose end.'

Jude felt a stab of alarm and looked around at the crowded street. Vin laughed.

'I just wanted a word.'

'I don't think that's necessary.'

'It'll just be a moment. It won't take longer than drinking a cup of coffee.'

'Sorry,' said Jude, and tried to walk past him. He stepped in the way.

'We can go to a crowded café,' he said. 'There's nothing for you to worry about.'

'I'm not worried about anything. It's just that we don't have anything to say to each other.'

'Ten minutes. Then you don't ever have to see me again. Otherwise I'll feel like we have unfinished business.'

Vin's tone and expression seemed affable, but

every word he said sounded like a threat. Would talking to him make him go away for ever or would it encourage him? Was she about to make the same mistake all over again?

She said okay, and a couple of minutes later she was sitting at a wooden table in a café much like the one to which she had gone with Liam almost a year earlier. Perhaps it was the same one. She couldn't remember. Vin bought a camomile tea for Jude and a cappuccino for himself. Before drinking he tore two sachets of sugar, tipped them into his cup and stirred it. He saw her expression and laughed.

'I suppose you're more a no-milk, no-sugar sort of girl.'

'Ten minutes,' said Jude.

'Come on,' said Vin. 'You must have something you want to ask me. You must be curious.'

'I know everything I need to know.'

Now Vin frowned. 'The police questioned me, just as they questioned you. They didn't find anything to charge me with, nothing at all. They went through everything. They searched the house. They took away my computer and my phone. They went through my texts and my emails and my Facebook messages and my Instagram and prob-ably other things I didn't even know I had. Nothing. *Nada.*'

Jude shrugged: it meant nothing to her. What Vin and Danny had done together, what they had planned, what they had concealed, wasn't the kind of thing you put in an email. She couldn't let it go entirely. She had to say something.

'I know you arranged the film. The film on YouTube that gave you an alibi.'

She expected him to look defensive but he only smiled again.

'We were having a good time at a party. I asked someone to film it. That isn't a crime.'

'You seem quite cheerful, considering your best friend and the woman you loved have both been murdered and you are responsible for both of those things.'

'Time has passed,' said Vin breezily. 'It was difficult at first but I've been through the stages of grief. I've arrived at acceptance.'

'I'd say you're stuck at denial.'

He laughed again. His laugh made her want to punch him.

'That's good. You're sharp. I always liked that about you. You know that night we had, exploring each other—'

'Stop that,' Jude hissed.

He had been speaking slightly too loudly and she sensed that the young couple at the next table had stopped their conversation and were eavesdropping.

'I just wanted to say that when two people have shared something like that, something intimate, then there's a connection. There'll always be a connection.'

'It was a mistake,' Jude said, in a violent whisper. 'A terrible, terrible mistake.'

Vin reached his hand across the table. Jude pulled her hand away before he could take it.

'We're almost done,' she said. 'Have you said what you had to say?'

His expression turned more serious and he leaned across the table and spoke in a quieter tone.

'You can ask me anything you want,' he said. 'I promise I'll tell you the truth. Anything.'

Jude stared across at him: at his broad, mirthful face.

'One thing. Do you feel bad?'

Vin looked genuinely surprised but more amused than angry.

'Is that it? That's a bit of a wasted opportunity. No, of course I don't.' He leaned forward once more. 'Now I get to ask you one question.'

'No, you don't.'

'I'll ask it anyway. You can answer it if you like or not.' He paused, as if thinking of how to phrase it. 'What was the plan?' he asked finally.

'What do you mean? What plan?'

'It's the only thing I keep wondering about. I know why Liam did what he did. Danny was going to destroy him. She was going to take Alfie and fight for sole custody. He'd lose it all. Obviously he made the mistake of telling Dermot about it. Nobody's perfect. But what was *your* plan? Or was it your idea in the first place? What was in it for you?'

Jude thought of not answering. She looked at him as he waited, so sure of himself, so blithe.

'There was no plan,' she said eventually. 'I didn't know what he was going to do.'

Vin nodded his head slowly.

'That's right, it couldn't have been your idea. The original idea was that Dermot would be his alibi. That makes sense. Your brother. That's someone you can trust. But Dermot said no and went and told Danny about it.'

Jude felt a jolt of understanding. Yes, that was it. That was why Liam had told Dermot. His brother was the one person he thought he could turn to. Vin continued speaking as if he was thinking aloud.

'He didn't know that Dermot had a big, big crush on Danny. That was bad luck. For Liam, I mean. Not for Danny.' Vin paused and thought for a moment. 'I guess in the end it was bad luck for Danny as well.' He grinned in a way that turned Jude's stomach. 'That was all in the future. When Dermot turned him down, he needed someone else who would give him an alibi for when he killed the mother of his child, so he turned to . . .' Vin stopped speaking and looked Jude full in the face for several seconds. 'His lost love.'

'I wasn't his lost love. And he wasn't mine.'

'Then what *was* it like? You were his big alibi. It all depended on you. When you heard that Danny had been murdered, you were the one who would have backed him up. He must have had a lot of faith in you and yet you say that there was nothing between you.'

He shook his head knowingly.

'I wouldn't,' Jude said. 'I would never have covered up for him.'

'Maybe.' Vin spoke as if it didn't matter very much.

'Do you really think you're going to get away with this?'

His expression remained as cheerful as ever. He lifted his right hand and wagged his forefinger at her reprovingly.

'Dr Winter. If I hadn't called on you by surprise, I would suspect you of wearing a wire and trying to trap me into admitting something.'

'You'll just have to live with it. What you know. What you've done.'

'I think I can manage,' he said cheerfully. 'You and me. We're the only ones who emerged from this undamaged.'

This was enough. Jude stood up and pulled her jacket on.

'I don't feel particularly undamaged,' she said.

He stood up. 'I suppose this is goodbye.'

'That's right.'

Outside on the pavement, Jude turned to leave. She hoped she would never see him again, but he put out a hand and touched her shoulder.

'I believe you,' he said.

'Believe what?'

'I don't think you would have given an alibi to a murderer. I was thinking that before, and now, meeting you here, I'm sure of it.'

'I don't care what you think.'

'You had his phone with you, right?'

Jude didn't answer but Vin continued as if she had said yes.

'That's all he needed. His phone was a hundred miles away. That was all the alibi he needed.'

'And I was there.'

He left a pause before replying.

'Think about it,' he said.

'Think about what?'

'We all know what Liam was like, what he was capable of. He was planning to kill the mother of his child. I think he was planning to kill you as well. Nobody knew you were there. Nobody knew he had met with you. You'd taken his luggage up to that cottage. That was all he needed from you. After that, it would be better if you were out of the way.'

For a moment Jude felt like the ground was moving beneath her. She looked back at that meeting with Liam. She tried to remember his demeanour, his tone. Could that really have been possible? Could Liam have been intending to murder her?

'No. I don't believe that's true.'

Vin gave a broad smile, the last of his smiles she would ever see.

'Maybe,' he said. 'But you'll never be sure.'

And he was the one who walked away, leaving her standing there.

CHAPTER SEVENTY

In the middle of October, on the day that Liam would have turned thirty-one, Jude walked from her flat in Bethnal Green to Walthamstow cemetery. It was a cool, windy day, and as she walked through Victoria Park and then on to the marshes, yellow leaves span through the air and she felt a few drops of rain on her cheek.

It had been nearly a year since that day in early November when Liam had found her and asked her for a favour. One year. It made her almost dizzy to look back at that feverish time when it seemed her life had turned on its axis and her sense of who she was had buckled and broken.

She walked through the gates of the cemetery and at once saw that many of the gravestones were tilted at odd angles. A placid angel leaned at almost forty-five degrees, and headstones were toppling together. It was as if the ground, and all its cargo of bones, was sinking.

She had thought it might take her some time to find where Liam was buried, but the place was smaller than she had expected. In only a few minutes she was standing in front of a plain grey stone, with Liam's name and his date of birth and death newly chiselled into it. Nothing else.

She remembered, with a sudden painful clarity, how, when they were lying in a field together, Liam had asked her to name the bones of the body. She had told him: talus, fibula, tibia, patella, femur, pelvis . . . She had put her hand on each bone as she spoke, holding his foot, placing her hand on his shin, his knee, his thigh, and at the end cradling his skull in her hands. Those beautiful bones were interred in this small space, all that was left of Liam Birch.

Now that she was here, Jude wasn't sure what she was meant to do or to feel. She wasn't even sure why she had come, carrying a little bunch of anemones, and she felt suddenly foolish. She thought of Liam as she had first known him, beautiful and dangerous, blazing with life and crackling with energy. She thought of him after that crash, casually throwing away his future in order to set her on her own path away from him. She remembered him sitting across from her in the café eleven years later, little laugh lines round his eyes, asking her for a simple favour.

She thought of what Vin had said, and gave an involuntary shiver. She would never know what Liam would have done, and perhaps that was okay. You have to live with doubt and uncertainty; you have to hold contradictions together and not struggle to resolve them. You have to learn that you're not as in control of life as you might like.

She squatted down. There were dead leaves heaped up at the base of the stone and she cleared them away, then placed her flowers there, bright as jewels. She thought of saying something, but what would she say? I was always in love with you? I was never in love with you? Was she here to say thank you or to say sorry, to ask forgiveness, to curse him, or simply to acknowledge that it was over, he was over – a glorious, terrible man now buried in a sinking landscape of the long dead?

Only when she stood up did she notice that a woman had turned up at the neighbouring grave, and was on her knees, digging out weeds with a miniature trowel.

'My Lewis,' she said, nodding towards the grave-stone. 'I come every day.'

'Was he your husband?'

'Yes. He died three years ago. Not young like your one there, just thirty. That's so sad.' She glanced at the flowers Jude had laid. 'I'm glad you've come to see him. I think no one ever comes. He's been left all alone. Isn't that a shame?'

'There are different ways of remembering someone.'

'That's true. Did you know him very well?'

Jude looked at the woman, then back at the headstone.

'No,' she said at last. 'He was like a dream. I don't think that I really knew him at all.'

ACKNOWLEDGEMENTS

While writing this story about places we weren't allowed to visit, we were helped and supported in so many different ways by people that we weren't allowed to meet.

They found extraordinary possibilities of being creative in a world turned upside down.

Our UK agents: Sarah Ballard, Eli Keren, St John Donald.

Our UK publishers: Suzanne Baboneau, Ian Chapman, Jess Barratt, Hayley McMullan, Katherine Armstrong, Louise Davies.

Thanks also to the booksellers, the book bloggers and the readers who have kept us going through a dark year.